FALSE WITNESS

Michelle Davies has been writing professionally for twenty years as a journalist on magazines, including on the production desk at *Elle*, and as Features Editor of *Heat*. Her last staff position before going freelance was Editor-at-Large at *Grazia* magazine and she currently writes for a number of women's magazines and newspaper supplements. She lives in London and juggles writing crime fiction with her freelance journalism and motherhood. *False Witness* is the third novel featuring DC Maggie Neville, following *Gone Astray* and *Wrong Place*.

Also by Michelle Davies

Gone Astray
Wrong Place

FALSE WITNESS

Michelle Davies

PAN BOOKS

First published 2018 by Pan Books
an imprint of Pan Macmillan
20 New Wharf Road, London N1 9RR
Associated companies throughout the world
www.panmacmillan.com

ISBN 978-1-5098-5682-4

1 3 5 7 9 8 6 4 2

A CIP catalogue record for this book is available from the British Library.

Typeset in Janson Text LT Std 11/14.5 pt by
Palimpsest Book Production Limited, Falkirk, Stirlingshire
Printed and bound by CPI Group (UK) Ltd, Croydon, CR0 4YY

To Granddad,
for being right about everything

1

Tuesday

Alan Donnelly's first thought on spotting the children on the ladder was to wonder whether it constituted a sacking offence under the terms of his contract.

His second was that he'd strangle the little sods when he got his hands on them.

One of them was already at the ladder's brow, the other not far behind. He couldn't see their faces clearly from that distance, but the girl in the lead had long blonde hair worn loose and wavy and was in a red gingham dress. From the size of her she looked as though she might be in Year 5, possibly 6. The boy in her wake had cropped dark hair and was wearing smart grey shorts and a white polo top. He looked physically younger, a skinny little runt.

Alan threw down his shovel on the soil he'd been using to fill in the cracks in the turf. It was Sports Day next week and the playing field was uneven underfoot, a potential safety hazard for egg-and-spoon and sack race competitors according to the head. Smacking his palms together to clean them, Alan set off across the grass towards the playground, angry at being pulled away from an important task to sort out misbehavers.

He'd warned Mrs Pullman something like this would happen if they didn't delay building work until the holidays started. During a tetchy meeting with her and the governors to discuss the plans, he'd likened cordoning off the playground while the kids were still at school to waving a bottle of vodka under the nose of an alcoholic. Far too tempting. They hadn't taken kindly to his metaphor and decided it would be far worse if they waited until the summer holidays and the work overran and the classes weren't finished for the new intake come September. Prepare for an early June start, he was told in no uncertain terms.

Yet here they were three weeks into the project and he was already being proved right. There wasn't time to be smug, though, because unless he got those kids down off that ladder before anyone else saw them he'd be right in the shit. It wouldn't matter how they'd broken into the school or got onto the building site, it was the fact that they had, and security was his responsibility as caretaker.

There were three new classrooms being built, in a single-storey, L-shaped annexe. An outer wall of the first one was already completed – about seven metres high, it was what the children were standing on now. They appeared to be alone, no sign of any others egging them on. He checked his watch quickly. It was ten past seven – he had about twenty minutes before the first members of staff would start arriving.

His breaths grew shorter as he picked up his pace and he reached into his pocket for his inhaler. He'd been using it a lot these past four days, since the heatwave baking Mansell and the rest of Buckinghamshire and much of the south-east had begun. He hated it, couldn't breathe it was so hot.

Yesterday the temperature had hit twenty-eight degrees and today was meant to be even higher.

The building site was separated from the playground by two-metre-high interlocking panels, but the door cut into the centre panel was ajar, its padlock swinging loose. Alan couldn't remember seeing it fastened when he did his rounds the previous evening but if anyone asked he would say it was and the kids must've forced it open.

He stepped through the doorway and his heart skipped a beat. Both children were on the top of the wall, backs to him. The girl was staring down into the hollowed guts of the new classroom but the boy was crouched low with his arms splayed out, as if struggling to keep his balance. Alan guessed the breeze blocks could take their weight but it wasn't a wide wall, not even for feet as small as theirs. One misstep was all it would take.

'What do you think you're doing?' he called up, loudly enough for them to hear but not so loud it would give them a fright and make them stumble.

The boy rose slowly to his feet, then reached out and grabbed the girl's hand. He whispered something and she angled her head towards him just enough for Alan to see her face. He didn't know her name but she was in Miss Felix's class, Year 6. Had a bit of a gob on her like most girls her age seemed to these days, but she wasn't one of the kids who usually warmed the row of chairs outside the head's office as they waited for a telling-off.

'You need to get down now,' he said.

The boy's shoulders began to heave as though he was laughing and that made Alan see red. If there was one thing guaranteed to wind him up it was being mocked by cocky little shits. He gripped the ladder and dragged it along the wall so it was closer to where they were.

'You first,' he said firmly to the girl. 'Take it steady though.'

'I can't,' she said, her voice cracking. 'He won't let me.'

The boy's head whipped round. It was the new kid, the one who a week earlier Alan had caught skulking in the cupboard where they stored the art supplies. He'd read him the riot act, told him it was out of bounds to pupils, but he didn't report it because the cupboard shouldn't have been unlocked in the first place. He was still trying to get to the bottom of whose fault that was.

The girl said something but Alan didn't catch it because his focus was on the boy who had started moving away from the ladder, pulling her with him.

'Come back here,' he shouted, too pissed off now to mind his volume. 'I'll have you excluded for this.'

They both ignored him.

Alan knew he had to act, and fast. The teachers who liked to start early would be arriving soon, not to mention the construction workers. He had to get the kids down from that wall. He started to climb the ladder, muttering all the swear words he wished he could say out loud but would get him sacked if he did.

A noise from above made him stop. The children were lurching ominously from side to side, holding hands, as though they were performing a dance.

'Stop that now!' he hollered. 'You'll fall if you're not careful.'

They stopped. The girl panted, her cheeks inflamed, but the boy was calm, his mouth curled into a lopsided grin.

'Right, let's stop this nonsense,' said Alan croakily as he scaled the rest of the ladder until his feet were only a few rungs from the top. He grabbed the rough-hewn ridge of the wall, hands shaking and legs like jelly.

'Walk towards me and I'll help you down,' he ordered. 'You'll have to let go of each other first.'

'Don't do that!' the girl suddenly screamed at the boy.

Alan shot out his right arm, stretching as far as he could, but his fingertips grasped only thin air and the ladder tilted violently under his shifting weight. Sights and sounds came at him like rapid gunfire and he cried out.

A lopsided grin . . . a blur of red gingham . . . a hand reaching out . . . streaming blonde hair . . . a high-pitched scream . . . a thud.

Then, silence.

2

Maggie didn't want the day to begin. She wanted to stay perched on the sill of the open window, her face, neck and exposed forearms warmed by the early-morning sun and the promise of another hot day. Tilting her chin up and closing her eyes, she imagined she was on holiday, on a balcony somewhere exotic, until the sharp blast of a guard's whistle below jolted her from her daydream.

Her flat overlooked Mansell railway station and she watched as a commuter train heading to London pulled away from the platform. Without thinking, she began counting under her breath as it disappeared out of sight, knowing that when she reached fifty-six the train would pass the house where her sister, Lou, used to live.

Her nephew Jude had made her time it once – him on the phone in the back garden where the tracks ran parallel, talking to Maggie as she stood at her lounge window above the station. She'd suggested they use a stopwatch for accuracy but Jude wanted them to count themselves and it had amused her that, despite a world of technology at his disposal, he was old-fashioned in his methodology. It was like her, a detective constable, preferring face-to-face instead of emailing witnesses.

The memory induced a smile from Maggie, though it was tinged with sadness. Seven months had passed since she'd seen or spoken to Jude, same for his siblings, Scotty and Mae, and their mum, Lou. Less than a year but more than half, it already felt like a lifetime.

The technical term for the current status of their relationship was 'estranged', a word that rolled off Maggie's tongue in a disconcertingly agreeable way when she said it out loud. But there was nothing pleasant about being as close as a person could possibly be to their family one day, the next being 'as good as dead' to them – as Lou had phrased it in a final, caustic text before cutting off contact completely.

In the crying-herself-to-sleep stage, Maggie wondered if it might be easier to think of her sister in the same way. Death allowed a person to grieve their loss, whereas estrangement meant being in perpetual limbo, with nothing but the hope things might resolve to hang on to. Now, seven months on, the hurt was levelling out largely due to the distraction of work and in particular the commendation she'd just received from the Chief Constable for her conduct on her last case as Family Liaison, the specialism she was trained for alongside being a detective with Mansell Force CID.

The second distraction stopping her from moping round the clock was gently snoring in her bed next door. Her mood began to lift as she pondered the noise Will Umpire made as he slept. It wasn't earth-shatteringly loud, rather a gentle, rhythmic hum she had grown accustomed to and liked very much.

She checked the time. Twenty past seven. She should wake him so he could leave hers before the roads became clogged with commuters and school-run parents. Umpire was a DCI and headed up the Homicide and Major Enquiry Team (HMET) at their force's area headquarters in Trenton, a town as far north in Buckinghamshire as Mansell was south. If the traffic was bad it could take him more than an hour to get there.

As though he'd sensed her thinking about him, Umpire appeared in the doorway. He was wearing her pale green silk bathrobe, which was indecently short on his six-foot-three-inch frame and revealed the soft, strawberry-blond hairs that densely covered his upper thighs. Maggie felt a stab of lust closely followed by regret that there was no time to drag him back to bed.

'Any more where that came from?' he asked, peering into her empty mug after he'd crossed the room to kiss her. His scent was a honeyed blend of laundered sheets and musky aftershave. She breathed in deeply, wishing the smell of him would stay with her all day.

'Pot's full.'

She got to her feet and used the heels of her hands to smooth the creases on the navy cropped trousers she'd plucked from her bedroom floor when she got up. Having a semi-permanent house guest had done nothing to improve her untidiness.

'I need to get going,' she said. 'I forgot to bring the leaflets home for my talk. I'll have to pick them up on the way.'

'Are you sure someone else can't do it?' Umpire called from the alcove kitchen.

She answered him as she crossed the lounge to retrieve

her bag, discarded the previous evening by the foot of the sofa.

'The head asked for me personally because she knows me and I said I'd do it. I'll be fine.'

Umpire came back into the lounge sipping from a coffee mug branded with the slogan 'World's Best Auntie'. It took every ounce of willpower not to duck away from his watchful stare, because if she did he'd know for certain she was lying.

She was giving a talk on cyber bullying at Rushbrooke Primary School, where until seven months ago her nephew Scotty had been a pupil. Not seeing him sitting amongst his little gang of friends during the assembly was going to hurt like hell but she couldn't pull out.

'You could've been honest about why it might be difficult for you,' said Umpire.

'Last time I checked, rowing with your sister doesn't count as a reason not to do your job,' she said wryly.

They both knew she was trying to make light of what had happened, when it went far deeper than a stupid argument. Maggie had done something to hurt Lou immeasurably and no apology or excuse was adequate enough to make up for what she'd done, or the many years she'd spent keeping it a secret.

'Will I see you tonight?' she asked, keen to change the subject. 'I can come to yours.'

Umpire owned a house in Trenton where they split their time together.

'Depends how manic it gets. I'll call you later.'

As he kissed her goodbye and went off to shower, Maggie was reminded again how seamless their transition had been from colleagues to couple. Perhaps it was because Umpire was older – forty-two to her twenty-nine – that it had been so easy: he didn't play games and was honest about his feelings, telling her he loved her far sooner than she'd expected.

That wasn't to say there hadn't been – and still were – hurdles. The start of their relationship had coincided with her falling out with Lou and it had cast a shadow over their nascent happiness. Fortunately, Umpire was enlightened enough to acknowledge that tears and passion didn't make for easy bedfellows and exercised patience when other men might have tired of her distress.

Besides, he'd had his own predicament: settling into a new custody arrangement with his two children, Flora, now fourteen, and Jack, two years younger. They spent every other weekend at his but their mother was railing against them meeting Maggie, saying they 'weren't ready'. Maggie suspected it was Umpire's ex-wife who had the problem but she made herself scarce on the weekends the kids were with him without complaint because, deep down, she wasn't ready to meet them either. The thought of stepping into a proxy stepmother role made her uneasy, yet she couldn't quite put her finger on why.

Outside the flat she was getting into her car when her phone went. It was a CID colleague, DS Anna Renshaw.

'I need you up at Rushbrooke Primary *now*,' said Renshaw. She was outdoors and sounded out of breath, and Maggie could hear other voices in the background.

'Am I late? My talk's meant to be at nine thirty.'

'It's not that. There's been a suspicious death in the school grounds. Victim's a pupil.'

'I'm on my way.'

3

The first person Maggie saw on arriving at Rushbrooke was a young male PC called Olly Talbot. Not long in the force, he had been tasked with logging the arrivals and departures of personnel at the crime scene and was hugging a clip-board to his chest like a soft toy as Maggie approached him to sign in.

'You okay?' she asked.

Talbot nodded but his eyes betrayed him. He blinked furiously to hide the evidence of his distress.

'Were you here first?'

He nodded, then cleared his throat.

'I was a First Responder, with PC Pritchard. There was nothing we could do for the poor lad.'

Maggie intuitively knew it was Talbot's first body and sympathy tugged at her. She could remember seeing her first corpse as vividly as if it'd happened yesterday. Her sister's fiancé, Jerome, run over and killed in front of her. His death was the reason she'd joined the police and trained as a FLO. She had wanted to help alleviate families' grief in the same way the liaison assigned to Lou and to Jerome's parents helped them.

'The first one's always the hardest,' she said, gently taking the clipboard from Talbot's clenched, white-knuckled hands.

'Mr Matheson asked me to describe what I saw when we arrived but my mind went blank. I couldn't remember anything. He must think I'm an idiot.'

'He won't,' Maggie reassured him. 'Mal understands more than anyone how awful it can be.'

Mal Matheson was the Chief Crime Scene Examiner for their force, a popular, grandfatherly figure known for his willingness to go the extra mile. His presence meant their young victim was in the best of hands now.

'I've been going over it and I've remembered what the eyewitness said to me the second we arrived. I know it's important, but I can't leave my post to tell Mr Matheson,' said Talbot anxiously.

'Anything to do with witness statements you should tell the SIO, not Mal. What did they say?'

'There was another kid on the wall, a girl, and the witness said he saw her push the victim on purpose. He was adamant.'

The idea of a child deliberately shoving another to their death brought Maggie up cold. The oldest kids at Rushbrooke were only eleven years old.

'You're right, that is important. I'll tell the SIO when I get to the crime scene. Make sure you record it word for word in your notes,' she said.

Talbot nodded as he took the clipboard and pen back. He pointed to his left.

'From here you need to go round the side of the main building, then across to the other side of the playground.

You'll see an area where they're building new classrooms and that's where the boy died. You can't miss it.'

Maggie declined to mention that she already knew her way around the school. Numerous mornings she had dropped Scotty off in the very same spot and she'd also attended plays and assemblies and even a couple of parents' evenings when Lou was unable to go herself. Stung by the memories, Maggie nodded at Talbot, then strode purposefully into the school grounds, her focus on the scene that awaited her.

She was paces away from the building site when Renshaw emerged through a gap in the hoardings dressed in the protective coveralls that forensics demanded. Her manner bore witness to what she'd seen on the other side of the wall – solemn and wan, her hands shook slightly as she removed her gloves and she greeted Maggie with a grimace.

'Sometimes I really fucking hate this job,' she said.

'That bad?'

'His head took the brunt. Didn't stand a chance.'

'Has he been ID'd yet?'

'Yeah, Benjamin Tyler, but everyone called him Benji. Just turned eleven. He only started after Christmas, moved here from Somerset with his mum. She's inside,' Renshaw added, nodding towards the main school building. Two-storey, red-brick, it had high arched windows that required a pole to open them on the inside.

'She wasn't here when it happened, was she?'

'No, thank God. She turned up about ten minutes ago. Another parent had texted her.'

'How did they know?'

'Usual Chinese whispers. The school didn't manage to get a message out in time to say it was shutting, so parents

13

started arriving as usual to drop their kids off and it didn't take long for them to work out what had happened when they saw us here. Benji's mum got the text, realized he wasn't in his bedroom like she thought he was, then ran all the way here.'

'Has she seen the body?'

'No. She keeps asking to but we can't yet, not in the state it's in,' said Renshaw, flashing Maggie a strained, knowing look.

'We're sure it's her son?'

'Yep. Benji's got a strawberry birthmark on his lower back and so's the body.'

Maggie hugged her arms to her chest, feeling a chill that didn't make sense on a day already so warm. 'His poor mum,' she said.

'I know, I've been thinking the same: how do you even begin to deal with something like this? The teachers say he was a lovely boy too. Not that it would be any easier if he wasn't,' Renshaw added hastily.

Maggie swallowed hard. If Benji was eleven, that put him in Year 6, the same as Scotty. Who knows, they might've ended up as friends if Scotty had stayed at Rushbrooke.

'What about his dad?'

'Looks like she's a single mum. We haven't confirmed that with her, though, she's too upset to talk right now.'

'Who's the SIO?' Maggie asked. 'I need to pass on something one of the first responders just told me.'

Renshaw pulled back the hood on her blue coverall and shook her auburn hair loose.

'As the ranking officer, I am. And before you ask, no, there isn't anyone else.'

'I wasn't going to.'

Their already cut-to-the-bone department was suffering from the recent departure of a DI and the failure to recruit another DC to replace the gap left by Renshaw when she was promoted to DS. The strained circumstances had made the rest of them a tighter operation, though, which in turn had facilitated a lasting thaw in Maggie and Renshaw's previously fractious relationship. Maggie wouldn't go so far as to call her a friend, but they were certainly friendlier.

'Good. What do you need to tell me then?'

'The eyewitness told PC Talbot that he saw the girl deliberately push the boy off the wall,' Maggie relayed.

Renshaw frowned.

'He must be talking about the caretaker – he was trying to get both children down off the wall when Benji fell. He's top of my list to interview after the girl.'

'Who is she?'

'Poppy Hepworth, same age, same class.'

Her name didn't ring any bells with Maggie – she wasn't one of the Rushbrooke girls Scotty used to talk about.

'We haven't been able to get anything out of her,' Renshaw went on. 'She's clammed up. Shock, probably, or maybe it's fear, because if she did push Benji she must know she's in serious trouble. A year over the age of criminality, old enough to be charged.'

'Okay, so what can I do?' asked Maggie.

'See to Benji's mum. She needs an experienced FLO and I want it to be you. I'll square it with DI Gant. I know he likes to put forward his own choice from his roster but you tick all the boxes for this one – you're used to dealing with cases where a child is the victim, you know the school because of your nephew and you're empathetic but not at the expense of being a detective.'

Renshaw's assessment was quite the compliment and Maggie was suddenly grateful she hadn't told anyone at work about being estranged from Lou. If Renshaw, or DI Tony Gant, the Family Liaison Coordinator for their force whose job it was to assign Maggie to cases, knew she was banned from seeing her nephews and niece they might think twice about putting her with a grieving mum with a child the same age as Scotty, in case it brought to the fore emotions she couldn't handle. Which, a voice in her head quietly cautioned, it well might.

'Benji's mum needs a FLO like you,' said Renshaw, as though she could sense Maggie wavering. '*I* need you to be her FLO.'

That made Maggie's mind up. A young boy was dead and his mum would be desperate for navigation and support as the investigation gathered pace. This was the role she was trained for and was bloody good at and there would only be conflict if she let there be. She dismissed any lingering doubt with a firm nod.

'Of course I'll do it.'

'Great, I'll call Gant after I've talked to Poppy. The head has said I can use her office for the interview.'

'You're not taking her in?'

'I thought I'd have a chat with her here before we do the whole formal bit at the station because I'm not ready to start the clock ticking,' said Renshaw. 'I want to see what she says, then ask for EIA.'

The police sought Early Investigative Advice from the CPS when they weren't sure about bringing charges. If the CPS said more evidence was needed first, you listened, and Maggie could see why Renshaw wanted to run this one past them. She was dealing with an eleven-year-old suspect who had potentially murdered another child. There was absolutely no margin for error with this case.

'What about her family? Are her parents here?'

Renshaw shook her head. 'I've sent uniform round. Considering the rest of the school seems to know what's happened it's weird they haven't turned up yet. Either they haven't noticed their daughter's not at home or they don't care.'

4

Bits of cereal were scattering across the table and onto the floor, a steady stream of rice and barley malt with added fortified vitamins.

'Dylan, watch what you're doing!' Julia Hepworth called across the kitchen to her son. 'Look at the mess you're making.'

Dylan dragged his gaze away from the back of the cereal packet, and the special offer for a plastic bowl with a built-in straw to drink up milk dregs, and looked down. Quickly he righted the box.

'Sorry, wasn't looking.'

'I can see that. I've already said no to you having that bowl as well. You don't need one with a straw, just tip the bowl up and drink the milk that way like everyone else does.'

Dylan grinned. Then, without needing to be asked, he set about clearing up the mess.

Smiling, Julia returned to making the sandwiches for their lunchboxes. Dylan was only nine but she never had to bribe him to help out around the house and his sister was the same. Friends would often ask what her secret was – how did she manage to have two such compliant children?

She wasn't entirely sure herself, but she liked to think that it was because while pregnant with Poppy she'd vowed never to be one of those mums who lost their rag over the small stuff, like spilled cereal, pen marks on walls or mislaid PE kits. So she didn't. Her children's upbringing was bathed in smiles and calm – although she would never say that aloud, because if it sounded trite to her ears God knows what other people would make of it.

'I hope those two aren't for me. They've got mould on.'

Julia jumped as her husband's voice rang in her ear. She hadn't heard him creep up on her and, looking down, saw why: Ewan's feet were bare and made no sound on the floorboards. She glanced at Dylan and saw he was hunched over his cereal bowl, shovelling spoonfuls into his mouth. She was grateful he'd cleaned up the mess before his dad saw it.

Ewan poked the two slices of bread that Julia had been about to butter, his fingertip leaving craters.

'See, there's blue bits on them.'

Julia looked closer and saw he was right. And, bloody typical, they were the last two slices in the loaf.

'I'll have these ones,' she said hastily.

'I should think so. People might think you were trying to poison me. Dylan . . . help me!'

Ewan staggered over to the table pretending to gag while clutching his throat. His scalp was still pink from his shower, visible through a receding hairline that he shaved down to dark bristle. Dylan giggled at the performance, which culminated in Ewan throwing himself on the floor.

'Honey, you'll get your shirt and trousers dirty,' said Julia, laughing along with her son.

'Doesn't matter,' said Ewan, picking himself up. 'The way they were ironed it looks like I slept in them anyway.'

Julia flushed. 'I did use the steam setting like you said.'

'I'm sure you did,' he said, turning his back to address their son. 'Your sister not up yet?'

Dylan, mouth full, could only shake his head.

'She's probably got her nose stuck in a book,' Julia interjected. 'Can you tell her to get a move on? It's twenty past eight and we have to leave in fifteen minutes.'

'Sorry, can't. I've got to leave now or I'll be late for the Arnold meeting. He's not happy with the blueprints.'

Ewan came over to grab his lunch and kissed his wife on the cheek. His lips felt dry and cracked against her sweaty skin. With another scorching-hot day looming, Julia's armpits were already telling her she'd need to reapply deodorant before leaving the house.

'I won't be home until late,' he added. 'Client dinner.'

'It's not on the board,' said Julia, glancing at the wall planner covered in multiple scribbles and crossings-out that denoted the family's coming and goings.

'I did tell you about it last week.'

'No, you didn't.'

'It's not my fault if you don't listen properly,' he snapped. 'You've always got too much on the go to pay attention.'

Julia felt a pang of guilt. He was right: between work, the children and running the house, Ewan did tend to slip in her priorities.

'I'm sorry. I should've listened. Who's the client?' she asked, thinking that might jog her memory, because she could've sworn he hadn't said a word about it until now.

'It doesn't matter,' said Ewan. He looked wounded, which made Julia feel even worse. 'Don't wait up for me.'

She forced a laugh. 'Of course I won't. I know what those client dinners are like. You'll come back drunk and bouncing off the walls before you crash out on the sofa until I come and put you into bed.'

Ewan held his hands up in a conciliatory fashion and grinned.

'Busted.'

He crossed the room and kissed her again, this time on the lips, harder and longer.

'I do love you,' he said.

'I love you too. I promise I'll do good listening from now on.'

They both laughed – that was what they used to say to the children as infants when they never paid attention.

'Good, otherwise it'll be the naughty step for you, young lady.'

At that he left and relief that a row had been averted washed over her.

'Dylan, can you please fetch your sister?' she asked, snapping the lids shut on the children's themed lunchboxes. 'We're going to be late.'

'Okay,' he grumbled, pushing his chair back.

The sound of the chair's metal feet scraping against the hardwood floor made Julia wince. As soon as he'd left the room she checked for marks. There was a tiny one, so she got out the special floor polish Ewan had suggested she buy and rubbed hard with a cloth until it was gone.

Sweaty from being on her hands and knees, she checked her make-up in a compact mirror only to wonder why she had bothered applying any as it had already melted off. Her dark brown hair, which she'd painstakingly styled in a sleek bob after her shower, was curling moistly into the nape of her neck like a fortune-teller fish from a Christmas cracker that flips over in your palm.

She shouted her children's names as she thrust her make-up bag back into the kitchen cupboard where she kept it for handiness alongside tins of beans and packets of pasta.

'Come on, you two, we've got to go.'

Hurrying into the hallway, she shoved her feet into the sandals she'd left by the front door yesterday. The paint was flaking off the skirting board next to where she'd discarded them and she made a mental note to remind Ewan that he'd promised to discuss redecorating in the summer holidays.

They'd lived in the house – a Victorian-era, white-rendered semi in a quiet road on the east side of Mansell – for seven years and the hallway, like most of the other rooms, hadn't been touched since the refurbishment they carried out when they moved in. Money wasn't an issue – both of them had decent jobs, Ewan as a self-employed structural engineer and her working as a project coordinator for their local council's Environmental and Community Services department – but time was. There weren't enough hours in the day for her to sort out decorators and builders on top of everything else.

She couldn't hear the children moving around on the floor above, so she went to the bottom of the stairs and called up to them. There was a cobweb spanning two banister spindles and she batted it away with her hand.

'We're going to be late. I hope you're dressed, Poppy!'

Dylan appeared at the top of the stairs.

'Is she ready?'

His face was pinched. 'She's not here.'

'Don't be silly, of course she is. Check –'

There was a noise at the front door. Not the doorbell but someone banging the letter-box knocker. Three short raps, a pause, then three more.

'She must be in the bathroom. You check while I get this,' she said.

The frosted glass in the door panel had warped the outlines of the unexpected callers but Julia knew instantly who they were. Trembling, she opened the door to them.

'Mrs Hepworth?' queried the taller of the two male officers. This one was wearing his hat but his colleague had his tucked under his arm, his face sheened with sweat.

She nodded.

'Can we come in?'

'What's wrong?' she asked, conditioning making her fear the worst. The police didn't usually turn up on doorsteps with good news.

Dylan appeared at her side and pressed his little body, sharp angled and skinny, into hers. Her arm snaked around his shoulders and pulled him closer.

'It would be better if we came inside,' said the tall one.

Julia let them in but the hallway was as far as she would allow them.

'Please tell me what's going on.'

It couldn't be Ewan. Even if he'd had an accident it was surely too soon for the police to show up.

'We need you to accompany us to Rushbrooke Primary School, Mrs Hepworth,' said the shorter one. 'There's been an incident on site involving your daughter.'

Julia was bemused. 'It can't do. She's still upstairs. We're running late,' she said apologetically, as if the officers would care.

Dylan prodded her in the side.

'Mum,' he whispered.

'Not now, Dylan, the grown-ups are talking.'

The short one gave her a solemn look.

'You need to come with us now, Mrs Hepworth,' he said. 'Your daughter needs you.'

'There's been a mistake,' Julia insisted. 'Poppy hasn't left for school yet.'

Dylan poked her again.

'Stop that.' The rebuke was brusquer than she'd intended and his face fell.

'Perhaps you should listen to your son, Mrs Hepworth,' said the taller officer.

Now it was her turn to be abashed. Cheeks growing hot, Julia looked down at her son.

'I'm sorry, darling,' she said as brightly as she could manage. 'What is it?'

'Poppy's not upstairs. I've looked everywhere. She's not here.'

Julia could tell he was frightened and a ripple of fear shook her body. She looked at the officers.

'You mean . . .' She couldn't get the rest of the words out.

The tall one nodded. 'There's been no mistake. Your daughter's in trouble.'

5

There was no template for the way a parent reacted to the news that their child was dead. The bewilderment that followed them being told almost instantly gave way to a scale of responses that, in Maggie's experience, stretched from eerily calm or catatonic with shock at one end, to hysterical and in need of sedation at the other. Right now Imogen Tyler was pinballing from one extreme to the other – inconsolable for the most part, but calming down long enough to mechanically answer Maggie's preliminary questions.

No, there was no reason for Benji to be in school so early. I thought he was in his bedroom getting ready.

He settled in well at Rushbrooke, made friends and had been invited to a couple of birthday parties.

We left Somerset because I wanted to come home to Mansell. I grew up here and need to be closer to my mum.

Now she was crying again, doubled over as though in pain, unloading her anguish into her lap. Only the crown of her head, the tiniest hint of dark roots striping her blonde hair, was visible to Maggie sitting opposite. As she cried, her small, delicate hands rhythmically clenched and unclenched on her knees, bared by the bright orange sundress she wore. Her nails were coated with blood-red varnish.

Maggie's gaze was drawn to the rings on the fourth finger of Imogen's right hand – a wedding band and an exquisite diamond solitaire. Relics of a former marriage moved to the opposite hand at its demise, or heirlooms passed on? Her left hand was bare.

Maggie waited for a lull in the crying, then leaned forward.

'Would you like me to contact Benji's father?' she asked gently.

The blonde hair slowly lifted. Imogen was short, much shorter than Maggie's five foot eight inches, and she had to look up to make eye contact. Her gaze was bloodshot and swollen.

'His father?' She spoke the word as though it was alien to her. 'He . . . I mean –' She sat up straight, the effort it took reflected in her weary expression. 'My husband died when Benji was a baby.'

'I'm sorry. Is there anyone else I can contact for you? Someone who can stay with you once we get you home?'

They were in the school's Welfare Room, sitting on low, brightly upholstered chairs designed for small frames and legs shorter than theirs. Maggie's back had stiffened in the hour they'd been sitting there but she wouldn't move. She didn't want to leave Imogen alone, not even for a minute.

'I'm a good mum,' said Imogen softly, as though she'd misheard Maggie. 'We've been doing fine, just the two of us –' She made a tiny choking sound and her hand flew up to cover her mouth. She squeezed her eyes tightly shut but still the tears spilled out.

Maggie moved across to sit next to her. With only a moment's hesitation she put her arm around Imogen's shoulders. You could never quite judge how someone might respond to physical contact and whether they would find it odd or inappropriate for a police officer to hug them, but Maggie's instincts about Imogen were correct and she felt the woman involuntarily shudder as she relaxed against her, cleaving to the physical support as she continued to cry.

It was impossible not to be moved by the woman's distress and it took every ounce of Maggie's self-control, and a lot of blinking, to stop tears filling her own eyes. It wouldn't help Imogen to see her mirroring her upset – what she needed from Maggie now was stoicism and a clear head to get things done. The poor woman was on the precipice of an indescribably painful process for which there was no definitive end. Her son was dead, he was never coming back, and there would be moments in the coming days, weeks and months when Imogen would barely be able to function, when even the simplest tasks like putting one foot in front of the other would be beyond her. She might even wish herself dead at times, asking herself what was the point of going on. Part of Maggie's role as her FLO would be to ensure Imogen had support around her to pull her back from the brink should she ever reach that point.

Eventually the crying eased into sniffles. Then, with an exhausted sigh, Imogen sat forward.

'There's my mum to tell, but she should hear it from me,' she said. Her voice was dull now, every inflection of emotion wrung from it. 'And my brother. He lives in Somerset still. I'll call him after I've spoken to her.' Imogen cradled her face in her hands. 'They're going to be devastated. They love Benji as much as I do.'

'It might help for you to talk to someone about what's happened, a counsellor who can help you process how you're feeling,' said Maggie. 'I'm not trained to do that, but I could arrange for someone from Victim Support to contact you, if you want?'

'Maybe . . . I don't know.' Imogen wiped her eyes again. 'Do I have to decide now?'

'Absolutely not, it's whenever you're ready. In the meantime, my job as your liaison is to answer any questions you have regarding our investigation into Benji's death. I might not always be able to tell you information straight away, like if we need to keep something quiet so it doesn't affect a future arrest or court proceedings, but I'll always let you know if that's the case.'

Imogen looked at her blankly.

'Hasn't Poppy been arrested yet?'

Maggie stilled. They hadn't discussed any details yet, so how did Imogen know another child had been present when Benji died, let alone who she was?

'She pushed him,' Imogen went on, her face now set with a discernible flintiness, 'and now he's dead. You should be arresting her.'

Maggie fought to keep her expression neutral.

'Where did you hear that?'

'One of the mums saw Poppy being led into the school and then she overheard a policeman tell another one that it looked like she'd pushed Benji off the wall.'

Loose-lipped coppers and playground gossips . . . just what the investigation needed, thought Maggie grimly.

28

'Is it true?' Imogen pressed.

Maggie had been in the same hot seat enough times to know what information she could impart without tying herself in knots or jeopardizing the investigation.

'There were two witnesses at the scene and we will be speaking to both of them. Only when we've got their statements and have gathered all the physical evidence will we have a clearer picture of what happened. I do understand you want someone to be held accountable for Benji's death, but we can't rush this process or mistakes will be made. For his sake we want to get it right.'

To her relief, Imogen nodded in agreement.

'I also understand people will be speculating about what happened,' Maggie went on, 'but I promise you that's all it is right now – speculation. They don't know anything. So unless I tell you otherwise, disregard what anyone else says. Now, do you have a recent picture of Benji we could use? We're not going to release it publicly, it would just be really helpful if we had one.'

She didn't air the thought that followed – that it would be helpful for her colleagues who'd seen his broken little body to see him as perfect and whole again.

'Yes, I do, his last school one, from just before Christmas. The original's at home but I've got a copy on my phone.'

Imogen reached for her mobile phone, which was resting on the chair next to her. In her haste to get to the school she'd brought only that and her house keys with her.

Maggie watched as she scrolled through a succession of images until she paused at one and held it aloft.

'This is Benji.'

'What a gorgeous picture,' said Maggie, meaning it. The

29

child filling the frame had short dark hair that stuck out at angles, richly lashed brown eyes and a smile that could power a funfair. As she studied Benji's face she felt a sudden pang: this was the first year she hadn't received copies of Scotty and Jude's school pictures. Just as quickly, she pushed the thought aside.

'He's such a smiler, always happy,' said Imogen. She faltered. 'Sorry . . . I mean he was.' Her face suddenly crumpled and she let out a wail. 'I can't talk about him like he's not here any more, I just can't.'

'Then don't,' said Maggie soothingly. She handed the phone back. 'Why don't you tell me a bit more about him? I'd really like to know.'

Imogen gently stroked the screen with her finger as she spoke.

'He's never been a boy's boy, if you know what I mean. He doesn't like football or any other team sports. He's a really good swimmer, though, can swim like a fish. That's probably because of us living in Somerset – I started him on lessons really young because we lived so close to the sea and I was scared he'd drown.'

For the next twenty minutes Maggie listened while Imogen painted a picture of her son as a funny, bright kid who rarely gave her any trouble, for which she was always grateful because life as a single mum was tough. Maggie could see his loss was going to have a profound effect on her, that their connection had been intense. Benji was, in Imogen's words, her little shadow and it had always been the two of them against the world, inseparable.

As Imogen's monologue drew to an end, Maggie asked

her again if she had any idea why Benji had gone to the school so early that morning.

'I honestly don't know. I don't know why he climbed up on a wall either. But I promise you Benji wouldn't have done something so stupid unless he was forced to, he's just not that kid. He's not a daredevil,' she stressed. 'I know in my heart it wasn't his idea to climb on top of it and anyone who says otherwise is lying.'

6

Alan slumped forward and buried his face in his hands. His palms smelled of the soil embedded in the lines criss-crossing them. His breathing was almost back to normal, though, his chest no longer burning as though it was on fire. But the subsidence of shock brought clarity of thought – and the realization that he had made a terrible, stupid mistake.

What he'd said to the copper who'd pulled him away from the body, the stuff he'd come out with . . . now the police were crawling all over the place and he kept hearing the words 'suspicious death' being bandied about.

Why the hell didn't he say it was an accident?

He played the moment back again in his mind, but already it was like watching an old cine film, all blurred, jerky and vague. It had happened so quickly, too fast for him to stop it. But there was no doubting *what* he saw. The girl pushed the boy, no question. And, really, the police should know that, because what she did was bad, so bad. But by being honest he'd dropped himself right in it.

Because the way he saw it now, if the police thought the boy's death was an accident, they'd probably poke around the building site for a bit, then pack up and leave. But now they were treating it more seriously than that – because of what *he* said he saw – and they could end up searching the entire premises, including opening up the Pavilion – and if that happened he was a dead man.

Just thinking about it made Alan's heartbeat accelerate again and his breaths grow shallower. He raised his head and checked around him. The playground was teeming with coppers, some in uniform, some not, but they weren't paying attention to him. Earlier, someone had pointed out the detective in charge and he could see her now on the other side of the playground. With a start he realized she reminded him of Ruby: her hair was the same shade of auburn and styled the same way, poker-straight to the shoulders. When the detective moved her head, her hair swished as one, like a curtain, same as Ruby's.

As he watched her talking to a bloke in a suit, another detective presumably, an idea suddenly came to him. There was something he should do while he had the chance.

Eagerly he got to his feet and went over to the nearest uniformed officer, tapping him on the shoulder to get his attention.

'I need my inhaler,' said Alan, surreptitiously placing his hand over the outline of the one concealed in his trouser pocket. 'I'm asthmatic. It's in my office – can I go and get it?'

The officer hesitated, as though he was weighing up whether he was allowed to give permission. He glanced around, then nodded.

'Come straight back, though.'

'I will.'

Alan's office was in the bowels of the main building, next

to the plant room. The head had offered him an alternative space on the ground floor when he started but he'd declined. The vibrating hum of the heating and water systems next door didn't bother him: it was an antidote to the high-pitched chatter of children's voices that often grated on him when he was going about his duties.

Few people ventured down to his office, unless Alan expressly asked them to. If any of the cleaning staff he managed wanted to speak to him they sent him a text or called him on the internal phone system, which is also what the head and other school staff did. Everyone knew the basement was Alan's domain and he didn't take kindly to people nosing around it.

He disentangled a silver Yale from the bunch looped to his belt – he was always careful to keep the door locked when he wasn't there. The latch was stiff and the bow of the key required an extra hard twist before it gave. Stepping inside the room, he quickly shut the door and secured it behind him, just in case.

Like the lock, his work computer had seen better days. Typing one key at a time with his index finger, Alan called up the school's CCTV system, which was password protected. Only he, Mrs Pullman and the chairman of the governors knew what the password was and Alan changed it once a month.

It was his predecessor who had fixed it so that whoever was Rushbrooke's site manager – Alan preferred being called caretaker because the proper title sounded too poncey to him – was also its Data Controlling Officer, responsible for running the CCTV system. Had his predecessor foreseen how the system could be abused? Did he ever do it himself? Alan had often wondered.

The cameras were installed in the main hall, front and side entrances, playground and some corridors; unions didn't like them in classrooms in case footage was used against teachers. Initially Alan hadn't given much consideration to being in charge of the system, apart from thinking that the extra few quid he received for the role would come in very handy. Now he knew exactly what it meant to be responsible for it, good and bad.

With the quick action of someone who'd done the same thing before, Alan pulled up the recording for one of the cameras that spanned the playground and rewound the footage until he saw the two children come into view. The time stamp read 07:02. He was curious to see how they'd been before they got on the wall and to his surprise he saw it was the boy leading the girl towards the building site, pulling her along by the hand – and she didn't appear too happy about it. He peered closely at the screen. Was she crying? It looked as though she was.

He shook his head, then closed the footage down. It didn't matter if she was crying, laughing or banging a bloody drum. She wasn't his biggest concern right now.

With a shaking hand he clicked on a camera labelled 'Corridor 8'. If anyone else at the school saw it they'd question its existence immediately – because there was no Corridor 8 inside Rushbrooke.

This was a camera Alan had secretly installed inside the Pavilion, a wooden, chalet-style building on the far side of the playing field that a lack of funding had allowed to fall into disrepair. Erected when the school was first built and used over the years as changing rooms, it was out of bounds to pupils now, and Mrs Pullman thought Alan used it for storing old sports equipment. Should she ever check for herself, she'd see the rotting gym mats and broken benches had long been removed and either side of the partitioned wall that once separated the girls' and boys' changing areas were two sofas that pulled out into double beds.

If she knew what they were being used for, the death of a pupil on school premises would be the least of her worries.

Alan steadied his hand as he clicked through a series of options to disable the camera and remove its technical presence from the CCTV system. The actual camera would have to stay where it was until he could sneak across to the Pavilion and remove it.

A couple more clicks later and every recorded frame of footage vanished with it.

7

The police had baulked at the idea of Dylan accompanying Julia to the school and insisted she ask a family member or friend to look after him while she was there.

Her first port of call had been her neighbour Cath, who lived two doors down and often minded the kids, but she wasn't in. So Julia was forced to call Siobhan, whose son Callum was Dylan's best friend. The mums weren't anywhere near as close as the boys and Julia knew it was a big ask, but luckily for her Siobhan had decided to work at home for the day because the school was shut and she agreed to take Dylan. Julia hadn't explained on the phone why she needed the favour, just that there was a family emergency she needed to sort out, and Siobhan's shock was therefore palpable when Dylan was dropped off at her house in a marked police car.

'Why have the police brought you?' she asked suspiciously, standing on the doorstep and eyeing the vehicle over Julia's shoulder. Dylan had already vanished inside the house with Callum.

'They're taking me up to the school,' said Julia falteringly.

Siobhan went pale. 'I got a text from Sam's mum to say that a kid had been hurt. It's not Poppy, is it?'

Julia matched her horrified expression.

'It can't be, they'd have told me, wouldn't they? They just said I'm needed at the school.'

Siobhan peered at the police car again. The two officers in the front stared impassively back at her.

'You're right, they would've told you before you left home if it was that bad.' Her gaze reverted to Julia. 'But it must mean Poppy's involved. Why else would they be taking you up there when the rest of us have been told to stay away? If she's not with you, where is she? Do you even know?'

'I should go,' said Julia tearfully, unable to stand a moment more questioning. 'Thanks for having Dylan. I'll text you as soon as I know how long I'll be.'

'Sure. I hope you get it sorted,' Siobhan called after her as Julia shot down the path.

'So do I.'

By the time they reached the lane leading up to the school Julia was stricken with anxiety. She tried to engage the officers in a conversation about what was going on but they kept insisting a more senior colleague, someone from CID, would explain everything.

She tried calling Ewan again, shifting sideways in her seat and turning her face to the window so the officer driving couldn't see her expression as he spied on her in the rear-view mirror. Her call diverted straight to voicemail again. She sent another text asking him to call her immediately, uppercasing the words for effect.

On arriving at Rushbrooke was struck by how quiet it was, the usual flow of parents in and out of the playground at that time eerily absent.

As the car pulled to a halt, panic overwhelmed her.

'Where's Poppy? I want to see her now.'

'Don't worry, we've been told to take you straight to her,' said the tall officer.

Inside the playground it was much busier. The sight of all the police and vehicles made her insides churn. The only person she recognized was the caretaker, Mr Donnelly, who was sitting on a bench at the edge of the playground. She could see he was using his asthma inhaler, his upper body rearing up as he sucked the vapour in. Their eyes met as she went past but he looked away before she did.

Julia followed the officers into the main building, the only part of the original red-brick structure built in 1910 that remained. Designed as a school for boys, half the school was bulldozed in the sixties and replaced with two bland concrete annexes to accommodate girls and an expanding catchment. Now, it was one of the best-performing primaries in Mansell, an Ofsted shining example, but its success was pushing it to bursting point: when Julia attended Rushbrooke in the early eighties there had been only one form per year; now there were three, with bulge classes being added to the lower years in September.

'Your daughter is in the head's office,' said the tall officer once they were inside.

Julia's head swam with confusion. Why had Poppy sneaked out to go to school early? Leaving the house without permission was a rule she knew never to break and there was no reason for her to be at school at such an early hour – no morning clubs for her to attend and no class trip scheduled that would require her being there ahead of the usual time. Her being there made no sense.

The corridor they were walking along was achingly familiar to Julia. Year 6 lockers on the left – Poppy's was number 23 and a quick glance confirmed it was unopened – then past the girls' toilets, the Welfare Room – in her day it had been Matron's – and the alcove where the head's PA sat until they reached a door with a sign proclaiming it as Mrs Pullman's office and a warning to knock before entering. The tall officer rapped softly on the door and it opened to reveal a woman with long auburn hair, dressed in a sober skirt suit. She slipped through the gap and closed the door softly behind her, thanked both officers and said she'd take it from here. They left without another glance at Julia, their pace brisk as they headed back along the corridor.

'I'm Detective Sergeant Anna Renshaw and I'm the officer in charge,' said the woman, shaking Julia's hand. 'Before I take you in to see Poppy I need to quickly explain why we want to question her, with you present as her appropriate adult.'

'Question her?' gasped Julia. 'About what?'

'Poppy was involved in a serious incident this morning. Another child fell off a wall inside the school grounds and was fatally injured.'

It took a moment for Julia's brain to catch up.

'Fatally injured? You mean . . .'

'Yes. I'm afraid he died from injuries sustained in the fall.'

'And . . . and you think Poppy had something to do with it? That's preposterous,' Julia spluttered.

'I'm afraid Poppy was on the wall with him when he fell,'

said Renshaw, her tone soft. 'I have a witness who saw her. Now, I need to question Poppy to find out exactly what happened, with you—'

Julia's shrill cry cut her short.

'No, no, this is crazy. You must have the wrong child.' She was overcome with dizziness. 'It's too hot in here . . . I'm going outside. I need some air.'

'Mrs Hepworth, I understand this has come as a shock, but Poppy needs you.'

But Julia was already backing away from her. When she was out of arm's reach she spun on her heel, the rubber sole of her sandals squeaking violently against the buffed floor. She was level with the door to the Welfare Room when it swung open and two women walked out. One was dressed in a vivid orange sundress but her demeanour didn't match the cheeriness of her attire – her face was a picture of devastation, her eyes bloodshot and swollen from crying. She looked up and as their eyes locked it was as though time had suddenly stopped.

Julia froze to the spot, breathless with shock.

The hair was different, far blonder, and the face older, but there was no mistaking who the woman was.

Imogen.

Panicked, Julia looked around for an escape route, like she was nine years old again and desperate for a hiding place where Imogen couldn't get to her. She could feel Imogen's gaze raking over her face and her skin blazed with a mixture of embarrassment and fear. Did Imogen recognize her after all these years . . . was she remembering what she did?

Before either of them could speak, Renshaw gestured to the woman who was with Imogen – a finger wag by her side

41

as though she was signalling 'no' to a dog begging for a treat. The movement was subtle but frantic and Julia suddenly knew why Imogen was so upset.

'Not your child –' she whispered in horror.

Imogen held her hands up to stop her, fresh tears streaking her cheeks. Her companion put a protective arm around her shoulders.

'Let's get you home,' said the woman, who was tall, with longish, honey-blonde hair and striking eyes. 'I'll call you later,' she added in an aside to Renshaw, who replied, 'Thanks, Maggie.'

As they walked away, Imogen slumped against the Maggie woman for support, Julia turned to Renshaw.

'Please tell me it's not her child who's died.'

'I'm afraid it is.'

Julia closed her eyes. The beginnings of a headache gripped her temples.

'I know this is difficult, but are you ready to see Poppy now?' asked Renshaw.

Julia ignored her.

'Imogen's child is a pupil at Rushbrooke? Since when? I mean, they moved away, didn't they? Imogen and her family. They left in the summer holidays after we left Rushbrooke. Isn't that right?'

The staccato of questions brought a frown to Renshaw's face.

'Mrs Tyler moved back to Mansell at Christmas. Her son was in Poppy's class,' she said.

Julia swayed on the spot. Imogen was living in Mansell again? Walking the same streets, breathing the same air as her? She couldn't bear the thought.

'Are you ready to see Poppy now?' Renshaw repeated.

Julia was suddenly overcome with guilt. What was she thinking, not going straight to her? Poppy needed her.

'Yes, I am. Please, take me to her.'

Julia's mind was in turmoil as she followed Renshaw back to the head's office.

What on earth had Poppy got herself caught up in?

What was she thinking climbing the wall in the first place?

And why did the child who died have to be the son of the one person Julia hated more than anyone else she'd ever met?

8

The house that until a few hours ago Imogen had shared
with her son was a terraced cottage set back from a busy
road, ten minutes from Rushbrooke on foot, three by car.
The downstairs was open plan but small, a lounge-cum-
dining room leading into a galley kitchen, with everything
wedged in its place. The decor was tasteful if a bit lacking
in personality for Maggie's taste: all muted tones and pale
wood furniture. Imogen had said there were two bedrooms
and a bathroom upstairs and Maggie imagined they were
done out the same.

She offered to make tea as Imogen wandered numbly
around the lounge area, picking up and putting down toys
that obviously belonged to and had been left out by Benji,
among them a hand-held games console. Eventually she sank
down onto the sofa, a light grey three-seater set against the
longest wall.

'Benji's usually waiting for me when I get home from
work,' she began, her voice hoarse from all the crying.
'Sometimes he'll be in his room but usually he's here, watching telly.' She stroked the seat beside her. 'He gives me this
soppy grin when I come in, like he's really pleased to see me

but he's too self-conscious to give me a kiss.' She looked up at Maggie beseechingly. 'Are you sure it's him? Maybe there's been a mistake, and it's another boy who looks like him? I wouldn't be cross if it was a mix-up, I promise. You can tell me.'

Maggie's heart ached for the woman. She would love nothing more than to be able to tell Imogen they'd got it wrong.

'I'm so sorry,' she said. 'But the birthmark . . . it matched.'

Imogen bit down hard on her bottom lip, nodding.

'I wish I could tell you differently,' said Maggie. 'I really do.'

She finished making them tea, then carried two full mugs back into the lounge. Imogen was reading texts on her phone.

'It's work, wondering where I am. I should let them know what's happened.'

'What do you do?'

'I'm a receptionist at the GP practice in Medley Lane.'

'I'll call them, save you having to deal with it,' said Maggie.

She went back into the kitchen to make the call, giving scant details to the inquisitive receptionist who answered. Maggie asked for the practice manager to call her back when they were next free.

Returning, she found Imogen shivering violently.

'I feel really cold,' she lamented.

Maggie felt the opposite. It was only mid-morning but it was already stiflingly hot and all of the windows downstairs were shut.

'It's probably the shock,' she said. 'Here, put this around you.'

She took a beige throw that was folded over the back of the easy chair and gently wrapped it around Imogen's shoulders.

'Is there anything else I can get you?' she asked.

Imogen looked up at her, eyes brimming once more with tears.

'I need to see him. I can't bear that he's on his own. He must be so scared.'

The woman's anguish was so raw that Maggie felt her own composure begin to flail. She nodded briskly to settle it.

'I understand. I'll find out when it can be arranged.'

She went off to make the call and when she came back Imogen had stopped shivering and was sipping her tea.

'Do you feel up to answering a few more questions?' Maggie asked. 'Only, one of my jobs as your liaison is to put together some notes to give to my colleagues so they can work out Benji's movements this morning. We call it a victimology, which I know might sound a bit scary, but it's really a list of his daily routine and habits, his likes and dislikes, the people he came into contact with, the places he regularly went to. Obviously it was unusual for him to be at school so early, so it might help us work out what made him deviate from his usual movements.'

While she spoke Maggie watched, hawk-like, for Imogen's reaction. The last thing she wanted was for her to think that gathering the victimology was an interrogation. Maggie saw it more like a conversation, going back and forth, teasing the details out.

'You think it will help?' asked Imogen, reaching across

and setting her mug down on the hearth, the hardest surface nearest to her.

'I do.'

'Okay.' Imogen pulled the wrap tighter around her. 'Ask me.'

Maggie pulled her notebook from her handbag. 'I'll use this to make notes,' she said. Then her gaze fell upon a copy of a well-known children's novel lying face down, pages open, on the sofa arm, waiting for Benji to come home and carry on where he'd left off.

'Let's start with likes and dislikes. You mentioned Benji loved swimming, and I can see the games console and novel here, so can I assume he was a fan of both?'

Imogen allowed herself a smile.

'He actually prefers reading to playing that thing. You know how some kids want to watch TV round the clock, or be on an iPad? With Benji it's always books. He's never happier than when he's got a good story to read. I have to bribe him to watch films with me at the weekend.' Imogen reached forward and gently ran a finger down the spine of the book. 'He's only halfway through this.'

Although Imogen was still referring to Benji in the present, Maggie deliberately didn't. It wouldn't help Imogen in the long run if the police too spoke as though he was still alive.

'What sort of films did he like when you managed to get him to watch one?'

They spent the next few minutes chatting about that, then Maggie asked what their usual morning routine involved.

'I get up around seven, Benji by half past, then we have breakfast together and I go off to work because he walks to school on his own. They're allowed to in Year Six,' Imogen explained. 'But this morning for some reason my alarm clock didn't go off, so it was gone eight by the time I woke up.'

'So Benji wasn't here when you got up?'

'I thought he was. I was in such a rush because I was running late that on my way into the shower I shouted for him to sort his own breakfast out.' Imogen's face crumpled. 'I could've sworn he answered. Then when I got out of the shower I saw the text on my phone saying something bad had happened at the school and that it was shut. I went to tell Benji and that's when I realized he wasn't in the house.'

'He hadn't said a word to you about needing to go to school early, or arranging to meet Poppy?'

'No, nothing.'

Spotting an obvious segueway, Maggie decided to deviate from her victimology questions. She knew that Renshaw, as SIO, would want to ask Imogen herself about Poppy, but it wouldn't hurt to give them a head start.

'Did Benji and Poppy get on well?'

Imogen's eyes widened apprehensively.

'I thought they did.'

'Did they often meet up outside school?'

'Not as much as Benji would've liked, but occasionally.'

'What do you mean by that?'

'If he had his way, she would come for tea every day. He adores her.'

'Are you aware of them ever falling out?'

Imogen grew teary. 'Please, I don't want to talk about her any more. I can't. It's too hard.'

'Of course,' said Maggie gently. 'It can wait.'

'I don't want anyone going around saying she adores him though. Because she can't do, not after this.'

'What do you mean?'

Imogen looked at her squarely.

'If she did, Poppy wouldn't have done this . . . you don't kill someone who's meant to be your best friend.'

9

The atmosphere in the head's office thrummed with tension. Ewan had finally arrived after switching on his phone once his meeting wrapped up to a bombardment of messages from Julia and he was now sitting one side of Poppy while she was on the other. DS Renshaw and another detective introduced to them as DC Nathan Thomas sat opposite, while Mrs Pullman stayed behind her desk, watching the proceedings solemnly and without interruption. The head was there at Julia's request, a familiar face to dilute the uneasy sense that it was now her family versus the police.

'Poppy, can you tell me why you were at school so early this morning?' asked Renshaw.

The woman had patience in spades, thought Julia. It must've been the twentieth time she'd asked Poppy that question and once again her daughter stonewalled her. Well, she wasn't refusing to answer as such – she simply wasn't saying anything, not a word. Her hands remained limp in her lap and her head bowed low so her face was hidden.

Julia took her daughter's right hand in hers and squeezed it, a gesture of reassurance that wasn't returned.

'Darling, you must say what happened,' she said, unable

to mask the panic she was feeling. If Poppy didn't open up soon, they'd think she was hiding something.

'This is ridiculous,' said Ewan, not bothering to hide his exasperation. 'My daughter needs a break, we all do.'

To Julia's surprise Renshaw agreed and rose to her feet.

'I need to talk to my colleague outside for a moment. Please excuse us.'

Julia flinched as the door shut behind them.

'Why don't I fetch some more tea? There might be some biscuits in the staffroom, too,' said Mrs Pullman, coming out from behind her desk. Whatever the head was thinking she hid behind a smile. Julia returned it weakly. Mrs Pullman gathered up the tray of empty cups on the table and left.

An uncomfortable silence settled over the room. Julia caught Ewan's eye for reassurance but his brow furrowed and he mouthed at her to 'say something'. Julia swallowed the flash of annoyance that rose inside her. He always left it to her to sort the kids out; why couldn't he step up for a change?

Then she looked at Poppy's bowed head and berated herself for being selfish.

'Sweetheart, you know we love you no matter what,' she said, squeezing Poppy's hand again. 'We're not cross, we just want to know what happened.'

Poppy gave the tiniest of nods.

'Take your time.' Julia kept her voice low, so the police outside couldn't hear. 'It's just me and Daddy here.'

A whimper, then, 'I can't.'

'Come on now,' said Ewan, his tone and volume rising

above his wife's. 'What Mummy's trying to say, rather badly, is that if you tell us we can help you.'

Julia smarted at the dig.

'You can't,' said Poppy. 'It's all my fault.'

Julia looked across at her husband, bewildered.

'But it was an accident, wasn't it?' said Ewan.

The pause between Ewan's question and Poppy answering 'yes' shook Julia and she suddenly became aware of how hot the room was. Just one of the windows was open, and only by a crack. Her vision swam as though she was about to faint.

'I can't – I'm sorry. I can't breathe.'

She got to her feet and rushed to the door.

'Where the hell are you going?' Ewan shouted.

'I need air.' She flung open the door and stumbled into the corridor. The two detectives were right outside.

'Are you okay, Mrs Hepworth?' asked Renshaw.

Julia clawed at her throat as she tried to catch her breath.

'Can't . . . breathe . . . too hot.'

'I think she's having a panic attack,' said Renshaw to her colleague.

They took her to the Welfare Room and, after rooting around the First Aid cupboard, found a paper sick-bag for her to breathe into. When Julia had calmed down, her heartbeat no longer thundering in her chest, DC Thomas pressed a small plastic cup of ice-cold water into her hand. She gratefully took a gulp.

'Better?' asked Renshaw.

Julia nodded.

'Good.' Renshaw folded her arms. 'I've decided it's best if you take Poppy home now, as we're not getting anywhere.

But you'll have to bring her down to the police station first thing tomorrow so we can continue questioning her.'

'She told us it was an accident, just now, after you left the room,' said Julia eagerly. 'It wasn't her fault.'

'Really? Let's go back in and see if she'll repeat that for us.'

But Poppy clammed up again the minute Renshaw spoke to her. The detective escorted Julia back outside with DC Thomas while Ewan stayed with their daughter.

'I cannot stress enough how important it is Poppy tells us what happened this morning,' said Renshaw. 'She needs to understand how serious this is.'

'I know. I promise we'll talk to her, make her understand. But can you not come to our house?' Julia implored. 'The police station will be scary for her.'

'It'll be fine – we have an interview suite specially for minors.'

That alarmed Julia even more. 'But she'll be more relaxed at home.'

'No, it has to be at the station,' said Renshaw firmly. 'A formal setting should convince her how much trouble she could be in if she doesn't tell us the truth.'

'In trouble?' Julia gasped. 'But it was an accident, she said so.'

'Mrs Hepworth, a boy has died in suspicious circumstances and Poppy was there when it happened. If she won't talk to us, what are we meant to think? Really, I should take her in to the station now, but I can see she's in shock so I'm prepared to wait. Hopefully she'll be more talkative tomorrow after some rest.'

Julia wanted to cry. This was like a bad dream, beyond

her control, with Imogen centre stage as her own personal bogeyman.

She'd been trying to ignore the emotions that had been churning inside her since she'd clapped eyes on Imogen in the corridor, pushing them to the pit of her stomach because Poppy needed her to stay focused on her. Now they were bubbling to the surface again: hate and anger, hand in hand.

Yet fear wasn't far behind them, fear of what Imogen might do and the trouble she could cause. Julia hesitated. Should she tell the police what went on between them all those years ago? Would it make any difference to Poppy's situation if she did?

Before she could utter a word, Ewan walked out of the head's office with Poppy in tow. Julia was startled by his expression – he looked shell-shocked.

'I want to take my daughter home,' he said.

Renshaw nodded. 'Your wife can explain what will happen tomorrow. But if Poppy wants to talk before then, call me. Doesn't matter what time it is.'

She handed Ewan a business card, which he pocketed.

Julia waited until the three of them were alone in the car park, by her husband's car, before she spoke.

'What's going on?'

'Maybe you should've shown more concern inside,' he answered tersely. 'I can't believe you just walked out on Poppy.'

'It wasn't like that,' she said lamely. 'I didn't feel well and—'

Ewan silenced her with a look.

'Let's get home.'

She waited by the driver's door until Poppy was strapped into the back seat, then, as Ewan went to open it, blocked his path.

'Did Poppy say anything else to you when I left the room?' she asked.

His answer came too quickly to be convincing.

'No, not a word.'

Julia stared at her husband as he yanked open the door and settled himself behind the wheel. After fifteen years of marriage she could say with confidence that she knew Ewan pretty much inside out. The qualities, beliefs, passions and foibles that stacked up to make him the person he was were an indelible part of her too, matrimonially etched on her psyche for better or worse.

Yes, she knew her husband exceptionally well – and she knew when he was lying to her.

10

Shortly after noon the officer who'd allowed Alan fetch his inhaler sought him out in the main hall. Not sure what he should be doing, what with the school being closed, Alan was busying himself buffing the parquet floor with the industrial polisher. It was so noisy he didn't hear the officer until he was right by his side, gesturing at him to turn it off.

'You can go home if you want, but CID wants you down at the station at two thirty to make a formal statement,' the copper said. 'Ask for DS Renshaw when you get there.'

Alan managed to hide his trepidation long enough to confirm that he'd keep the appointment. He'd been hoping for at least a day's grace to get his thoughts straight and fathom a way out of this mess, but now he had two and a bit hours to come up with a plan to divert the police's attention away from Rushbrooke and, more importantly, the Pavilion.

He decided to wait in his office until it was time to leave; it would at least give him respite from all the commotion above ground, with police vehicles coming and going and people in overalls and masks traipsing all over the place. But as he reached the stairwell to his basement workplace Mrs Pullman stopped him.

'I understand the police want to interview you,' she said. 'Why don't you go home first? You've had a terrible shock.' She looked him up and down, taking in his bottle-green combat trousers and sweat-stained grey T-shirt, and pulled a face. 'It probably wouldn't hurt to smarten up a little as well.'

Alan managed his first smile of the day. He and the head got on well, always had, and he was not in the slightest bit offended by the remark because she was right, he looked a state.

'Actually, I wouldn't mind nipping home to change, if you're sure.'

She nodded sadly. 'There's nothing either of us can do here at the moment.'

Alan's house was two streets away from the school and came with the job. It was a decent size and the rent was reasonable enough for him to not mind the six-monthly poke-around by the council – in its guise as the local education authority and therefore his employer – to make sure he wasn't trashing the place.

If anything the inspectors were always taken aback by how staid it was, its interior more reflective of a pensioner's home than a man of forty-seven. The house was filled with decrepit dark wood furniture and fussy ornaments that Alan had taken possession of when his dad went into the nursing home and the front room was pretty much a replica of the one he'd grown up in. But as he'd taken nothing from the house he had shared with his now ex-wife and their three children, he couldn't afford to be picky and he certainly couldn't afford new furnishings on top of paying maintenance for the kids.

After a quick shower, Alan changed into the one smart shirt he owned and a pair of old suit trousers that he struggled to fasten because a few years had passed and a couple of stone been added on since he'd last worn them.

The shirt was soaked with sweat within five minutes of him leaving the house, even though he was keeping to the shadiest side of the road. The back way into town, along alleyways and down side streets, would've been cooler but Alan wasn't confident enough of the route, even though he'd been living in Mansell for almost three years now. He didn't venture into town much – apart from a nightly pint in his local and shopping at the nearby Co-op, he spent all his time at Rushbrooke.

He was halfway to the police station when his phone rang. He wasn't surprised by who was calling, just that it had taken him this long. Alan had half expected to see him up at the school but knew exactly why he'd stayed away.

The Pavilion.

'Alan?'

'Hi, Gus.'

'How are you doing?'

He sounded genuinely concerned and Alan was taken aback. He'd been expecting Gus to be angry with him, as though it was his fault the police were crawling all over the school.

'I'm okay.'

'Horrible business with the kid.'

'Yeah, it is.' An image flashed before Alan's eyes and he shuddered. He'd never seen so much blood before.

'I've got to say I'm concerned though, with the police involved. Alan, I need you to sort it out for us.'

'What?'

'Well, I can't do it, can I? No one's going to listen to what I say because I wasn't there. But you, you witnessed it. You're on the inside.'

'But it's the police,' said Alan, cupping his hand over his mouth and phone to buffer the sound of traffic rumbling past.

'You need to make this thing go away, Alan,' Gus implored. 'Make *them* go away.'

'I can't tell the police what to do,' said Alan fearfully.

The tone of Gus's voice changed abruptly.

'The Pavilion would never have happened without you,' he said ominously. 'You're up to your neck in this as much as the rest of us. Figure it out but do it quick. We're all counting on you, mate.'

The line went dead.

Half an hour later, when Alan was sitting in the witness interview suite watching an irritated DS Renshaw and her colleague fiddle with the recording equipment to get it to start, the answer hit him. It was so blindingly obvious he couldn't believe he hadn't thought of it sooner.

He exhaled heavily. Could he really do this? It could get him in serious trouble . . . but then the alternative didn't bear thinking about either. Another image of the boy popped into his head but he forced it away. If he let himself dwell on it . . . And he had to do this . . . The Pavilion *had* to stay a secret.

Recording equipment running, Renshaw asked Alan to describe what he'd seen take place on the wall.

'We want as much detail as you can remember,' she said. He swallowed hard.

'There's not much to tell. I could see kids mucking around and I told them to get down. At first they wouldn't, so I moved the ladder nearer to them. They were about to climb down when the boy lost his footing and fell.'

The two officers exchanged glances.

'You're sure about that?' said DS Renshaw sternly. 'He just slipped?'

'Yes, I'm sure.'

'Mr Donnelly, that's not what you told PC Talbot, one of the officers first to arrive at the scene. He said you told him you saw Poppy push Benji off the wall and that it wasn't an accident.'

Alan shook his head vehemently.

'I never said that.'

'PC Talbot is certain you did.'

'Well, I'm telling you I didn't.'

'You must've been extremely distressed by what happened. Maybe that's confusing your recollection,' said Renshaw pointedly.

'Of course I was upset: it's the worst thing I've ever seen. I mean, the way he landed –' Alan suddenly pictured the boy lying on the ground, blood everywhere, and felt genuine anguish. He took another deep breath to steady himself. 'But he definitely wasn't pushed.'

Renshaw leaned forward on her elbows and stared at him.

'Mr Donnelly, are you absolutely certain you didn't see

Poppy Hepworth push Benji Tyler off that wall to his death?'

Alan hid his trembling hands beneath the table. He never was a good liar.

'I am. She didn't lay a finger on him.'

11

Imogen's brother, Ed, arrived from Somerset as the afternoon ebbed into early evening. He had gone directly to the
mortuary to make a formal identification of his nephew,
then collected their mother, Grace, from her home on the
outskirts of Mansell on his way to Imogen's house. Maggie
had wondered why Grace didn't make the trip earlier on her
own when she lived only two miles away but didn't question
it. Some people were brought closer together by a death in
the family, in others it widened the cracks already showing.
Only time would tell which camp the Tylers would fall into.

The presence of Ed and Grace allowed Imogen to fully
succumb to her grief. With them she didn't have to pretend
to be strong, to try to hold it together, and she cried with
abandon in her brother's arms. Maggie knew it was time for
her to withdraw and leave them to mourn alone for a while.
She left her number and told Imogen she could call her at
any point during the evening, no matter how late. Then
she'd be back in the morning.

Driving back to the station Maggie mulled over what
Imogen had said about Benji and Poppy not being the
friends she thought they were. Before leaving, she'd asked

her to elaborate on what she meant and Imogen explained that Poppy knew Benji was a cautious boy who shied away from anything too adventurous so it must've been her who persuaded him to climb the wall, and a friend wouldn't have done that.

'He's so timid he wouldn't try going down the smallest water slide on holiday and he turned down an invitation to a party at a climbing centre because he was scared. It's my fault – I tend to be overprotective and I should encourage him more to take risks. But that's also why I know it can't have been an accident – Benji's so careful he'd never willingly put himself in danger.'

Maggie had promised she would share what she'd told her with Renshaw and the rest of the team. In the meantime Imogen was going to compile a list of the other friends Benji had made at Rushbrooke, as they would need to talk to them all.

The traffic crawled to a halt as she neared the town centre so Maggie called Umpire on her hands-free. He sounded frazzled.

'Sorry, I meant to call earlier but I'm swamped. I'll be working late, so it's probably not worth you coming over,' he said.

'That's fine. My day's not been great either.'

She told him about Benji. 'I'm FLO to his mum now.'

Umpire was blunt in his response.

'Is that a good idea?'

Maggie's skin prickled. 'Meaning?'

'You know exactly why.'

Usually she liked that he could second-guess her so easily. Now wasn't one of those times.

63

'I'll be fine.'

'How can you be so sure? You still get emotional whenever you talk about Lou and the children, you haven't slept properly since they moved away and there isn't a day that goes by that you don't miss them.'

He was saying nothing that she hadn't thought herself but his inference irritated her.

'You think I'm so unprofessional that I'd let it get in the way?' she snapped back.

'That's not what I'm saying. I just think you might not be in the right frame of mind for this particular case because it involves a child dying who was the same age as Scotty, and at the same school. You have a duty to his mother and your colleagues to make sure you are.'

'Actually, it was because of those things that I'm now the FLO.'

'Have you told them about your family circumstances then?'

Maggie lost her temper.

'Instead of lecturing me like an SIO, how about you talk to me like my boyfriend?' she sniped.

'That's what I am doing,' said Umpire quietly. 'I'm worried, that's all.'

'Don't be. Look, I have to go, I'm at the station now.'

She wasn't, she was still five minutes away, but she wanted to end the call.

'Fine. I'm sorry if you're upset but you do need to be rational about this.'

'I am being.'

But as she said the words out loud, she wasn't sure she believed them any more than Umpire did.

12

CID was on the top floor of Mansell police station and still buzzing with the sound of hard graft despite the late hour. Almost every desk in the open-plan office was occupied as Maggie weaved through it to reach her own. Up ahead she could see Renshaw talking to Detective Superintendent Andreotti. Whatever was being discussed, Renshaw appeared happy with the outcome and she grinned at Maggie as she returned to her own desk across the walkway.

'I'm staying as SIO on the Rushbrooke case. Boss says he still hasn't had the go-ahead to bring in anyone more senior.'

Nathan groaned in protest but Maggie knew he didn't mean it. He and Renshaw were close and worked well together, so it suited him having her in charge. Maggie was mildly surprised to find she was happy about it too – Renshaw must be growing on her more than she realized.

'Another DC will be on board by tomorrow morning's briefing, though. Boss says we can have Incident Room Five.'

This time Nathan's groan was genuine. Incident Room 5 was barely bigger than a horsebox and it was a running joke in the station that it was the place where investigations were sent to die.

'Let's make the best of it,' said Renshaw briskly.

Maggie and Nathan followed her into Room 5, which was eleven metres square, the same size as the average double bedroom. Desks were pushed up against the walls so everyone would be working with their backs to each other.

'It's not that bad,' said Renshaw, catching the looks on their faces. 'Once we get the board up it'll feel like we're getting somewhere. Then I'll brief everyone on what the CPS said.'

Maggie frowned. Renshaw had a tendency while in charge to keep back the best intel until briefings, so she could deliver it with a theatrical 'ta-da!' rather than sharing it as and when it came in, which would be more helpful to the team slogging away under her.

'Just tell us now,' said Maggie wearily.

'Okay, they've said that because the caretaker's account has changed we need to find cast-iron evidence of Poppy pushing Benji before we can even think about charging her,' said Renshaw darkly. 'And right now we've got sod all in that department.'

'He's changed his story?' queried Maggie.

'Yep. Donnelly's saying Benji slipped and he denies telling PC Talbot that Poppy was to blame. We pressed him on it and he's sticking to the version that the fall was an accident.'

'Could Talbot have been mistaken? I saw him at the scene and he was in a bit of a state. Maybe he misheard him,' said Maggie.

'Yeah, I thought that too, but I've spoken to him again and he's certain that's what Donnelly said.'

'What's Mal's take?' asked Maggie.

'His prelim report says Benji landed with force, like he was propelled to the ground, but that could also be because he was small and slight and went down harder. It doesn't necessarily translate as him being helped on his way,' said Renshaw.

'Benji's mum says he was risk averse and wouldn't try anything remotely scary,' said Maggie. 'She's certain it wouldn't have been his idea to climb the wall.'

Renshaw was thoughtful for a moment.

'Let's just say it was an accident and he slipped,' she said. 'If we can prove Poppy coerced him into climbing onto the wall, and that led to him dying, we could go after an involuntary manslaughter charge for death caused by reckless behaviour.'

'You'd really be happy to prosecute an eleven-year-old for that?' Maggie asked. 'She should be blamed for him slipping?'

'If Poppy's reckless actions caused Benji's death she should be held accountable regardless of her age,' said Renshaw. 'No?'

Maggie hesitated. She always believed no criminal deed should go unpunished but with this one she found she couldn't be so sure. Even if Poppy had forced Benji up on the wall against his better judgement, should she be punished for him losing his footing? Scotty was the same age and Maggie knew she would hate for him to be tried for a death he probably never meant to happen. His whole life destroyed because of a mistake? But the answer came to her as an image of Imogen crying popped into her head.

'Benji's mum would be devastated if the person directly or indirectly responsible for his death didn't answer for their actions in some way,' she said reluctantly. 'There needs to be some kind of resolution for her sake.'

'Even if we make a case for involuntary manslaughter, the CPS could decide it's not in the public interest to prosecute because of Poppy's age,' Nathan said. 'Plenty of cases with minors where that's happened.'

Renshaw glared at him.

'Before we decide to roll over and give up, let's gather that evidence, shall we? *Then* we can decide what case there is to answer and whether it was deliberate or not. First and foremost I want to know about the dynamic between Benji and Poppy – were they friends, was there any bad blood between them, any reported incidents of bullying, was she the class mean girl? I want to know why she and Benji were on that wall in the first place and whose idea it was.'

'Imogen and I have talked a little bit about it already,' said Maggie. 'She described the kids as best friends who socialized out of school.'

Renshaw frowned. 'That's odd. Julia Hepworth said she hadn't seen Imogen for years until this morning. You know the mums went to Rushbrooke together?'

'No, Imogen hasn't mentioned it.'

'If Julia didn't even know Imogen was living back in Mansell, who was organizing the play dates with the kids?'

'I don't think they call them play dates when they're eleven,' Maggie grinned.

'You know what I mean. But I'm right, aren't I? Parents usually arrange for their kids to get together.'

'It must be Poppy's dad then,' said Nathan.

'The way Julia reacted to Imogen I don't think they were friends at school,' said Maggie. 'Did you see her face?'

'I did. Like she was chewing a wasp,' said Renshaw.

'So I'm going to hazard a guess that Mr Hepworth hasn't told his wife he's been organizing play dates with Imogen,' said Maggie.

'That's going to make for an interesting line of questioning tomorrow,' said Renshaw with a smirk. 'What's the story with Benji's dad?'

'He died when Benji was a baby.'

'Shit, Imogen's young to be a widow,' said Renshaw. 'She's only forty, isn't she?'

'Thirty-nine,' Maggie corrected.

'So she had Benji at, what, twenty-eight? That's younger than we are now,' said Renshaw. 'Christ, I'd best get a move on. You too, Maggie.'

Maggie shifted awkwardly in her seat. Renshaw made no secret about wanting children now she was in a serious relationship; her partner, who she lived with, was also a higher rank in their force – Assistant Chief Constable Marcus Bailey. But having children was not a topic Maggie and Umpire had addressed. For all she knew he might not even want more.

She didn't need reminding how old she was either – in three days she would be turning thirty. Maggie hadn't told anyone at work it was her birthday and she planned to mark the milestone with a low-key dinner with Umpire on the day, then at the weekend nipping off to a hotel in Brighton overnight, just the two of them. She didn't want anything more elaborate: it would be the first birthday she'd ever spent without seeing Lou at some point during the day or evening, and without her and the kids, what was the point of a big celebration?

'Right, let's reconvene in the morning,' said Renshaw. 'Hopefully we can get something out of Poppy when she comes in.'

'For argument's sake, what happens if we get her to admit she pushed him on purpose, knowing he'd most likely be killed?' asked Nathan.

Renshaw grimaced. 'Then tomorrow we'll be charging an eleven-year-old with murder.'

13

Dinner was beans on toast washed down with a glass of rosé and accompanied by the latest period-drama. Even with every window flung open the flat was uncomfortably hot and Maggie lay stretched out on the sofa in a futile bid to stay cool.

Her mobile was cradled in her lap, ostensibly in case Imogen called. But part of her hoped, as it did every evening, that Lou might ring or text. Maggie knew her sister had changed her number because the last time she tried to call there was a message saying the old one was unobtainable. Now every time an unknown number came up on the screen her heart leapt into her mouth.

She tried to concentrate but the TV couldn't hold her interest. She sat up and opened her laptop, moving her phone aside to make way for it. Opening Facebook, she went straight to the search box and typed in Lou's name. Her sister's profile came up but there was nothing to see apart from her profile picture: the rest of the page had been blocked from Maggie's view since Lou unfriended her.

Fortunately, their mum, Jeanette – who along with their dad, Graeme, had taken Lou's side in the row – was less strict with her privacy settings. Her cover photo was a picture of Jude, Scotty and Mae on a picnic blanket in the back garden of the Nevilles' house near Portsmouth. It was impossible for Maggie not to be rankled by it – her parents had done little to support Lou over the years, disapproving of her having three children by three different men, yet all of a sudden they were happy to do the dutiful grandparents bit. Their hypocrisy made it easier for her to not miss them since they'd cut her off too.

Sighing, Maggie clicked off her mum's profile. She had no idea whether Lou and the kids were staying with her parents or if they had a place of their own by now. It made her miserable to think they could be carving out a new life that she knew nothing about. Would Mae, a two-year-old, even remember who she was if she saw her now?

But she knew she only had herself to blame. Twelve years previously, when she was seventeen, she'd had an affair with Lou's fiancé, an unemployed twenty-year-old called Jerome. Lou was pregnant with Jude at the time. When Jerome was killed in a road traffic accident while the affair was ongoing, Maggie, grief-stricken and wracked with guilt, had vowed her sister must never find out.

But Lou had, seven months ago, by chance. And on discovering the betrayal she had moved away from Mansell with the kids, saying she could no longer bear to live in the same town as Maggie, much less have anything to do with her. It didn't matter how long ago the affair took place, it was the fact that it had, and the fact that Maggie had continuously lied to her.

Feeling shaky just thinking about it and in need of comfort, Maggie called Umpire. He was still in his office.

'I'm glad you called. I'm afraid I've got some bad news. Sarah's changed her mind about this weekend.'

'Are you serious? What about Brighton?'

Sarah was Umpire's ex-wife and the mother of Flora and Jack. This weekend should've been his turn to have the children, but he'd asked to swap as a one-off because it was Maggie's thirtieth and Sarah had agreed. Umpire would then have them two weekends in a row.

'She's saying she's had a think about it and thinks for the kids' sake we should stick to the agreed custody plan.'

'What did you say?'

'I had to say yes. It's the kids. Look, I know it's disappointing, but we'll still have the dinner on Friday on your actual birthday, then we'll rearrange Brighton for another weekend.'

'But it won't be my birthday weekend then.' Maggie knew she was being petulant but the thought of not seeing him all weekend filled her with dread. She didn't want to be sitting at home alone obsessing over her family and why they hadn't sent a single card between them.

'I know, and I'm sorry. I did try but I couldn't talk her round.'

Maggie bit down the angry retort about to escape her lips. It wasn't Umpire's fault his ex-wife was being a bitch. But is this what it was going to be like, at least until the kids were older, her always coming second to them?

'Maggie? Are you still there?'

'Yes, I'm here,' she said sulkily.

'I am sorry. Really I am.'

His conciliatory tone had the effect of softening hers. 'I

know. I was just looking forward to going away,' she said with a sigh.

'So was I.'

They chatted for a few more minutes, then said goodnight.

Maggie went back to scrolling through her news feed. She clicked 'like' on a picture posted by her friend Belmar Small, who she'd met when he partnered her as FLO on the Rosie Kinnock abduction case a year ago and who was part of Umpire's unit. The picture was of him and his wife, Allie, clinking glasses in a bar on the Caribbean island of Saint Vincent, where they were visiting his relatives. She was pleased to see how relaxed they looked after a difficult few months undergoing IVF for the first time with no success. They were due back on Saturday and had promised to celebrate her birthday belatedly. At least that was something to look forward to.

She was about to close down Facebook when curiosity got the better of her and she typed 'Imogen Tyler' into the search box.

Imogen's profile page was like Lou's – set to private and giving nothing away. The profile picture was a blurry shot of Imogen taken at a distance. Typing Julia Hepworth's name into the search box yielded more than just a profile page, though – other mentions of her name appeared on screen too.

Maggie clicked on the first one and her heart sank. A woman called Iris Sharp had posted a gossipy, semi-illiterate item on a community group for Mansell residents that named Poppy as the pupil present when Benji died – and had tagged Julia in it.

It was bad enough that Poppy was named but Maggie couldn't understand what had motivated Iris to tag her mother as well. Was it so Julia would be compelled to reply? To set trolls on to her? The replies to the post made Maggie even angrier – adults playing judge and jury by deciding Poppy must've killed Benji if the police had spoken to her. Why else would they question her?

Despite the late hour, Maggie called Renshaw.

'Poppy's been named on a local Facebook group,' she said. 'People are writing all kinds of crap.'

'Shit. That's all we need.'

'Can we ask Facebook to take it down?'

'I can try, but technically they aren't obliged to. There are no reporting restrictions in place yet because we're still treating her as a witness. Right now there's nothing to stop her being named.'

'No, but she is a minor and they have a responsibility not to allow the witch-hunt of an eleven-year-old,' said Maggie tetchily.

'Given some of the stuff Facebook lets people post I wouldn't bet on them taking the moral high ground,' said Renshaw. 'I'll apply to have the mentions of her removed on the grounds that she's a witness who's a minor and see what they say. I wonder if the Hepworths have seen it.'

'Probably – the person who wrote the post tagged Julia.'

'Nice of them,' said Renshaw sarcastically.

Maggie was scrolling through the comments again when one jumped out at her.

'Hey, listen to this comment,' she said. 'It's a bit inarticulate but you get the gist . . . "Police should look at whole family, not just girl – if she's violent it's 'cause she's learned it.'"

'Could be nonsense, someone trying to make themselves seem knowledgeable?'

'Maybe, but the rest of the message is pretty emphatic. They even used caps.'

'What's it say?'

'"Trust me – I KNOW."'

14

Wednesday

At 4 a.m. Julia gave up any pretence of sleeping and got up. Ewan stirred as she let herself out of the bedroom but didn't wake. On the landing she stalled for a moment outside Poppy's room and with her fingertip traced the pink, sparkly nameplate Ewan had fixed to the door when they moved in. It was worn around the edges now and faded from where sunlight hit it as it streamed through the landing window.

A few weeks ago she and Poppy had rowed about taking it down. Poppy said it was babyish and stupid and her friends had 'Keep Out' signs on their doors, so why couldn't she? Julia wasn't comfortable allowing such a combative message to be visible inside the house and said no – but now it seemed such a trivial thing for them to have argued over.

Poppy had kept up her wall of silence when they got back from the school and Julia had been unable to fight the creeping unease that Ewan knew something she didn't. He rebuffed her attempts to talk to him in private, telling her she was making Poppy feel worse. That in turn made Julia feel wretched, so while he and the kids watched a film –

they'd collected Dylan from Siobhan's on their way home – she sat alone in the kitchen.

She couldn't sit still, though, so had cleared out the food cupboard instead, a chore she'd been putting off for weeks. Systematically checking the 'use by' dates on tins did distract her for a bit, but then her thoughts resumed their torture: what if the police decided it wasn't an accident and charged Poppy? What if she went to court and was found guilty even though she wasn't? What if the court took her away from them?

It wasn't until the children were in bed that she was able to corner Ewan, when he came into the kitchen to get a drink.

'Not that again,' he'd grumbled.

'But something happened. You came out of that office looking as white as a sheet.'

He'd made her wait before he answered, deliberately taking his time as he poured himself a glass of water and gulped it down.

'Why does it bother you so much that me and Poppy are close?' he'd said, setting the glass down on the side.

Her stomach had clenched. It was a subject he'd raised before and she'd come out of the conversation looking rather pathetic.

'That's not what I'm talking about,' she'd said quickly.

'But it is, Julia,' he'd sighed. 'I wish you weren't so jealous. It's not an attractive trait.'

'I'm not jealous; I'm concerned. Please tell me what happened. What did she say to you?'

Ewan had rolled his eyes. 'All that happened was that I hugged Poppy and told her everything will be fine, like a good parent should. That's what she needs to hear right now, not hysteria like this.'

That had stopped Julia in her tracks. Was she being hysterical? She didn't think she was.

'You're being a bit selfish, darling,' Ewan had added, wrapping his arms around her and kissing her. She'd wanted to protest that she wasn't, that her only concern was for Poppy, but let it go and relaxed into his embrace. Ewan could argue his way out of a paper bag and after the day they'd had she was too exhausted to take him on again.

Downstairs was in darkness. Julia tiptoed through the kitchen without bothering to switch on the lights. The room was stuffy, the warmth of the day still lingering, so she threw open the back door to let the cooler night-time air flood in.

It was a clear night, the sky an inky expanse peppered with stars. At the bottom of the garden loomed the kids' trampoline and the sight of it prompted an unexpected wave of sorrow that sent her sinking to the doorstep.

She silently wept with her face buried in her hands, but after a minute or so forced herself to stop. How would it help Poppy if she fell apart now? Her job was to hold the family together. However awful the circumstances were, she needed to stay strong for her daughter.

Gazing up at the stars, Julia wondered if Imogen was managing to get any sleep. She couldn't begin to fathom what she must be going through. Devastated probably didn't come close. But as an image of Imogen took root in Julia's mind it was not as she'd seen her today, but a younger version, the one she'd known at school – and a familiar sick feeling began snowballing in the pit of her stomach. With a start Julia realized the passing of time had done nothing to dilute her body's physical response to her former class-mate, nor had her mental reaction softened: she hated her just as much now as she had done then.

She was eight when the bullying began. It started with teas-ing and name-calling, then rapidly escalated to shoving and pinching and hitting when no one was looking. For a while Imogen acted alone but then she realized there was more fun to be had in a crowd and roped in the rest of the class to ape her behaviour. Pretty soon it was twenty-odd kids pitched against Julia, friendless and defenceless.

She'd spent many tearful hours trying to work out what she'd done wrong to provoke Imogen, but she always came up blank.

Imogen bullied her just because.

It only ended when the girls left Rushbrooke three years later and went their separate ways. Imogen had sailed through the test to gain a place at one of Buckinghamshire's renowned grammar schools but Julia, who was expected to pass too, deliberately flunked hers so she could attend the secondary modern nearest her home. She preferred to fail, even if it meant disappointing her parents, than spend another five years at the same school as Imogen. Then she heard Imogen's family had moved away, so it was all for nothing.

But even though the bullying thankfully ended, Julia never quite shook off its effects. Imogen's treatment of her had ingrained a tendency to retreat at the first sign of confrontation and in adulthood she was a people pleaser who put others' needs above her own, often to her detriment, because she couldn't bear the thought of being disliked and feared being shunned again.

It was only when she met Ewan, at a work event, that she began to believe she wasn't ugly, boring and stupid – just a few of the insults Imogen and her classmates would toss out daily. Ewan told her she was beautiful and that he'd always look after her and while Julia's self-esteem would forever be bruised and never quite sure of itself, he'd helped raise it to a level where she could look in a mirror and not see her eight-year-old self staring back, reminding her how hideous she was.

Aside from her parents, he was the only person she'd ever confided in about the bullying. She had to, because of what happened when they rowed for the first time. It had been over something so inconsequential that she couldn't remember the details now, but she could vividly recall how she'd curled up in a corner of the room and sobbed at him to leave her alone. He was horrified, thinking he must've done or said something really abhorrent to make her react in such an extreme way, and at first had struggled to understand how embedded the effects of the bullying were, thinking she should be over it given that it happened a decade previously. Now, after almost sixteen years together and having witnessed Julia's reactions, he understood.

There was a rustling in a bush nearest the back door. It was probably a hedgehog or next-door's cat but it made Julia jump and hauled her focus away from her memories. She decided to go back inside and make herself a cuppa, but as she got to her feet she was suddenly gripped by another uncomfortable thought.

There was a time when she used to daydream constantly about making Imogen suffer the same kind of mental torture she was forced to endure, when she would've given *anything* for Imogen to experience a fraction of the distress she experienced.

Now, with her son dead, Imogen was.

Julia knew she shouldn't think it, that it was wicked to let it cross her mind even for a second, but part of her was glad.

15

Half a mile away Alan Donnelly was also awake. He'd drunk three double whiskies at bedtime to knock himself out, but now he was fully alert and the hangover he wasn't expecting until morning was banging on the inside of his skull and churning up his insides. He'd moved from his bed to the sofa, hoping that lying propped up against the cushions might help, but still he couldn't settle so just after four thirty, as the first hint of dawn smouldered at the horizon, he let himself out of the house and walked the two streets to the school.

He felt unsettled and anxious as he stood in front of the building site. It would remain out of bounds to anyone but the police for the next day at least, until all the physical evidence had been gathered. They'd confiscated the ladder and had even removed some of the bricks along the top of the wall for examination. The project manager hadn't been too happy when Alan told him, but he could hardly kick up a fuss under the circumstances.

Alan cupped his mouth with his hand and shook his head as he contemplated the scene before him. Gus was mad to think he was in a position to make the police pack up and go home. They were suspicious of him now and had him in their crosshairs: he could tell by the way DS Renshaw spent a good hour hammering away at him after he'd said the boy wasn't pushed – any longer and he might've cracked.

The guilt at what he'd done kicked in on his way home. Now, without the whisky to make him forget, it smothered him like fog. He'd lied to save his own skin and in doing so had deprived the boy's family of the truth – unless the police found some other way to prove the girl did it. But Alan knew she wouldn't confess: after it had happened she'd simply stared down at the boy's body as though she had no idea how it had ended up there. Alan had tried talking to her but it was like she couldn't hear him or was pretending not to. Then, just as the police arrived, she'd calmly climbed down the ladder and waited at the foot of it. She was like a bloody robot.

Turning his back on the building site, Alan headed across the playing field. With Sports Day now cancelled out of respect, the cracks in the turf could wait, but he might come in over the weekend to finish up. He didn't usually work when he wasn't paid to, but he felt he owed it to Mrs Pullman to get the school looking as normal as possible before all the pupils returned. God knows how they were going to be coming back to school when a kid had died.

He reached the other side of the playing field and stopped. Ten strides further on was a line of thick undergrowth, beyond that the back gardens of a new housing estate still in its first phase and mostly uninhabited. The children were banned from venturing into the undergrowth and only the foolish tried – the scrub was virtually impenetrable and all they got for their efforts were vicious scratches from branches and thorns.

Alan knew how to get through it unscathed. He walked to the far-left corner and squeezed down the side of a large blackthorn bush. Once through, he followed a well-worn path, ducking beneath a couple of low-lying branches, until he hit a small clearing bordered by a wooden fence. It was the only part of the boundary that didn't have new houses on the other side.

One of the fence panels could be pulled loose and swung open to reveal a sizeable gap. Depending on which direction you were coming from, it was either a hidden entrance into the school or a stealth exit to a dirt track where cars could be parked without being seen from the main road.

Alan was tempted to fetch his toolbox and nail it up so it couldn't be used again. But it would be a waste of time – Gus would just badger him to create another opening somewhere else along the fence. Gus could do that, because of who he was.

The moment they'd been introduced Alan had known Gus was going to cause trouble for him.

He just hadn't realized how much.

He retraced his steps until he was back on the edge of the playing field and a few metres from the back door of the Pavilion, which was accessed up some rickety wooden steps. The front of the structure had a porch running its entire length that was visible from the school, so Gus had insisted only the back door was used.

The stretch of grass leading up to the rear of the Pavilion was flattened, despite Alan's best and repeated attempts to make it look otherwise.

But it wasn't him treading a regular path there, and it only happened during night-time hours, long after the kids and teachers had gone home and the school was locked up. The footfall belonged to the women who worked for Gus – and the eager punters lining up to have sex with them.

16

Maggie was draining the glass of orange juice that constituted her breakfast when Imogen rang. She was surprised at the earliness of the call – it wasn't even seven thirty yet. But clearly what Imogen had to tell her couldn't wait until later: she was in such a rush to get her words out that Maggie had trouble understanding her.

'Sorry, can you repeat that?' she asked, putting the glass in the sink alongside last night's dirty crockery.

Imogen slowed her voice.

'I said, one of the mums from school messaged me overnight to say did I know that Benji and Poppy had a big fight at school last week,' said Imogen breathlessly. 'I didn't: he never mentioned it to me and neither did his teacher, although it sounds like she might not have known about it.'

Maggie dashed into the lounge to grab her notebook and flipped it open to make notes as Imogen continued.

'Poppy attacked Benji during lunch break last Thursday. She pulled his hair and slapped him on the arm.'

'And he never said a word?'

'No, not a peep.'

'How did this mum know about it?'

'Her daughter Lucie saw it. She's in their class as well.'

'Did she know what sparked the fight?'

'She didn't say; all she wrote was one minute they were standing there chatting, the next Benji was yelling because Poppy had grabbed his hair.'

'Have you got a name for the mum?'

'Tess Edwards. She messaged me on WhatsApp. It proves I was right about Poppy and Benji not being as good friends as I thought. Tess also said that Lucie said it's not the first time Poppy's lashed out at school.'

'At Benji?'

'She didn't say specifically. But she did say Poppy was known for being a right madam.'

'Had you ever seen them fight in your presence, when they hung out after school?'

'Never. She was always really well behaved when she came round for tea. They got on well when they were together.'

Maggie remembered the conversation between her, Nathan and Renshaw about who organized the play dates.

'Was it her dad who brought her round and picked her up?'

'Yes, Ewan. I haven't met her mum yet. She works long hours, I think.'

'That explains your reaction when we bumped into her leaving the Welfare Room yesterday, before I brought you home,' said Maggie.

There was a pause.

'Julia I went to school with is Poppy's *mum*?'

Imogen's shock seemed real enough to Maggie.

'Yes, she is.'

'I – I had no idea. I mean, Ewan's mentioned his wife in conversation but now I think about it I don't think he's ever told me her first name. And when we were at Rushbrooke her surname was Cox.'

'It's Hepworth now,' said Maggie. 'I think she was quite taken aback to see you too after all this time.'

'I didn't really notice, not with everything . . . well, you know,' said Imogen.

'That's understandable. Did you manage to get any sleep last night?'

'Not really. I kept thinking I could hear Benji calling for me from his bedroom. In the end I got into his bed.' Her voice broke. 'I want him back, Maggie. I want my little boy home. He was all on his own last night. Usually he sleeps with his old teddy – not to cuddle, just on his bed. He can't get to sleep unless he knows the bear is there. It should've been with him last night.'

'You'll be able to see him today,' said Maggie softly. 'It's being arranged for this morning. I'm waiting for the time to be confirmed.'

'Thank you. Can I ask you something though?'

'Of course, ask me anything.'

'Will there be a post-mortem?'

'Because of the circumstances and nature of Benji's death, I'm afraid so.'

Imogen's voice wavered. 'Can I see him before they do it? I don't want to see him after he's been . . .' She stifled a sob.

'I'm sure that can be arranged. I'll talk to the pathologist right away.'

Maggie knew the pathologist would agree to push it back

an hour or two to accommodate Imogen's request. He wouldn't want to make the viewing any worse than it already would be.

She hesitated for a moment; what she was about to say might distress Imogen and she needed to frame it right.

'When someone dies from a serious head injury the pathologist usually makes sure that part of them is covered up before their family sees them. So Benji might be shrouded when you see him,' she said carefully. 'I want you to be prepared for seeing him like that, so it doesn't come as a shock.'

'I don't care – I still want to see him. I never got to kiss him before he went to school yesterday and I hate myself for it,' said Imogen, openly crying now. 'I need to see him to say I'm sorry.'

17

Returning home, Alan managed a couple of hours' fitful sleep on the sofa before being woken by the phone ringing. It was Mrs Pullman, telling him that he needn't bother coming into work.

'Take the day off,' she said. 'The police will be back again and I'll be on site all day to assist them if needs be, so you get some rest.'

Most people would've relished an unexpected day's leave but not Alan. He wanted to be at the school so he could keep an eye on what the police were up to, and try to make sure they went nowhere near the Pavilion.

'I'm fine,' he said, panic scratching at his insides. 'I'd rather come in and keep busy.'

'Nonsense. What happened yesterday has taken its toll on us all, but you've suffered more than most, watching it happen. Stay at home and put your feet up,' Mrs Pullman ordered. 'I'll call you later with an update on when we might reopen. I'm hoping it will be tomorrow or Friday if the police allow it. We need to get back to normal.'

Alan spent the rest of the morning moving twitchily from room to room, unable to relax. He did contemplate going back to bed but his room was like a furnace with no breeze to temper the heat and no fan to artificially produce one.

He decided to sit outside but even the small patio out the back held no respite, its stone surface too hot to stand on for long. So he took one of the plastic garden chairs and positioned it under the shade of the cherry tree that loomed into his garden from the one next door. Then he checked his phone again, scrolling anxiously through his messages as though he suddenly expected to find a summons from the police because they'd found the hidden entrance in the boundary fence, or had opened up the Pavilion and gleaned what it was being used for, or had worked out that he had lied to them about Poppy Hepworth.

Not finding any such message did nothing to calm him and for a moment he toyed with ringing Gus, knowing he'd be up to speed with what the police were doing at the school. But then Gus might be angry he wasn't there himself and hadn't done anything beyond altering his statement. Alan had heard enough alarming stories about the way Gus treated people who'd crossed him to know he needed to keep him sweet at any cost.

Alan wiped the sweat dripping from his brow. Even sitting in the shade was too uncomfortable so he went back inside, switched on the telly and managed to distract himself watching *This Morning*.

At noon he made a sandwich, ham and pickle on doorstep-thick white bread. He'd only managed one bite when his phone went. He snatched it up, thinking it would be Mrs Pullman, and was so surprised to see who was calling that the mouthful caught in his throat and he had to cough forcibly to dislodge it.

'Al? Is that you?'

The quiet, mellifluous voice made his heart shudder in his chest. How long had it been since they'd spoken? Three years? Surely it couldn't be that long? Christ, he realized with a start, it *was* three years ago – on the day he'd moved to Mansell.

'Yes, it's me,' he managed to croak, dashing into the kitchen to get a drink of water. The signal was stronger in there as well and he didn't want to risk cutting out mid-sentence; if that happened his ex-wife might wait another three years to speak to him again.

'You're the last person I was expecting to ring, Gayle,' he said, throat cleared.

'I wasn't sure if this was still your number,' she said falteringly. 'It's been a while . . . I thought you might have changed it.'

All their communication was done via email or solicitors, her choice. He wanted to point out the obvious, that if he had changed his number the kids would have no way of speaking to him, but he bit down hard on the comment before it escaped his lips. There was no point antagonizing her for the sake of point scoring.

'How are the kids?'

They had three – Lacey, thirteen, Kyra, nine, and Freddie, five. He'd stopped all physical contact eighteen months ago, because the younger two were becoming so distraught every time it came to saying goodbye that he thought it was unfair to put them through it. Less upsetting for him too. So instead of him travelling to Newark once a month they chatted on the phone fortnightly and sent messages whenever the urge took them, which was never as often as he'd like, and he never missed a maintenance payment for their keep, which equated to half his salary.

The lack of physical contact was something Alan had learned to endure, like a sprained ankle that only hurt when you walked on it. But now, hearing Gayle's voice out of the blue, he yearned to see them again.

'They're really good.'

'Do they miss me?'

The kids never said it to him when they spoke: usually they nattered on about school and the chats were heartachingly brief.

The line went quiet and for a second he feared Gayle had put the phone down.

'Yes, especially Freddie,' she answered. 'He's a Liverpool fan now. I told him you used to go to matches sometimes so when they're on the telly he looks for you in the crowd.'

Tears began to course down Alan's face, the grief he carried inside him every waking moment finally breaking through the dam of self-restraint. He was missing so much of his children growing up.

'What about the girls?' he sobbed. 'Does Lacey still hate me?'

Lacey had been old enough to assimilate snippets from the rows she overheard to form a picture of what was behind them and Alan couldn't bring himself to lie to her when she confronted him about what he'd done. Theirs was the most precarious of his relationships with his children and the day he moved to Mansell she had shown no emotion as they waved him off.

Kyra had been the opposite, clinging to him in tears, and begging him not to move so far away. But he had no choice – the job at Rushbrooke was the only one he'd been able to get in his situation. Yes, it meant moving hundreds of miles away from Newark but jobs in caretaking were thin on the ground round there and he didn't have the means or the time to retrain. At that point Gayle wanted him as far away from her as possible – he'd irrevocably broken her trust with all the debts he'd run up and it was only thanks to her parents that they hadn't lost the house after he'd secretly remortgaged it behind her back and then defaulted on the payments.

'Please don't cry,' she was saying to him now. 'I hate it when you get upset.'

Alan had not once blamed Gayle for throwing him out. It was his actions that had destroyed their marriage, not hers. He also knew it could've been a hell of a lot worse: had she reported him to the police for fraudulently remortgaging the house the way her parents wanted her to, he probably would've been convicted and imprisoned. Banishment down south was a small price to pay by comparison.

'I'm sorry,' he said, darkening the grey marl hem of his T-shirt as he mopped his tears with it. 'It's just, hearing your voice after all this time . . . Freddie and the girls – I wish I could see them.'

'They wish they could see you too. But listen, I have to be quick because I'm on my break. I'm calling because I wanted to check you're okay. I heard about the boy dying and you being there. Are you okay?'

Alan was confused. 'How do you know about that?'

The news had broken online but details were sparse and

none of the reports mentioned him, the caretaker, being a witness. Not even the boy had been named.

'I've had a call from someone you know, a man called Gus Campbell.'

Alan's legs almost gave way.

'You what?'

'He said he worked—'

'I know who he is,' Alan interrupted frantically. 'What did he say?'

'He thought I should know, because it was obviously awful for you and you don't have anyone in Mansell to support you. You and I aren't exactly family any more, but is there anything I can do to help?'

'No, no, there isn't. But thank you. It's good of you to call.' He hoped he sounded appreciative but he was so livid he could barely speak. 'Look, I'm sorry, I have to go. There's something I have to do. Can I call you back on this number?'

'Yes, of course.'

He called Gus the second Gayle hung up.

'What the hell are you doing calling my ex?' he shouted.

To his fury Gus chuckled.

'Oh, I was just doing my rounds. Prominent councillor . . . tick. High-ranking police officer . . . tick. Star player for the local football team . . . tick. Half a dozen bosses of the town's biggest firms . . . tick. Mother of the caretaker's children who would be most upset if they knew what Daddy was up to . . . tick. It's called getting my ducks in a row, Alan.'

For the first time Alan realized the enormity of what he'd done by helping Gus, and how widespread his prostitution racket was. Alan had never seen or met any of the punters

involved – he'd always stayed out of that side of things –
and was shocked at the list Gus had reeled off. These were
men who had standing in Mansell, who people looked up
to. Men with the power and influence to make his life even
more hellish than Gus could.

'How did you get her number?'

'She's down as your next of kin.'

Gus must've got hold of his personnel file. There was no
level the man wouldn't stoop to.

'Please don't involve my kids,' Alan begged. 'You're a dad
– how would you feel if I told yours?'

'Don't you even dare speak of my children,' said Gus
icily. 'My family stays out of this.'

Alan had often wondered about Gus's wife and whether
she had any inkling of his business interests. He'd met her
once, fleetingly, and was struck by what a looker she was.
Gorgeous blonde – Gus was punching way above with her.
It made Alan think that Gus couldn't possibly sleep with the
escorts he employed – with a wife like that waiting at home,
why would he need to?

'Why can't mine be left alone too?' he asked.

'Alan, you're in no position to barter. You never have
been.'

Crushingly, he knew it was true. By the time it had
dawned on him exactly what Gus had in mind for the Pavilion, it was too late to deny him access to it. He'd already
banked the sizeable 'arrangement fee', as Gus called it. After
that, his cooperation was secured not with cash but with the
threat of losing his job, which he could ill afford to do.
Whichever way he looked at it, Gus had him cornered.

A thought crossed his mind. 'If you know a copper, why

not get him to make the rest of them finish up at the school?'

'Too many questions would be asked. He's important, you see. A VIP in the ranks.'

Alan felt even worse hearing that.

'Gus, you've got to do something,' he said desperately. 'I've told the police the boy's death was an accident. There's nothing else I can do now.'

'Was it?'

'Was it what?'

'An accident.'

'Well, not exactly –'

Gus made an 'uh-uh' sound like a game-show buzzer going off.

'Wrong answer! If you're going to lie, Alan, at least be consistent. Look, mate,' he said, suddenly conciliatory, 'you've done the right thing and I'm grateful. Keep sticking to your story and before you know it we'll have the Pavilion up and running again and things will be back to normal.'

'No, no way,' Alan exclaimed. 'Find somewhere else, Gus. It's too risky now.'

'Why? The Pavilion is perfect.'

'It's inside a *school*. Can't you see how fucked up that is?'

'Of course I can. But that's why I'm chairman of the governors and you're not – because I recognize a perk of the job when I see one.'

18

There was a strange man sitting at Maggie's desk when she arrived in CID. She slowed her pace as she approached, giving herself time to digest his appearance. He was younger than her, late twenties at most, with cropped brown hair and heavy, black-framed glasses. He was wearing a mismatched suit of navy trousers and dark grey jacket with a crisp white shirt and a visitor's pass on a lanyard in lieu of a tie. He had the rumpled air of a college lecturer about him.

She was about to say hello when Renshaw intercepted her.

'Need a quick word,' she said, ushering Maggie towards the water cooler at the rear of the office.

'It's been decided there should be two FLOs on this case, given the sensitive nature of it,' she said.

'Oh, right.'

Usually DI Gant called ahead to warn her someone was joining her but she wasn't unduly concerned. Force guidelines stated that FLOs should work in pairs wherever possible because of the 24/7 nature of the job and the strain of being sent into emotionally charged households for weeks or even months at a time. Two FLOs could give each other a break and offer support if things got tough.

'I know you enjoyed working alone on your last case so I hope you don't mind,' said Renshaw.

'That was down to cutbacks. I'm fine to partner up,' Maggie reassured her. 'It'll be good to have someone to bounce off.'

'Good, because that's your new partner,' grinned Renshaw, head jerking towards the man at Maggie's desk. 'DC Jamie Byford. Fast-tracked into CID straight from uni, been a detective for a few years, but this is his first case as a FLO.'

Now Maggie was less enamoured. She didn't want to be saddled with a rookie. Why *hadn't* Gant warned her himself?

'I know he's a newbie but make sure you share the load with him, okay? This case is a tough one because it involves kids and it's important none of us take on more than we can handle. You must say if you find it hard.'

Maggie frowned. Was it her imagination or did that little speech sound unnaturally stilted, as though Renshaw was repeating words that weren't her own?

'You've never been this bothered about me before,' she said suspiciously, thinking back to her conversation with Umpire yesterday, when he had urged her to rethink her involvement. Would he have dared to share his concerns behind her back? She'd like to think not, but if he hadn't, where else was Renshaw's sudden empathy coming from?

'Has someone said something to you?' she asked.

'Don't be so paranoid – of course not. This is a big case for me and I need you on the ball to make me look good.'

Maggie wasn't convinced but let the matter drop.

'Come on, I'll introduce you,' said Renshaw.

Byford got to his feet as they walked up.

'Maggie, this is DC Byford. Or do you prefer Jamie?'

'Byford's fine. You must be DC Neville. Good to meet you.' He had a deep, sonorous voice with no discernible accent and no trace of a smile on his lips as they shook hands.

'Call me Maggie. Good to meet you too,' she said.

'There's a briefing now,' said Renshaw. 'Maggie will show you where to go.'

'Once it's done, I'll bring you up to speed on where I am with the victimology,' said Maggie. 'Do you want tea or coffee before we go in?'

'Water's fine.'

The briefing was to the point, with the most significant new information being what Maggie had to report about the fight between Poppy and Benji at school and the comment left on Facebook that implied violence within the Hepworth household.

'Imogen Tyler thought the children were close, but the fight suggests that might not be the case,' Renshaw extrapolated. 'I want every single one of their classmates interviewed to find out if the fight between them was an isolated incident or not. Let's also ask if Poppy Hepworth has form for lamping other kids. Teachers can't see everything that goes on in the playground but kids might. Nath, that's your job for today.'

'How am I going to interview twenty-eight kids if the

school's still shut?' Nathan asked grumpily. 'I can't go round their houses, it'll take ages.'

'Talk to the headteacher and see if she can get the parents to bring their kids into school today at timed intervals,' said Renshaw. 'You can whittle it down to seven interviews if you speak to them in batches of four. If any of the kids say anything of significance, we can do a one-to-one follow-up interview.'

Nathan pretended he couldn't work out Renshaw's mathematics and made a show of counting the sum on his fingers. The rest of them laughed, but Byford sat stony-faced and Maggie hoped his lack of response wasn't an indication of dour things to come.

His wasn't the only unfamiliar face in the incident room that morning – DC Karl Burton had also joined them, seconded overnight from another division by the Superintendent.

'The Hepworths are bringing Poppy back in for questioning this morning, so I'll raise the fight at school and see how she reacts,' Renshaw added.

'Aren't you forgetting something?' piped up Byford suddenly. 'Even if the kids say there was a history of bullying, what does it matter if our only eyewitness is saying the death was an accident? It's irrelevant.'

Maggie was surprised by the snotty way Byford addressed Renshaw – underlined by him lounging so far back in his seat he looked like he was about to take a nap – but she wasn't surprised when Renshaw glowered at him as though she could cheerfully strangle him. The DS might look serene with her immaculate suits and shiny, always brushed hair – something Maggie coveted, seeing as hers could go days without being acquainted with a comb – but beneath that haughty poise lay a temper so blistering it could strip wallpaper.

'It *matters*,' Renshaw seethed, 'because one, I don't believe his new account, and two, even if he's telling the truth I still want proof Poppy Hepworth is capable of hurting another kid. Deliberate or not, I believe she's culpable for Benji's death and I intend to build a case against her. Being a kid doesn't mean she's off the hook.'

Nathan finished his counting.

'I'll be stuck at school all day,' he moaned.

Renshaw smirked. 'Best take a packed lunch then.'

19

The room wasn't at all what Julia had imagined. Her expectations were moulded by the police dramas she'd watched on TV and she assumed Poppy would be interviewed across a table in a small, bleak, windowless room. Instead they were in a suite with a sofa and two armchairs, floor cushions, brightly patterned rugs, and an array of toys occupying one corner, which Poppy ignored.

'This is our ABE suite,' said DS Renshaw, inviting them to take a seat. Poppy sat ramrod straight between her parents.

'What does that stand for?' asked Ewan.

'Achieving Best Evidence,' said Renshaw. 'We want Poppy to feel as relaxed as possible while we talk and this is much nicer than the rooms we interview grown-ups in.' She said this to Poppy with a smile but was rewarded with a blank look. 'We'll get started as soon as DC Burton joins us.'

The wait, although less than a minute, was interminable. Julia fidgeted in her seat, crossing and uncrossing her legs and tucking her hair behind her ears. She had left it uncombed after showering and the natural kink she normally blow-dried straight was doing its unruly best to get in her eyes. By contrast Poppy and Ewan sat perfectly still.

The door opened and a young man in T-shirt and jeans came into the room carrying a few bottles of water and a carton of Ribena, which he gave to Poppy.

'Thought you might like this,' he said. 'I'm DC Burton but you can call me Karl.'

Poppy gave him a shy look, then said 'thank you'. They were the first words she'd spoken all morning and the fact that he'd managed to elicit a response forced Julia to bite back her objection to the Ribena. Now was hardly the time to fuss about tooth decay and sugar intake.

'Poppy, we've asked you to come in because we still need to know what happened yesterday morning at school. You haven't been arrested, just so you're clear about that,' said DS Renshaw.

Despite the assurance, Julia couldn't shake off the feeling that the police had already decided Poppy was to blame and it worried her that they hadn't sought legal advice. She had tried to, but Ewan went ballistic when he found her on her laptop looking up the names of local solicitors who dealt with juvenile crime just before they were due to leave for the station. He accused her of thinking that Poppy was guilty and said she should be ashamed of herself. She'd tried to argue that it was folly to face the police for a second time without any legal advice but he wouldn't back down. So in the end she did.

When Polly didn't respond, Renshaw nodded to Burton, who took a swig of water from one of the bottles, then set it down by his feet. He leaned forward and rested his elbows on his knees.

'Do you like school, Poppy?' he asked.

'Well, she's in the top—' Julia began, but Renshaw held a hand up to stop her.

'Please, Mrs Hepworth. We need Poppy to answer.'

Julia sank back in her seat, cheeks burning at the rebuke.

'I wasn't a fan of it myself. I hated being stuck inside a classroom,' Burton added. 'I was only happy when it was break time and I could be outside playing with my mates.'

Julia felt Poppy stir beside her.

'The only subject I liked was PE,' he went on. 'What's your favourite?'

'Science,' came the reply, so quietly that Julia had to strain to hear it. 'I like it when we do experiments.'

Ewan caught Julia's eye. She thought, like her, he'd be relieved that Poppy was talking – the sooner they cleared this up and went home the better – but he looked anxious.

'What sort of experiments?'

With some gentle coaxing, Burton got Poppy to talk about her favourite science test, which involved Fairy Liquid, a balloon and a sewing needle.

'You mean you stuck a pin right through the balloon and it didn't burst?' Burton blurted out. 'That's impossible!'

'It's not,' said Poppy, smiling. 'The washing-up liquid you coat on top is what stops it popping.'

Tears suddenly pricked Julia's eyes as she watched her daughter grow more animated as she explained the experiment to Burton. How could her beautiful, clever, funny little girl have ended up being questioned in a police station over the death of another child? Of all the nightmare scenarios her imagination had conjured up to scare her with since becoming a parent – illness, road accident, stranger-danger

– never once had it occurred to her that her children might end up on the wrong side of the law. Aware Renshaw was staring at her, Julia blinked the tears away and straightened up in her seat.

'Were you due to do science yesterday morning? Is that why you were at school early, because you were keen to get started?'

Poppy hesitated, then shook her head.

'We need you to answer out loud,' said Renshaw. 'Remember at the start I told you we were going to record the interview? The audio can't tell if you only nod.'

'No,' said Poppy tremulously. 'That's not why I went in early.'

'So why did you?' asked Burton, not taking his eyes off hers.

'Benji asked me to.'

Julia held her breath, unable to drag her gaze away from her daughter.

'What reason did he give?'

When Poppy hesitated, Ewan stepped in. 'It's okay, honey; just tell them.'

'Benji said he'd worked out how to get into the building site and that it was really cool because you could climb on stuff. I thought it sounded cool, so I said I'd go with him.'

'Where did you meet?'

Ewan again prompted her when she clammed up.

'Tell the truth,' he urged.

'It was by that new housing estate at the back of the school. There's a gap in the fence that comes out by the playing field.'

'What time did you meet?'

'Six. I set my alarm to wake up early.'

Julia was stunned. How had they not heard it? Poppy's room was right next to theirs.

'Whose idea was it to get on the wall?' asked Burton.

'His. I didn't want to. It was really high.'

'What made you change your mind?'

'Benji started calling me names. He said I was a crybaby. I'm not,' said Poppy hotly.

'So you got cross with him and decided to prove a point?' asked Renshaw carefully.

'Not cross, no. I was upset, like, crying, 'cause he kept on at me. In the end I said yes to make him stop.'

'Who went up the ladder first?'

'He did.'

Poppy began chewing anxiously on her bottom lip. Julia felt so tense it was a struggle to remember to breathe.

'It seems very clear the boy coerced my daughter onto that wall,' said Ewan firmly.

Both Renshaw and Burton ignored him.

'When you reached the top of the ladder, then what happened?' asked Burton.

Poppy stopped chewing. There were flecks of blood visible on her lip.

'Can I say something?' she asked.

'Of course,' said Renshaw.

'It's not my fault Benji died.' Her voice splintered with grief. 'I'm really, really sorry for what happened but it wasn't my fault. I said it was too high but he wouldn't listen.' She rubbed at her eyes, now wet with tears. 'I wanted to get down but he wouldn't let me. When his foot slipped I tried to grab hold of him but it happened too fast and I thought I was going to fall too and I was so scared. But it was an accident, I swear.'

20

Imogen was confused by Byford's sudden appointment as another FLO when Maggie called ahead to say he was coming round to meet her. She had tried to explain it would be better for Imogen to have both of them as a point of contact – if one wasn't available, the other would be – but it raised an awkward question.

'Which one of you is in charge though?' Imogen asked.

It was a good point and Maggie decided to raise it with Byford on the drive over, politely expressing her belief that liaison ran more smoothly when one FLO took their cue from the other. It had worked well for her and Belmar on the Rosie Kinnock case with her leading, and as Imogen already trusted her it made sense for her to lead again on this investigation.

Byford disagreed.

'What, you should be in charge just because you've had a twenty-four-hour head start?' he'd scoffed. 'I don't think so.'

'This is your first case as a FLO,' Maggie shot back. 'You need to learn to walk before you can run.'

'You make it sound like I'm a total novice when in fact I

know I've been in CID longer than you have, because I checked.'

They agreed, after arguing back and forth, that neither of them was the lead officer and they'd work together. Maggie then spent the rest of the journey inwardly cursing Gant for pairing her with someone so evidently competitive. No wonder he hadn't rung himself to tell her about Byford.

When they arrived at Imogen's, Maggie made a point of explaining that neither of them was in charge, so everyone was clear on where they stood. By that point Imogen seemed unbothered by Byford's presence – as she was waiting for them to arrive she'd turned on the TV for the first time since yesterday morning and it went straight to Benji's favourite channel and one of his favourite programmes, prompting a fresh tidal wave of sorrow.

Ed and Grace were doing their best to comfort her but her tears had had a ripple effect and now the three of them were in pieces. Maggie glanced at Byford to gauge his reaction and saw that, thankfully, he wasn't discomfited by their distress. A good FLO needed to soak up grief like a sponge and not let it show when it got to them. Maybe he wouldn't be so bad after all.

A round of tea later, the Tylers had calmed down sufficiently for Maggie to explain that they would like to have a look through Benji's bedroom, to see if there was anything that might be relevant to the case.

'Such as?' asked Grace.

'Any indication of what his friendship with Poppy was really like. Did he keep a diary?' Maggie asked Imogen.

'Not that I'm aware.'

'Did he have access to a computer?' asked Byford.

'He uses my laptop but under supervision. I'm very strict about screen time.'

Maggie noted that Imogen was still using the present tense.

'Can we take a look at it?' she asked.

'Sure. It's in my room, I'll go and get it.'

When Imogen left the room, Grace rounded on them.

'My daughter was too accepting of that girl. She's a horrid, horrid child.'

Maggie was caught off guard by the venom that dripped from Grace's every word.

'I take it you aren't a fan?'

'No, I'm not, and neither was my grandson. She was rude to him, and bossy. I don't know what possessed Imogen to encourage the friendship.'

'Did you and Benji ever talk about it?'

Grace nodded. 'He told me once he was unhappy being paired with Poppy in class. He told me she rode roughshod over his ideas and always wanted her way. Liked being the centre of attention. But I didn't say anything because I knew Imogen liked them being friends.'

'Any idea why?' asked Byford.

Grace shared an uneasy glance with Ed, who quickly looked away.

'I don't know,' said Grace.

Maggie's instincts told her Grace knew exactly why but wasn't saying.

'Did Benji mention a recent incident at school where Poppy hurt him?' she asked.

'Do you mean the fight that Imogen was messaged

about?' Grace shook her head. 'No, he never said anything to me about it. But I'll tell you something, if my grandson could've stayed out of that girl's way he would've.'

21

There was an awkward moment when Imogen came back downstairs with the laptop, and Byford airily announced he was off to 'poke around' Benji's room while Maggie asked them some more questions. Maggie shot into the hallway after him and a heated, furiously whispered argument kicked off.

'You need to be more sensitive,' she snapped. 'You should've asked them first if it was okay to go upstairs.'

For a second she thought he was about to roll his eyes but he caught himself.

'Fine. I'm sorry. Chalk it up as my first mistake. I'll know for next time.'

Bristling with anger, Maggie let him go. Then she took a deep breath and returned to the lounge. Fortunately for her and Byford, the Tylers were too distracted to have noticed anything amiss.

She sat down on the easy chair opposite the sofa where they were sitting.

'If you feel up to answering, I'd like to talk more about Benji,' she said.

'Yes, whatever you need to know,' said Ed, taking his sister's hand. 'We want to help.'

Staying gentle in her approach, Maggie eased Imogen through the history of her and Benji moving back to Mansell and him starting at Rushbrooke.

'The first couple of weeks were tough but he's settled in well,' said Imogen. 'The teacher told me he's been keeping up in class.'

'Aside from Poppy, who I'll come back to, had he made friends at school?' Maggie asked.

'There's one boy called Imtiaz that he talks about all the time. Really bright child, top of the class, but shy, like Benji. I think that's why they've hit it off. They don't see each other out of school though. I've tried to arrange stuff but his mum's not very receptive. He's on the list you asked for, along with a few others,' she added.

'I know you said this morning that Benji hadn't mentioned the fight between him and Poppy, but had he talked about any other issues with her?'

'They're a lot like siblings – one minute they get on, the next they're bickering. He was upset a few weeks ago when she called him "butt breath" in front of the class but I told Ewan and he made her apologize,' said Imogen. 'After that they were fine again, or at least I thought they were.'

'Did they have their play dates here? Sorry, I know that's not what they are when children are eleven, but I can't think what else to call them.'

Imogen frowned thoughtfully. 'Yes, now you come to mention it. But Ewan did say Poppy's little brother always got in the way when she had friends over, so maybe that's why she preferred coming here.'

'How often did she come round?'

'Um, I'd say every other week. Usually on a Tuesday because neither of them had activities after school that day.'

'It was always her dad who facilitated the play dates, never her mum?'

Grace made a scoffing sound.

'Mum, be quiet,' Imogen hissed.

'Oh, for heaven's sake, just tell her,' said Grace. 'It might be relevant. Ed agrees, don't you, Ed?'

He nodded, much to Imogen's annoyance.

'Tell me what?' asked Maggie.

When Imogen refused to respond, snatching her hand away from her brother's and crossing her arms angrily in front of her, Grace spoke instead.

'Poppy's mum tried to get Imogen expelled when they were at Rushbrooke.'

Maggie's eyebrows shot up. 'Oh.'

'Yes, oh, indeed,' said Grace. 'There was a bit of nastiness in the playground, nothing serious, but it got completely blown out of proportion and Imogen was falsely accused of being the ringleader. I had to go down to the school to sort it out, but fortunately the teachers saw fit to believe that she hadn't hurt anyone.' Grace leaned forward. 'Don't you think it's odd my grandson was pushed to his death by the daughter of the classmate who tried to get Imogen expelled?'

Maggie took a moment before responding, carefully forming the words in her brain before she engaged her mouth.

'Firstly, we don't know Poppy did push him; we're still gathering evidence,' she said firmly. 'Secondly, Imogen wasn't aware Julia was Poppy's mum until yesterday morning, so how can we be sure the children knew about the history between their mums? Thirdly, even if they were aware, why do you think it has any bearing on Benji's death?'

'I can answer that,' said Ed quickly. 'To address your first point, we know Benji wouldn't have got on that wall without being bullied into it and once he was up there he was so careful he would've clung to it for dear life. He wouldn't have fallen, he'd have had to be pushed to move him off it, and she was the only person with him at the time,' he said. 'Secondly, you're right, Benji probably wasn't aware of the history because, as you said, Imogen didn't know Julia was Poppy's mum. But that's not to say Poppy didn't know.'

'Julia accused my daughter of some terrible things,' said Grace. 'Didn't she, darling?'

'To be honest, it's a bit hazy,' said Imogen, her cheeks colouring. 'I mean, I remember she was in my class, but I'd forgotten all about getting into trouble until Mum brought it up. I doubt Julia remembers it either, it was so long ago.'

'Unless she's held a grudge all this time,' Grace crowed. 'She could have been biding her time, waiting for revenge because you showed her up to be a liar all those years ago. Then Benji started in her daughter's class and the opportunity was suddenly in front of her.'

'You think Julia manipulated Poppy into harming Benji to get back at Imogen for something that did or didn't happen years ago?' Maggie asked, eyebrows disappearing into her hairline.

'It's not implausible,' said Grace huffily. 'People do terrible things in the name of revenge; history is full of examples. Take Queen Boudicca—'

Ed mercifully interrupted.

117

'Mum loves history programmes,' he said wryly.

Beside him, Imogen shifted awkwardly in her seat.

'Do you think it's plausible?' Maggie asked her.

Imogen wrung her hands, obviously agitated. 'I guess . . . I mean, it sounds ridiculous, and on the one hand I think it's total nonsense . . .'

'But on the other?' Maggie prompted.

'I'm scared it might be true.'

22

The Wheatsheaf was set back from one of the main arterial roads that ran through Mansell. The front entrance was reached down a flight of steep, narrow stairs and Alan's hand skimmed the metal handrail as he made his way down them.

It was far earlier in the day than he'd normally start drinking, but the phone calls with Gayle and Gus had left him feeling rattled and he needed a pint to take the edge off his nerves. He wasn't expecting the pub to be busy at two in the afternoon – most of the regulars who drank there arrived at the end of the working day, just as he usually did.

He'd come across The Wheatsheaf on his first weekend in Mansell, on a walk to familiarize himself with his new neighbourhood. It was one of only a few town pubs that hadn't been converted into a mini supermarket or knocked down to make way for flats and as a consequence did a healthy trade amongst locals. Soon it had become a daily habit for him to take a detour home from the school to duck through its shabby doorway.

The front entrance led into a lounge bar conspicuous for its sparse furnishings: a few tables circled by some uncomfortable-looking hard-backed chairs. This was where infrequent customers tended to drink, away from the locals who noisily dominated the snug bar next door that was rammed with overstuffed easy chairs, small round tables and stools that wobbled precariously when sat upon.

Alan had kept to the lounge the first few times he'd visited, until he felt brave enough to venture through.

The landlord, Doug, didn't question why he was drinking so early – he simply set a pint of Adnams on the bar and batted away the £10 note Alan proffered.

'On the house,' he said. 'I bet you need it after what's been going on at the school. Gus was in here last night talking about it.'

The colour drained from Alan's face and his hand shook as he picked up the glass. Beer sloshed over the side, depositing a puddle on the bar that dripped onto the carpet next to his feet.

'Watch where you're slinging that about, that's good beer you're wasting,' said Doug with a chuckle.

'Sorry, if you give me a cloth I'll wipe it up,' said Alan.

Doug leaned over the pumps and mopped up the spillage himself.

'Must've been a shock for you, seeing the kid hit the deck like that.'

Alan couldn't meet his eyes. 'What did Gus say about it?'

'He said you told the police it was an accident.'

'That's what it looked like,' said Alan uncomfortably. He didn't want to discuss it, certainly not in the pub.

'He said it was nasty, the way the kid fell.'

Alan wondered if Doug knew about Gus's set-up in the Pavilion. It wasn't a long shot to assume he did: the landlord was no fool and his vantage point behind the bar made it easy for him to notice huddled conversations and money passing hands. He was unlikely to be a customer though: Doug was gay and Gus had only female escorts on his books.

'Sorry, I shouldn't pry,' said Doug. 'I can see you're upset.'

Alan gulped down another mouthful of beer. 'Yeah, can we talk about something else?'

They spent the next few minutes discussing football and whether United or City would win the Manchester derby that weekend. Then, just as Alan had begun to relax and savour his pint, Doug leaned over the bar and beckoned him closer.

'I want to give you a word of advice,' he said in a hushed voice. 'If the police find out what's been going on at the school, Gus will throw you under the bus, no question about it. So you get yourself some insurance, Alan. Something you can use against him.'

So Doug did know. Alan stared at him, suddenly afraid. 'Insurance?'

'Something that proves the Pavilion wasn't your idea.'

'I didn't know,' said Alan desperately. 'By the time I realized what he was up to, it was too late to back out.' He dropped his voice to a whisper. 'He's chairman of the fucking governors.'

'I know he is, that's what's so sickening. I'd tip off the police myself if it wasn't for the fact that Gus would see to it I'd lose all my custom and I can't afford the risk. I also don't want to drop you in it, Alan. You're a good bloke. So do yourself a favour and get that insurance sorted, because I can bet you Gus has his get-out-of-jail-free card all nice and ready.'

Alan felt sick, because he knew Doug was right. But what could he do? He'd wiped the incriminating CCTV footage from 'Corridor 8' and, besides, Gus could easily explain away any of his appearances on it, what with him being the school's leading governor.

Then it dawned on him. If he couldn't force Gus and the girls from the Pavilion, he'd have to take the Pavilion from them.

23

'When I was at primary school it wasn't called bullying,' said Imogen, sinking back against the sofa cushions. She looked spent, as though every syllable was an effort to pronounce. 'It was playground bickering, kids being mean to each other. None of us gave any thought to how the person on the receiving end must've felt, mostly because the next week it would be our turn to be picked on. It was cyclical for everyone.'

Maggie was trying to listen, but Grace kept muttering over the top of her daughter and interrupting. If she wanted Imogen to speak freely, she needed to get rid of her.

'Would you mind giving me a minute alone with Imogen?' she asked as pleasantly as she could manage. 'It's a bit difficult to concentrate and the quicker I get through these questions the better, because we don't want to be late for seeing Benji.'

The pathologist had agreed to delay the post-mortem to allow Imogen to see her son after Maggie's earlier phone call. They needed to leave in an hour to get there.

'I'll put some coffee on,' said Ed, heading for the kitchen.

'Come on, Mum.' Grace did as she was asked but sounded her annoyance in the huffing noises she made as she went.

Once they were next door, Maggie resumed her questions.

'Are you saying you did bully Julia Hepworth then?' she asked.

'As I said, I don't remember her specifically. She doesn't stand out in my memory,' said Imogen apologetically. 'We didn't share the same group of friends. She was one of the quiet ones. Julia could say that I bullied her and I wouldn't be able to say if it was true or not, because I don't remember.'

'Why are you worried there might be some truth in your mum's theory?'

Imogen let out a long, deep sigh.

'I'm not, not really. It's just that when Mum brought it up yesterday she was so convinced it wasn't a coincidence that Poppy was Julia's daughter that she got me thinking the same. I'm sorry, you must think we're wasting your time here.'

'You're not. It's important I gather every bit of information I can about Benji's relationship with Poppy and for that reason it's good for me to know any history between your families. Me and my colleagues can work out what's relevant and what's not.'

'You're very kind,' said Imogen. She glanced towards the hallway. 'How much longer do you think he'll be in Benji's room?'

'I don't know. I can see how he's getting on if you want.'

'Do you mind if I go? I just feel a bit weird about a stranger going through Benji's stuff.'

'That's fine, but Jamie will need you to wait outside on the landing while he finishes.'

'I understand.'

Maggie slipped into the kitchen while Imogen went upstairs. Grace had gone to sit outside on the terrace but Ed was leaning against the sink unit, his face desolate.

'I don't know how Im's going to cope without Benji,' he said, choking back tears.

'I know it'll be harder because she's on her own, having already lost her husband so young, but there's so much help out there for her,' Maggie reassured him. 'We'll make sure she gets it.'

Ed's eyes narrowed. 'I'm not sure "lost" is the right word.'

'Sorry, I didn't mean to sound insensitive. I meant him dying.'

'Dying? Stephen isn't dead,' Ed exclaimed. 'When I said "lost" wasn't the right word it's because "abandoned" would be more accurate. He walked out on my sister when Benji was two months old.' He clocked the expression of surprise on Maggie's face. 'Ah, I get it. She told you he was dead. She prefers telling people that rather than saying he left.'

'What she did tell Benji?'

'The same: that Stephen died just after he was born. I didn't agree at all – I felt Benji deserved to know the truth – but Im thought it would be too confusing for him and that he wouldn't understand why Stephen didn't want to see him.'

'Bit of a risky strategy – what if Stephen turned up one day asking to see him?'

'True, but by the time Im told Benji it was pretty clear

Stephen was long gone. He hasn't been in touch since the day he left and none of us have a clue where he is.'

Maggie started to wonder what else Imogen might've revised for the sake of appearances. What if Benji wasn't quite the little angel she was painting him to be? She said he was too timid to dare climb the wall by his own volition, but he did sneak out of the house to get there . . . Then again, she of all people could sympathize with Imogen wanting to spin a different story about her ex-husband – she'd spent the past decade revising her own past to cover up her affair with Lou's fiancé.

'So where do you stand on the theory of Julia Hepworth taking revenge?' she asked.

She expected Ed to dismiss it as Imogen had done out of Grace's earshot, but to her surprise he said he thought there might be something in it.

'There's got to be a reason why my nephew fell off that wall and you and your colleagues haven't come up with anything else to explain it.'

'We deal in facts and evidence and proof, not wild supposition,' said Maggie.

'Fine. Then prove to us that Mum's theory isn't true.'

24

The high street felt claustrophobically muggy after the cool confines of the police station. Wednesday was market day and the stalls lining the pavement brought with them the bustle of shoppers browsing their wares.

Ewan led the way through the throng with Poppy clinging to his hand and Julia bringing up the rear. She was surprised the police had agreed to his suggestion they take Poppy outside to get some lunch: she thought they would be obliged to stay put until she'd answered all their questions. But after her earlier outburst Poppy had reverted to one-word answers and, with the process becoming painstakingly slow again, the detectives needed a break as much as they did.

Julia had wanted them to go for a walk in the town park, next to the stretch of water known colloquially as The Puddle. The fresh air and sunshine would do them all good and there was a Tesco Express on the way where they could buy sandwiches. But Ewan said they should let Poppy decide and she'd promptly asked to go to McDonald's, knowing Julia would never let her eat there under normal circumstances. Ewan had pretended not to notice his wife's look of disapproval.

As they joined one of the queues snaking back from the counter, Julia tried to engage her husband in speculation about what else the police might ask Poppy next – in her mind they had covered a lot of ground already; what else could they possibly want to know?

'Can you please give it a rest,' he said tightly. 'Let's just get our food.'

She tried to lighten the mood. 'Does McDonald's even count as real food?'

The young woman in front of them shot Julia a filthy look over her shoulder.

'Stop it,' said Ewan in an angry whisper. 'You're embarrassing Poppy and yourself.'

'But I was joking –' Julia protested.

Poppy pressed herself closer into her dad's side, a hostile barrier between husband and wife. Julia shrank away from them.

A couple of minutes later it was their turn to order.

'What do you want, darling?' Ewan asked Poppy.

'Um, cheeseburger, fries and a chocolate milkshake, please.'

Poppy looked warily at Julia as if waiting for a rebuke and the sight of her big blue eyes filled with apprehension brought a lump to Julia's throat.

'Have what you want, darling.'

'Thanks, Mum,' said Poppy delightedly. 'Can I have a McFlurry too?'

To anyone watching they were an ordinary family having lunch together, albeit without Dylan, who was being looked after by their neighbour, Cath. Julia went through the pretence of trying to be excited about the chicken salad she'd ordered – she was sure she'd read somewhere that the McDonald's version had more calories than a bowl of carbonara pasta – when really she wanted to rail against the awfulness of the situation they were in. But if she did that, Poppy might think she was blaming her and as she watched her daughter and husband banter over their lunch and pretend to steal each other's fries, she didn't want to be the one to spoil the mood.

But she needed someone to blame and as she picked at her salad her thoughts returned to Imogen again.

Julia still bore a scar from one of her attacks – a thin, silvery line running vertically down her shin from where Imogen had pushed her over in the playground. When she went to tell the teacher what had happened, Imogen persuaded her friends to say they all saw Julia trip and the teacher had once again believed the chorus of voices over Julia's lone protest.

Given how devious and manipulative Imogen herself had been at that age, it wasn't a stretch to assume her son might've been the same. Poppy wouldn't have risked being punished for sneaking out of the house unless she was more fearful of what might happen if she didn't. Julia was becoming more and more convinced that Imogen's son must've threatened her in order for her to meet him.

She pulsed with anger as more memories of the cruel treatment Imogen doled out came flooding back. One of the worst occasions was the Christmas when Julia was given the part of Archangel Gabriel in the school nativity. She was minutes from going on stage, wearing the costume her mum had lovingly handmade, when Imogen threw red paint down her front. The costume was in such a state and her face so drenched in paint that there was no way she could go on, so their teacher ripped off Julia's halo and promoted one of the angels from the chorus into the role. When Imogen was quizzed about it, she claimed Julia poured the paint over herself and blamed her because she didn't want to perform in front of an audience. Everyone believed Imogen because, well, Julia was so timid that *of course* she had stage fright.

Ultimately her time at Rushbrooke was one long cycle of humiliation and distress because of Imogen. Complaining made no difference: the school's stance was that she should make an effort to get along with her and their classmates, as though it was Julia's fault for not being more likeable.

She did tell her parents but they were too caught up in their own problems to appreciate how bad it was. Her mum, Ruth, had gone back to work full time after Julia started school but her dad, Malcolm, wasn't happy about the long hours she worked. At one point they even separated and her mum went to stay with her sister for a bit. Then one day, just as suddenly, she came back.

Twenty minutes later the three of them headed back down the high street in the direction of the police station. They'd just drawn level with the taxi rank when the sound of someone yelling made them turn round.

'How have you got the nerve to show your faces in public?'

Marching across the road towards them, her face contorted by a look of disgust, was a mum Julia recognized from drop-offs. She was one of the scarier-looking ones to frequent the playground, with an abundance of tattoos, dyed purple hair and a ripe vocabulary that needed moderating around children but never was. Neither of her children was in the same class or year as Poppy or Dylan, and Julia had never exchanged so much as a 'hello' with her.

'She should be locked up!' the mum yelled, pointing at Poppy.

Julia was horrified. 'Don't say that, she's done nothing wrong.'

'She killed that poor little lad. Everyone knows it.'

Julia went to say something but Ewan got there first. Purpling with anger, he strode over to where the woman was and stood so close they were toe to toe.

'Don't you dare say that about my child.'

'Why? I'm only saying what's true,' the woman spat.

Every muscle in Julia's body was primed to run away from the confrontation.

'Come on, Ewan, let's go.'

He shot her a look of disgust. 'Just because you're too weak to stand up for our daughter.'

Tears pricked Julia's eyes. Why did he always have to make her feel like such a failure?

He turned back to the woman. 'You say one more lie about my daughter and I'll make you wish you'd never been born.'

He said it in such a blithe, matter-of-fact way that the woman laughed. So he said it again, this time more menacingly.

The mum stepped backwards, stunned into muteness. It

was clearly an alien sensation for her, lips moving but no sound coming out.

'Ewan, come on, leave it,' said Julia, who was now trying to shield a sobbing Poppy from rubberneckers. 'She's not worth it.'

The mum's voice was hoarse when she spoke again.

'You need to take a long, hard look at yourself,' she said, but the fire had gone out of her and her delivery was as feeble as her insult was weak.

Ewan spat out a last retort as he walked away.

'I've done nothing to be ashamed of and neither has my daughter.'

25

Arranging for Imogen to view Benji's body had been the easy part; it was getting her there that was proving impossible.

'Why can't I see my grandson?' Grace asked for what felt like the twentieth time.

'I've told you, I want to see Benji on my own,' Imogen replied in a tight, clipped tone that suggested she was about one answer away from blowing her top.

The stand-off was happening in the cramped hallway. Maggie was pinned against the front door, trying to calm the two women down, while Ed hovered on the stairs and Byford stood in the doorway leading back into the lounge. His search of Benji's room had been fruitless – no diary, notes, or anything else relating to Poppy.

'It's not fair,' Grace retaliated.

'I want to be on my own with him for a bit. Why can't you accept that?'

'Because you're being selfish.'

'He's my son!' Imogen yelled. 'Not yours, mine!'

Grace went puce and began to cry. Ed swore loudly.

'Right, that's enough,' he said. 'Mum, I'm sorry, but you

need to let Im do this alone. He's her son and she needs to say goodbye. I'll take you to see Benji when he's moved to the funeral director's.'

Grace seemed stunned to have been spoken to with such firmness by her son and nodded meekly.

Relieved, Imogen turned to Maggie.

'You don't have to come either. Jamie's offered to take me.'

Imogen didn't need the two of them to accompany her and Maggie had little desire to see Benji on a mortuary slab, let alone bear witness to Imogen seeing him, but she didn't appreciate being frozen out by Byford, who at that moment was staring at his feet. He'd overstepped the mark by excluding her without a discussion first but Maggie smoothed over her annoyance with a smile.

'No problem. I'll wait here until you get back,' she said.

'Don't stay on my account: I'm driving back to Frome in a bit,' said Ed. 'Our youngest is only six weeks old so my wife needs me. But I'll be back in a few days.'

'I don't need to be babysat by a police officer either,' said Grace witheringly.

'Fine, I'll head back to the station, see if there are any updates.'

Suddenly the doorbell chimed. Maggie was closest and squeezed round to open it. When she saw who was on the doorstep she stepped outside and pulled the door shut behind her, telling the others she'd be a minute.

'Why am I not surprised to find you here, DC Neville?' said Jennifer Jones. 'You get all the juicy ones.'

Maggie made no effort to hide her contempt. Jennifer was Chief Reporter for the local paper, the *Mansell Echo*, and had demonstrated on previous cases an appalling lack of sensitivity for someone sent out to speak to grieving relatives. She'd also provoked Maggie's ire when she covered a fire at Lou's house and had written a horribly speculative piece about why an investigation was being carried out, flagging up Maggie's status as a police officer. That story was published on the front page but when the inquiry cleared Lou of any fault, the follow-up was buried on page 21 and only a paragraph long, pissing Maggie off no end because hardly anyone would see it.

'I don't think that's how the families see it,' she said. 'Keep your voice down or I'll force you off the property.'

Jennifer had the sense not to push her luck and walked down the path away from the house, gesturing for Maggie to follow her.

'I came to see if Benji's mum was in,' she said, once they were out of earshot. 'I was hoping she might give me a few quotes for the obit.'

'How did you get his name? We haven't released it yet.'

'Oh, you know, sources,' Jennifer smirked. 'So, is she in? I only need a few minutes. It'll be a lovely way for her to pay tribute to her son.'

'I would respect you so much more if you didn't come out with such bollocks,' said Maggie scathingly. 'Why don't you be honest and say why you're really here? You don't want to write a nice tribute, you want all the juicy details and you don't give a toss about how that will make his mum feel.'

Jennifer was visibly taken aback. 'That's a bit harsh. I'm only doing my job.'

'Well, you're not doing it here, not today.'

'Can you give her my number then?' said Jennifer, proffering a business card. 'If today's too soon she might feel differently tomorrow.'

Maggie snatched the card from her hand.

'All requests go through the press office as you well know and they won't agree to any interviews that might prejudice the case.'

'I don't see how me getting a few quotes about Benji being a lovely boy is a problem when no arrests have been made or charges brought or even a warrant issued. Proceedings aren't active yet.' Jennifer wagged her finger at Maggie. 'Don't tell me you don't know contempt law, DC Neville.'

Maggie hated that she was right. Had Poppy, or anyone else for that matter, been arrested already, the media would be bound by a set of reporting restrictions that ruled out an interview with Imogen discussing Benji's death in case it harmed future court proceedings. Until then, there was nothing to stop her granting the *Echo* or any other media outlet an interview about him.

'It happened inside a school so there are other minors involved who can't be named,' Maggie pointed out.

'The *Echo* isn't an irresponsible newspaper. We wouldn't name the girl allegedly involved.' Jennifer hooked her fingers in the air as she said 'allegedly'. Maggie glared at her. 'Fine. In the interests of not upsetting anyone, I'll go through the press office. But can you at least mention to Benji's mum that I came round?'

It was a compromise Maggie knew she'd be foolish to reject if it meant Jennifer would stop badgering the Tylers.

'Okay, I'll tell her.'

Maggie tapped on the front door to be let in and Grace opened it. The others had gone back into the lounge.

'Was that a reporter?' Grace asked.

'Yes, for the *Echo*. I told her she has to go through our press office, so don't worry, she won't be back.'

Grace caught sight of the card in Maggie's hand.

'What's that?' she asked.

'Her business card. I'll hold on to it for now.'

'Can I see it?'

Maggie reluctantly passed the card to Benji's grand-mother. Her eyes gleamed as she scanned it.

'The Chief Reporter? Gosh. Imogen, look at this,' she trilled, scurrying into the lounge. 'The *Echo* sent its top reporter to talk to you.'

Maggie followed her with growing unease. She had a very bad feeling about this.

26

Back at the station Maggie found Renshaw and Burton eating lunch in the incident room and discussing their strategy for when they resumed questioning Poppy.

'You did a great job getting her to open up over the science stuff,' Renshaw was saying to Burton as Maggie sat down with them. 'A bit more of that kind of chat might get her to open up even more.'

'What's her version?' Maggie asked.

'That it was an accident,' said Renshaw, balling up the cardboard wrapper from her sandwich and tossing it like a basketball into the bin. 'She claims she tried to help Benji when he slipped but didn't get to him in time. No physical contact, in other words. Then she got upset and we had to take a break. Anyway, how come you're back already?'

Maggie gave a detailed account of the morning, repeating what Grace had said about Benji not being as enamoured with Poppy as Imogen thought he was; Imogen being falsely accused of bullying Julia back when they were at school; Byford not finding anything in his search of Benji's room; the row about viewing the body. She also told them Benji's dad wasn't dead after all.

'Why would you make up something like that?' asked Burton.

'Embarrassment, I guess,' said Maggie, who having watched Lou struggle with the humiliation of her ex-husband leaving to set up home with another woman, understood why Imogen hid the truth. Self-preservation. 'There doesn't seem to be any sinister reason for her lying.'

'Yeah, but telling Benji he's dead is a bit cruel. What if he suddenly showed up asking to see him?'

'That's what I said, but it sounds like he's done a complete runner,' said Maggie, reaching over and helping herself to a crisp from the packet Burton was holding. 'Did you ask Poppy about the fight with Benji?'

'That's for round two, once our child whisperer here has softened her up again,' said Renshaw, poking Burton in the arm. 'If we go straight in with it she'll clam up again.'

'What if history *has* repeated itself?' mused Burton. 'One mum bullies the other at school, then their kids have a similar fall-out years later, only this time one of them dies. What if Poppy found out her mum got beaten up by Benji's and turned against him because of it?'

'Well, that scenario sounds more likely than Benji taking up the baton for his mum, because she hardly remembers Julia,' said Maggie.

'What, she's forgotten bullying her?' asked Renshaw, frowning.

'She's saying she can't recall and Grace told me the school believed Imogen over Julia anyway. Imogen remembers some kids having playground spats but doesn't recall any specific incidents involving Julia,' Maggie explained. 'But is it really a surprise if Imogen is woolly on details? I'm ten years younger than her and I struggle to picture most of the kids from my class when I was eleven, let alone remember stuff I said or did to them –'

The expression on Renshaw's face made her stop.

'Lucky for you,' Renshaw said bitterly. 'I remember mine only too well. Being called copperknob, Duracell, ginger nut and carrot head day in, day out tends to stick in your mind. The teasing was so bloody relentless I once tried to shave off all my hair with my mum's Ladyshave. Didn't work.'

Burton laughed but Maggie was more surprised than amused. She found it hard to imagine Renshaw ever being picked on. If anything, she'd have put money on her being the antagonist – Renshaw had certainly displayed enough of the character traits in the time before the two of them became friendlier.

'There was this one girl in particular who wouldn't leave me alone and was always picking on me,' Renshaw went on. 'Then I saw her in a pub in town a couple of years ago and she acted like I was her long-lost best friend. It was so bizarre. Although she soon scarpered when I mentioned I was in CID.'

They all laughed at that.

'But in all seriousness I don't think the history between the mums relates to Benji's death,' said Renshaw. 'Because if it did, we're basically saying we think Julia put her daughter up to pushing Benji off that wall and I can't see any parent manipulating their child like that for their own ends. People talk about confronting their school bully, but who really does that? I was as bloody nice as pie to mine in the pub.'

'I agree,' said Maggie. 'Yesterday was the first time Julia and Imogen had seen each other in years. They're grown women now.'

'Okay, so Julia didn't put Poppy up to it, but there's no harm in asking Poppy if her mum ever mentioned being bullied,' said Burton. 'Maybe she was doing the same to Benji out of misplaced loyalty and it got out of hand.' He tipped the remains of the crisp packet into his palm and sucked up the salty crumbs.

'It would give us a motive,' Renshaw conceded. 'Maggie, I want you to watch the interview on a monitor and gauge Julia's response when I ask Poppy. Imogen reckons she's wiped her from memory – let's see if Julia's done the same with her.'

27

Julia was still shaking from the confrontation in the high street as they returned to their seats in the ABE suite. There had been no time to discuss it properly with Ewan between them calming Poppy down and arriving back at the station, and her mind began to spin as they waited in silence for the detectives to join them.

What on earth had possessed him to threaten that mum? Julia knew she would tell everyone at school and people would turn against them even more for it. The worst thing was, they didn't know Ewan the way she did and would just think badly of him. Yes, he could be fearsome when he was riled and blurt out cruel comments to spite people, but he was also loving and generous. She'd learned long ago, even before they were married, to let his outbursts wash over her. He was a good husband and dad and it troubled her that people might get the wrong end of the stick.

They'd met at a council Christmas party sixteen years ago. She'd recently started in Environmental and Community Services as assistant to the director, Ewan was doing some contract work with another department, and their eyes met when they both reached for a tinfoil platter of sausage rolls and mini quiche at the same time. By the end of the evening, emboldened by a steady supply of Chardonnay, she'd thrown caution to the wind and invited him home with her. She wasn't in the habit of taking strange men back to her flat for sex but Ewan felt like someone she'd known for years. He was so easy to talk to and so attentive and complimentary. He made her feel as though together they could conquer the world.

They got engaged three weeks later, on New Year's Eve, and were married within six months. The speed at which she became his wife shocked her family, while her two best friends, who she'd known since secondary school, expressed concern that Ewan was pushing her too quickly into making such a big commitment. Now she wished they were still in touch so she could show them how wrong they were. But after the wedding Ewan said he felt uncomfortable in their presence, which she could understand after what they'd said about him, so she'd let the friendships fizzle out.

The door opened and Renshaw and Burton entered. Ewan relayed the incident to them, omitting the part where he'd threatened the woman.

'You need to put a stop to people thinking Poppy is to blame,' he said, still simmering with anger.

'I agree,' said Renshaw, 'and the quickest way for us to do that is if Poppy finishes telling us what happened. We can't set people straight if we don't know the full facts ourselves.'

'Are you ready to tell us, Poppy?' asked Burton.

Julia felt her frustration build as Poppy kept her gaze focused on her lap. Why didn't she just tell the police what they wanted to know, then they could collect Dylan, go home and put this nightmare behind them. Ewan shot her a glare that made her flinch, as though he'd sensed what she was thinking.

Burton tried again. 'Poppy? Are you ready?'

Finally she looked up and nodded.

The tension in the room shifted, as though a blast of cold air had unexpectedly blown in from outside. Julia's anxiety rose to match it, suddenly fearful of what her daughter might say.

Burton glanced down at his notebook, then cleared his throat.

'Poppy, you told us earlier that Benji wanted you to meet him at school because he knew how to get into the building site. Were the hoardings unlocked when you got there?'

'Benji had a key for the padlock. I don't know where he got it from.'

The sound of Renshaw's phone pinging made them all jump. The officer frowned as she read the text she'd been sent, then looked across at Poppy.

'Did Benji seem scared at all to you?' she asked.

'No.'

There was another ping. Renshaw studied her phone again.

'Was it definitely his idea to climb the wall?'

'Yes, it was. I didn't want to do it.'

Julia glanced up at the camera in the corner of the room. She hadn't given any thought to it while sitting there, but the timing of the texts and Renshaw's subsequent questions made her suddenly suspect others were watching them. The thought chilled her blood.

'The thing is, Poppy, Benji's mum's told us that he wasn't very adventurous and that he would've been far too scared to break into the building site, let alone climb the wall,' said Renshaw. 'Which makes me wonder if all this was *your* idea and not his.'

The mention of Imogen, even abstractly, made Julia tense.

'No, it wasn't me!' Poppy cried. 'I didn't even know about the fence way in until he told me. He said he found the gap when he was out playing. That's how he knew how to get into school when no one else was there.'

'Right, can we put a stop to this nonsense now?' Ewan butted in before Burton could pose his next question. 'My daughter's told you everything.'

'Not quite,' said Renshaw coolly. 'She still hasn't talked us through the moments before Benji fell.'

'I did, I told you he slipped.'

'I'd like more detail, Poppy. Like, how long were you on the wall?'

'I'm not sure. I don't think it was long.'

'Ten minutes?'

'Less than that.'

'Five?'

'I suppose.'

'Do you remember the caretaker trying to get you to come down?'

'It's what I said before – I remember someone shouting but I didn't know it was Mr Alan until after, when Benji was –' Poppy swallowed hard – 'on the ground.'

'Mr Alan? You mean Mr Donnelly?'

Poppy shrugged. 'The teachers call him that but we all call him Mr Alan.'

'What was the last thing Benji said to you?'

She thought for a moment. 'Um, I think he said we were so high up he felt like Superman. Or maybe it was Spider-Man.'

'Did that make you laugh?'

Poppy eyed Renshaw warily. 'I guess.'

'So you were definitely laughing before he fell to his death, not arguing?'

Poppy burst into tears. Ewan pulled her into a hug before Julia could.

'I don't like your tone, officer,' he snapped.

'And I don't like dealing with liars, Mr Hepworth. I don't think your daughter is telling us the truth.'

'I am, I am!' Poppy wailed.

Julia couldn't help herself and began to tear up too. 'Please stop,' she cried to Renshaw and Burton. 'She's just a child.'

'That's it. We're out of here,' said Ewan, getting to his feet and pulling Poppy to hers. 'If you want to talk to my daughter again you'll have to do it in the presence of our solicitor.'

'If that's what you'd prefer,' said Renshaw, rising out of her seat. 'Oh, one last question before we go. Mrs Hepworth, are you aware Poppy was having regular play dates at Benji's house?'

It was like the floor suddenly shifted beneath Julia's feet. 'What?'

'Your husband hasn't mentioned it? He arranged them with Benji's mum.'

Bewildered, Julia looked to Ewan for reassurance. 'But you wouldn't do that. Not with her.'

'Oh, for God's sake,' Ewan snarled at Renshaw. 'I can see

146

what you're trying to do but it won't work. Come on, Julia, let's go.'

Reluctantly she followed him but her mind was in overdrive. Ewan was in touch with Imogen? Poppy had been going to her *house*? No, no way, the police must be making it up. Ewan wouldn't dream of being friends with Imogen, not knowing how upset it would make her. She stalled for a second, desperate to stay and have it out with Renshaw, but then Ewan barked at her from the doorway to get a move on and she knew that if she didn't he'd blow his top.

But as she reached the open doorway she saw her husband and daughter were already halfway down the corridor, backs to her, so she paused and turned back.

'Really?' she whispered to Renshaw.

'Yes, really.'

28

Maggie left the room where she'd been following the interview on a monitor and joined Renshaw and Burton in the ABE suite.

'That was some grenade you lobbed in at the end,' she said as she sat down. 'I think it's safe to say Julia had no idea what's been going on behind her back.'

'Did you see the dad's face?' remarked Burton. 'I thought he was going to lose it.'

'He's definitely volatile, that one,' said Renshaw pensively. 'I'm thinking there might be some truth in that Facebook comment about Poppy being exposed to violence at home. Karl, get on to social services to see if they've ever had a file on the family, then check the PNC for any previous. Him and his wife.'

'What about speaking to the person who left the comment?' Maggie suggested.

'Already thought of that, but the account's been deactivated.'

'So the comment's gone?'

'Yep, and Facebook's removed all mentions of Poppy too.

I did screen-grab it but it's going to be hard to track the poster down.'

'Why?' asked Burton.

'Their user name was Lady Jane.'

'That's the title of a Rolling Stones track,' he mused.

Renshaw rolled her eyes. 'Exactly. I've asked Facebook to hand over the account details so we'll see if we get a proper name from that. So, what did you both make of Poppy's version of events?'

'I think she was lying about Benji's last words,' said Maggie. 'That Superman comment sounded contrived.'

'That's what I thought,' said Burton.

'But, I have to say, I did believe her when she said it was all Benji's idea,' Maggie went on. 'Obviously that doesn't tally with what Imogen's been saying about Benji being scared of his own shadow, but I think she wants us to believe he was too timid to instigate it because she's worried it reflects badly on her.'

'Because she let him play out in the evenings?' Renshaw retorted. 'It's hardly child neglect.'

'No, it's not, but if he spent the time breaking into private property and trespassing, then that's not good,' said Burton.

'Talk to Imogen again,' Renshaw said to Maggie. 'Make it clear Poppy's blaming it all on Benji, see how she reacts.' Her phone began to ring. 'It's the mortuary.'

She got up and went to the other side of the room to take the call. One-sided though it was, Maggie could tell it wasn't good news being delivered and when Renshaw hung up she was enraged.

'I could quite happily kill someone right now,' she said.

'Imogen got hysterical after seeing Benji's body and started saying that she wouldn't allow the post-mortem. So to calm her down some bright spark told her about digital autopsies and what a great alternative they are because they don't involve scalpels and now she's demanding one.'

'Can she do that?' asked Maggie.

'Evidently, yes. And it looks like the coroner is going to agree to it.'

'How does a DA work exactly?' asked Burton. 'I've never been present for one.'

'Me neither, but it's like an MRI scan,' said Renshaw. 'They're being used all the time now for routine coronial deaths, which is why I'm pissed off because this case is anything but routine. We need evidence of Benji being pushed but I don't know how good DAs are at picking up internal bruising.'

'If the coroner says yes, where will it be done?' asked Burton.

'There's a place in West Bromwich that's going to do it. But the coroner said it could take a day or so to sort the paperwork for the body to be shipped up there, and I can't see us getting the results until Monday at the earliest. We're in sodding limbo until then.'

'You can't blame Imogen for not wanting her son to have a traditional PM,' said Maggie reasonably. 'It's a common reaction from parents, one I've seen before. It's traumatic enough to lose your child without having to consider his or her body being flayed open on a gurney and their insides plopped onto a side table.'

Burton recoiled at Maggie's vivid description, while Renshaw sighed.

'I know you're right and I'm not angry with her. I'm pissed off with the person who suggested it, because they should've thought about the consequences for our investigation and the delay it might cause.'

'Whose idea was it?' asked Maggie.

Renshaw shot her a look.

'Your new partner's.'

29

Maggie spent the next hour dealing with the fallout from Imogen's decision to request a digital autopsy. Renshaw was furious with Byford for planting the idea in her mind but Maggie stood up for him and pointed out he wasn't actually at fault. FLOs were meant to offer practical advice to families about the coroner process and if Imogen was distraught at the thought of her son being cut open, a digital autopsy was an acceptable alternative. But Renshaw wasn't swayed and insisted Byford had acted unprofessionally by not consulting her first, so she'd tasked Maggie and not him with talking to the coroner about the logistics.

Yet far from being troubled by Benji's body being dispatched to the Midlands for examination, the coroner, an amiable chap called Tim who was also a prominent and long-serving solicitor in Mansell, told Maggie he welcomed the advancement of non-scalpel post-mortems.

'There were lots of families who objected to a post-mortem on religious grounds and telling them that we didn't need their permission to carry one out was distressing for everyone involved,' he said. 'It felt like we were riding roughshod over their wishes, so I think it's marvellous these scans are now available.'

'But are they as thorough?' asked Maggie. She found it difficult to believe they would be.

'Yes, they are. Some police forces now request them as the first option in forensic cases because a digital autopsy enables the body to be secured in its natural state. I would say that in the majority of cases a DA is rigorous enough to establish cause of death. However, if for some reason it doesn't, a traditional post-mortem can still be carried out.'

'So you think it's fine in this case?'

'I do. The cause of death should be straightforward given the head injury the child sustained in the fall, so if it brings the mother comfort to know her son's body remains intact I'm all for it. But I also believe it is prudent to warn her that if the results are inconclusive we shall have to insist on a surgical post-mortem. Prepare her for every eventuality.'

Maggie didn't relish that conversation.

Phone call to the coroner done, she sneaked in a quick call to Umpire.

He sounded so pleased to hear her voice when he picked up that for a moment she felt bad about sulking.

'I missed you last night,' he said. 'I'm going to leave at a decent time tomorrow night so I can come to yours and be there on your birthday morning. You might need helping out of bed now you're getting on a bit,' he teased.

'If turning thirty makes me old then you are officially ancient,' she laughed.

They chatted a bit about work, then Umpire said he needed to go.

'Before I do, I have some good news,' he said.

'What's that?'

'I felt bad about us having to cancel going away so I had a long chat with Sarah last night and she's agreed it's time you met the kids.'

'Oh. Right.'

'I thought you'd be pleased,' he said, sounding confused. 'It means we can see each other when the kids are here.'

'I am pleased,' she said, trying to sound convincing. 'I'm just surprised by the sudden change of heart.'

'Sarah admitted that she's been worried about the kids getting attached to you and then being upset when we broke up.'

Maggie bristled. 'What makes her think we'll break up?'

'She thought you might not see it as a serious relationship, because you're younger and haven't had kids of your own. In a way I can see what she means – it *is* a big thing, taking on someone else's children.'

'I think you're forgetting I had a pretty big hand in raising my niece and nephews,' she said, outraged by the suggestion that she was clueless when it came to parenting. 'I did everything for them a mum would do.'

'I know, that's what I told Sarah and that's what changed her mind. So, you do think we're serious?'

'Why, don't you?'

'Absolutely.' His voice dropped to a whisper. 'These last few months with you are the happiest I've been in years.'

Despite her anger at his ex's comment, Maggie found herself smiling.

'Me too.'

'So you'll meet Jack and Flora?'

'Yes, of course.'

'Amazing. They're great kids, I know you'll like them.'

Maggie was gripped with apprehension. Yes, but would they like her?

30

Ewan had always been adept at dodging discussions he didn't want to have, but since storming out of the police station he'd excelled himself. He knew Julia was dying to ask him about Poppy's visits to Imogen's house but he was making certain she had no opportunity to get him on his own.

After leaving the station he marched the three of them straight round the corner to a street that was lined with legal practices, not far from the magistrates' court. They went into the first to be told there was no one free to see them, so Ewan huffily told the receptionist to forget it and went two doors along to the next one, where a solicitor who specialized in criminal law was happy to squeeze them in.

The solicitor's name was Darren and Julia wasn't sure she liked him much: he spoke flippantly and aggressively and his manner was as oily as whatever it was he'd rubbed in his hair that morning to slick it down. She also found his approach baffling – Darren didn't ask Poppy any questions directly and didn't seem concerned with knowing the details of what had happened. But Ewan clearly liked him and Julia knew it was a done deal when the solicitor took the names of the detectives investigating the case and said he would make them aware he was now Poppy's legal representative.

Afterwards they drove directly to Cath's house to collect Dylan; Ewan turned the radio up so loud that conversation in the car was impossible. Cath invited them to stay for a coffee, which Ewan eagerly said yes to, so Poppy plonked herself down on the sofa next to her brother to watch TV and the adults retreated to the kitchen so the kids couldn't hear them talking.

'She did really well,' said Ewan, 'right up until the police got nasty.'

'In what way?' asked Cath.

'They tried to imply it was all her idea to break into the school.'

As Ewan filled Cath in, Julia sipped her coffee in the hope it would settle the gnawing in her stomach. Had they made things worse by pulling Poppy out of the interview? To her horror, Cath seemed to think they had.

'I understand why you walked out, but refusing to co-operate might force the police's hand to arrest and interview her under caution,' she said. 'Rather than go in all guns blazing with a lawyer, try to smooth it over.'

Ewan's face darkened but he didn't retaliate straight away as he would with most people. Cath was one of the few people he held in high regard and in return she was one of the few people who thought nothing of putting him in his place when he was being out of line.

Perhaps it was because of her age that Ewan respected her. Cath was two decades older than them, a retired civil servant who lived alone, her husband dead five years now and their two sons grown up and both living in London. She appeared on their doorstep the day they moved in, clutching a bottle of wine and a lasagne she'd made, to save them the worry of cooking on their first night. Ewan's initial critique was that she was pushy and entitled but over time he'd come to like her as much as Julia did.

'What should we do?' Julia asked her worriedly.

'Tell them you were upset and that you'll bring her back in whenever they want,' said Cath. 'You're gambling with Poppy's future if you don't.'

'I'm not sacking the solicitor,' said Ewan huffily.

'I'm not suggesting you do. Frankly, you should've had a solicitor with you from the first moment—'

'That's what I said,' Julia interrupted. 'I even started looking for one.'

Ewan wasn't impressed. 'Really, Julia, you think this is the time to start point scoring? I'm sorry I'm such a crap partner that I didn't back you up,' he pouted.

'I wasn't saying you were!'

An uncomfortable silence fell over the kitchen. Cath offered to make more coffee.

'No, thanks,' said Ewan. 'I thought we could take the kids somewhere fun before tea. I was thinking swimming at the Lido.'

Julia was alarmed. What if someone had a go at them like earlier?

'I don't think it's a good idea,' she began.

'I think you should go,' said Cath. 'The kids can't stay indoors roasting all afternoon. It'll be nice and cool in the water.'

'But what if someone sees us?' Julia fretted.

'If we hide ourselves away it looks worse,' said Ewan.

'He's right,' Cath nodded.

'That's settled then,' said Ewan. 'We can go for pizza after. I'll tell the kids.'

Cath waited until he was gone.

'You okay?'

'I've had better days, but it'll be fine. I'm sure the police will believe Poppy,' said Julia, trying to sound positive.

'That's not what I meant. I mean you and Ewan. I get that he's stressed but that doesn't excuse him talking to you like that.'

Julia's cheeks mottled. 'Like you said, he's stressed. I've been snappy with him too.'

'But he's always like that with you.'

'No, he's not.'

'But he—'

Julia hastily got to her feet.

'We'd best get going if we want to take the kids swimming. Thanks for the coffee and for having Dylan.' She quickly hugged her friend and made for the door.

Cath called after her. 'I'm here if you ever need to talk.'

But Julia had already bolted from the room.

31

Thursday

Alan's lunchtime pint in The Wheatsheaf had led to another, then another, until it was eight in the evening and Doug was calling time on him, saying he'd had enough and wouldn't be served anything else even if he asked nicely.

Alan didn't remember much about getting home – he had a vague sense of weaving along a street he didn't recognize, past houses whose occupants were strangers to him – then the next thing he knew he was waking up in his own bed at six in the morning with a clanging headache, parched mouth and a soreness down the right-hand side of his face.

Stumbling to the bathroom, he checked his reflection in the mirror over the sink and saw there was a thin but vivid red graze scoring his cheek from temple to chin. He rubbed it gingerly and winced. He must've caught it on a bush on his walk home.

He checked his phone and there was no message from Mrs Pullman telling him to stay off work again, so he had a bracingly cold shower that took the edge off his headache, downed two cups of strong black coffee, gagging only the once, and made a sandwich for his packed lunch using the few scraps of ham left in his fridge.

His stomach clenched with nerves as he walked through the school gates at ten to seven, only relenting when it became apparent that he was alone as usual.

This was his favourite time of day . . . a brief window of solitude before the rest of the school descended. His first task was to walk round the site and complete a Health & Safety check – once that was done he could open up the gates. He knew he'd have to give a statement at some point to H&S inspectors to explain how the kids had managed to get into the grounds so early; their investigation had begun in tandem with the police's.

Bang on seven thirty Alan bumped into Mrs Pullman and the deputy head, Mr Lincoln, as they headed into the main building on their way from the car park.

'How are you?' asked the head, cupping Alan's elbow briefly as a gesture of comfort.

'I'm okay,' he said, hoping his rigorous teeth brushing had eradicated the worst of the stale alcohol on his breath. 'I know you said I could stay off but I want to get back to work, get on with things.'

'What happened to your face?' asked Mr Lincoln.

'Gardening. I caught it on a twig.'

The deputy head smirked.

'We're closed to pupils again today but I'm sure you'll find plenty to keep you busy,' said Mrs Pullman, before taking a pause. 'There will be counsellors on standby when the school reopens to talk to the children affected by Benji's death. Would you like to talk to someone too?'

'Not really my cup of tea,' said Alan. 'But thank you.'

'Didn't see you as the stiff-upper-lip type,' said Mr Lincoln mockingly.

Alan let the comment slide, unwilling to be drawn into a conversation with the deputy, who he didn't much like. Mr Lincoln was among the handful of staff that spoke to Alan in a way that made him feel subservient and lacking. By way of payback he always put those teachers' names to the bottom of his list if any of them wanted jobs doing.

'Well, the offer stands should you change your mind,' said Mrs Pullman.

She looked weary, the wrinkles around her eyes and mouth more pronounced than usual. Her hair, although cropped short and its natural grey, looked lank. The boy's death must be weighing heavy on her heart and mind, thought Alan. It didn't matter that it wasn't her fault or that there was nothing she could've done to prevent it, he knew as head teacher she would feel responsible regardless. It made him feel even guiltier about what he was facilitating in the Pavilion.

'Trust me, I won't. Are the police going to be here today?' he asked.

'I think they'll be popping in and out. It sounds like they've exhausted their search of the grounds, though.'

Alan's stomach flip-flopped.

'The grounds? I thought they were only checking the building site where it happened.'

'That's what I meant by grounds,' said Mrs Pullman.

'Right. Well, I should get on,' said Alan, feeling more reassured.

The head nodded. 'Thank you for coming in today, Alan, I do appreciate it. But if at any point you feel you'd like to go home, that's absolutely fine. Just come and see me.'

He said he would, then excused himself and set off for his office below ground.

Paranoia made him double-check everything – the lock on his door to see if it had been forced open, the files on his computer to see if they'd been accessed, even whether his private stash of coffee had been tampered with. Everything about his office looked exactly as it should, with no signs of interference, yet still Alan couldn't shake the feeling that someone had been inside, poking around.

He checked the list of jobs he'd been forced to abandon on Tuesday. Most were simple to rectify, such as a radiator cover coming loose in one of the classrooms and a toilet door that kept jamming. He then accessed the email account he'd set up on the school system for teachers to message him with repair requests and wasn't surprised to find none had been sent in the past two days.

He decided to tackle the radiator cover first. His tools were secured in an outbuilding so after locking his office behind him he headed outdoors.

Yesterday's phone call with Gayle was still weighing heavy on his mind and his preoccupation meant he didn't notice someone following him until he reached the out-building and a hand grabbed his shoulder, making him yelp in surprise.

'Sorry, did I startle you?' said Gus, grinning.

'You could say that,' he wheezed, as his heart pounded against his ribcage.

'I think we need a chat, don't you?'

'I've done my bit,' Alan protested. 'I told the police I thought it was an accident.'

'You did, and that's great. You did good, mate. But it's the girls I'm here about now.'

'The girls?' Alan stammered.

'I hear you went round to Ruby's house last night, saying all sorts about me.'

There was an edge to Gus's voice that scared him. Ruby was one of six girls who operated out of the Pavilion. Her, Lila, Celeste, Krysia and two others whose names he didn't know.

'Did I? I don't remember doing that. I was absolutely bladdered last night – I'd been down The Wheatsheaf since lunchtime.'

He wasn't lying either. He had no recollection of going to see Ruby, much less anything he might've said to her.

'She was very upset you called her a whore.' Gus took a step towards him. 'But not half as upset as I am that you told her I was evil and that you were going to put a stop to my enterprise.'

Alan reeled back. Had he really said that? *Shit.*

'She's making it up,' he said feebly.

'Really? Is that why she scratched you down your face?'

Alan's hand flew to his cheek. Ruby did that to him? But surely he would've remembered her clawing his face, her fingernail marking him?

'I honestly don't remember going to see her.'

Gus inched closer. 'Are you calling me a liar now?'

'No, no, I'm not.'

'Good. I don't like it when my girls are upset.'

The way Gus said it made them sound as though they were his pets.

'I'm sorry,' said Alan.

'Lucky for you I'm prepared to let it go this once, because I know it's been a tough couple of days for you and because I don't want to screw up the grand reopening.'

'For what?'

'The Pavilion, of course. Now the police are wrapping up I want it up and running again as soon as possible.'

Alan's insides turned to mulch. 'By when?'

'Tomorrow. Friday night's always our busiest time with everyone looking to let off some steam after a long week. So be a good lad and make sure it's ready.'

As Gus sauntered off, Alan staggered into the outbuilding and sank down onto the floor in despair. He sat hunched over, forehead resting on his bent knees, feeling like he might be sick. What the hell was he going to do? Last night in The Wheatsheaf, before he'd got drunk enough to forget, he'd decided the only way out of this mess was to remove the Pavilion from Gus's control. But how?

After a few minutes he raised his head. The outbuilding was dingy inside and Alan could barely see as he sat there in the gloom. Then, gradually, his eyes began to focus and they lit upon a container stacked on a pile of boxes right in front of him. As he idly read the lettering printed on the side, an idea came to him in a flash.

He'd found his way out.

32

Maggie set off for Imogen's alone after that morning's briefing. Byford had been ordered to area HQ in Trenton to tie up loose ends on a previous case and it would be lunchtime before he'd be back in Mansell.

Grace and Imogen were in the midst of a row when she arrived. Grace was insisting they choose a coffin from a glossy brochure she'd somehow procured and Imogen was understandably distressed. Maggie managed to diffuse the argument by saying they might want to hold off planning the funeral until the digital autopsy was completed. Grace didn't take kindly to being silenced and stomped upstairs in a huff, brochure wedged under her arm.

Maggie and Imogen went to sit in the small paved courtyard at the rear of the cottage, the only outdoor space. Benji's bike was propped up against the fence, helmet dangling off the handlebars. Maggie was grateful Grace had gone upstairs – it was easier to talk to Imogen without her chipping in every other sentence.

'How are you today?' she asked.

'Like everything's gone numb,' said Imogen. 'I haven't

even cried. I think it's because of yesterday, seeing Benji. It took it out of me.'

'It can't have been easy,' said Maggie, wishing she'd been with her.

'Will the scan thingy prove Benji was pushed?'

Preparing relatives for every possible outcome was a requisite skill for a FLO and one of the toughest parts of the job. It meant having to dash the hopes of a family praying their relative would return alive when you knew your colleagues were looking for a body, or breaking the news that the conviction they were depending on for closure wasn't assured. Maggie had to make sure relatives understood the grim odds they faced in the gentlest way possible.

'If Benji was pushed there may be physical signs that show up on the digital autopsy,' she said carefully. 'But it won't tell us whether it was accidental or deliberate, so that's where other evidence comes in, like witness statements. Only when we've gathered enough conclusive evidence can my senior officers present it to the CPS to see if there is a case to answer.'

Imogen's eyes narrowed.

'Is it because Poppy's a kid?'

'No. She's a year above the age of criminality so she can be charged if the evidence is there. But we're still gathering it, so you'll need to be patient. It could be weeks before anything is decided.'

Imogen tucked her feet up on the chair and rested her chin on her knees. She looked almost child-like herself, especially dressed in red shorts and a black vest top. It was the most anyone would want to be wearing on a sweltering day like this but Maggie was sweating again in trousers because she couldn't stand wearing skirts.

'How is Poppy?' Imogen asked. 'How are her parents?'

Maggie stalled for a moment. Would it help Imogen to know they were managing to hold it together, or would telling her they were falling apart ease her pain? Whichever she said it probably wouldn't be the right answer, so she decided to fudge it.

'I don't really know. My priority has been you, not them.'

'I keep thinking I should hate Poppy, but I can't.' Imogen sighed and lowered her legs back to the ground. 'She has the same lovely thick hair that Julia used to have, except Julia's was dark brown. I used to be so jealous of it – my hair's as thin as cotton thread. Julia's mum would put it in a gorgeous French plait every morning.'

'I thought you didn't remember her that well?'

Imogen shrugged. 'I don't. Her hair stuck in my mind because it was so lovely.'

'I'm surprised you never bumped into each other after Benji started at Rushbrooke.'

'The older the kids are, the less involved parents are. Benji walked there and back alone and I only met Ewan because we helped out on the same school trip.'

'Where to?'

'London Zoo, just before Easter.' Imogen picked at the hem of her shorts. 'He's a nice man, and a good dad. We have a laugh.'

'I wonder why he never mentioned Julia was his wife.'

'Why would he?'

'Well, because of your history. It looks like he might have known about it.'

Maggie was careful how she worded it; she didn't want Imogen to know she had watched Poppy being interviewed with her parents present and had seen Julia's reaction on discovering Ewan had been setting up the play dates.

'I'd be amazed if she had told him, because, like I said yesterday, it wasn't that big a deal. I doubt Julia gives it a second thought now. I think you're making more of this than I am.' She flashed Maggie a weak smile.

'Maybe I am. So, was it after that trip when the play dates began?'

Imogen nodded. 'Poppy and Benji got on well that day so Ewan suggested we swap numbers and arrange for the kids to meet up after school. Poppy came here for tea and they had a great time. She was polite, said her pleases and thank-yous, thanked me for having her as she left. Not in a million years did I worry about her being horrible to Benji. That's why I invited her back.'

'And you never noticed any change in Benji in the last few weeks? No mood swings, being grumpy, bottling things up?'

'Not at all. Why?'

'When kids have problems at school, like a fall-out with their friends, it often shows up in their behaviour at home.'

'Benji was no different,' said Imogen. The hem picking became more urgent but her eyes remained dry.

'Was he happy about moving to Mansell?'

'He wasn't at first, because he thought he'd miss his friends. But we came up a few times when I was house hunting and he started to get used to the idea and he liked Rushbrooke when we had a look around. By the time the move happened he was really excited about going there.'

'Why did you come back?'

'I had to.'

It occurred to Maggie that Imogen had never mentioned being forced to leave Somerset. She'd made it sound as though it was her choice.

'It was nothing to do with Benji,' Imogen added hastily. 'I got made redundant and I was struggling to find another job. Mum thought I'd have better luck up here.'

Her gaze strayed to the bike in the corner.

'She wants me to start clearing his things away. She thinks it's worse for me if I have to see them all the time. But if I do that it'll seem like I'm getting rid of him and it's only been a couple of days.'

'There's no rush to do anything,' said Maggie. 'Wait until you're ready . . . Sorry, I think I hear my phone ringing. I'd better get it in case it's important.'

Dashing inside, Maggie plucked her phone from her bag, which she'd left on the small dining table. It was Renshaw.

'Have I got an update for you,' she said excitedly.

'What's happened?'

'Forensics have come back to say they found blood at the spot where Benji died that wasn't his. Lots of it, in fact.'

'Eh?'

'I said, there's blood on the building site that wasn't his.'

'Maybe one of the builders cut themselves, bled out, didn't bother to clean up?'

'That's what I said, but Forensics are ruling that out because of the splatter pattern. It looks like someone suffered serious blood loss at the foot of the wall where Benji fell. So –' Renshaw took a deep breath – 'I've put in a request for

EVR dogs to be brought in. If I get the nod it might happen this afternoon.'

'Seriously?' Maggie exclaimed. 'You're asking for dogs that sniff bodies through concrete?'

'I'm acting on what Forensics have said. Based on the amount of blood at the scene and the way it was spilled, they suspect that Benji isn't the only person who's died there.'

33

When Maggie went back outside Imogen was perched expectantly on the edge of her seat, waiting for her.

'What's happened?'

'That was DS Renshaw, the SIO. They're going to be doing another search of the school grounds as something significant has come to light. We're not sure if it's linked to Benji's death though, so I can't really give you any more details until the search is completed.'

'I heard you mention sniffer dogs.'

'Yes, they're being brought in to assist the search.' Maggie pulled a face. 'I'm sorry that I'm having to be vague, I find it frustrating too.'

'It's okay, I understand.'

'I do need to clear up a couple of things that could help move the investigation on,' said Maggie, opening her notebook and casting an eye over the scrawled entries she'd made during the briefing earlier, when Renshaw had outlined the information she needed from Imogen today. 'Do you feel up to a few more questions?'

Imogen immediately crossed her arms protectively in front of her but she also nodded.

'Benji told Poppy he knew a hidden way to get into Rushbrooke because he'd found it while out playing,' said Maggie. 'Were you aware he was going up to the school when he went out to play?'

'I wondered if you were going to ask me about that. Yes, I knew,' said Imogen, visibly abashed. 'I didn't realize at first he was actually getting into the grounds, and when I did I told him he mustn't, because it was trespassing and he could get into trouble. But at the same time I *wanted* him to go off exploring. I know this is going to sound terrible, but sometimes I hated that he was so bloody sensitive and could be a bit of a wimp. I'd watch other kids racing around all over the place and it would drive me mad that Benji was always on the sidelines, sitting things out. I thought that if he went out on his bike in the evenings he'd become a bit braver and learn to take risks.' Tears slid down her face. 'Now I wish I'd kept him wrapped up in cotton wool all the time so he'd be here with me, safe.'

'Was Poppy one of the kids you saw racing around?'

'Yes. That's why I was happy for them to be friends. I thought she might be a positive influence on him, get him to come out of his shell a bit.'

'Your mum told me that Benji thought Poppy could be bossy and overbearing.'

'I guess she could be at times, but I thought it was good for Benji to have someone be a bit bolshie with him, to push him into trying new things. I saw the kind of parent Ewan was with Poppy and how it toughened her up and I was trying to do the same.'

'What does Ewan do?'

'He's very no-nonsense, so if Poppy ever got upset and

said she didn't want to do something because she was scared or was being lazy, Ewan wouldn't let her duck out. He'd make her join in. And, of course, once she did she was fine.'

Maggie wasn't sure she agreed. Forcing kids against their will to participate when they were upset seemed cruel.

'I thought I should do the same with Benji,' Imogen continued. 'I was never scared of my own shadow as a child and I hated that he was like that.'

'Did it help his confidence, being tougher on him?'

Imogen wiped her cheeks dry with her fingertips. 'It did. He started going out on his bike after school and he seemed much happier.' Her face suddenly clouded for a moment. 'There was one day he came back upset though. He was crying.'

Maggie flipped on to a clean page in her notebook.

'Did he tell you why?'

'I didn't ask. I was really cross because he came home with his school trousers covered in chalky mud and I had to get them washed for the morning. I made him get in the shower and then go straight to bed.'

'Can you remember what day it was?'

'Um, it was the Tuesday before last.'

Exactly two weeks before his death, Maggie noted.

'What time did he get home?'

'It was late, gone nine,' Imogen admitted. 'His curfew was usually seven.'

'He was two hours late?'

'Yes, but we were talking on the phone the whole time, so it wasn't like I didn't know where he was. He begged me to let him stay out a bit longer and because I was so happy he was being adventurous I stupidly agreed. I did make him text me every fifteen minutes to let me know he was okay but I feel terrible about it now. What kind of mum lets her eleven-year-old son roam around the streets that late?'

'I think you're being a bit hard on yourself. When we were kids we played out until it was dark.'

'Those were different times,' said Imogen. 'It's not as safe now.'

'Sometimes I think it's the perceived threat of danger rather than the actual threat that makes us worry it's not as safe,' said Maggie in an attempt to placate her. 'I mean, increased traffic is definitely an issue – there are way more cars on the roads than when we were kids – but it's hard to tell if the other dangers exist in greater numbers because comparing statistics from then and now is too simplistic. The numbers aren't always reliable. I don't think it was nec-essarily a bad thing you let Benji stay out and nor should you.'

'But it was bad, because now he's dead!'

'Do you think him coming home upset the week before might have had something to do with what happened to him?' Maggie checked her notes. 'You said you knew where he was because he kept texting you. Where was he?'

Imogen grew tearful again. 'He was cycling round that new housing estate at the back of Rushbrooke, the one that's half built. But I don't know if it's related, because I was too angry about the mud to bother listening to what he was trying to tell me. My poor baby came home crying his eyes out and I never asked him why.'

34

Byford turned up not long after two, so Maggie took advantage of his presence to return to the station to update her FL log and catch up on emails. She also did some digging on the housing development behind Rushbrooke and discovered that the same construction company putting up the new classrooms was behind it. What had happened to Benji while he was there to make him so upset? She made a note to raise it at the next briefing.

Maggie was alone in the incident room when Omana, one of the admin assistants, popped her head round the door.

'Is DC Byford around?'

'No, he's with Benji's mum. Can I help?'

'Mind if I leave this with you?' She handed Maggie a sealed foolscap envelope with Byford's name written on the front. 'He knows what it is.'

'Sure, I'll leave it on his desk.' She dropped it in his in-tray.

By six she was finished for the day. But rather than drive straight home she took a detour, heading along the main route out of town, then cutting up a side street before swinging left into the road where Lou used to live. Drawing level with her sister's old house, she pulled into a vacant space opposite.

Maggie spotted immediately that the front door had been repainted since her last visit and the unexpected change floored her. The paintwork was now fire-engine red, glossily coated on to cover the sky blue of old. She lowered her window and stared at the house. Did the new owners see the irony in choosing a shade that represented the reason why they were able to buy it for such a low price in the first place?

The fire had begun in the kitchen but was contained before it could cause widespread damage. The few lingering traces had been obliterated by the installation of new double-glazed windows downstairs to replace the ones blown out by the heat, while the sooty exterior brickwork had been power-washed back to clean. The house looked loved again.

Maggie knew that going there was a habit she should break but she couldn't help herself. She was welded to the memories the house held within its walls and with her birthday tomorrow they were more acute than ever. Last year Lou had thrown a BBQ for her on the Saturday before – it had been a brilliant afternoon that staggered hazily into the evening and Maggie remembered feeling overcome with happiness to be surrounded by her family and close friends. Lou had raised her glass at one point and said, 'Next year we'll have the mother of all parties for your thirtieth!' But Maggie wasn't interested. 'No. Let's do this again,' she'd said. 'This is perfect.'

She swallowed the tears building in the back of her

throat as her fingers clenched the key in the ignition. Turn it, start the engine, drive away. Seconds ticked by but still she didn't move. Then her phone rang, forcing her out of her stupor.

'Hey, I was going to call you when I got home,' she answered, thankful for the interruption. 'What time will you get to mine?'

'I know where you are,' said Umpire, his voice unexpectedly tender.

'What?'

'Look in your rear-view mirror.'

Three spaces behind her, he was leaning against the bonnet of his car dressed in a white T-shirt, navy shorts adorned with more pockets than one person would ever need, his feet sockless in trainers. She smiled through her tears. Seeing Umpire in casual clothes still took some getting used to.

She climbed out of her car, legs wobbly from sitting still. He didn't wait for her to come to him, his long stride covering the tarmac between them in seconds. Without a word he wrapped his arms around her and held her as she cried.

'I miss them so much.'

'I know you do.'

Umpire knew every detail of her row with Lou and the affair that had precipitated it. It was to him Maggie had turned in the early hours after her sister walked out. He hadn't judged her, he'd simply listened and comforted her and tried to reassure her that she could make things right again.

He disentangled himself from her and immediately she missed the feel of his body against hers.

'I understand why you keep coming back here but it's not healthy. It makes you more upset,' he said. 'It's why I'm concerned about you being on this case.'

'I'm doing okay, I promise.' She gave him a potted version of the day's events.

'As I was leaving tonight Renshaw got the green light to use the EVR dogs. The search is happening in the morning,' she said. 'She's convinced they're going to find something.'

'The blood find warrants it. I'd be bringing them in if I was her.' His eyes searched hers. 'You ready to go?'

'Sure. What do you fancy doing tonight? Pub? Take-away?'

'I was hoping for an early night. I'm yours for the taking, basically.'

Maggie grinned. Umpire had an innate knack of making her feel better no matter how low her mood was. He was good for her and she hoped the sentiment was reciprocated.

'I'll race you back to mine,' she said, moving to open her driver's door.

'Keeping below the speed limit, I hope,' he pretended to admonish. 'Yeah, I'll meet you back there.' He watched as her gaze strayed back across the road to the newly painted door.

'I bet she misses you too,' he said softly. 'She won't stay away forever.'

Maggie sighed. 'Knowing Lou, I wouldn't be so sure.'

35

Julia went through the motions of her usual night-time routine. She washed her face, applied moisturizer and was just finishing brushing her teeth when Ewan came into the bathroom without knocking.

'You going to be long? I'm bursting.'

She needed a wee too, but she let him use the toilet first and went to their bedroom to wait, sitting on the edge of the bed and idly flicking through the paperback on her bedside table because she'd lost her place and hadn't marked where she was up to.

When Ewan came into the room minutes later she tensed. It was the first time they'd been alone all day and they still needed to discuss the police's revelation that Poppy had been going to Benji's house for tea. Julia had so many questions she wanted to ask her husband – who instigated the children getting together, was it him or Imogen? Had he been to her house too? How often were they in contact? Had they ever met up *without* the kids?

But she still hadn't been able to ask because once the kids had gone to bed a surprise guest turned up on the doorstep – her dad, Malcolm. It transpired Ewan had called him and

asked him to fly over from southern Spain – where he'd
retired to a year previously – because he thought Julia could
do with the support and an extra pair of hands with the kids
while they were off school.

She'd been pleased to see her dad but also wary. He and
Ewan got on brilliantly but her relationship with Malcolm
was more distant, a hangover from her childhood when he
ruled their household with an autocratic fist. As a teen she'd
avoided being in his presence as much as she could and it
was only when she got married that, at Ewan's urging, their
relationship improved.

Ewan began stripping off his clothes and laying them out
on the blanket box at the foot of their bed, so Julia got up
to go to the toilet.

'Where do you think you're going?'

He grabbed her by the wrist and pulled her towards him,
then started nuzzling her neck. She could feel he was
already hard and was filled with dread.

'I don't think we should, not tonight,' she said. 'Dad'll
hear us in the next room.'

'We'll have to be quiet then.'

'No,' she said, pulling away. 'It doesn't feel right, not with
everything going on.'

This time he encircled her completely with his arms,
making it almost impossible for her to move.

'But I want to,' he murmured.

The touch of him made her agitated. How could he
possibly be thinking about sex when their family was in
crisis?

'Ewan, no, I don't want to,' she said, and she wriggled to
free herself from his clasp.

Swearing, he shoved her backwards so she landed heavily on the bed.

'You never want to,' he huffed.

'That's not true,' she protested.

'Yes, it is. You should count yourself lucky I'm still here – other men wouldn't put up with what I have to and would've started an affair by now. But I wouldn't, because I'm not some awful bastard.'

Please, not another row, she thought despairingly.

'I'm sorry, I'm just not in the mood.'

'Do you not fancy me any more? Is that it?'

Julia's smile was genuine. 'Are you kidding? Of course I do.'

'It doesn't feel like it.'

She got up and went over to him. 'Ewan Hepworth, you are the most gorgeous man I've ever laid eyes on and I love you.'

'Show me.'

'What?'

'Show me you love me. Right now, on this bed.'

'But I – I don't –'

He went to grab his boxer shorts. 'Fine, but don't say I didn't warn you. I don't want to live like a bloody monk the rest of my life.'

Julia was torn between wanting him to leave her alone and feeling as though she had no choice but to give him what he wanted. As she watched him pull on his boxers, resignation washed over her.

'I need the loo first,' she said.

The boxers were discarded in an instant.

'No, you don't,' he grinned as he pulled her onto the bed.

'It'll hurt if I don't,' she protested.

But he'd already stopped listening.

36

The day had dragged even more than it did when the children were in school. Alan had tried to keep busy but invariably he found himself checking his watch again, only to be disappointed that so little time had passed since he'd last checked.

Eventually, to his relief, home time for the grown-ups came around. Teachers were expected to stay and work after the bell went at 3.30 but Mrs Pullman was that rare breed of head teacher who wanted her staff to have a work–life balance and insisted everyone go home by 6.30, instructing Alan to turf out any stragglers so he could lock up for the evening.

He walked out with the last teacher to leave and locked the main gates behind them. Heading down the lane, he made a point of waving as she drove past him.

Then he went straight to the pub as usual.

Keeping to his routine was important. Most people never noticed if you did the same thing day in, day out – but they paid attention when you didn't.

The snug was busier than usual as Thursday night was quiz night and Doug, being the generous sort, always stumped up a decent prize for the winning team: free beer for the rest of the evening. Alan wasn't one for quizzes, so there was nothing unusual in him declining invites to join in. Instead he stayed in his usual spot, at a table close to the bar, and chatted to a couple of the other regulars who, like him, preferred to be spectators.

At nine o'clock he rose from his seat on the pretext of going to the toilet. He'd only had a couple of pints, less than usual, but he pretended to be weaving drunk as he crossed the snug, as was his typical state most evenings at that time. If he got a shift on, he could be back before anyone noticed he'd disappeared. And if anyone did ask, he'd say he fell asleep on the loo, which he'd done once or twice before when he was bladdered, so nothing out of the ordinary there.

But instead of going into the men's, Alan pushed open a door marked 'Private'. It was the entrance that led upstairs to Doug's personal quarters, but there was also a door that went outside into the back yard. To Alan's relief it wasn't locked, so he slipped out.

On the other side of the yard was a pair of double wooden gates leading into the street beyond but, as he expected, these were bolted shut and fastened with a padlock. He scanned the gates, then around him. He could probably get over the top of them if he had something to stand on . . .

Barrels. There were a couple of empty ones in the corner next to the wall. Alan managed to heave one across to the gates without making too much noise. Then he hauled himself up and reached for the top of the gate. His fingertips had just managed to make contact when he heard someone clear their throat behind him.

'Where do you think you're going?'

His hands betrayed him, letting go before he was ready, and he landed heavily on the barrel. It wobbled but stayed upright. Deflated, he rested his forehead on the fence.

'Alan?'

The voice was next to him now. He looked round.

'I'm sorry, Doug. I know I shouldn't be out here. I just –' he could feel tears building – 'I want to put things right. I thought I could do it without anyone seeing.'

Doug helped him down off the barrel.

'This about the Pavilion?'

'Gus wants to reopen it tomorrow night. I can't let him do that.'

Alan told him his plan and Doug stood there for a moment, thinking. Then he pulled out a set of keys from his pocket and unlocked the padlock on the gates.

'If anyone asks where you are I'll say you've passed out in the loo. I'll lock one of the cubicles from the outside.'

'That was going to be my excuse,' said Alan with a shaky grin. Overwhelmed with gratitude, he gripped the landlord's hand and shook it. 'Thank you.'

'I'm doing this because you're a good bloke, Alan, and I don't think you realize the shit you're in. I'll leave the gate unlocked so you can get back in. But don't be too long: if you're not here by closing I can't cover for you.'

Ten minutes later Alan crossed the playing field to the outbuilding, mindful to hug the path that kept him out of the watchful stare of the CCTV. He unlocked the door, flung it wide open and grabbed the plastic container he'd seen earlier, which held spare petrol for the school's engine mower. Then he rifled through a drawer where he kept odds and ends until his fingers folded over the small wallet of matches he knew was somewhere in there.

The back door to the Pavilion was locked, as it should've been. Conscious that he needed to make it look as though vandals were responsible, Alan kicked it open. It took a few attempts before the frame splintered, the steel toecaps on his work boots taking the brunt of it.

He paused for a moment in the open doorway. To anyone else it would look like a lovely little hideaway, the sofas making the space seem inviting and comfy. Bile rose up and scorched his throat.

He went to the sofa nearest the door, a blue corduroy number, and splashed some of the petrol onto the seat cushions, but not much – just enough to get the flames going. With a bit of luck it would be mistaken for lighter fuel: kids messing around with cigarettes, being careless.

Returning to the doorway, Alan lit a match; his hands were trembling so violently it took multiple strikes for the spark to catch. Then he tossed it onto the sofa and left as quickly as he'd arrived.

37

Friday

Renshaw insisted everyone be in at 7 a.m for the briefing, no exceptions. Maggie had joined in the chorus of moans but was secretly grateful for the early summons – it gave her a convenient excuse not to mope about her flat wondering if Lou or her parents were going to get in touch to wish her happy birthday.

She hadn't given much thought to turning thirty, not in the way some people fretted; it was another year to tick off rather than a milestone to dread. But as she applied her make-up in the bathroom mirror, skin illuminated by the bright daylight streaming through the window, she did peer at the fine lines feathering out from the corners of her eyes and resolve to invest in a decent eye cream the next time she went shopping.

The one present she had received she left on the coffee table as she went to work. Confirmation of two flights to Rome, a gift from Umpire who'd got up at 5.30 to make her breakfast in bed. She was both thrilled and shocked at his generosity – Rome was a city she'd never visited but had always longed to. The fact that he'd booked the trip for September also gave her reason to smile – they hadn't discussed the future so it was nice to receive confirmation that he saw them still being together months down the line.

Renshaw was in a tetchy mood as the team gathered in the incident room.

'Right, settle down,' she said as DC Burton, the last through the door, slid into a seat at the front of the room between Maggie and Nathan. Byford was seated in the row behind them.

'We've got the go-ahead to bring in the dogs. But something else of significance has happened that I want to discuss first. Last night, one of the outbuildings in the grounds of Rushbrooke was set on fire.' Renshaw slapped a picture of what appeared to be a sports pavilion on the board behind her. 'This was how the building looked before. Someone driving past spotted smoke and called it in before the fire took hold completely, so it's still standing, just about. But it looks like someone set fire to a sofa inside by pouring some kind of fuel on it. The fire service are treating it as suspected arson.'

'Do you think it's related to Benji's death?' asked Nathan.

'I'm not ruling anything out,' said Renshaw. 'Someone took a massive risk breaking into the school grounds last night to set it on fire when we've been crawling all over the site for days.'

'It'll have been kids,' said Byford nonchalantly. 'Daring each other because we've been hanging around the place.'

'Yes, it could've been,' Renshaw admitted, 'but my gut tells me not. The timing is too much of a coincidence.'

'Do we know why there was a sofa in there?' asked Maggie. 'The Pavilion – that's what it's known as – used to

189

be the old changing rooms, but it's been out of bounds to the kids for ages. A sofa seems a bit weird.'

Renshaw frowned. 'How do you know that?'

'A couple of years ago some parents organized a big fundraising drive to pay for a refurb but it ended up being too expensive. So it's been abandoned for ages. Last I heard the school was trying to get a Lottery grant to do it up.'

'That's interesting, because there were actually two sofas inside. We can check with Mrs Pullman exactly what the building was being used for when we head up there,' said Renshaw.

'Why not ask the caretaker?' said Burton, cocking an eyebrow. 'It's his job to keep check on the entire school.'

'He's right,' said Maggie, her mind whirring. 'He'll have unfettered access.'

'I'll be speaking to Donnelly this morning, don't worry . . .' Renshaw caught Maggie's pensive expression. 'What's on your mind?'

Maggie took her time answering, ruminating on her theory as she said it aloud.

'If you knew something bad was going on but you didn't want anyone to know, you'd do anything to stop people finding out. And by people I mean us, the police,' she said. 'Donnelly's changed his story to say Benji's death was an accident, right? What if he did that not because it was true, but because he wanted to wrong-foot us?'

Renshaw's eyes narrowed.

'You mean Donnelly thinks that if we chalk Benji's death up as an accident we'll pack up and go home?'

'Exactly. Only we're not going anywhere, especially now Forensics are saying there's unidentified blood at the scene.'

Burton sat up excitedly. 'So he burns down the building in the middle of the night as another distraction.'

'Yes,' said Maggie. 'Another incident in another part of the school is bound to turn our heads.'

'So you think Donnelly might have something to do with this other blood that's been found?' said Byford sceptically.

'Unfettered access,' Maggie reminded him.

But Renshaw shook her head.

'For everywhere *except* the building site,' she said. 'Mrs Pullman's already confirmed Donnelly was supposed to check the hoardings were locked up at night but he wasn't the key-holder. The project manager is, a bloke called Neil Simpson. If there was any problem relating to the site, the school called Simpson to sort it out.'

'So Neil Simpson is a person of interest?' asked Byford.

'Let's see what the dogs find first,' said Renshaw.

Maggie tried to hide her disappointment as her theory unravelled in front of her. She had been certain she was on to something.

'I agree with you that Donnelly's lying about Benji,' Renshaw acknowledged. 'I just don't see the rest stacking up.'

'Honestly, you should've seen his face when he changed his statement,' Nathan chipped in. 'Smug as anything because he thought he'd convinced us. My cat's a better liar than he is.'

Laughter rippled around the room.

'We do need to find out why he's spinning us a load of crap,' Renshaw added.

Byford lazily raised his hand. Renshaw stared at him. 'Yes?'

'I think you're being too quick to condemn the man,' he

said. 'It's like you're determined to prove he's hiding something because if Benji's death *was* an accident it's not our problem any more and you don't get to be SIO. Sorry, but I think you're putting your personal agenda before the truth.'

Maggie's mouth dropped open. It was an outrageous accusation for Byford to make against Renshaw, especially in front of the rest of the team.

The room stilled as they waited for Renshaw to let rip, as Maggie thought she would, but instead the DS falteringly outlined the team's objectives for the day and called the briefing to a close. As she quickly left the room, Nathan turned on Byford.

'That was fucking out of order,' he snapped.

Byford remained unruffled. 'If you want to sit by and say nothing as she puts Donnelly in the frame for God knows what, be my guest. But I'm not having my career screwed up because of it.'

'We're a team, she's our boss, we do what she says,' said Nathan.

He stalked from the room. Burton, looking equally peeved, followed him.

'What about you, Maggie? Are you going to stand by her to the bitter end? Although, judging by that ridiculous theory you came up with, I'm pretty sure I already know the answer,' said Byford scathingly.

'Thrashing out theories, however crazy they might seem, is part of being a detective, or did you miss that bit in training?' she retaliated. 'As is knowing when to disregard them, which is what I'm doing. I get what you're saying about not rushing to assume the worst of Donnelly, but the way you spoke to DS Renshaw was so disrespectful. She could have you thrown off the case for insubordination.'

'She won't,' said Byford blithely. 'Look, it's really simple to me: Donnelly changed his statement because once the shock had worn off he knew he couldn't be certain Poppy had pushed Benji and he felt he had to say so. But instead of believing him we're searching for angles to punish him for not wanting to convict an eleven-year-old girl for something she didn't do. And that's because Renshaw wants to make a name for herself with this investigation. Don't even try to pretend like you don't know that's true, Maggie.'

She couldn't bring herself to contradict him.

'I won't apologize for trying to inject some rational thinking into this case,' Byford added. 'Because right now it doesn't look like anyone else is going to.'

38

Julia barely slept again and the fitful night left its mark with dark circles under her eyes and a foul mood she couldn't shake off as she made breakfast. Pancakes, Poppy's favourite, meant to be a treat and something to take their minds off what was happening. Instead, the formality of them sitting round the table together on a Friday morning simply reinforced the grim turn their life had taken.

'You'll break the plates if you slam them down any harder,' remarked Ewan as she laid the table.

'You do it then,' she said, dropping the stack in front of him.

Ewan swore, then threw his phone onto the table with a loud clatter, making them all jump. Immediately she apologized.

'I'm sorry, I didn't mean to snap,' she said. 'I didn't get much sleep.'

'Neither did I but you don't see me using you as a verbal punchbag,' said Ewan. 'Nor am I complaining that I've got a ton of work to do and should be seeing a client to sign off the deal I've been working on for six months, but because you can't cope I'm staying at home.'

'I'm really grateful you are,' said Julia, wishing desperately she'd kept her mouth shut.

Ewan shot her a look and returned to checking his emails.

The kitchen door swung open and Julia's father, Malcolm, walked in.

'Surprise!' he shouted.

'Grandpa!' shrieked Poppy, shooting out of her chair and racing across the kitchen with Dylan in hot pursuit. Julia smiled as she watched them fling their arms around him.

'Good morning, Malcolm,' chuckled Ewan. 'Did you sleep well?'

'Like a king,' said his father-in-law, slapping him on the shoulder.

'Tea or coffee?' Julia asked him.

'A decent cuppa would be great. That's the one downside of living in Spain – dismal tea.'

The children retook their seats and resumed their breakfast.

'Everything all right?' said Malcolm, glancing between his daughter and son-in-law.

'We're fine, Dad,' said Julia, worried he'd picked up on the tension between them.

Malcolm didn't look convinced.

'I was thinking, why don't we go down to The Puddle today and hire one of the boats? My treat. Then Ewan can get on with a bit of work while we're out.'

Ewan looked pleased, but Julia shook her head. She didn't think another outing was appropriate. What if the police wanted to talk to Poppy and they weren't at home when they called?

'I think we should stay here today,' she said.

'Well, that's a selfish attitude,' said Ewan. 'I need to work, your dad wants to spend time with you and the children, and they love boating. Blimey, isn't Mummy being a right selfish so-and-so today?'

As the children chimed in to agree with him, Julia could feel her resentment building. Why did she always have to be the bad guy in every scenario?

'Fine, we'll go,' she snapped.

As the children cheered and Dylan began excitedly discussing with Malcolm whether they should hire a boat shaped like a swan or a dragon, Julia glared at her husband, but he was already too absorbed in his phone to notice.

The boats were hired from a cafe next to The Puddle, which, despite its nickname, was in fact a large, man-made lake. As they stepped inside the cafe, Julia was overwhelmed with apprehension that they might run into someone they knew and as they joined the queue at the counter her fears were realized: two mums she recognized from Rushbrooke's PTA were chatting animatedly at one of the tables, two half-drunk lattes in front of them. One made eye contact with Julia and her expression changed from friendly to hostile in a heartbeat as she dug an elbow into her friend's ribs and cocked her head in their group's direction.

Julia smiled feebly but both women shot her a look of disgust. Malcolm must've seen it because he squeezed Julia's arm.

'Don't say anything, love,' he whispered. 'They want you to react and if you do you'll make things worse.'

Her heart swelled with gratitude that he was there to support her. It hadn't been until she was an adult that she'd grasped how similar she and her dad were. Despite how overbearing he could be, he always walked away at the first sign of conflict too. It was probably what infuriated her mum so much about their marriage – Malcolm always got the last word because he walked away before she'd had the chance to say it.

'You know what they say,' said one of the mums in a loud voice to her companion. 'Liars breed liars. Like mother, like daughter.'

'Is she talking about you, Mummy?' Dylan asked, his little face pinched with worry. 'Why is she saying that?'

'Probably because of what Benji's mum's been saying,' said Poppy with a matter-of-factness that left Julia stunned.

'What do you mean?' she croaked.

'Samira told me that Lucie's mum had messaged Benji's mum and she said she never bullied you at school and you're making it up.'

Julia burned with anger. Lucie's mum was Tess, the playground gossip – trust her to wheedle her way in with Imogen.

'When did you speak to Samira?' she asked, trying to keep her temper in check.

'We FaceTimed last night.'

It hadn't occurred to Julia that Poppy might've been in touch with her friends while all this was going on. She was usually strict about how much screen time the children had and monitored their online communication, but amid all the stress and upset she hadn't been as vigilant in the past couple of days.

'It's probably not a good idea to be chatting to your friends about Benji or his mum while the police are still investigating his death,' Malcolm said.

'Did you make it up?' asked Dylan curiously.

Julia stared at her son, flabbergasted.

'No, I did not. It's not often I say this about someone, but she is not a nice person.'

'She's lovely to me. I really like her,' said Poppy nonchalantly.

The statement was so unexpected it punched the breath from Julia's lungs. On seeing her reaction, Malcolm took Dylan by the hand.

'Let's wait outside while these two sort out the boat hire.' When Dylan protested he said, 'Don't worry, you'll get your dragon.'

Julia barely noticed them leaving as she stared at her daughter.

'You think Imogen is lovely?'

Poppy gave a shrug. 'Yes.'

Julia was shocked by how betrayed she felt.

'Nicer than me?'

When Poppy didn't answer, Julia burned with fury. That bitch smarming over her child, pretending to be nice. The thought made her skin crawl.

'Has she said something to you about me?' said Julia, raising her voice.

'No.'

'Go on, what has she said?'

Poppy looked uncomfortable and shuffled awkwardly on the spot. 'Nothing.'

'I don't believe you,' Julia scoffed. 'What the hell has Imogen been saying?'

Poppy threw her mum a look of defiance, then started walking away. Without thinking, Julia grabbed her by the upper arm and pulled her back.

'Ouch!' Poppy yelped.

'Tell me what she said.'

'Let go, you're hurting me!'

But Julia held on, determined to get an answer out of her. Then she heard a voice behind her.

'Madam, I think you should let her go,' said a heavily accented voice.

She turned to be confronted by the white-haired Italian man who'd been serving behind the counter. His face was veiled with disapproval and immediately Julia relaxed her grip.

'I wasn't –' she stuttered, aware of how bad it looked and horrified the owner had come over to stop her.

'You were hurting her,' he said.

Only then did Julia notice the cafe had come to a stand-still and everyone was staring at her. Her gaze immediately fell on the two mums, who were both looking at her as if she'd suddenly grown another head.

One turned to the other.

'See, it's like I said – like mother, like daughter.'

39

Maggie went in search of Renshaw and found her in the ladies' toilet washing her hands.

'Hey, are you okay?'

Renshaw was looking ahead into the mirror so it was her reflection that answered.

'Sure. Why wouldn't I be?'

'Byford should never have spoken to you like that,' said Maggie. 'We all told him so.'

'I don't need you defending me.'

There it was, a flash of the old Renshaw, the one that used to make their working environment so combative and fraught that Maggie couldn't stand her. With a start Maggie knew she would do anything for them not to regress to that.

'I know you don't,' she said. 'But if I think someone's being a prick to the SIO I'm not going to sit back and say nothing.'

Renshaw's reflection grinned.

'Thanks. Where is he now?'

'Downstairs in the car park. I told him to wait there until I was ready.'

'Good.' Renshaw wiped her hands dry with a paper towel.

'Can you do me a favour? I was going to call the mum who sent Imogen that message about the fight between Poppy and Benji, but I've only got half an hour before we go up to Rushbrooke with the dogs and I need to pop to the chemist. I feel like crap; I think it's something I've eaten.'

Renshaw did look a bit peaky now she mentioned it, her pale skin more wan than usual against her auburn hair.

'Do you need to go home?'

'No, it's not that bad, it comes and goes. I just need something to settle my stomach.'

'What's the mum's name?'

'Tess Edwards. Her contact details should've been uploaded to the case file.'

'I'll go and do it now. Good luck with the search.'

'Thanks. We need a breakthrough and I'm hoping this'll be it.'

Tess Edwards answered her phone on the second ring and became animated when Maggie introduced herself.

'I did wonder if Imogen might pass on my message,' she trilled.

'I was hoping you could tell me more about the fight between Benji and Poppy,' said Maggie.

'Well, according to my daughter Lucie the pair of them had to be separated in the cloakroom outside their class. They really went for it: hair pulling, the works.'

'Does your daughter know what the row was about?'

'It sounded quite trivial, to be honest. Poppy accused Dylan of knocking into her, then she accused him of telling lies for attention. She was quite het up, apparently. Lucie didn't know what the supposed lies were and I don't think any of the other kids knew either.'

'You said in your message that it wasn't the first time Poppy had lashed out at school and –' Maggie had a screenshot of the text in front of her – 'she could be a "right madam".'

Tess noisily sucked in a breath.

'Oh, it sounds really spiteful when you say it like that.'

'But that is what you said, isn't it?'

'Well, yes.'

'Why do you think she's a madam?'

'Because of something else that happened at school. But I'm a bit embarrassed to talk about it, because Lucie was involved too.'

'I just need to know what Poppy did.'

'Well, one of the girls in their class had a notebook which she took into the playground and some of them started writing horrible things in it about the other kids – descriptions of how they looked,' said Tess.

'Poppy was writing the comments?'

'No, that was Lucie and her friends. I know, it's awful, but I did tell her off when the school told me. She had no iPad time for a week as a punishment.'

'What was Poppy's involvement then?'

'She heard about the book and confronted the girls. They hadn't even written anything about her and offered to show her, but she didn't believe them. She started yelling at them and then she punched the girl whose notebook it was.'

'She punched her? Was the girl hurt?'

'Yes, she had a black eye. Poppy got away with it though.'

'How do you mean?'

'The teachers came running, obviously, but Poppy said it was an accident and that she'd raised her arm to get the girl's attention and it grazed her eye, so the head let her off with a warning to play nicely. But it was no accident, believe me.'

'You presumably weren't there, so how can you be so sure?'

'Because I believe Lucie and she said Poppy definitely punched the girl.'

'When was this?'

'Just before Christmas.'

Before Benji joined the school, Maggie noted.

'Is there anything else you can tell me that might be useful to our investigation?'

Tess pondered for a moment. 'Not that I can think of right now.'

'Do you know Poppy's parents at all?'

'I know Ewan because he does most of the school runs. But Julia we don't see that often.' Tess paused. 'You know about her, don't you?'

'That depends what you mean,' said Maggie evenly.

'About her not being well.'

'She's ill?'

'Not now. But she was when Poppy was little. Ewan said he had to do everything. She was in bed the whole time.'

'What was wrong with her?'

'Oh, I don't think it's my place to say.'

But that's not going to stop you, thought Maggie shrewdly, and she was right.

'It was depression,' Tess ploughed on. 'Quite severe by

the sounds of it; enough for social services to keep an eye on her, anyway.'

'Ewan told you this?'

'Oh, yes, he's been quite open about it. It was obviously very tough for him, having to carry the can for both of them. He's a great dad, though, terrific with both the kids.'

Maggie's mind flashed back to Tuesday evening and the comment posted on Facebook.

'Someone has indicated to us that Poppy's home life could be volatile. Do you know anything about that?'

Tess sounded shocked. 'No, I don't. I would be amazed, though. Ewan's not the sort.'

'Sort?'

'He doesn't come across like someone who loses his temper or is a bit handy with his fists.'

Maggie winced at the crude description.

'I've never heard him so much as raise his voice to the kids,' Tess added.

'I've heard he's very strict with them,' said Maggie, remembering what Imogen had said.

'He'll tell them off but he's not rough with them. If I had to say either of them was the nasty type, I'd say it was Julia, no question. You can tell by looking at her she's moody.'

Maggie could see they were heading down a conversational cul-de-sac. As much as she wanted the police to think so, Tess didn't know what went on inside the Hepworths' house and her comments were guesswork.

'I think that's all the questions I have for now,' Maggie said. 'You've been really helpful. If anything else occurs to you please give me a call.'

She recited her direct phone line for Tess to take down,

then hung up as Byford appeared in the doorway looking pissed off.

'I've been waiting downstairs for ages.'

'Sorry, I had to make a call, and now I've got to check something else with Burton – can you give me another minute?'

With a sigh, Byford threw himself into the chair at his desk.

'What do you need to check?'

'He was meant to be speaking to social services to see if the Hepworths are known to them.' She quickly told him what Tess had said about Julia being depressed and how she suggested she might be aggressive.

'Why does it matter if she was?' asked Byford.

'It's a known fact that children raised in violent house-holds are more likely to commit acts of violence themselves,' said Maggie. 'If there's a pattern of behaviour that might've influenced Poppy we need to know about it.'

'So you do want her to be guilty,' said Byford.

Maggie bristled. 'I want to be satisfied I've done my job by looking at every possibility. You should try it.' Irritated by what he'd said, she decided to change the subject. 'By the way, Omana dropped a document off for you last night. It's in your in-tray.'

'Thanks.'

Byford leaned over, picked up the envelope and ripped it open. Whatever was detailed on the document triggered him to raise his eyebrows, then he slid the paper back inside.

'Anything important?' asked Maggie.

'Nope.'

Byford unlocked his bottom desk drawer to toss the envelope inside. The drawer was one of those deep ones that could accommodate hanging files but there was nothing in it except two notebooks: one A5 size and patterned with footballs, the other slim and covered in flowers.

'Footballs *and* flowers?' Maggie queried with a smile.

Byford shrugged. 'That's me, a mass of contradictions.'

With a bang he slid the drawer shut, then locked it.

40

Alan was taking a break in his usual spot, at a picnic table adjacent to the playing field. Normally it would be assembly at this time and he'd either be lurking at the back of the hall or using the minutes to complete a repair in one of the classrooms while they were empty. But with the school still closed to pupils there seemed little point sticking to routine. No one was going to berate him today for having an early, unscheduled tea break.

The smell of smoke still permeated the air around him, even though the fire that had turned the Pavilion into a charred wreck had long been extinguished. The warmth of the day – still hot, but a more bearable temperature than previous days – gave it no means of escape, no breeze on which it could be carried away.

He'd been there when the last flame was extinguished; the call summoning him to the school came only minutes after he'd sneaked back into the pub. Being caretaker made him the first point of contact in an emergency, so off he'd dashed – conspicuously, via the pub's front door this time – to offer his assistance to the fire crews putting out the blaze they had no idea he'd started.

He'd made a point of telling anyone who'd listen that he suspected kids were to blame, that there were always gangs of older ones skirting around the school grounds after hours. He'd sounded convincing and even though they were treating it as suspected arson he wasn't worried. His mood today was jubilant, in fact – there was no way Gus's girls could use the Pavilion the state it was in now.

'Excuse me, are you Alan Donnelly?' a voice interrupted him.

He looked round to see a very short woman bearing down on him. Sometimes suppliers requested an appointment to peddle their products but Alan didn't recall any in the diary for today and he was certain he'd have remembered arranging to meet this one. With wild curly hair and a disarming smile, she was exceptionally pretty.

Reaching the table, she stuck out her hand.

'I'm Jennifer Jones, Chief Reporter with the *Mansell Echo*. Have you got a minute to chat?'

Alan stumbled to his feet, jolting the table in his haste and spilling what coffee was left in his mug, which crashed to the floor.

'How did you get in?' he asked tetchily. 'You can't just walk around the school unaccompanied.'

'I couldn't find anywhere to sign in. The reception is shut.'

'That's because the school is shut today,' he shot back. 'If you want to talk to anyone, you need to speak to Mrs Pullman, the head. She's in charge.'

Jennifer ignored him and plonked herself down at the picnic table across from him.

'But it's not her who has the story I want. You were there, you saw the boy die.'

'Oh, come on, if you think I'm giving an interview about that –'

'I'm not going to sensationalize it, if that's what you're worried about. We're a local paper, not a tabloid. I'm only after a few quotes about what the boy was like.'

'I didn't know him,' said Alan shortly.

'So tell me how sad you are about what happened, then. Did you try to save him?'

'I don't mean to be rude, but I really shouldn't be talking to you. It's not my job to give statements to the press. If you want, I can ask Mrs Pullman to call you?' He ducked beneath the table to retrieve his mug.

Jennifer's voice rang over his head.

'You left your last job very abruptly, didn't you, Mr Donnelly?'

Alan froze, his arm still stretching towards the mug. How did she know that?

'You were groundsman at a sports facility in –' he heard the sound of paper being flicked through – 'Newark.'

He was grateful she couldn't see his face below the table.

'It sounds like you've been doing your homework,' he replied with forced joviality as he straightened.

She gazed up at him, a smile playing on her lips.

'It's always good to get some background context,' she said. 'Your ex-wife was very helpful.'

Alan's mouth gaped open. 'You've spoken to Gayle? What the hell for?'

Jennifer stood up. She barely reached his shoulder.

'Look, I think we're getting off on the wrong foot. I want

to write a piece about the hero caretaker who tried to save the boy who fell, but the school turned me down when I requested an interview so I—'

Alan cut her dead. 'Who told you I tried to save him?'

'I have my contacts.'

He didn't like where the conversation was going. He was certainly no hero.

'I don't want you to write about me. I don't want to be in the paper.'

'I understand. You want your privacy. The thing is, Mr Donnelly, your wife said . . .'

They were both suddenly distracted by the sight of two marked police cars and a van turning into the school entrance. Pulling to a halt, all four doors opened on both cars and a number of people got out. Then the back doors of the van opened to reveal two dogs.

'Sniffer dogs? I wonder what that's all about,' mused Jennifer. 'I'd better go and find out.' She gave Alan another teasing smile. 'You're off the hook for now, Mr Donnelly. We'll have to chat another time.'

As she walked away, Alan called after her.

'What did Gayle say to you?'

Jennifer didn't bother to turn round, shouting dismissively over her shoulder.

'Nothing for you to worry about.'

41

Julia didn't even wait to put her bag down before confessing to Ewan what had happened in the cafe.

'I know it must sound awful but I didn't realize I'd grabbed her so hard. She was being rude and walking off and I hadn't finished talking,' she explained.

But Ewan was furious.

'Isn't it enough that we've got the police investigation hanging over us?' His voice was low so it couldn't be heard in the next room where Malcolm and the kids were watch-ing TV, but anger sharpened its tone. 'I can't believe you manhandled Poppy in public.'

'I lost my temper. It won't happen again.'

'That's what you said the last time.'

Julia stood motionless but her heart was racing.

'Why are you bringing that up now?' she said quietly. 'That was years ago. It's not the same.'

'Isn't it?'

'I wasn't well then, you know that.'

'And now?'

'I'm fine.'

He scoffed. 'I think I'll be the judge of that. You're

211

definitely not helping the situation, that's for sure. Getting hysterical doesn't help Poppy – and nor does abusing her in public.'

Julia was horrified. 'It wasn't like that! I only grabbed her arm.'

'It's always "only" something with you, Julia. I'm so tired of you trying to excuse your behaviour.'

The words were out of her mouth before she could stop them.

'What about *your* behaviour? Why is it always me in the wrong?'

Ewan appraised her coolly. 'My behaviour?'

'Sneaking around with Imogen behind my back!'

He threw back his head and laughed.

'Oh my God, is that what this is about? Because I've been talking to some woman you don't like?'

Julia was shaking now. 'You know how awful she was to me, how she made my life hell. I can't believe you've been arranging for Poppy to go to her house behind my back.'

'Oh, but she keeps a very nice house, as my nan used to say.' As Ewan said this, his gaze flitted around the kitchen. 'I wish we could get rid of some of this clutter,' he sighed.

Julia burned with humiliation. There was a pile of clean laundry on the side she hadn't got round to taking upstairs and some empty glasses that needed to go in the dishwasher once the current load had been put away, but apart from that the kitchen was spotless.

'Please don't compare me to her.'

Ewan gave a sigh of exasperation. 'Come on, Julia, it's thirty years since you were at Rushbrooke with Imogen and yet you're behaving like it all happened yesterday. She's a grown woman now, as are you. But frankly she's the only one acting like it.'

'That's a horrible thing to say,' said Julia, close to tears now.

'Well, I don't see her bleating about a girl not liking her at school. It's pathetic.'

His words landed on her like slaps.

'How can you say that? You know how much it affected me.'

'I know how much you've *let* it affect you. There's a difference.' He suddenly changed tack. 'Honey, all I'm saying is that if you got to know Imogen now, as adults, I think you'd probably get on. Do you honestly think I'd have let Poppy go round there if I didn't think Imogen was okay? Besides, I could hardly say no. Poppy thought the world of Benji and she wanted to hang out with him. I didn't really have a choice. Now you're making me feel terrible for being a good dad.'

Julia dropped her head, unwilling to let him see her cry. All this anger and hurt she'd carried around for years – was she being pathetic? She heard footsteps on the tiled floor, then felt her husband's arms curl around her waist. She exhaled with relief as she buried her face in his chest.

'I'm sorry, I didn't mean to be so harsh,' said Ewan, gently kissing the top of her head.

She hesitated before speaking again, unsure how he'd react to what she had to say. But it had been playing on her mind and since he'd raised the subject, she needed to know how much it had crossed his too.

'What happened with me back then, with Poppy . . . Do you think I should tell the police?'

Her voice was muffled where she was pressed against his shirt and she wasn't sure if he'd heard her properly. But after a few seconds he replied.

'I was wondering when you'd ask,' he said, his voice hoarse.

They disentangled themselves in silence, then sat down at the table.

'Should I?' she asked.

'I've been thinking about it a lot and I think you shouldn't, because I'm worried the police might see it as an admission, that we think Poppy did push Benji off that wall.'

'But you said it might be the same –'

He took her hand in his and with his thumb stroked her palm. Unlike the previous evening, this time she found his touch a comfort.

'I'm sorry, darling. I was lashing out because I was angry. I don't think it's the same. But you shouldn't have grabbed Poppy in the cafe,' he admonished.

'I know, and I'm so sorry.'

'The police may find out anyway if they dig hard enough.'

'It happened eight years ago, though,' said Julia worriedly. 'They wouldn't think it was connected, surely?'

'What if they do?'

She could hardly believe what she was hearing. She had expected Ewan to dismiss the thought out of hand and tell her she was being silly. The last thing she anticipated was for him to give weight to it.

'Look, we know our daughter is innocent, but if anyone knew what she'd been exposed to, they might think otherwise. I mean, given the similarities . . .'

Julia let out a sob. The episode was a dark, petrifying moment in her past, her lowest of low points. What she had done would haunt her for the rest of her days and she would never be able to make it up to Poppy or Ewan.

'I don't know how many times I can say it before you'll believe me,' she cried. 'I wouldn't have hurt Poppy . . . I never would've jumped.'

42

Burton had gone up to Rushbrooke with Renshaw so Maggie had to call him to see if he'd heard back from social services yet.

'Not yet, no. I was going to chase them this morning but it looks like we'll be here for a while,' he said.

'Have the dogs found anything yet?'

'The search is about to start. There's been a delay because the head teacher got very upset when we told her why we're back. Between this, Benji's death and last night's fire, she's pretty on edge.'

'I'll bet. Having to keep the school closed indefinitely must be a huge pressure. Text me the number for social services and I'll call them now.'

'Will do. Hang on a sec, Anna wants a word.'

Renshaw came on the line.

'How did you get on with Tess Edwards?'

Maggie relayed the conversation to her. 'That's why I was ringing Burton, to see if social services have anything on the family. He hasn't heard back so I'll chase them myself.'

'Good. After that I want you and Byford to go round to check on the Hepworths. They've got a solicitor acting for them now, but I think if you say you're not there to question Poppy but want to see how they are, they might not call him.'

'Okay, but what's the real point of us going?'

'You spend every case as a FLO in close proximity with relatives and that means you're brilliant at picking up on dynamics. I want you to see what's going on in that house right now between Poppy and her parents and the parents themselves.'

'But why?'

Renshaw lowered her voice. 'Because if this search doesn't amount to anything, I need to make sure we've still got a case to fall back on. Proving Poppy's involvement in Benji's death is still our priority.'

Byford wasn't happy when Maggie revealed they were taking a detour on their way to see Imogen.

'Isn't it a conflict of interest us visiting the suspect when we're the victim's mother's liaison?'

'We're detectives as well as FLOs and when everyone else is busy we have to muck in. Besides, it's just a house call, nothing formal. Can you call Imogen and let her know we'll be round a bit later? I've got to call social services first.'

'Sure. I'll do it now while I grab a water. Want one?'

Maggie said no. Byford got up and left the incident room.

The number Burton had texted her was for a social worker called Esther Wicklow.

'I'm chasing up a subject access request on behalf of my colleague, DC Karl Burton,' said Maggie, after giving her own credentials.

'Oh, yes. I have the information he requested. It's not a

big file so I can email you the information if you give me your details.'

Social services weren't obliged to give the police any information unless served by a court order. But a subsection of the Data Protection Act allowed them to circumvent it as long as the information was necessary to prevent or detect a crime, or facilitate an arrest or prosecution. The police could also argue that social services not sharing the information would hamper their investigation.

Maggie duly recited her email address and thanked the woman for her help. She debated whether to hang around at the station until the information came through, but decided she could look at it on her phone. Byford was back and she could tell he was getting restless from the way he was hovering around her desk.

'Was Imogen okay about us coming later?' she asked him.

He stared at her coldly. 'We didn't exactly give her a choice, did we?'

43

Julia was hanging washing out in the back garden in an attempt to regain a semblance of normality when Ewan dashed outside holding his phone aloft.

'The police are on their way,' he panted. 'I've just had a message.'

Julia stopped. 'What do they want now?'

'I don't know. I'm going to call Darren. He did say they shouldn't question Poppy again without him present.'

As Ewan rushed back inside to call their solicitor, Julia was overcome with rage. Desperate to vent, she began ripping down the clothes she'd pegged to the line and stamped them into the grass. The angrier she got, the harder her foot landed.

'Julia! What on earth are you doing?'

Malcolm had appeared at the back door and he looked horrified.

'Why won't they leave us alone?' she screamed at him. 'Poppy told them it was an accident, why can't they accept that?'

Malcolm didn't come any closer, knowing better than to try to comfort her when she was so angry.

'What's happened, darling?'

Julia came to a standstill, feet planted on one of Ewan's work shirts.

'The police want to interview Poppy again. Ewan's calling our solicitor.'

'I imagine they're simply being thorough in checking her statement,' said Malcolm.

'For God's sake, Dad, don't be so bloody reasonable.'

Malcolm shrank back from the heat of her temper. 'There's no need to be rude.'

She stormed past him into the house. Ewan was nowhere to be seen.

'You need to calm down before they get here,' said Malcolm, following her into the lounge. Dylan looked up from the Lego he was assembling in the middle of the carpet.

'I'm too bloody angry to be calm! Christ, Dad, you're not helping.'

Still needing an outlet for her anger, she started picking up cushions from the sofa and throwing them back down.

'Mummy, what are you doing?' asked Dylan, clearly alarmed.

'Dylan, go upstairs and see what Daddy and Poppy are up to. Mummy's a bit upset right now.'

Malcolm's pious tone was the last straw.

'I can't stand another minute in this house. I'm going out.'

'Where are you going?' Malcolm called after her. 'What about Poppy?'

'Let Ewan sort it out,' she yelled back as she yanked open the front door and shot up the path into the street. Her feet were bare and she had no money or phone with her but she didn't care. She didn't think about where she was going, only that she needed to get as quickly away as she could.

44

The elderly man who opened the door looked disappointed to see Maggie and Byford standing there.

'I thought you might be someone else,' he said forlornly.

Maggie gave him their names and apologized for not calling ahead.

'It's only a quick visit while we were passing,' she said.

'Oh, it's not that, we knew you were coming. I thought you might be my daughter, Julia. She's gone out without her keys.'

Maggie was puzzled. 'How did you know we were coming?'

'Does it matter?' said Byford in an aside. He smiled kindly at the man. 'Is everything okay, Mr . . . um?'

'Cox. Malcolm Cox. No, it's not. My daughter is under tremendous stress and I'm worried about her. When are you going to put an end to this nonsense with Poppy?' he asked them angrily.

'We're doing everything we can to make sure the investigation progresses as quickly as possible,' said Maggie. 'We do understand how difficult this is for everyone involved. Can we come in for a quick chat?'

'I think I should check with my son-in-law first. Wait here.'

He shut the door on them. Maggie turned to Byford.

'How could they have known we were on our way?'

'The DS must've let them know.'

'No, the whole point was she didn't want them fore-warned.'

'She probably changed her mind. She does tend to flip-flop on decisions.'

Maggie was about to deliver another rebuke when the door opened again and Ewan Hepworth stood before them. His face pinched with anger as his gaze settled first on Maggie, then on Byford.

'What is it?'

'Our SIO asked us to pop round to see if Poppy has any new information for us,' said Byford, eyeing him squarely back.

Maggie was annoyed. That wasn't the script they'd agreed. Byford was making it sound as though they were there to interview Poppy again, which was bound to inflame her father.

It did.

'I've told you, if you want to question my daughter again you'll have to do it in the presence of our solicitor. You can't just turn up here demanding answers,' Ewan hissed.

Maggie went to placate him but her phone rang. It was Renshaw.

'I'd better get this. Excuse me for a moment.'

She walked down the path until she was back on the street and out of earshot. Byford and Ewan continued to have words.

'Maggie, are you at the Hepworths'?'

'Yep, here now. The welcoming committee isn't exactly rolling the bunting out, if you catch my drift.'

'Don't worry about that now. I need you to bring Poppy up to the school instead.'

'Why?'

'The dogs have found some items of clothing and I need Poppy to tell us whether she recognizes them.'

'What kind of clothes?'

'A fuchsia dress that looks like it was made for Funtime Barbie and a G-string that's about as substantial as a piece of tissue paper. I don't think we're looking for another kid, let's put it that way. They were buried beneath some rubble close to the spot where Benji died and I want to know if they were visible when he and Poppy were on that wall.'

'Can't I just ask her?'

'No, I want her to see the items in situ, before Forensics take them. I want to gauge her reaction, to see if she tells us the truth. Maggie, they're covered in blood.'

'Shit.'

'Yes, shit. We're going to start excavating the building site. The way the dogs have reacted it's very likely there's another body here.'

45

When the door opened Julia reacted with surprise, as though she hadn't thought it would be a consequence of her ringing the doorbell.

'Oh, you're in,' she said.

'I'm working from home again,' said Siobhan.

'Can I come in?'

Her friend looked awkward. 'Now's really not a good time.'

'Please, I need to talk to someone before I go mad,' Julia implored.

Looking far from happy about it, Siobhan moved aside to let Julia across the threshold.

'Where are your shoes?' she asked.

Julia looked down at her bare feet, smudged with dirt. Only then did she notice her soles were hurting from walking along warm pavements.

'I left them at home,' she said.

'Let's go in here,' said Siobhan, opening the door to the lounge. 'Callum and Evie are playing out the back.'

Unlike Julia and Ewan, Siobhan and her husband had invested in their home and aluminium trifold doors now separated the newly landscaped garden from the newly refitted kitchen. If they went in there to talk and the doors were open, the children might overhear them.

Once inside the front room – all stark white walls, immaculately ordered alcove shelving and a feature fireplace – Julia was at a loss for what to say. She hadn't planned on coming to Siobhan's and now she was there she felt a bit silly. Fortunately Siobhan broke the silence herself.

'How are you?'

'I've had better weeks.'

Siobhan pulled a face. 'I imagine Imogen's saying the same thing.'

'I didn't mean it like it's a competition,' said Julia wearily.

'How did you mean it, then?'

Julia fished for the right words, unnerved by the animosity that was coming off Siobhan in waves. They'd always got on well because their sons were best friends and this was a side of her Julia hadn't experienced before.

'It's been very hard, that's all. The police are coming round again.'

'They can't be satisfied with what Poppy's told them so far.'

Julia sank down onto the sofa, exhausted. She had no fight left in her.

'She didn't hurt him,' she said quietly.

Siobhan sat down opposite, on a leather upholstered armchair.

'Are you certain of that?' she asked in a tone that matched Julia's in volume.

Julia stared at her through a glaze of tears.

'How can you ask me that? You know Poppy. You know she isn't capable of hurting anyone.'

'She is known for picking on other kids though.'

'Once, that's all. The teacher spoke to us about it and we told her off.'

'That was the one time she got caught.'

'I doubt she's any worse than the rest of the class,' Julia said weakly.

'You would say that because you're her mum. But ask any of the other parents and they'll tell you it's always Poppy who's the ringleader. The school does nothing to stop it because she always blames it on someone else and the teachers believe her. You know Archie in their class? He was put into alternate lunch for a week because of something Poppy did.'

'If she's such a nightmare, why haven't any of you ever said anything to me or Ewan?'

Siobhan looked apprehensive for a moment.

'You're not the most approachable of people.'

'Us? That's ridiculous.'

'I actually didn't mean you, I meant Ewan. He's – how can I put this – unbending, yes, that's the right word, he's unbending when it comes to listening to anyone else. It's like he can't be challenged and that you guys have this perfect life where your kids are perfect and well behaved and the rest of us can't compete.' Siobhan was warming to her part now, her tone resolute. 'It gets on people's nerves.'

Julia was floored. She couldn't believe what she was hearing.

'The thing is,' Siobhan went on, 'Poppy's the same as him. She swans around the school like she owns it.'

Julia clasped her hands over her mouth as tears spilled down her cheeks.

'I didn't mean to upset you, I just think you should know what people say about her.' Siobhan cocked her head to one side as though a thought had suddenly occurred to her. 'I hear you've told the police Imogen bullied you years ago.'

Julia prised her hands from her mouth.

'She did. She was awful to me.'

Siobhan sat back, arms crossed, clearly unconvinced.

'It didn't sound like that the way she described it.'

Julia was appalled. 'You've talked to her about it?'

'We've messaged a couple of times on WhatsApp, after I texted my condolences. She has no idea what you're talking about and she doesn't even remember you from school. Spinning stuff to take the attention away from Poppy isn't very nice, Julia.'

'You believe her? I'm the one telling the truth, not her. She was horrendous to me, a complete bitch.'

Siobhan was unimpressed.

'Will you listen to yourself? You sound worse than the kids. This isn't about what did or didn't happen to you at school, Julia – this is about Benji dying and the police finding out who is responsible.'

Julia had heard enough. She stood up.

'You and everyone else can believe whatever you want, but my daughter did not cause that boy's death. She didn't do anything wrong and I'll expect a grovelling apology from you and everyone else when it's proved.'

46

Mrs Pullman didn't bother to hide the fact that she'd been crying when Alan entered her office after knocking.

'It's all too much,' she said, reaching across her desk to pluck a tissue from the box sitting on it. 'It's devastating enough that we've lost one of our pupils without the stress of the police being here again.'

'That's why I've come to see you. I wondered if there's anything I could be doing to help them?' Alan hoped that by offering his assistance he might find out why they'd returned. 'What's brought them back? Is it to do with the fire last night?'

'I thought that too, but no, it's something to do with some evidence they found when they examined the place where Benji fell,' she said, sighing heavily. 'They won't tell me what it is.'

'Do the governors know they're here again?' asked Alan, fearing what Gus would make of this latest development.

'I've just got off the phone with the chairman. He's coming in.' Mrs Pullman welled up again. 'I was already deeply concerned about how Benji's death might affect Rushbrooke going forward and now I'm even more fearful.'

'I'm sure it will be nothing,' said Alan. 'I was there as well, don't forget, and there was nothing where he landed except a pile of rubble. I wouldn't be surprised if the girl's behind it, that she's made up some story about there being something there to get herself out of trouble.'

Mrs Pullman stared at him. 'Why would she need to do that if it was an accident?'

'It was,' said Alan quickly, kicking himself for not catching the mistake before he said it.

'I do hope you're being truthful with the police, Alan,' she said.

Her cool tone shook him.

'I am, I swear.'

'An official from the fire service came to speak to me this morning about the Pavilion.'

Alan's next breath caught in his throat.

'I was very surprised by what they said.'

He could barely look at her, but knew that to avert his gaze now would be tantamount to confessing.

'Where has all the old sports equipment gone, Alan? Because the fire official said the only things destroyed in the blaze were two old sofas.'

This he could answer.

'It's all in the other shed,' he responded swiftly. 'I decided to have a clear-out, see if I couldn't fix up the Pavilion so the kiddies could use it again. I know the school can't afford a major repair, so I've been doing bits and bobs in my spare time. It was going to be a surprise.'

She looked as though she was weighing up whether to believe him.

'If I looked in the shed I'd find every last bit of the missing equipment, is that what you're saying?'

Alan was baffled, then appalled when he realized what Mrs Pullman meant.

'I haven't nicked anything, or sold it, if that's what you're getting at? Are you calling me a thief?'

Mrs Pullman's face fell. 'I'm sorry, Alan, but I had to ask. I was very shocked to hear the Pavilion was virtually empty. I shouldn't have been so quick to judge.'

'I should've said something before now. I'm sorry.'

'Did you organize the sofas?'

'I did. I got them from a mate who does bulk collections for the council. You'd be amazed at the perfectly good furniture people throw away.'

In reality they were two hundred quid each off Gumtree. Both pulled out into beds. The thought of what they were used for made Alan feel sick and he was glad they had been destroyed.

'I wanted to see whether it could be used like a common room or something,' he said feebly. He wasn't sure she was buying any of it.

'If the Pavilion was to be used for anything it should have been sports related. But I do appreciate you taking the initiative,' she said, finally smiling.

'Did the bloke from the fire service say who they thought set it alight?'

'They believe it was opportunist vandals.' Mrs Pullman raised her hands in a gesture of surrender. 'As if we didn't already have enough on our plate that someone thought we deserved a fire on top of everything else. I desperately want to reopen the school but heaven knows how long it will be before Rushbrooke is back to normal.'

Alan was filled with dread. If the Pavilion's secret was ever discovered, it never would be.

47

'I can't believe you got me drunk. You are such a bad influence.'

The sun lounger creaked ominously as Julia rolled off it and planted her feet unsteadily on the decking.

'You can't blame me if you didn't eat any breakfast,' said Cath, grin rendered sloppy by smeared lipstick. 'Besides, you looked like you could do with a drink.'

Julia was still so angry when she arrived home from Siobhan's that she couldn't bring herself to go inside and had continued down the road until she reached Cath's house.

It had been a relief to see a friendly face. Cath had taken one look at her, ushered her into the kitchen and thrust a glass of neat vodka into her hand. Without any breakfast to buffer its effects, the alcohol had gone straight to Julia's head and then she hadn't the willpower to turn down the Cava-filled Bucks Fizz her friend had offered as a follow-up.

'Christ, look at the state of you,' said Cath with a honk of laughter. 'Anyone would think you'd never had booze before.'

'I'm not used to daytime drinking,' Julia groaned. The

garden was spinning now. Even when she stood stock-still it spun.

'That's the joy of retirement,' said Cath, tilting her glass. 'Besides, I think a drink is allowed under the circumstances.'

'What's the time now?'

'Ten past one. Time for another.'

Julia shook her head vigorously, then immediately regretted it as a fresh wave of nausea hit.

'No, I need water. Oh God. Ewan's going to be wondering where I am.'

'No, he's not. I sent him a text to say you're with me.'

'Did he reply?'

'Well, no.'

'See, he's going to be mad.'

'Nothing unusual there, then.'

Julia stared down at her, trying to focus. 'What's that supposed to mean?'

'Nothing.'

'Come on, spit it out.'

Cath took another swig of drink. 'Don't get me wrong, I like Ewan. But I think he's very hard on you. He treats you like a third child.'

'Don't be like that. He's put up with a lot from me.'

'For Chrissakes, Julia, you had post-natal depression. You were ill. Ewan shouldn't use it as a stick to beat you with.'

'He doesn't,' said Julia, enraged. 'He's a good man. Look how he's been with Poppy this past week. He's been there for her, while I'm here getting pissed with you. Who's the worst parent really?'

'You need a break, there's nothing wrong with that.'

'She didn't do it,' Julia slurred, swaying perilously.

'I know, I believe you.'

'And you believe me about Imogen, don't you?'

When Julia arrived at her door Cath had listened intently and without interruption as she vented her frustration that Siobhan seemed more inclined to believe Imogen over her, and that she was going to prove her child was no monster. It was only when she'd finished that Cath finally spoke – and in a few sentences she'd made more sense to Julia than anyone else had in the past few days.

'Of course people will view the other mum more sympathetically,' Cath had said. 'She's grieving the death of her only child. However you feel about her, you need to respect the fact that she's lost her son – going on about the way she treated you at school right now makes you seem irrational and unfeeling, and I know you're neither of those things.'

'I can't help it,' Julia had protested. 'When I think about how she treated me I hate her so much I can barely breathe. Her bullying really screwed me up – I didn't appreciate how badly until I've had to face up to it.'

'I understand that,' Cath had remarked, 'but the more you go on about it while this police investigation is under way, the more negatively people are likely to react to you. For Poppy's sake, you need to put a lid on your anger.'

Julia wasn't certain she could, but knew Cath was right and that she at least had to try. Then they'd gone outside to sit on the sun loungers on Cath's decking as they drank.

Still standing, Julia shoved the borrowed pair of Cath's sunglasses she'd been wearing onto the top of her head.

'I think I'm going to be sick,' she said, clamping a hand over her mouth.

'Quick, inside,' Cath yelped.

Julia staggered across the decking but didn't make it to the house and threw up in a terracotta tub. Specks of vomit pebbledashed her dress.

'I'm so sorry,' she said, appalled.

'You really are in a state,' said Cath, more amused than cross. 'I'll put some coffee on.' As she reached the back door a phone inside began to ring. 'I'll be back in a sec once I've got this.'

Cath went inside and Julia marvelled at how sober she seemed. The woman had the constitution of an ox.

A second later she reappeared at the back door.

'It's Ewan wanting to talk to you.'

Julia groaned again. 'Tell him I'm on the loo or something.'

Cath stood in the open doorway, shoulder and hip resting against the frame.

'Sorry, Ewan, she's popped to the toilet. Can I pass a message on?'

The colour drained from her face as she listened to Ewan's reply. Julia dragged the back of her hand across her mouth to wipe it clean and tried to stand upright.

'What is it?' she hissed.

Cath held a hand up to quiet her.

'Really? But why do they need Poppy to see it?'

Julia's brain swam with confusion. See what?

'Yes, I'll get Julia to meet you there. The thing is, we've both had a drink so we'll have to get a cab . . . No, really, I can't risk it . . . Well, just a couple . . . Look, do you want to speak to her?' Julia went to take the phone, but Cath shifted awkwardly so it remained out of reach. 'Fine, I'll tell her.' She hung up.

236

'You're never going to believe this, but the police have found some clothing covered in blood near to where Benji fell and now they think there's another body buried on the building site. The police have taken Poppy up to the school so she can tell them if she remembers seeing the clothes when she and Benji were on the wall. Ewan wants you to meet them there.'

Julia snapped out of her post-sick slouch.

'I'll walk. I need to sober up.'

'A cab will be quicker. I'll come with you.'

'I'll be fine walking.' Julia made a move towards the back door but stumbled.

'You can't go on your own. Come on.'

Julia went to take Cath's outstretched hand but stopped.

'Sorry, was I hearing you right? Did you really say a dead body?'

'I did. The police think there might be one buried where the classrooms are being built.'

This time Julia didn't even make the tub.

48

It was a phrase he'd heard before, might've even used himself once or twice, but it was only now that Alan understood what 'shocked to the core' really meant. It was as though his insides were paralysed. He couldn't swallow; there was no movement in his throat to enable the action, nothing he could do to trigger it.

He'd been sitting in the same position for half an hour, on one of the low benches in the playground. In front of him a few of the teachers were milling around, Mr Lincoln among them. The deputy head was going through the motions of trying to appear in charge but his expression suggested he was incapable of stringing a sentence together. None of them could; they were in shock. Meanwhile Mrs Pullman was in her office being checked over by a first aider: when she'd heard what the police dogs had found, the head teacher collapsed and had to be helped inside.

The bloodstained clothes had been bundled in a carrier bag and jammed into the foundations. From what Alan had gleaned by eavesdropping, the garments definitely belonged to a woman and now the police were going to excavate the site because the way the dogs had reacted suggested there might be a body nearby. The dogs had only been able to recover the bag because the foundations were partly accessible – the concrete floor that would seal them beneath the classrooms had yet to be poured in and set. There was talk of them ripping the wall down as well.

Someone sat down next to him and with a jolt he saw it was Gus.

'What the fuck is going on?' he asked Alan in an undertone.

'They found some bloodstained clothes. They think there's a body buried,' said Alan, keeping his voice to a whisper as well.

'How did they know the stuff was there?'

'I don't know.'

'They probably think it's something to do with you.'

Alan glared at him. 'You what?'

'A kid falls off a wall and dies. Three days later, bloodied clothes are found in the same place. Who has the most after-hours access? The school's site manager. *You.*'

'I don't know anything about the clothes.'

'But you know about the fire, don't you, Alan? I know it was you and I am very, very upset,' said Gus in a voice that was chillingly calm.

It was as though someone had flicked a switch: the air evaporated from Alan's lungs and he couldn't breathe.

'My inhaler. Pocket,' he gasped, unable to move to get it.

Gus retrieved it for him, then glanced round to see if anyone was watching. Satisfied nobody was, he pressed his thumb down once on the metal canister, and there was a long hiss as the vapour disappeared into thin air. Alan's eyes bulged in horror as he desperately tried to catch his breath.

'No, don't,' he wheezed.

'I'm just making certain you understand what's at stake here, Alan,' said Gus, giving the canister another burst. 'If you mention my name to the police in any way, a bit of breathlessness will be the least of your worries.'

Gus got to his feet and tossed the inhaler onto the ground as he walked away, leaving Alan scrabbling to reach it.

49

Poppy Hepworth's composure was remarkable for a girl her age. She hadn't been at all flustered when her dad informed her she had to accompany Maggie and Byford up to Rushbrooke, nor had she reacted when, on arriving at the school, Renshaw explained what it was they needed her to do. She'd compliantly followed Renshaw through the gap in the hoardings without so much as a backwards glance.

Ewan Hepworth was a different matter. Clearly agitated he wasn't allowed to chaperone his daughter on the other side of the hoardings – he was made to stay put to avoid scene contamination – he paced the playground while whispering furiously into his phone. Maggie suspected he was talking to his solicitor, who, if he was worth his fee, was presumably telling Ewan to cooperate for Poppy's sake.

A few metres away Byford was also on his phone. Maggie wondered who he was talking to – it can't have been Imogen because she'd called herself to let her know they were still delayed. Except it hadn't been Imogen who answered but Grace, keen to express her annoyance they were being made to wait around when they were desperate for an update.

Maggie had apologized profusely and said they'd get there as soon as they could.

As she watched Byford, her phone pinged to signal a received text. She opened the message without a thought, then gasped when she read it.

Happy birthday, Auntie Maggie. We really miss u. I wish u and Mum wud make up. xoxo Jude

Maggie was overwhelmed with delight. The message was the most unexpected birthday present she could've hoped for. Immediately she texted her nephew back.

It's SO lovely to hear from you. How are you? How are Scotty and Mae? Send them my love. I miss you all so much. I wish I could see you. Let me know how you're doing. xxx

Minutes ticked by but no more texts arrived. She was toying with ringing Jude when Byford appeared at her side.

'I've got to go.'

'What do you mean?'

'I'm needed in Trenton. That case I had to go back for is about to collapse and I've been told to be there this afternoon to review my notes again.'

For someone facing a work crisis Byford didn't seem unduly troubled. Maggie wished she could be as laid-back about things.

'You'll need to let DS Renshaw know,' she said.

'She already does. ACC Bailey's called her.'

It must be serious if the Assistant Chief Constable was

involved. Byford made no acknowledgement of the fact that Bailey was Renshaw's boyfriend and Maggie wondered if he even knew.

'Fine. I'll call you later and let you know the latest here. Good luck. I hope you can sort it out,' said Maggie.

Her comment seemed to startle him.

'Right . . . thanks, appreciate it.'

A thought occurred to her. 'How will you get back to the station to pick up your car? We came in mine.'

'I'll walk.'

'Don't be daft, I'll drop you off, then I'll go round to see Imogen.' She glanced over at Ewan. 'I don't think there's anything for me to do here. Someone else can chauffeur the Hepworths home.'

As they neared her car, Maggie remembered the file that was being sent to her by social services.

'You get in,' she said, unlocking the vehicle. 'I need to check an email first.'

But Byford waited, watching her intently as she opened the message and scrolled down, her eyes widening as she did.

'Wow, this is a turn-up,' she said, explaining who the email was from and why they'd asked for it. 'The Hepworths came under the social services' radar in 2009 after Julia had a breakdown triggered by post-natal depression and Poppy was considered at risk. There's one specific incident that's mentioned, which you are not going to believe,' Maggie breathed. 'Julia disappeared with Poppy one afternoon when the kid was about two and Ewan found them on top of the disused viaduct at Hawley Ridge, the one where they do abseiling now.'

'I know it,' said Byford, nodding.

'According to this, Julia was threatening to jump off it – and she was going to take Poppy with her.'

50

The taxi driver stopped twice on the way to Rushbrooke so Julia could be sick. By the time they arrived at the school she had nothing left in her stomach to expel and felt marginally better for it, but her coordination was still impeded by the alcohol and when she tried to get out of the car she lost her footing and sprawled to the ground.

Cath, no longer finding the state of her amusing, hauled her to her feet.

'You've got to hold it together,' she said desperately. 'For Poppy's sake.'

Julia nodded and together they walked across the playground. Julia was wearing a pair of Cath's flat-soled sandals that were two sizes too small for her feet and her heels scraped painfully against the tarmac as she walked.

She spotted Ewan first. He was standing with a uniformed officer on the playground side of the police cordon, pensively watching the entrance to the building site. The nearer they got, Julia could see flashes of people walking past the doorway on the other side.

'Where's Poppy?' she asked on reaching him. She had

hoped she sounded more sober than she felt but Ewan's reaction told her she'd failed.

'Look at the state of you,' he said through clenched teeth. 'What the hell are you thinking turning up here drunk?' He swung round to vent his wrath at Cath. 'You said it was just a couple. My wife is fucking hammered while my daughter is through there having to walk around the place where she watched another child die.'

Cath was remarkably calm in replying. Julia, meanwhile, was fighting the feeling that the playground was tilting and was trying not to be sick again.

'I'm sorry you're upset but this is not the time to have a pop at Julia or me. We're here now, that's what matters.'

'But it's not even the afternoon and she's drunk,' said Ewan. 'What message does that send to the police?'

The officer near the cordon was trying and failing to pretend he wasn't listening.

'It tells them your poor wife is under a huge amount of strain at the moment. Why aren't you with Poppy anyway?'

'They wouldn't let me be. Something about avoiding contamination of the scene.'

Julia burst into noisy tears.

'I'm sorry. I didn't mean to make things worse.'

'Take her home,' Ewan snapped at Cath. 'I don't want Poppy to see her like this.'

'I want to see my daughter!' wailed Julia. 'Where's my baby?'

She lurched forward to duck under the police tape but the combination of poorly fitting shoes and drunken incapacity proved too much and she went flying, knees and palms bearing the brunt of the heavy landing. As she yelped in pain DS Renshaw chose that moment to come back through the doorway with Poppy in tow.

'Mum, what are you doing?'

Julia was relieved to see Poppy hadn't been crying. She struggled to her feet.

'I can't believe you made her go in there without one of us,' she bawled at DS Renshaw. 'She's just a kid.'

'I'm very well aware of Poppy's age,' said the officer, unmoved. 'You can take her home now.'

'Oh, we can, can we?' Julia responded tartly. 'That's big of you.'

Ewan intervened, taking Julia's hand.

'Let's get Poppy home,' he said. It was an order rather than a request.

'Hang on,' said Julia, shrugging her hand out of his. 'I want to know what happens next. How long are you going to keep us in limbo?'

'We're still making inquiries,' said Renshaw.

Julia flung her hands skywards. 'If I hear that one more time I'll scream. What you're doing is barbaric. She's a kid and you're letting everyone think she's guilty.'

'What would you rather us do, Mrs Hepworth? Arrest her right now? Charge her with a crime? I could do either of those things but I'm not going to because I have to be certain it's in your daughter's best interests.' She stepped forward so she and Julia were practically bumping noses. 'Let me give you some advice, Mrs Hepworth. Losing your temper like this isn't helping your daughter one little bit. In fact, it's making me seriously wonder how bad her home life must be when her mum's losing her shit all the time. Like, what kind of behaviour she might be picking up. Do you see what I'm getting at?'

Julia was stunned.

'Now, if you don't want to be arrested yourself for being drunken and disorderly, I suggest you do what your husband says and take Poppy home,' said Renshaw. 'I won't warn you again.'

51

'I thought we were supposed to be your priority,' was Grace's opening barb, delivered before Maggie had even crossed the threshold into the house.

'You are, but sometimes I have to do other tasks relating to the investigation. We don't have finite resources, I'm afraid.'

Imogen appeared at Grace's shoulder.

'Mum, let the poor woman come in.'

Maggie followed them into the lounge. Imogen was wearing the orange sundress again but it no longer hugged her figure; it hung from it. The deterioration in her appearance was worrying.

'I'm sorry I couldn't get here earlier,' she said.

'Was it because of what you've found at the school?' asked Imogen.

Maggie's brow furrowed. 'How do you know about that?'

'All the mums are texting about it. One of them said you've found a body,' said Imogen anxiously. 'It's not another child, is it?'

'So far we've only found items of clothing and we're certain they don't belong to a child.'

Imogen sagged with relief.

'We don't need to get involved in any more nonsense,' Grace butted in. 'You –' she stabbed a finger at Maggie – 'should be concentrating on my grandson's death. That's what your job is, isn't it? Being our liaison?'

Maggie considered herself pretty robust when it came to standing up to overbearing people, having had plenty of practice with her sister among others, but there was something about Grace's disapproval that made her less sure of her responses.

'Yes, that is my job,' she began warily, 'and I can assure you mine and the rest of the team's commitment to the investigation into Benji's death hasn't lessened in any way.'

God, she sounded like a poorly written police manual. She could only imagine how intimidating it must've been growing up in Grace's household and felt a surge of pity for Imogen.

'Make sure you keep it that way,' Grace ordered. 'If I think that you're not fully committed to solving my grandson's case there will be severe consequences. It will not end well for you, DC Neville.'

Grace stalked from the room and went upstairs. Maggie did her best to reassure Imogen.

'Our focus is still on finding out what caused Benji to fall.'

'Mum's upset because we thought there would be more progress by now. Are you going to arrest Poppy?'

Maggie sat down beside her.

'It's not that simple. We have an eyewitness who is corroborating her story that it was an accident.'

Imogen went pale. 'You mean he might've fallen by

himself? No, I don't believe it. I won't accept that. The witness is lying too.'

'That's what we're trying to establish. The results of the digital autopsy might give us a clearer idea of whether Benji was pushed or not, but at the moment we don't know when we'll be getting those.'

'What about the notebooks Jamie took? Did they help?'

Maggie's insides fluttered with consternation as she tried to think on her feet.

'I'm not sure where we're at with them. These were the ones he found in Benji's room the other day?'

'Yes, in his treasure box. One was his, the other I hadn't seen before.'

A flashback to the office, to Byford's bottom drawer: one notebook patterned with footballs, the other with flowers.

Maggie took a punt. 'The football one was a diary, wasn't it?'

'No, Benji used it for writing short stories. Jamie seemed to think there was something in it that might be useful.'

'I think he's still checking through it,' said Maggie, angry at being forced to cover for him. What the hell was Byford playing at? Why hadn't he submitted the notebooks for evidence and told the rest of the team about them?

'Have you seen the other one? I told Jamie it was going to take him ages to ring all those phone numbers. Pages and pages of them.'

'You still haven't remembered where Benji got it from?' Again, another punt.

Imogen shrugged. 'I thought at first it might be his because of all the code alongside the numbers, but it wasn't his handwriting. He must've found it somewhere and decided to keep it to see if he could crack the code. Pretending to be a spy was a favourite game of his.'

It was another hour before Maggie was able to excuse herself to make a phone call. Grace had come back downstairs and wanted her to tell them what happened when an inquest was opened, as Benji's was due to be on Monday morning. So she'd explained the process, making both women aware it would be a brief hearing that would end in an adjournment so the police investigation could continue. They could attend if they wished and she would be more than happy to accompany them. Imogen wanted to know whether any photographs of Benji after he'd died would be shown during the hearing and Maggie was pleased she could reassure her they wouldn't be, not at this stage.

She went outside to her car to make the phone call, on the pretext of fetching something from it.

Byford didn't pick up. She left a message saying she needed to speak to him urgently, but didn't mention the notebooks so he couldn't use the time before calling her back to invent an excuse as to why he hadn't handed them in.

She toyed with ringing Umpire to see what he thought, but decided against it, knowing Renshaw wouldn't thank her for soliciting his advice. So she dialled another familiar number instead.

'Maggie, how's it going?'

DI Tony Gant was markedly ebullient for someone so famously grumpy and Maggie felt a pang that she was about to ruin the FLO coordinator's good mood.

'I'm fine, but I'm not ringing about me, though. I wanted to talk to you about Jamie Byford.'

'Is this because he keeps being yanked back to HQ to deal with that case? Sorry, Maggie, there's nothing I can do about that.'

'It's not that. I don't think he's cut out for family liaison.'

She didn't want to wade straight in with her concern about him withholding evidence, knowing the shit storm it would unleash.

To her utter shock, Gant agreed with her.

'He's not the most obvious candidate, no. If I had my way this wouldn't be his first case.'

'But you're the coordinator, you must've put him forward.'

'Well, not exactly.'

'You were *told* to?'

'He was suggested to me, yes.'

Maggie's mind whirled. Gant was scrupulous about making sure he assigned FLOs with the right qualities to each case – why would he let someone else call the shots on an investigation as sensitive as Benji's?

'Has Byford even completed the training?'

The pause was all the answer she needed.

'Look, Maggie, I can't get into this. Just do your job and don't worry about Byford. He *is* a great detective, that's not up for dispute.'

'But if he's not a trained FLO—'

'Drop it, Maggie, please. This goes way above my head and yours.'

She fell silent, frustration leeching through her every pore.

'Now we've sorted that, I can tell you my news. It's being announced first thing on Monday, so consider it a heads-up. I'm moving on.'

'What?' Maggie was stunned. 'Moving on to where?'

'I'm transferring down to Cornwall. My wife wants to live somewhere more rural and I'm ready for a job change. You know, it's a shame you're not a higher rank, Maggie, because you'd be great to take over this job.'

'You think I could be the Liaison Coordinator for the entire force?'

'Absolutely. The job requires someone who is considered and organized and above all thinks about the families' needs when assigning their FLOs. I think you'd be terrific at it.'

'As are you, which is why you can't leave!'

She was shocked how upset the thought of him leaving made her feel. She couldn't imagine not working with him. He was the one who'd recruited her to family liaison in the first place and had overseen her training and every assignment. He was more than her senior officer: he was her mentor and a friend.

'That's very kind of you, Maggie, but my bucket and spade are packed. But I'm serious about your potential – you need to think about moving up. It's time. I know how much you love family liaison and if you're determined to continue with it there is scope to take what you do to a much higher level. The Met is always looking for officers of your calibre. I know someone who works for the Homicide and Serious Crime Command, I could put in a good word for you.'

'Joining the Met would mean moving to London.'

'What's wrong with that? You're young, you're not sad-dled with kids: this is the perfect time to further your career. Do you really want to spend your entire working life in the town you grew up in?'

Maggie leaned back against the headrest and took a deep breath. She'd never contemplated moving away from Mansell before, mostly because of Lou and the kids. Could she really up and leave? What about Umpire? Yet she knew what he'd say – ever since they'd first worked together he'd been pressing her to apply for promotion. If she moved to London, he'd find a way for them to make it work.

'I don't know. It's a big step,' she said.

'Say the word and I'll make some calls. But don't let opportunity pass you by, Maggie – there's a career waiting for you beyond Mansell if you want it.'

52

Maggie felt oddly exposed as she walked into the incident room two hours later, as if her nerve endings were twitching for everyone to see. She wasn't sure which of Gant's bombshells had unsettled her the most – him quitting his position or Byford being foisted upon her by someone higher up the chain of command than him.

She sat down at her desk and surreptitiously leaned over to open Byford's bottom drawer. It was locked. She made a decision: she would stay late until everyone else had gone home so she could break into it. Even if Byford came up with a perfectly plausible excuse as to why he hadn't told anyone about the notebooks or submitted them as evidence, she wanted to see what was in them before he could. Suspicion that he was hiding something other than the notebooks themselves nagged away at her.

Staying late would mean cancelling her birthday dinner with Umpire. With a sigh, she called him to break the bad news. Fortunately he'd had enough birthday celebrations of his own cancelled at short notice because of work to not get angry.

'There's so much going on now,' she said, cupping her

hand over the mouthpiece so he could hear her. The room had suddenly got noisier with the return of Renshaw and Burton; Nathan, who was at a desk in the corner double-checking the typed-up statements he'd taken from the class-mates and their teacher, gestured at them to pipe down.

'I'll cancel the booking,' said Umpire. 'I've heard there might be another body at the school site. Is that right?'

Bad news travelled fast.

'Possibly. I'll know more after the briefing. I am sorry about dinner.'

'It's not your fault. I feel bad because first Brighton and now this.'

Maggie smiled. 'I think it's a sign I should ignore turning thirty. Actually, there is one good thing that's happened – Jude texted to wish me happy birthday.'

'Really? That's great he's made contact.'

'He said he misses me and wishes me and Lou would make up. I texted him back but he's not replied.'

'If he's texted you once I'm sure he will.'

'I hope so. I have to go now. I'll miss you this weekend, but have a great time with the kids. Call me when you can.'

'I will.'

As she hung up, Renshaw called her over to join her and Burton.

'How's Imogen holding up?' she asked.

'Not bad, although the family is concerned attention is being diverted away from Benji with the dog search. It might help if you go round to see her, reassure her.'

Renshaw nodded. 'I'll do that.'

'When's the excavation going to start?'

'First thing tomorrow – we can't get everything on site before then. So I'm afraid we're all on call this weekend.'

'Fine by me,' said Maggie. 'I don't have any plans.'

'I had a night in planned with a bottle of wine,' said Burton resignedly. 'Talking of which, you missed Julia Hepworth's drunken antics. She turned up absolutely hamm—'

He never got to finish the sentence.

'For fuck's sake!' Nathan suddenly shouted, making them jump. 'I don't fucking believe it.' He rushed across to them holding a printout, so worked up his face was scarlet.

'I've just found this mixed in with the pile of statements – it's the transcript of the caretaker's 999 call. I don't know why the fuck we weren't given this sooner. Anna, you really need to read this.'

Renshaw snatched it from his hand. As her eyes scanned the document, her cheeks burned like Nathan's.

'He's been lying to us from day one. According to this, when the dispatcher asked him to describe what had happened, Donnelly replied – and I quote – "The boy was on the wall and the girl pushed him. Oh God, oh God, I think he's dead." The dispatcher then asks if he's sure the girl pushed him, and Donnelly replies, "I saw her do it – she put her hands on his chest and pushed him with all her might."'

53

Alan knew as soon as the door went that he was in trouble. The head walked in first and on her heels were DS Renshaw and the male officer Alan had seen milling around the school interviewing some of the teachers.

His little office suddenly felt very crowded.

'I'm sorry to disturb you,' said Mrs Pullman, sounding anything but, her expression set like stone. 'These officers need to speak to you as a matter of urgency. As it's nearly four o'clock I've told them you can be relieved of your duties for the rest of the day.'

Alan nodded but was distracted by the male officer, who had walked over to his desk and was peering closely at his computer screen. There was nothing incriminating open on the desktop, but still Alan's pulse juddered with fear.

'You're welcome to use my office,' said Mrs Pullman.

'I think it would be better if Mr Donnelly came down to the station with us,' said Renshaw. 'You don't mind that, do you?'

'How long will it take?' he asked worriedly. 'I need to lock up at the end of the day.'

'I'm sure Mrs Pullman can find someone else to do that.'

The head nodded. 'I'll do it myself if needs be.' She fixed her eyes on Alan's. 'Can I please ask that you cooperate with them? It would be in everyone's interests if you did. Rushbrooke needs to get back to normal.'

The head made it sound as though he was the reason the police had been swarming all over the place and not the kid who fell, and he was stung by the rebuke. He was also scared. Why did they want to question him again? Had they found out he started the fire? Did they know about the Pavilion?

The scratch on his face suddenly itched like mad but he kept his hands clenched at his sides, not wanting to draw any more attention to it. He could say with some conviction that he had no idea how he did it – whatever Gus insisted otherwise, he still had no recollection of going to talk to Ruby. And even if he had approached her, what would her response have been anyway? He might not use her and her friends the way others did, but he was as bad in many respects. He was the enabler and coward who turned his back and ignored what was going on to save his own skin.

It bothered him that he couldn't lock his office door as the police marched him outside, but if he insisted they might become suspicious, as might Mrs Pullman. Instead he unfastened the bundle of keys he carried on a loop on his belt and handed it to her. Some of the keys were labelled and for the ones that weren't he explained their function as quickly as he could. The look on the head's face suggested she'd forgotten which key fitted which lock the moment he'd told her, but she said she'd work it out.

Alan was grateful there were no children around to see his walk of shame across the playground to the staff car park,

where the officers had left their car. He was also grateful
their vehicle was unmarked, its plain, dark navy bodywork
making it indistinguishable from any other car on the road.

They made the drive into the centre of Mansell in
silence, the two of them up front and Alan sitting in the
back. He debated asking if he needed a solicitor but feared
doing so was tantamount to admitting he was in trouble.

Renshaw didn't bother with preamble: she simply slipped a
piece of paper across the table and asked him to read it
aloud.

As his own words leapt off the page at him, Alan swallowed hard. So this wasn't about the fire.

Shit, shit, shit.

'That's a very different account to what you told us on
Tuesday, Mr Donnelly.'

He pushed the piece of paper back towards her.

'I was in shock. I made a mistake.'

'Your statement on Tuesday was a mistake?'

'No, when I dialled 999. I didn't know whether I was
coming or going. What happened . . . it was horrible. I still
can't get that kid's face out of my mind.'

'I imagine it has been a very difficult experience for you,'
said Renshaw frostily. 'But here's the thing. I've got an eleven-
year-old boy lying dead on a mortuary slab and his mum is
beside herself wanting to know how he ended up there. You
swore blind it was an accident but then I'm given this transcript and suddenly it appears that you're lying. So I'll ask
you again, Mr Donnelly, why did you give us a different
account to the one you told the dispatcher?'

Alan could feel the sweat beading on his forehead but didn't dare wipe it away. He knew every movement, every gesture, was being scrutinized.

'I told you. I was confused and upset.'

'Did you or did you not see Poppy Hepworth push Benji Tyler off the wall to his death? Hang on, what does it say here?' Renshaw picked up the transcript and began to read as though she was rehearsing for a play. 'Oh, yes, here we go – "I saw her do it – she put her hands on his chest and she pushed him with all her might."' She put the paper down on the table and stared at him. 'Well?'

'That's what I thought I saw, but when I calmed down I realized I'd got it wrong. There was no way she could've pushed him from where she was standing – they were too far apart. It might've looked like she had, but what I saw was her reaching out to try to grab him to stop him falling.'

The lie was convincing enough to send a flicker of doubt across Renshaw's face. Her colleague looked equally uncertain and Alan experienced a surge of confidence. He might actually pull this off.

'That's what you believe now, that she tried to help, to stop him falling?'

'Yes. They were too far apart for it to be anything else.'

Renshaw looked far from happy.

'Listen, I'm not going to get a little girl into trouble for something she didn't do,' Alan continued, sensing he was on the home stretch. 'I couldn't live with myself if I did. I'm very sorry the boy died, I wish I could've saved him myself. For as long as I live I will never be able to wipe the memory of him lying on the ground bleeding like that. But I know what I saw and I'm sorry, but I can't change that.'

54

Julia had managed to force down a couple of slices of dry toast when they got home and was now napping on the sofa. The rest of the house was as quiet: Malcolm had spirited Dylan to the cinema, Poppy had shut herself in her room and Ewan was working at the kitchen table.

Drifting in and out of sleep, Julia's mind replayed snatches of the morning's events but she couldn't tell which bits were real and which were scenarios conjured in her dreams. Her falling over had definitely happened – she had bruised knees and bloodied palms as evidence – but Ewan swearing at her, telling her to go home? It wasn't like him to use the F-word in public. That bit can't have been real.

She must've rolled over onto her side and fallen into a deeper sleep, because when she came to again the digital clock on the DVD player said it was 18:05. She ungainly got to her feet in an ungainly fashion and walked to the kitchen, clutching the walls for support. She could no longer be classified as staggeringly drunk, but she felt terrible. Mouth parched, head pounding, the makings of an epic hangover.

She went straight to the sink and gulped down two large glasses of water.

'Sore head?' asked Ewan from behind his laptop.

'I feel awful.'

'You won't get any sympathy from me,' he said curtly. 'You were a disgrace.'

His anger shook her.

'I know, and I'm so, so sorry. I didn't know the police were going to call us.'

'DS Renshaw warned us at the police station that they might need to see us at short notice, when she asked us to stay in Mansell. You couldn't even stay sober for a few hours.'

'It was only a couple of drinks,' she protested.

'You were threatened with arrest, for crying out loud.'

'Was I?' Julia was appalled she couldn't remember. 'By who?'

'DS fucking Renshaw, that's who,' Ewan shouted at her. 'Can you imagine if she had nicked you? The officer questioning Poppy arrests her mum for being abusive and too fucking pissed to stand up straight.'

Julia quailed, his tirade pinning her to the kitchen unit. She had never seen him so angry.

'Daddy, don't.'

Neither of them had noticed Poppy coming into the kitchen. She was teary-eyed and trembling as she looked from one parent to the other.

'This is all my fault you're arguing,' she cried.

'No, it's not. It's mine,' said Julia. 'Daddy's right, I did a stupid thing.'

She went to hug her daughter but Ewan got there first.

'I'm very sorry we upset you,' he said, kissing the top of

Poppy's head and smoothing her hair. 'I just got a bit angry at Mummy, but we've sorted it out now.'

Watching Ewan lie so effortlessly to their daughter when they both knew the row was far from over reminded Julia that she still hadn't got to the bottom of what Poppy had told him on that first day in the head's office.

'Are you two keeping something from me?'

Ewan stared at her as though she was mad. 'What are you going on about?'

'On Tuesday, when I left Mrs Pullman's office to get some air, something happened. You looked shocked. Poppy, what did you tell Daddy?'

Poppy stonewalled her.

'Daddy, can I have some ice cream?'

'Of course.'

'No, she can't, we haven't had tea yet,' Julia snapped. 'Poppy, I asked you a question.'

'Why are you getting cross with me?' her daughter answered, growing tearful.

'See, now look what you've done,' said Ewan. For once Julia ignored him.

'Honey, did you tell Daddy what really happened when Benji fell?'

Poppy's expression slowly morphed as her eyes flickered from her mother's face to her father's and it pinned Julia to the spot with shame. For the first time she saw her daughter was every bit as intimidated by Ewan as she was.

55

The discovery of Donnelly's 999 transcript had triggered a witch-hunt to find out whose fault it was that it had been mislaid in the first place. The admin assistants, led by the irrepressible Pearl, were refusing to take responsibility, saying it had been delivered to the team as procedure demanded, while Renshaw was arguing that it hadn't and their sloppiness had thwarted the investigation.

The stand-off between the two women was taking place in the middle of the CID department, in the full view of everyone, and Maggie admired Pearl for not backing down in the face of Renshaw's fury.

'I don't know how it ended up mixed up with those other statements but I know it wasn't my girls who put it there,' she said.

'So who did, the fucking Tooth Fairy?' Renshaw shouted back, her anger fuelled by Donnelly's own refusal to back down from his statement that Benji's fall was accidental. He was currently downstairs in an interview room, cooling his heels until Renshaw had another crack at him.

'I gave it to one of your detectives like he asked me to,' Omana piped up.

Maggie, who was standing behind Renshaw, froze.

'Who asked you to?' Renshaw demanded to know.

'I think I know,' said Maggie. 'It was Byford.'

Renshaw spun round.

'Why the hell would he need the transcript first?'

'I don't know, but I think there's something else he's got that he shouldn't have.'

Leaving Pearl simmering about wanting an apology, Renshaw followed Maggie back into the incident room.

'We need to get into his bottom drawer,' said Maggie. 'But he keeps it locked.'

Renshaw tried it anyway but it was firmly shut. 'Anyone know how to jimmy this open?'

'This might do it,' said Burton, holding up a lock pick.

'I won't ask where you got that from,' said Renshaw wryly.

She and Maggie stood aside as Burton got to work. In less than ten seconds the drawer was open.

'Are these what you're looking for?' he asked, holding up a notebook in each hand. Renshaw took the one with flowers while Maggie flicked through the football one.

'Imogen told me Byford found these in Benji's room,' Maggie admitted. 'I was going to give him a chance to explain himself before I told you.'

Renshaw shot her a look that made it clear how unimpressed she was at Maggie not telling her sooner.

'What's in that one?'

'It's a story by the looks of things,' said Maggie, reading on.

The writing was clearly that of a child, a spidery, lopsided scrawl, and the story about a boy called Leo who sneaked out of his house at night because he was a secret spy. On the evening the story was set Leo came across a man shoving a body into the ground. The man was tall, with 'a grin that showed his teeth like a wolf' and a round, shiny head like a skeleton's. It wasn't the most coherent piece of creative writing she'd ever read, but instantly Maggie knew it might be crucial and she relayed the story to Renshaw and the others.

'Is it dated?' Burton asked.

'Sadly, no.'

Nathan chimed in. 'So, do we think it's a work of fiction, or is it Benji's account of seeing someone bury a body in the grounds at Rushbrooke masquerading as fiction?'

They all looked at each other as the prospect of it being the latter sank in.

'We should ask Poppy and the rest of his classmates if he mentioned anything about seeing a body, even as a made-up story,' said Burton. 'Worth checking with his mum too.'

'Yes, let's,' said Renshaw. 'Nathan, can you do the kids?'

He nodded. 'I've got email addresses and phone numbers for all the parents now.'

'Good.' Renshaw flicked through the pages of the flowered notebook. 'This one's just pages of phone numbers with random letters after them.'

'Imogen thinks Benji must've found the notebook somewhere and was trying to crack the code. He fancied himself as a spy, hence the story he wrote,' said Maggie.

Burton peered over Renshaw's shoulder.

'It's code, but not like you think. I've seen this before, on another case. The letters next to the phone numbers denote the person's sexual preferences – what you've got there is a prostitute's little black book.'

Renshaw looked baffled. 'Wouldn't it be simpler to put the client's initials down next to their number to remind you who they are?'

'You'd think, but these girls aren't stupid. If their clients are important people they're going to be careful not to write their names down anywhere,' explained Burton. 'For their sakes as much as their clients'.'

Renshaw flipped back to the opening page. 'There's nothing here to ID the book's owner.' She slowly leafed through the pages, then stopped. Maggie heard a little gasp escape from her lips.

'What is it?'

Renshaw couldn't speak. The colour had drained from her face.

'I – I need a word with Maggie in private,' she rasped.

Burton and Nathan shared a look of concern. 'Is everything okay?' Nathan asked.

'Give us a minute. Please.'

The two of them left the incident room, shutting the door softly behind them.

Maggie's heart rate soared as she watched Renshaw slump into a chair.

'Anna, what the hell's wrong?'

'I recognize one of these mobile numbers.'

She looked up at Maggie, crestfallen.

'It's my boyfriend's.'

56

Saturday

Maggie was woken by the sound of her doorbell ringing continuously, like someone was pressing down on it with their finger and not letting go. She rolled over to check the time on her alarm clock and groaned when she saw it was only nine o'clock.

She'd had precisely four hours' sleep, having stayed up drinking wine with Renshaw, who was now passed out in her spare room.

As she pulled back the covers the doorbell suddenly stopped. She gave it a few seconds to make sure it didn't start up again, then, when it didn't, flopped onto her back, and stared up at the ceiling.

She still couldn't believe it. ACC Bailey, Renshaw's boyfriend, paying for sex.

The situation had snowballed after Renshaw told Maggie she'd spotted his number in the notebook. Despite Maggie urging restraint – because they couldn't be sure Burton's theory about it belonging to a prostitute was even correct – Renshaw had called Bailey in his office at area HQ in Trenton and asked him outright why his phone number was listed in the notebook alongside other punters.

He didn't even try to deny it.

There were tears, shouting and, from what Maggie could glean, desperate attempts by Bailey to apologize for his indiscretion. All the while Maggie sat there wishing she didn't have to play witness to Renshaw's life imploding and watch her become more and more broken by her boyfriend's admissions of guilt. He couldn't even tell her whose book it might be – the owner could be one of half a dozen girls he regularly used.

Then, after refusing his pleas to let him drive home so they could sort it out, Renshaw lit the fuse she knew would detonate his career as well as their relationship.

'The notebook was found in the bedroom of a child whose death we're investigating. How do you explain that?'

The snowball had avalanched after that, and by the time Maggie had persuaded Renshaw to leave the office and come home with her around midnight, ACC Marcus Bailey was suspended pending an inquiry, while Renshaw had been given a leave of absence on compassionate grounds, the first few hours of which she spent getting drunk on Maggie's sofa.

Still woolly-headed herself, Maggie clambered out of bed to get a drink of water. In the kitchen was a bouquet of flowers she'd come home to find outside her front door last night, signed for and brought up to the top floor by one of her neighbours. A vivid explosion of orange and pink roses, lilies and flora, they were from Belmar and Allie Small to wish her a happy birthday. When Renshaw saw them she had berated Maggie for not revealing it was her thirtieth and insisted they open a bottle of champagne Maggie had been saving for a special occasion.

As Maggie downed the water, she wondered who was going to be brought in to take over now that Renshaw was no longer SIO. Their Superintendent had agreed that Burton could oversee the excavation at the school that morning but a new lead detective would be appointed by Monday.

She went back to bed and drifted off again, only to be woken an hour later by Burton ringing.

'What's up?' she answered groggily.

'Is Renshaw with you?'

'Yeah, but she's asleep.'

'I thought she'd want to know that she was right. We've found a woman's body wedged into the foundations.'

Maggie bolted upright.

'Seriously? How did she die?'

'Looks like strangulation but she was also badly beaten, which would account for the blood. We're treating it as murder.'

'Do we know who she is yet?'

'Yep, her name's Violet Castle. She's got a distinctive tattoo, a peacock with its tail fanning across the top of her back, and when we ran it through the PNC it came up that she's been picked up before for solicitation.'

Maggie's hungover brain needed a minute to slot the pieces together.

'She's a prostitute? Do you think the notebook was hers?'

'I'm willing to bet it was. Benji must've found it on the building site or somewhere close to it. Mal's going to run it for prints to make sure.'

'Christ. So let me get this straight – ACC Bailey was the client of a prostitute who's just turned up dead in the grounds of a school where an eleven-year-old boy died – the same boy who appears to have found the prostitute's client list with ACC Bailey's phone number on it.'

'I'd say that's pretty much it.'

'How the hell am I going to explain this to Anna when she wakes up?'

There was a noise behind her and Maggie looked round to see Renshaw in the doorway, her face twisted in anguish.

'It's okay, you just did.'

57

Monday

The weekend passed in a comatosed blur for Alan. Not at The Wheatsheaf – he'd bypassed that on Friday evening and gone straight to the off-licence where he bought three bottles of the cheapest Scotch it stocked with the intention of drinking every last drop. By last night, Sunday, there was only a quarter left in the last one, so he'd finished it off for breakfast and was now sprawled out on the sofa with the empty bottle on the floor beside him, watching TV through blurred vision.

He drank because he didn't have a job to go to. Mrs Pullman had told him the school was going to be shut today even before he'd left on Friday. Apparently the police couldn't be sure two days was long enough for their search, so they wanted to take the precaution of keeping the school closed on Monday as well.

His phone had been switched off all weekend, his curtains drawn. He wanted to keep the world at bay for as long as he could. A couple of times, in his stupor, he thought he might've heard a knock on the door, but he hadn't been able to rouse himself off the sofa to check.

But there was no mistaking the knock that had been

sounding intermittently for the last ten minutes or so, nor the voice echoing through the letter box demanding he open the door.

'I know you're in there,' said Gus, voice clenched with anger. 'I can hear the TV.'

The letter box clattered shut again. Alan held his breath and counted, hoping Gus had given up and gone away. But after less than sixty seconds, the knocking started up again and the letter box reopened.

'If you don't answer this fucking door right this second I'll call the police. I mean it. I'm dialling them now –'

Alan knew he meant it. He managed to roll himself off the sofa and landed heavily on all fours. He dragged himself upright, then wove drunkenly down the hallway.

The front door was on the latch, as it had been since Friday evening. It took him three attempts to open it, his brain and fingers so alcohol sodden that they failed him at the first and second goes.

Gus pushed his way in before the door was even open a crack, sending Alan flying. He slammed the door shut behind him, put the latch back on, then grabbed Alan by the upper arm and hauled him into the kitchen at the rear of the house. He shoved Alan into one of the two chairs either side of the small foldaway table, then lowered the window blind, cursing as the pulley became tangled and the right side of the slats finished up lower than the left.

Then he turned on Alan, his expression devoid of any warmth.

'What the hell did you do?'

Even as drunk as he was, Alan still managed to summon up outrage.

'Me? What about you?' He wobbled to his feet. 'The police think there's a dead woman at the school.'

Gus seized hold of Alan's shoulders and shoved him back down onto the chair.

'There *is* a dead woman – and it's Ruby.'

Alan stared up at him, confused.

'She hasn't been seen for days, no one can get hold of her,' said Gus. 'You know what that means, don't you?'

'That you'll be going down for murder, most likely,' said Alan. He wouldn't normally dare speak to Gus like that, but the Scotch was making him braver. 'You and your foul, disgusting mates.'

To his surprise, Gus laughed.

'Me? I didn't kill her and nor did anyone I know. But *you* were definitely the last person to see her alive.'

It took a few seconds for Alan to register what Gus was insinuating.

'No way, it wasn't anything to do with me,' he slurred. 'I saw Ruby on – wait, what day is it now?' He counted backwards on his fingers. 'That's it, Wednesday. I saw her on Wednesday, although I still don't remember that I did.'

Gus bent down so his face was level with Alan's.

'That was the last day the other girls remember seeing her, which makes you the last person to talk to her, when you went round to her house, called her a whore and she scratched you.'

Alan fumbled his cheek and felt the line that was still there, scored into his skin.

'It wasn't me,' he said, suddenly panicking. 'I didn't do anything to her.'

Gus straightened up and smiled, then held his arms out as though offering Alan an embrace.

'Let's think logically about this,' he said. 'Neither of us wants the police at our door, so I'm prepared to give you an alibi for Wednesday evening – I'll say you came round to mine after the pub and that you went nowhere near Ruby's house. In return, you continue to keep quiet about the Pavilion.'

The thought of being accused of murder terrified Alan into agreeing. Who wouldn't believe an alibi from the school's chair of governors? It was only after Gus left, when he was trying to take everything in, that Alan realized something crucial, something he had overlooked himself until that point.

He didn't actually know where Ruby lived. How could he have gone round to see her, let alone have harmed her in any way, when he didn't actually possess her address? Why had Gus lied to him about her scratching him, when it was obvious now that he must've caught his cheek on a bush, as he originally assumed?

The answer that came to him was horrifyingly simple: Gus was setting him up.

58

Monday morning the station car park was almost at capacity as Maggie eased her old Toyota into a space. A blast of chilly air swirled around her as she climbed out and her exposed arms showed their indignation by covering themselves in goosebumps.

'Looks like the heatwave's over,' said a voice behind her. It was Burton, wearing his usual jeans-and-T-shirt combo, but with a lightweight navy bomber jacket over the top. A shivering Maggie, again in a short-sleeved shirt and thin cotton trousers, mentally berated herself for not checking the weather report before getting dressed that morning.

'Have you spoken to Anna since Saturday?' he asked as they fell into step.

'Only briefly on the phone. After your call she left mine to go home. Her parents have convinced her to go and stay with them in Newcastle for a bit.'

'I didn't know she was a Geordie. She doesn't have an accent.'

'Not even a hint of one.'

'So how is she?'

'Awful. It's bad enough her finding out that her boyfriend

has been sleeping with prostitutes, but she's also got to contend with everyone at work knowing. She's heartbroken and humiliated. He's moved out.'

They were almost at the outer door. The rear of the station was its modern half, a sleek, secretive facade of smoked-glass windows and reinforced-steel doors. What it presented to the world on the street side was its welcoming face: red-brick, preserved from history, it preened at passers-by like an ageing beauty queen. Maggie punched in the access code to get through the outer door, then swiped her pass to enter the foyer where the lift was.

'Any word on who's coming in as SIO?' she asked.

Burton chuckled. 'Yeah, nice one.'

'What's that supposed to mean? I'm asking if you know who it is.'

'You're joking, right?'

'I'm not. No one's told me anything. I don't even know who's replacing Byford as my new liaison partner. I've been trying to get hold of DI Gant to find out but he's not answering.'

'You know it was Bailey who suggested Byford as a FLO?' Burton continued. 'They're good mates; they play for the same five-a-side football team at the weekend and socialize afterwards. I still can't believe he put his neck on the line for the ACC. He must be seriously regretting it now he's been suspended as well.'

'He didn't seem very remorseful on Friday night,' said Maggie.

Under questioning, Byford confirmed ACC Bailey sent him to keep an eye on the investigation into Benji's death because he was aware some of the prostitutes he used operated near the school and it was too close for comfort. Byford then admitted to concealing evidence by hiding the notebooks in his drawer. He knew when he found them in Benji's room that the flowered notebook would expose Bailey, recognizing his phone number in it just as Renshaw had, and he'd made the decision to protect his mate at the expense of the investigation.

'Do you think Anna knew Byford was Bailey's mate?' Burton queried.

'She can't have done. She didn't react when he turned up; I never got the feeling they already knew each other.'

They were in the lift now, going up to CID. As it juddered to a halt on the third floor, Burton shot Maggie a curious look.

'Do you really not know who the new SIO is?'

'I told you, I'm out of the loop.'

'I think you're in for a surprise then.'

The department was even busier than usual. Three officers Maggie had never seen before were loitering by the back of the room, chatting quietly amongst themselves. On recognizing Burton, one of them came over to greet him and then introduced himself to Maggie as DS Abram Joseph.

'We're joining the investigation,' said Abram.

'Which one? The boy's death or the murder?' asked Maggie.

'The murder, and also the prostitution ring. Bailey's saying he wasn't the only high-ranking officer involved but he's refusing to name names because he wants to cut a deal to save his job. That's not going to happen, so it's down to us to find out who the rest are.'

'I hope that doesn't mean Benji's case is now less of a priority,' Maggie frowned. 'I'm the FLO and we owe it to his mum not to let it slide.'

Someone standing behind her laughed.

'Always the defender, Maggie.'

She spun round at the sound of the familiar voice.

'What the hell are you doing here?' she exclaimed.

Belmar Small adjusted his tie with a wink.

'I've come to work.'

'You're on the case now?' She locked eyes with Burton as the penny slowly dropped. 'You mean . . .?'

'Yep. That's why I was surprised you didn't know.'

Nathan chose that moment to barrel up to them.

'Can someone please tell me what the bloody hell is going on?'

'We're discussing the new SIO,' Burton told him.

'Who is it?'

'Me.'

The group swivelled round and Maggie's insides gave a violent lurch.

'Right,' said Umpire. 'Let's get this briefing started.'

59

Maggie could barely concentrate on what Umpire was saying. She was livid beyond words. Not only had he not bothered to warn her that he and a team from HMET were being brought in by the Chief Constable to investigate the murder and prostitution ring, but he'd made her look an idiot in front of her colleagues for not knowing. They were in a relationship and yet she hadn't warranted so much as a text in advance.

She stared resolutely ahead, determined not to make eye contact.

'What we know about our victim so far,' he was saying, 'is that her name is Violet Castle but she was known to friends as Ruby because of her hair colour. She's eighteen and spent most of her adolescence in foster care. She's not a Mansell native, but moved here from Wales with her mum as an infant. Her last known address is a bedsit on Creighton Avenue. Abram, I want you round there this morning talking to neighbours. We need names of known associates, colleagues.'

'Sure, boss,' said Belmar, prompting Maggie to be

inexplicably angry with him too. Why hadn't he let her know either? They were meant to be mates.

Actually, they were closer than that now – Belmar was one of her best friends. When they'd first met she'd thought he was faintly ridiculous – he strutted about the place in three-piece suits and pointy shoes like a *GQ* model, and still did – but he was kind and gracious and funny and, with his wife, Allie, to whom she was also close, had been incredibly supportive since her fall-out with Lou, filling up her social calendar with nights out to take her mind off it. In return, she was their hand-holder as they dealt with the stress of failing to get pregnant.

Belmar was in the front row, next to Nathan and another detective Maggie didn't know. She was in the middle row with Burton on her right and Joseph on her left. She didn't know any of the officers in the back row. They'd been up-graded to Incident Room 1, the biggest and plushest the nick had to offer.

'Establishing Ruby's last movements is our priority,' said Umpire. 'We understand she was a regular at the Marshall Smith drop-in centre for adolescent drug users and addicts. Ruby used the centre a couple of times a week until about a month ago. Apparently there's been chatter amongst the regulars this week that she'd not been seen in her usual haunts and that her friends didn't know where she was.'

'They weren't concerned enough to report her missing though,' Belmar commented.

'It wasn't entirely out of character for Ruby to duck in and out of the area,' said Umpire. 'She had friends in London she would sometimes crash with for weeks at a time.'

Maggie raised her hand to ask a question.

'What's on your mind, DC Neville?' Umpire asked evenly.

She could feel eyes upon her as she cleared her throat. Everyone within the force knew that they were a couple and for the first time she minded that they did.

'Was Ruby going to the centre because she was an addict?'

Umpire levelled his gaze at her and a million unspoken words passed between them. He knew she was angry with him.

'Crack was her drug of choice, but according to the outreach workers at the centre she'd been clean for three months. If any of you locals have any idea who her dealer was, speak up.'

Nathan suggested a few names, which Umpire jotted down on the evidence board.

It wasn't why Maggie had asked though – she was thinking about Renshaw and what Bailey might've exposed her to by sleeping with prostitutes.

'We are systematically checking every single phone number in Ruby's notebook—'

'How do we know for sure it's hers?' Nathan interrupted.

'We've had it corroborated. She was known to carry it on her person.'

His caginess led Maggie to the conclusion that Bailey must've verified it. She wondered if Umpire had interviewed him and knew that, if he had, it would've been difficult. Bailey had been Umpire's biggest supporter and it was under his auspices that HMET was set up with him in charge. How ironic that the same team was now tasked with investigating him.

'Now, I know some of you are concerned about the Benji

Tyler investigation being overshadowed by the murder. Don't be. I'm the SIO for that as well and I want it solved as much as you do.' He inhaled sharply, then his voice quickened. 'I've decided that DC Neville will act up as DS for the remainder of the investigation into Benji's death. DS Andrew Finnegan, who joins me from HMET, will be Deputy SIO for both cases.'

Maggie was dumbstruck. He wanted her to do *what*?

'DC Hazel Carmichael is stepping in as FLO to the Tyler family. For the time being she'll work alone under Acting DS Neville's guidance. Welcome to the team, Hazel,' he added, nodding towards the back of the room.

Maggie spun round in her seat to see an older woman with cropped, silvery-grey hair nodding back.

Slowly she turned round to face Umpire but he wouldn't meet her gaze. She could barely contain her fury but knew that if she exploded now it would be force-wide gossip by the end of the day. Instead she raged internally, calling him all the names under the sun. How dare he remove her from liaison without a word of warning? How many times did she have to tell him that she didn't want a fucking promotion if it meant giving up the role she loved?

He must've known how pissed off she was because as he checked his notes she saw high spots of colour on his cheeks, which only ever appeared at times of extreme stress. She felt a bit better for seeing them.

'Right, it's been almost three days since Poppy Hepworth was last questioned,' said Umpire. 'That's far too long. We should be keeping up the pressure on her. Maggie, I want you to bring her in this morning and put the 999 transcript to her. If she thinks we believe it she might buckle. Belmar will do the interview with you.'

Oh, so we're back on first-name terms, are we, thought Maggie resentfully. Like that's going to get you off the hook. Belmar looked over his shoulder at her and winked. She tried to glower at him but ended up smiling. That was the thing about Belmar – he was the kind of guy who could charm Eskimos into buying ice cubes. She must remember to thank him for the birthday flowers.

She was seriously worried how Imogen would react to her stepping aside at such short notice. With Byford gone too, who could blame her for feeling even more unsettled and deserted by the police? She'd need reassurance she was in good hands with Carmichael, which was tricky when Maggie didn't know the first thing about the woman. She'd have to call Gant, although he wasn't in her good books either because he must've known she was being moved off and that's why he'd been dodging her calls all morning.

'In the meantime, the rest of us need to track down and question every person involved in the construction of the new classrooms. I want to know exactly who had access, from delivery men to labourers.'

'We should bring Donnelly in again,' said Burton.

'You read my mind,' said Umpire, consulting the evidence board behind him. 'School caretaker, unfettered access to the grounds, saw all the comings and goings. He has to be top of our list to be questioned about Violet Castle.'

'He's still not off the hook for altering his statement,' said Nathan grimly. 'I've been thinking about it, and what if he changed his story so we'd think Benji's death was an accident and we closed the case?'

Maggie tensed. It was the theory she'd put forward to Renshaw, the one Byford had rubbished and made her doubt. Would Umpire give weight to it?

'I think you may well be right, DC Thomas,' said Umpire, his eyes gleaming. 'And for suggesting it you get the enjoyable task of ruining Mr Donnelly's Monday morning. Bring him in.'

60

Julia was sitting up in bed swaddled in her dressing gown with her tablet on her lap. The curtains were still drawn, even though it was gone eleven.

Ewan was at work, the kids downstairs with her dad, by now on their third film of the morning. She should care that they had already exceeded their daily screen time by half but she didn't have it in her to go downstairs and deal with them whining at her when she switched the TV off.

Up here, on her own, she could pretend everything was normal. Her manager had granted her a week's leave of absence 'to deal with things', informing her by email over the weekend. Julia hoped it was borne of kindness and a desire to lessen what her family was going through, but she suspected the offer was really a ruse to put some distance between her and the council. No one wanted to be tainted by association.

She checked the *Echo* website again. Benji's death had been eclipsed by the discovery of the body at Rushbrooke. There was lots of speculation about how it got there but little in the way of detail. The police were saying nothing and the identity of the woman – they had at least confirmed it was a she – wasn't being made public until next of kin had been informed.

Julia's visits to the *Echo* website that morning already numbered in the dozens. But when events shifted like sand and could be updated every second, let alone every hour, she didn't want to miss anything. So she sat and she read, and refreshed, and read, and refreshed, over and over, until her eyes started to smart and her neck and shoulders throbbed in protest at being kept still for so long.

At midday Malcolm came up with a cup of tea and a cheese sandwich. He'd cut the crusts off, the way her mum used to do when she was little.

'Thought you might be hungry,' he said.

He tiptoed into the room as though he didn't want to disturb her and set the plate and mug down on her bedside table.

'Shall I open the curtains, let some sunshine in?'

She was about to say no and ask that he leave her alone, but something stopped her.

'Yes, please.'

She squinted, her eyes adjusting to the flood of daylight as he pulled back the lined drapes.

'Why don't you come downstairs for a bit after you've eaten? If you feel up to it?'

'I'm not ill, Dad,' she said, chewing a mouthful of sandwich. It was white bread, which wasn't their usual, and it felt spongy and alien against the roof of her mouth.

'That's the only bread the shop on the corner had left,' said Malcolm as she laid the rest back on the plate, uneaten. 'I didn't want to leave the kids for too long to go to one of the bigger supermarkets. But we are running out of food.'

Julia picked up her tablet again. 'I'll order an online shop.'

'Poppy's been asking what's wrong.'

She looked away, unable to answer him.

'You can't punish her like this,' her dad admonished.

'I'm not punishing her.'

'You've barely spoken to her since Friday evening, nor have you hugged her, kissed her or offered any other kind of comfort.' Malcolm lowered himself onto the edge of the bed. 'I've been watching you. The way you're behaving you may as well just say you think she's guilty. While you're up here doing heaven knows what, that poor child is downstairs beside herself. You think this is hard for you, Julia, but what about her? Imagine how she's feeling. She watched another boy die, her classmate, and then she's accused of hurting him.' Malcolm shook his head. 'Poppy hasn't deviated from her story once. If she doesn't doubt herself, then you shouldn't doubt her either.'

Julia stared at her dad, wide-eyed with fright. His angry tone was an unwelcome flashback to her childhood when he would yell and posture at her mum.

'I'm sorry, you're right,' she stuttered.

'I know you're feeling het up about the boy's mother, but you need to get some perspective. Are you even sure the bullying happened like you think it did?'

Julia was horrified. 'How can you ask me that?'

'I recall you having a bit of a fall-out with some girls during your third year at Rushbrooke but the vast majority of the time you were happy there and did well. Your reports said the same thing. Your mum and I never had any concerns about you.'

Julia lost her cool.

'You probably don't remember how upset I was because you were too busy being horrible to Mum!'

Far from being annoyed by her comment, her dad nodded sadly.

'I wasn't always the best husband.'

'You were terrible. Sometimes I don't know why Mum came back.'

'Oh, Julia, if only things were that black and white.'

She stared, open-mouthed, as her dad's face crumpled. The only time she'd ever seen him cry was at her mum's funeral.

'Dad, why are you upset?'

'I loved your mum so much.' He removed his glasses and wiped his cheeks. 'But she didn't love me in the same way.'

'That's rubbish,' Julia retorted.

'I know you don't want to believe it but it's true. Her moving out was nothing to do with me forcing her to leave. She went because she was having an affair.'

Julia was furious at his distortion of the past. She remembered how upset her mum had been before she left, how Malcolm had given her no alternative but to go.

'That's not what happened. She went because you didn't want her working and she got fed up with you nagging her.'

'Julia, your mother moved out for about three months to set up home with another man. She wanted to take you too but I refused – there was no way I was going to let him raise my child.' Malcolm faltered. 'Your mum didn't want to give you up so she gave him up instead and came home. But she resented me for forcing her to choose and never let me forget it was him that she loved. It was very hard for me to deal with and I can see how, to you, it must've looked as though I was difficult to live with. But the constant rejection wore me down.'

Everything Julia had believed about her parents' marriage was suddenly turned on its head. She'd always thought her mum was unaffectionate and closed off because of the way her dad behaved towards her.

'But if she didn't love you, why stay together long after I'd moved out?'

'I guess we'd got used to each other by then. When you went to university I told your mum we could sell the house and split everything, but she said there was no point. I think, by then, she had started to love me again, in her own way.' He began to cry again. Julia reached over and hugged him.

'Why didn't you tell me this sooner?' she implored. 'All this time I thought you were the problem.'

'Is that why you hated me? We were so close when you were little but as you got older it was like you couldn't stand me.'

Julia was horrified. 'You could tell?'

'I could, yes. But I never let on how upset it made me because I didn't want to make things any worse. Life at home was already bad enough.'

A tidal wave of sorrow rose up and crashed over her. All those years she'd blamed her dad for being a nightmare to live with, yet all that time he was trying to hold their family together. How could she have got it so wrong?

'I'm so sorry,' she said.

Malcolm smiled as he wiped more tears away.

'It's in the past and all I care about is that you and I get on fine now. But you can't hold on to the bad stuff because it eats away at you. Don't let what happened at school thirty years ago cloud your judgement over Poppy.'

'But it was awful, Dad. Imogen was vile to me and I can't seem to get beyond that. Who I am, everything I've done, everything I do, is a result of what she did.'

'Only because you let it be,' he replied. 'Poppy needs you to believe her, to be on her side. Ask yourself this, Julia – do you really want to lose your daughter the way I lost you for all those years?'

61

It took two phone calls to finally rouse Alan from the sofa, upon which he'd stayed slumped after Gus's earlier visit.

The first was from his ex-wife, Gayle, incandescent with rage and shouting the odds.

'If you ever threaten me like that again I'll report you to the police!'

He didn't have a clue what she was talking about, and said so.

'The text you sent me at four this morning, saying you'd kill me if I spoke to any reporters again.'

He had no recollection of sending any texts but when he checked his phone, there it was.

'Oh God, I'm so sorry. I didn't mean it. I was pissed when I sent it.'

'I haven't even spoken to anyone.'

'The woman from the *Echo* said you'd been telling her stuff about me.'

'It's rubbish. She did call me but I put the phone down on her. I can't believe you thought I would sell you out.'

'She made it sound like you had. I shouldn't have texted

you and I promise, swear on my life, that I'll never do it again.'

'You shouldn't be drinking, Al,' she said, calming down. 'It makes you worse.'

'I've got nothing else to do,' he said piteously.

'Oh, Alan.'

'I miss you. I miss the kids. I still love you, Gayle.'

Her voice wavered. 'You didn't love me enough, though. If you had, you wouldn't have squandered every penny we had and run up tens of thousands' worth of debt behind my back.'

'How many more times can I say I'm sorry? I wanted to give us a better life.'

'I didn't need flash cars and holidays for a better life. I needed a husband who didn't lie to me about his spending habits and make me and my kids destitute.'

'Haven't I been punished enough? I know I did wrong but I lost you, the kids, my job and my home. What more do you want?'

'I can't do this. I can't keep having the same conversation with you, Al. It's the same thing, over and over. You tell me you're sorry and I tell you that I understand, but it still doesn't make things right.' She stifled a sob, which made his heart splinter. 'I have to go.' She hung up.

When the phone rang again twenty minutes later he raced to answer it, hoping it might be her ringing back to smooth things over. But it was Mrs Pullman, informing him that Years 5 and 6 would be returning to school tomorrow but the remaining years and Reception were going to be set up in temporary classrooms at sites across town, including two other primaries and the town hall.

'It's devastating to think of the children scattered across Mansell,' she said, her voice full of emotion. 'Children crave routine and they need the structure that school gives them. But I don't see what choice we have. The children's education cannot be disrupted any longer.'

'I'm so sorry,' said Alan lamely.

'It's not your fault. I do need you back on site tomorrow though. Are you fit enough to return to work?'

'Why wouldn't I be?'

'You've been through a lot this past week, Alan. I want to make sure you are feeling mentally capable of doing your job with everything that's going on. I have a duty of care to my staff as much as to the children.'

He was touched by her concern and it gave him the impetus to shake the sleep from his leaden limbs and resolve to freshen up, starting with getting rid of the bristles puncturing his chin and having a shower. He would pop to the shops after and get some decent food in for dinner, no processed crap. And no booze: he was done drinking for at least the rest of the week.

'I'll be fine,' he assured her.

He meant it. Talking to Gayle made him realize the job at Rushbrooke was all he had now, and like children with their routines he cleaved to the security it gave him. He needed to get back to normal too.

62

There were too many people still milling about for Maggie to confront Umpire. Instead she shot him furious looks across the incident room while she prepared to brief Carmichael about Imogen. Once or twice he glanced back, but his expression was impenetrable, which annoyed her even more.

Carmichael was, to her relief, as competent as she looked. She listened intently as Maggie went through her log and brought her up to speed on where the investigation into Benji's death was. She was older than Maggie, at least late forties, and she had the air of someone who stayed calm in a crisis. She was also astute.

'I get the feeling you're not happy about this,' said Carmichael, quiet enough so the others couldn't hear.

'No, I'm not. Well, not because of you,' Maggie said hurriedly. 'I'm annoyed because I wasn't warned this was happening. I'm worried about how Imogen will take it. She and her mum are already concerned they're being bumped down our list of priorities and this will convince them their fears are valid.'

'Don't worry, I'll reassure them that this is in their best interests.'

Maggie frowned. 'I'm not sure I follow.'

'They already know and trust you, so who better to step up and take more responsibility for the investigation? I can make it clear to them that you'll still be in regular contact, while I'll be there to ease them through procedural stuff. Between us I'm sure we can allay any concerns they have.'

Begrudgingly Maggie had to admit to herself that Carmichael was going to be a great replacement.

'How long have you been a FLO?' she asked.

'I've lost count,' said Carmichael with a smile. 'I was one of the first wave when they brought in the new training, so that's going back to 2000, 2001.'

'Have you never wanted to do anything else?'

Carmichael gave her a shrewd look.

'No, I love liaison. Nothing else has appealed to me in the same way. I did do a stint as an Acting DS myself once, but I knew pretty quickly it wasn't a good fit for me.' She leaned forward and dropped her voice even lower. 'Don't do anything rash because of today. You might find you like it.'

'I wouldn't be too sure.'

Carmichael grinned. 'I'm guessing someone will be getting it in the neck tonight. He should've warned you.'

Maggie blushed. 'You know about us?'

'I know from what others have said that you're a couple who have always acted professionally when working together and that's all I care about.' She leaned forward again. 'But make sure you give him hell when you get him home.'

63

Feeling better after his shower, Alan rifled through the cupboard under his kitchen sink to find some old carrier bags to take to the supermarket, save himself some money buying new ones.

Rising up, his cheek itched again and he rubbed it furiously. He'd decided against shaving when it occurred to him the bristles were doing a good job of masking the scratch on his face. The fewer questions he solicited about that, the better. But bloody hell it itched.

Leaving home, he was pleased to see the weather had cooled a bit; having not ventured outside the entire weekend and with the curtains kept shut he'd had no idea whether it was sunny or raining. The cloying heat that made it difficult for him to breathe had dissipated but it was still pleasantly mild.

There was a Co-op not far from The Wheatsheaf but Alan turned right out of his garden gate to head in the opposite direction. He didn't want to bump into anyone he knew and he didn't want to be tempted into having a drink. He needed to keep a clear head.

As he ambled along the pavement his thoughts strayed

uncomfortably to Ruby. He hated to think what might've happened to her. She seemed like a nice girl, all things considered, and no one deserved to be discarded like unwanted rubbish under a pile of cement.

He expected the police would want to question him about her, but he didn't mind. This time he had nothing to hide, because he knew nothing. He had no idea who killed Ruby or why. He wouldn't be lying this time.

Encouraged, his stride became brisker and he whistled a tune as he walked. The tunnel had a glimmer of light at its end: Gayle hadn't said anything to the reporter, the police couldn't force him to change his story back about the Hepworth girl and Gus was willing to alibi him for Wednesday evening in return for his continued silence.

His step faltered as he dwelled on Gus for a moment. He didn't want to rely on him, but what else could he do? Then he had a thought, and reached for his phone. Get it down in writing – don't just accept his word for it.

Hi, Gus. Cheers for letting me say I was at yours on Weds. Owe you one. Alan.

It took about six seconds after he'd pressed send to realize what he'd done. He stopped in the middle of the pavement, white as a sheet, staring down at his phone.

He'd set up a false alibi in a text and he'd made it sound as though it was all his idea.

Fuck.

Alan clutched his phone, wondering how he could retract the message and make it vanish from existence. Perhaps he could call Gus, ask him to delete it from his phone. Would that be enough?

Alan's thumb was about to press down on the green handset symbol to make the call when a car screeched up to the kerb beside him. The passenger door opened and a man got out. For a split second he thought it was Gus and his stomach did a somersault. Then he realized it was the detective who'd interviewed him on Friday about his 999 call, DC Thomas.

'A word, Mr Donnelly.'

'I'm on my way to the shops,' he said feebly.

'I need you to come down to the station with me.'

He could feel himself backing away, even though he knew he shouldn't and that it was a bad idea to, but it was as though he had no control over his legs.

'Mr Donnelly, don't make this more difficult for yourself.'

He turned to run but Nathan was too quick and his grip on Alan's upper arm too firm.

'If you don't come with me now, I'll be forced to arrest you on suspicion of perverting the course of justice,' Nathan said.

Alan's legs gave up on him.

64

Imogen took instantly to Carmichael and seemed mollified by her and Maggie's explanation of how things would work from then on. Grace, on the other hand, raged with indignation.

'My grandson hasn't been dead a week and we're on our third family-liaison person. This is outrageous,' she said. 'I've a good mind to make a complaint.'

'This isn't how we want to do things either,' said Maggie.

'Mum, Maggie said she's still involved in the case,' said Imogen. 'She's not leaving us to it.'

Grace made a harrumphing noise that made it clear she thought otherwise.

'The books that Jamie took, have they been helpful?' asked Imogen.

Maggie let Carmichael answer. She wanted to be sure she knew how to handle questions that required a considered answer. Patronizing, yes, given that Carmichael was far more experienced than her, but the guilt Maggie felt at being removed from her post made her crave the reassurance.

'Benji had written a story in his notebook about a boy who saw someone disposing of a dead body. We have reason to suspect it was actually a true account of something he'd witnessed himself in the school grounds,' said Carmichael steadily.

'Benji saw a dead body? You don't mean the woman you found on Saturday?' Imogen gasped. 'Oh, that's horrible.'

'Did he ever give you any indication he'd witnessed something like that? Like making funny comments or dropping hints?'

'Only what I told you about him coming home crying that day. Maybe that was it? Mum, can you think of anything else?'

Grace was too shocked to speak, shaking her head vigorously instead.

'Are you sure the story is really about that?' Imogen pressed. 'He could've just made it up. He had a great imagination.'

'We did consider that, but the other notebook found in Benji's bedroom belonged to the deceased woman.'

Imogen clamped her hand over her mouth in horror.

'We believe Benji found the notebook either where the woman's body was buried or close by,' Maggie added. 'Apparently she carried it on her at all times.'

Grace floundered for words.

'But if Benji had seen something so . . . so . . . serious, he would've said something. Imogen raised him to be honest and open, he would tell her anything.'

'Maybe he was too scared,' said Carmichael. 'Maggie is going to be interviewing Poppy again this morning to see if she knew. There was a reason the children went to the school last Tuesday morning and it might be that Benji wanted to tell her what he'd seen and where it happened. He might've wanted to confide in a friend first for advice.'

Imogen unclenched her hand from her mouth.

'That doesn't explain why he fell to his death though.'

'No, it doesn't,' Maggie admitted, 'and just because we're pursuing this other angle doesn't mean we've given up on finding out. We have a new senior officer in charge, DCI Umpire, and he's determined you'll get the answers you want.'

'It's not answers we're after, it's justice,' said Grace.

'We understand,' said Carmichael.

'I'm not sure you do. My grandson was the most precious thing in the world to us and we're bereft he's gone. I feel like my heart has been ripped from my chest and it hurts so much I can barely breathe.'

Imogen's tears came suddenly, unbidden.

'Mum's right. Every time the door goes, I expect him to run in calling my name. I wake up in the middle of the night craving a cuddle, like my body is literally aching for him. I want to feel the weight of him again, feel his arms around my neck, and I can't. I miss him so much,' she cried.

'So you can tell us you understand, but really you don't,' said Grace. 'The only thing that's keeping us from going completely mad right now is the idea that someone will pay for his death, and soon.'

65

Maggie left Carmichael comforting Imogen and Grace, and made the short drive to the Hepworths' house. She parked in a side street around the corner because she wanted to check her phone before going in; it had pinged twice on the drive over and she didn't want to be sitting in full view of the Hepworths' front-room window as she checked her messages.

The first was an email from Burton and the news it imparted was frustrating: the digital autopsy results were in but there were no visible signs to show Benji had been pushed, no bruising or contusions to his chest or back. However, the conclusion did echo Mal Matheson's preliminary report that the severity of Benji's head injury suggested he had fallen with unnatural force.

Burton's email finished by saying Umpire was now deciding whether the scan could be trusted and if they should insist on a scalpel PM being carried out, in case there were signs of internal bruising. He was going to seek advice from the head of Legal Services before taking the request to Imogen. Maggie dreaded to think how she would react.

The other message she'd received was a text – and to her delight it was from Jude. She scrolled down its length, her pulse beginning to race. Her nephew hadn't messaged her to say hello again, he was asking for help.

I hate it here. I want to come home. I want to go back to my old school. Can I live with u? Mum's got a new bf and he's nasty.

She messaged back immediately.

That doesn't sound good. Can you talk now?

Ten long seconds passed until the next ping.

Can't now, Mum's here. But I'll try soon.

I'll be waiting. But if you need me before then, call ANY TIME.

I will. XXXXXX

I love you kiddo. And Scotty and Mae. XXXXXX

Maggie stayed parked for another ten minutes, until she was sure Jude wasn't going to text back again. Then she got out of the car, her joy at him getting in touch again overshadowed by heart-clawing worry for him and his brother and sister, and for their mum as well. Lou's taste in men had never been stellar, but none of her past boyfriends or her ex-husband had ever been aggressive towards her or the kids, assuming that's what Jude meant by him being nasty.

What on earth was going on at home that Jude was desperate to leave?

66

Julia checked through the bags one last time to satisfy herself both children had everything they needed for the following day. For Dylan that meant his PE kit, for Poppy her library book to be exchanged. With shaking fingers she fastened the bags and moved them from the kitchen table to by the front door, so they could pick them up on their way out in the morning.

If she had her way she'd have kept them off school for longer, but Ewan agreed with Mrs Pullman that they shouldn't miss any more lessons and should return tomorrow. Poppy would be going back to Rushbrooke but Dylan's class was going to be taught at a primary school fifteen minutes by car. Julia was grateful she had the week off to take Poppy, while her dad was going to drive Dylan.

Mrs Pullman had reassured them during her phone call that Poppy would be supported on her return. She seemed to think that because the police hadn't taken any action against her that was the end of the matter.

'We have pastoral-care measures in place to ensure her welfare, including the opportunity to talk to a counsellor. I think it will be good for Poppy to return to her normal routine,' she'd said.

Julia knew she should've been grateful that the head was being so accommodating but she wasn't sure they shared the same idea of normal. To Mrs Pullman that meant re-integrating Poppy into the classroom as if nothing had happened, but Julia knew that her daughter's return to school would still be frowned upon by some parents who thought she was to blame for another child dying. She'd read the comments online, the slurs against her family, the insinuations and falsehoods about Poppy, about her as a parent. The temptation to reply to each one was overwhelming until she forced herself to shut down her tablet and silence the sniping.

Poppy was upstairs in her room, reading. Julia asked if they could have a chat.

'How are you feeling about going back to school tomorrow?'

'Mum, that's the hundredth time you've asked me. I told you – I'd rather be at school than here. I want to see my friends.'

Her happiness at returning to Rushbrooke seemed genuine enough and this was the most upbeat she'd been in days. Julia had taken on board her dad's criticism of her behaviour towards Poppy and had made a huge effort to hug and kiss her as normal. His other comments were buried at the back of her mind to deal with another day; she had too much going on to dwell on her mum's affair right now.

'I'm pleased to hear it,' said Julia, although it wasn't

strictly true. If Poppy had protested about going back she'd have kept her at home in a heartbeat.

They chatted for a minute about the book Poppy was reading, then, as Julia got to her feet, the doorbell went.

'I'd better see who that is,' she said, planting a kiss on her daughter's crown.

Passing Dylan's bedroom, she could hear the noise of him pretending to be a dragon tamer. Oh, to be nine and able to switch off to the horrors that surround you.

She still had a smile on her face when she yanked open the door. It dropped the second she saw the warrant card being held up.

'Mrs Hepworth, I'm Acting DS Maggie Neville. I'm here for your daughter.'

67

Alan turned down the offer of a duty solicitor, fearing it might make him appear guilty if he accepted. It was already bad enough that the police had misconstrued the panic attack he'd experienced on arriving at the station as him being deliberately obstructive. He tried to explain it was because of his asthma that he was getting anxious and that he felt better after using his inhaler, but they'd still put him in a cell to 'cool down'.

Half an hour into his confinement, it dawned on Alan that his only option was to stick to his story and brazen out the text message to Gus if they asked him about it.

He wasn't worried about the police finding any other incriminating messages on his phone, because the arrangement with Gus to use the Pavilion was done through the school email system. It was genius when he thought about it – who'd query messages from the chairman of the school governors to the site manager asking for a building in the grounds to be unlocked? More specific messages had been passed on in person, like the request for Alan to source the sofa beds.

Reclining onto the hard rubber mattress rolled out on a concrete bench inside the cell, Alan debated which of Gus's cohorts was responsible for Ruby's murder. Deep down he knew it wouldn't have been Gus himself because he never got his hands dirty when others were willing to do it for him. Alan wasn't sure if Gus even availed himself of the services Ruby and her friends provided – he suspected he simply profited from them. Gus's profession, the day job that occupied his hours outside of being a governor, was accountancy, and Alan always got the impression that money trumped everything for him, even sex.

Poor Ruby, though. Alan had only spoken to her the once, when she'd arrived early at the Pavilion one night just as he was opening up. She seemed like a sweet kid, friendly and polite, if out of it, like she was on something. She'd mistaken him for her first punter and when he explained who he was, she said she could squeeze him in if he wanted, for mates' rates, on account of him knowing Gus. Her proposition horrified him and he said no. He hadn't slept with anyone since Gayle.

Really, whoever was behind Ruby's murder could be any man out of hundreds. Gus had boasted to him once about the number of clients his girls had, of the men queuing up to pay to sleep with them. From all walks of life they came, even community stalwarts who ran in the same circles as Gus, whose faces were familiar to readers of the *Echo* . . .

Alan sat up suddenly, remembering.

What was it Gus had said after he'd spoken to Gayle? Getting his ducks in a row. A councillor, business leaders, a police officer . . . and the star player of the local football team. Alan never went to matches but he knew the striker's name: Marky Gates. Playing for a top-table second-division side meant the player's involvement in a prostitution ring would make headlines.

He'd have to be clever about it, though.

He got up and banged on the door until the duty officer came to see what the fuss was about.

'I want my phone call now,' said Alan.

'Are you calling your solicitor?'

'No, a friend. I want to let them know I'm here.'

As Alan trailed the officer along the corridor, past identical cell doors, he remembered what Doug had said to him in The Wheatsheaf about making sure he had some insurance in place for when the shit hit the fan.

Well, the fan was spinning. This was his insurance.

He huddled over the phone so the duty officer couldn't hear.

'Gus, it's me, Alan.'

'Why are you whispering?'

'I'm at the police station. They want to question me about the body at the school.'

'Shit.'

'The thing is, I've heard them mention Marky Gates. I think they know about him.'

There was a drawn-out pause.

'Gus? You still there?'

'Yes, I'm thinking.'

'You need to get me out of here now. Ask that police officer you know to help.'

'I can't. He's been suspended.'

Alan's heart sank.

'But there is someone else I can try. Leave it with me.'

Twenty minutes later the duty officer was back at his cell door. Alan was free to go.

68

Maggie took Poppy and Julia straight to the ABE suite, where Belmar and another woman were already waiting for them. Her name was Ayse and, Belmar explained, she was a social worker who was going to be sitting in on the interview as an appropriate adult instead of her parents.

'No, I'm not having that,' said Julia. 'I should be with her.'

'I'm sorry, but we don't need your permission for this,' said Maggie firmly. 'You can wait outside until we're done.'

Julia tried to protest, but Maggie wouldn't budge. 'DC Small will show you where you can wait.'

As Julia left the room Poppy started crying as though her life depended on it.

'You think I'm guilty! That's why she's here,' she sobbed, pointing at Ayse.

Maggie handed the girl a tissue and tried to assuage her anxiety.

'Ayse is simply here to make sure you're okay while we have our chat with you.'

The child still looked terrified. 'Why can't my mum stay with me?'

Ayse answered before Maggie could. She knelt down next to Poppy's chair so they were on the same level. She had the kind of face you trusted immediately, with beguiling, deep-set brown eyes, and a wide, kind smile. Poppy seemed calmed by her friendliness, wiping her tears with the tissue as she listened.

'You know how sometimes you don't always want to say stuff in front of your parents, because they might not understand or get the wrong end of the stick? Well, that's why I'm here instead today,' Ayse explained. 'So you can talk freely without worrying about what they'll say. Your mum is just outside the room waiting for you. Answer the questions as quick and as fully as you can and then you can go and see her.'

Belmar returned and settled down on the sofa next to Maggie. He was more casually attired than normal, his preferred three-piece suit dispensed of presumably in deference to the warm weather.

Ayse sat with Poppy.

'We want to talk to you a bit more about how you got along with Benji, because I'm a little confused about it,' said Maggie. 'Are you okay to do that?'

Poppy looked to Ayse for reassurance and received an encouraging nod in return.

'I am,' she replied.

'That's great,' said Maggie warmly. She wanted Poppy to feel as though the interview was in her control, that she wasn't being strong-armed into talking. It was a strategy she and Belmar had agreed beforehand, as well as their line of questioning.

'We've been told you had a big fight with Benji at school two weeks ago. Is that right?'

Poppy hesitated for a moment, her gaze flitting to the door that separated her and her mum.

'We did.'

'What was the fight about?'

'Benji kept shoving me really hard and it hurt. When I told him to stop he started saying stuff and I got cross, so I whacked him. It wasn't hard.'

'Why was he shoving you in the first place?'

'He wanted me to listen to him but I was talking to someone else.'

'Listen about what?' asked Belmar.

Poppy shuffled awkwardly in her seat. 'I don't know.'

Maggie appraised the girl carefully and decided she did know: she just wasn't saying.

'Was it about something he'd seen in the school grounds, something that might've been shocking or scary?'

The head shake was too quick, too eager.

'No.'

'Poppy, on Saturday we found a body buried in the school grounds, close to where Benji fell. We're pretty certain he knew it was there. Did he say anything to you about it?'

Any pretence at playing it cool was lost as Poppy's mouth gaped open.

'He wasn't lying?'

'Benji had said something then?'

Poppy looked around wildly.

'I want my mum.'

'You can see her in a minute.'

'No, I want to see her now.'

She leapt to her feet and began screaming for Julia. Ayse tried to calm her but Poppy shrugged her off and ran to the door.

'Mum! Mum!'

Maggie went after her.

'Poppy, please sit down,' she urged, gently holding her shoulders. 'I'll go and get your mum now.'

Ayse took over and led a sobbing Poppy back to the sofa. Maggie darted out of the room where she found Julia almost hysterical with worry.

'What have you said to her? Why is she screaming like that?'

'Please, come in, she needs you.'

Julia elbowed past Maggie and raced across the ABE suite to Poppy, who wailed even louder as she fell into her mum's arms.

'Honey, what is it? What's upset you?'

Poppy was crying so hard that none of what she said made any sense. Julia kept shushing her and eventually her words became clearer. She was saying the same thing over and over, like a mantra.

'He wasn't lying. He wasn't lying. He wasn't lying . . .'

69

Maggie and Belmar went outside to give Julia and Poppy some space. Ayse stayed with them, a silent but comforting presence.

'Bloody hell,' said Belmar, clearly rattled. 'That was some scream.'

'Benji told her about the body,' said Maggie, trembling from the adrenaline spike Poppy's outburst had triggered. 'He told her and she didn't believe him.' She took a breath. 'I think she pushed him. I think she was telling him to shut up on the wall because she didn't believe him. Kids shove each other when they're annoyed. He'd got her out of bed early in the morning but when they got on the wall there was nothing to see and she thought he'd lied and so she shoved him. She didn't mean to kill him, but she did, I'm certain of it.'

'I think the same. So what do we do? Talk to Umpire about bringing charges?'

This, Maggie knew, was her first test as Acting DS. If they went to Umpire now Poppy's fate would be sealed, because there was cause for the CPS to recommend charging her with manslaughter on the grounds of gross negligence. Once the CPS was involved, Poppy was in the system.

Maggie stared up at her friend as she tried to think. However angry she'd been with him earlier, now she was grateful he was there. Belmar was the best partner she'd ever worked with and she trusted him to back her.

'Let's see if we can get her to admit it first,' she finally said.

'You mean give her a chance?'

'Yes. She's eleven years old and she's no Mary Bell. I want to make sure we've got this right.'

Belmar pulled a face at her mention of Bell, one of Britain's most notorious juvenile killers. Bell was the same age as Poppy when she was convicted in 1968 for murdering two boys, one three years old, the other four.

'No, Poppy's not. Bell's actions were far more savage,' he said. 'But . . .'

Maggie groaned. 'I know I'm not going to like this "but".'

'Mary Bell was also convicted of manslaughter and not murder. She successfully pleaded diminished responsibility because her mother was an alcoholic prostitute who tried to kill Bell as a baby, then let clients sexually abuse her for money from the age of four.'

'What are you getting at?'

'The jury believed the psychiatrist who testified in the trial that Bell had developed a psychopathic personality that impaired her mental responsibility. I'm not saying Julia's been exposing Poppy to similar depravity, but the social services file is very revealing about that episode on the viaduct. I went through it earlier,' he added.

'That happened when Poppy was *two*,' Maggie pointed

out. 'There's no way she'd remember it and, besides, what Julia did wasn't an act of violence but of desperation, brought on by PND.'

'What about since? The Facebook post said Poppy was most likely violent because of what was going on at home. For all we know the viaduct was the catalyst.'

'If we pursue this line we're saying we think Poppy meant to kill him.'

'I'll go along with whatever you think is right,' said Belmar.

She exhaled slowly. 'Let's go back in.'

70

Alan barely had the energy to turn the key in the lock, let alone push the front door open. He stumbled into the hallway, then collapsed on the bottom step of the staircase, too fatigued to move any further.

The enormity of his situation bore down on him like a ten-tonne weight. Whoever Gus had called to secure his quick release from police custody had to be someone high up, with clout. And now Alan was indebted to them as well as Gus.

It was seriously beginning to look as though running away might be his only option. He'd already done it once when he moved to Mansell and this time it'd be even less of a wrench because he wasn't leaving behind anyone he loved. He could start again in a new town, maybe somewhere coastal this time, get some fresh air in his tired, aching lungs. God knows they needed it.

Eventually he dragged himself off the bottom step and into the kitchen. He was starving, his last meal now hours ago. But on opening the fridge he remembered he still didn't have any food in the house. Could he be bothered to go out again? The gnawing hunger in his stomach convinced him he had to, so he trudged back down the hallway. But as he pulled open the front door to leave, he was jolted to find someone on the doorstep, knuckles poised to knock.

'I hope you don't mind me coming round unannounced,' said Mr Lincoln, the school's deputy head and not a person Alan ever expected to see on his doorstep, let alone in a social context. 'I heard that the police questioned you again today and I wanted to see how you were.'

'Did Mrs Pullman send you?'

'No, she doesn't know I'm here.'

Alan couldn't understand why Lincoln had taken it upon himself to come round. Unless –

'Did Gus Reynolds tell you?' he asked sharply.

Lincoln's expression instantly gave him away. Alan was stunned. He was one of them. He knew about the Pavilion.

The teacher tried to brazen it out.

'I happened to bump into him on my way home,' he said, 'so I thought I'd pop round to check you were okay.'

'You can see that I am, so, bye.'

Alan went to close the door, but Lincoln put his hand out to stop him.

'Mrs Pullman thinks really highly of you,' he said. 'I would hate to see her faith in you destroyed.'

'What's that supposed to mean?'

A look of utter desperation seized Lincoln's features.

'I'm sorry. I didn't come round here to threaten you. I'm at my wits' end. I only did it the once.'

'That's what they all say,' said Alan flintily. Lincoln had lorded it over him at every opportunity, yet all this time he was the real lowlife at Rushbrooke.

'It's true, I swear. Afterwards I knew what a terrible mistake I'd made, what I stood to lose if my wife found out, so I never went back. But if it comes out now, I'll be ruined. I'll lose her, my kids and my job.'

Alan wavered. He knew what it was like to wish you could turn back the clock and choose a different path, one that didn't hurt the people you loved and rob you of your self-respect.

'I came here to ask if you know what the police suspect. Please, I'm going out of my mind with worry.'

'I wasn't questioned in the end. They let me go. I don't know anything.'

Lincoln went grey. Alan decided to throw him a bone.

'Gus knows people high up in the police – that's why I wasn't questioned. Trust me, they're not going to let the truth about the Pavilion get out.'

Lincoln's posture went limp as he exhaled.

'That's good to know,' he said.

'Was it Gus who told you about it?'

Lincoln looked haunted for a moment.

'Yes, but not outright. He told me he was having a few after-hours drinks and did I want to join him and his friends. I didn't guess what the set-up was until it was too late, and then I was too weak and too pissed to say no. I can't believe I was so stupid.' He looked like he might cry. 'I want to tell the authorities what he's been doing, because of the girl they found, but I'm scared because of where it'll leave me.'

'I know that feeling. Look, do you want to come in and talk about it?' asked Alan companionably. 'I can only offer you water, mind. The milk's off and I was on my way to the Co-op when the police came for me again.'

Lincoln lifted up the carrier bag he was holding, the bottles it contained clinking as he did.

'I came prepared.'

71

It was soon apparent that Poppy was physically incapable of answering any more questions. She had stopped crying but was curled up against Julia on one of the sofas, her face buried into her shoulder, eyes tightly shut. She wouldn't look up despite Maggie and Belmar doing their gentle best to coax her and after half an hour of trying Maggie called time on their efforts.

'This isn't getting us anywhere,' she said to Belmar. 'I think we all need a break. Julia, can I get you a tea or coffee? What would Poppy like?'

'I'll have a tea please, milk, no sugar. Do you have any lemonade?'

Poppy suddenly raised her head.

'Really?'

Julia smiled at her. 'I think it's allowed today.'

'I wouldn't say no to a tea either,' said Ayse. 'I take mine the same.'

Maggie and Belmar left the ABE suite and as they went Julia felt the tension begin to seep from her limbs. Poppy uncurled herself and yawned.

'You tired, honey?'

The girl nodded and it alarmed Julia how awful she looked, her face puffy and red from all the crying.

'Hopefully we'll be able to get out of here soon and go home.'

Poppy's eyes widened with fear and she shook her head. 'Do we have to?'

'Go home? Of course we do. Where else would we go?'

'Can't we go and stay with Grandpa in Spain?'

'Poppy, that's a crazy idea. For one thing the police have asked us not to go too far from Mansell. I don't think they'll be happy with us going on holiday.'

'Not a holiday. For good.'

Julia was baffled. 'Poppy, what's all this about?'

'I don't want to stay here any more. This place is horrible. I hate it.'

Julia caught Ayse's eye and blushed.

'Sweetheart, we can't just move away from Mansell. Our jobs are here, our friends are here –' She stopped herself, fearing Ayse might think it was inappropriate for her to say that because one of Poppy's friends was now dead. 'What I mean is, moving away is not an option right now.'

Poppy slumped back in the chair and closed her eyes. Julia was at a loss what to say and was grateful when the door opened and Belmar and Maggie came in bearing their drinks.

'I need the toilet,' Poppy suddenly announced.

'So do I,' said Ayse. 'I know where the nearest one is, if you want to come with me?'

Poppy eyed her warily. 'I guess.'

'Mrs Hepworth, can I ask you something?' asked Maggie,

as the door shut behind them. 'It's a bit of a personal question but it does relate to Poppy.'

Julia was midway through swallowing a mouthful of tea and began to cough as it went down the wrong way. Maggie waited until her spluttering had eased, then raised an eyebrow expectantly at her.

'Yes, ask me,' she said.

'Does Poppy know about what happened on the viaduct?'

This time it was her breath that caught in her throat. Even though she'd known there was a good chance the police would find out and want to question her about it, hearing Maggie mention her past still rocked her to her core.

'Mrs Hepworth?'

'You can call me Julia,' she said, desperately scrabbling for the answer Maggie was waiting for.

'Okay, Julia. Does Poppy know what happened?'

'Yes, she does. My husband, he, um . . . well, he thought she should know.'

The reality was that Ewan used it as a stick to beat her with, or rather undermine her with. From Poppy's tantrums as a toddler to her pre-teen back-chatting, any behaviour their daughter exhibited that Ewan deemed unacceptable was because of what Julia did that day on the viaduct. Instead of castigating Poppy, he would tell their daughter it wasn't her fault because she couldn't help herself – Mummy was to blame, for exposing her to such awfulness at an early age.

She wasn't going to tell the police that though.

'Does she remember anything of what happened?' asked Maggie.

'I very much doubt it,' said Julia. 'I can barely remember it myself.'

She had the drugs to thank for that, the tranquillizers her doctor had prescribed to help her cope with PND but which turned her into a zombie incapable of rational thought. They made her think she had no other option, that jumping off the viaduct was the only thing that would save her and Poppy from the terrible dark cloud enveloping her. It was only weeks later, once she was out of hospital and weaned off the drugs, that she could comprehend what she'd done. So she didn't blame Ewan for being unable to forget – he was the one who had witnessed it, after all.

'I don't really see why you're asking me,' she said. 'It's got nothing to do with –' she waved her hand – 'all this.'

Maggie said nothing.

'How does Poppy get on with her brother?' asked Belmar. 'It's Dylan, isn't it?'

'Yes. They get on fine. Well, like siblings. One minute they adore each other, the next they're squabbling over the remote.'

'Has she ever hurt him?' asked Belmar.

Julia reared up like a lioness bearing her claws to protect her cubs.

'How dare you! I know what you're trying to suggest but you can forget it. Poppy doesn't hurt other children, especially not her brother.'

Neither officer responded: they simply sat there watching her. Julia's instinct was to fill the uncomfortable silence but the thought of saying the wrong thing kept her lips tightly shut.

Maggie checked her watch. It was a big, chunky one, more like a man's than a woman's.

'They've been ten minutes. I'm going to go and check on them.'

Julia watched Belmar as she sipped her tea. He was scribbling notes on a pad.

'Can I ask you something?' she ventured.

He looked up and smiled.

'Sure.'

'What will happen to Poppy, if . . . if she can't make you believe her?'

He looked uncomfortable. 'I don't know if I can—'

'Please,' she implored. 'I want to know.'

'Well, if we thought there was a case to answer we would formally charge her. Then there would be an initial court hearing to decide if she was eligible for bail.'

Julia was horrified. 'Why wouldn't she be?'

'Even children can be denied bail if the charge is serious,' said Belmar sombrely.

'What, you'd send an eleven-year-old to prison before they've stood trial?'

'No, no, she would be remanded into the care of the local authority. It's called youth detention accommodation.'

Julia felt sick to her stomach at the thought of Poppy being taken away from them.

'She didn't do it, I swear she didn't,' she said tearfully. 'You have to believe me—'

A commotion outside in the corridor cut her short. She could hear raised voices, then shouting.

Suddenly the door burst open and Ewan walked in

flanked by their solicitor, Darren. Maggie came after them, with Poppy and Ayse trailing close behind.

'How could you be so stupid?' Ewan yelled at her. 'You should never have let them interview Poppy without me or him here.'

Julia scrambled to her feet. 'I'm sorry, they said we had to come.'

'God, you are such an idiot,' he sneered.

Maggie put herself between the couple.

'Mr Hepworth, you need to calm down.'

He looked incredulous. 'You can't tell me how to talk to my wife.'

'Ewan, let me deal with this,' said Darren hastily. 'Did you interview Poppy under caution?' he asked Maggie.

'No, she is here as a material witness.'

'Do you have any further questions for her?'

Julia could see Maggie hesitate. 'Not right now, no.'

'Then my client will be exercising her right to leave.'

Maggie nodded, but Julia could tell she wasn't happy.

'Right, let's go home,' said Ewan, shooting Julia a look that made her cringe. 'Come on, honey,' he said, holding a hand out to Poppy.

'No!'

Everyone looked at her with surprise.

'I don't want to go with you,' she said, scuttling over to Julia and taking her hand.

Julia was stunned. She couldn't remember the last time Poppy had chosen to go with her over Ewan. Judging by his expression, neither could he.

72

Anyone observing Maggie and Umpire's exchanges during the final briefing of the day who didn't know them would never have guessed they were even friendly, let alone a couple. They were the epitome of icy professionalism, trading information in clipped comments that belied their feelings for one another.

Maggie wasn't sure how much longer she could keep it up though. The intense anger she'd felt earlier had waned to mild irritation and she found that, contrary to her expectations, she hadn't minded her first day as Acting DS. If nothing else it had been good to work with Belmar again, even if they hadn't got much further with Poppy. Now, with the end of her shift in sight, there was nothing she wanted more than to head to the nearest pub garden with Umpire, order herself a large glass of chilled white wine and enjoy the last of the heatwave.

Umpire, however, had other ideas, as he concluded the briefing with details of a number of arrests the team were to make first thing in the morning.

'The majority of numbers in Violet Castle's book have turned out to be for burner phones – those clients were clever enough not to use their registered mobiles to arrange to see her.'

Unlike ACC Bailey, thought Maggie. She wondered why it had never occurred to him to cover his tracks more.

'So we've concentrated on tracing the clients who were that stupid,' Umpire added, 'and those are the ones we'll be picking up. We're struggling to build a timeline of Violet's movements before her death and these men might be able to help . . .'

Maggie's heart sank as he began detailing which officers would be covering the arrests. The operation put paid to them having a night out: Umpire wouldn't want a late night with the arrests happening as the sun went up. It'd have to be tea, telly, then bed.

But Umpire had other ideas about that too.

Briefing over and the team dispersed, he called her to the front of the room.

'Well done for today.'

'I didn't get Poppy to confess to pushing Benji, though,' she said. 'But I think I can: it was obvious to me and Belmar that she knew Benji had seen the body. We just need to keep up the pressure.' She paused. 'Unless you think we have enough to go on to convince the CPS to bring charges?'

'I think the gentle approach is better. Bring her back in tomorrow morning, but make sure this time her solicitor sits in.'

'I will. What time will you be finished here? I want to pop round to see Imogen on my way home.'

Umpire crossed his arms and Maggie started when she saw he was annoyed.

'What's that look for?' she asked.

'You're not Imogen's FLO so you don't need to go round to check on her in person. That's why I brought in Hazel.'

Maggie bristled, her anger of earlier rearing back up. 'But I want to.'

'You need to focus on the job I've given you,' he said sternly.

That did it.

'A job I didn't want,' she hissed, lowering her voice so the others couldn't hear. 'You know how much I love being a FLO but you've forced me to give it up.'

'It's one case. You're overreacting,' he said, his voice dropping to match her volume.

'That's not the point. This is about you deciding what's best for me and me having no say in it. I don't like being manipulated. How would you like it if I made decisions that affected your career without consulting you? You didn't even tell me you were coming in as SIO.'

'There wasn't time.'

'Bollocks,' said Maggie, heat rising in her cheeks. 'You could've texted me.'

'Okay, I should've let you know, but funnily enough I was too occupied with taking over the investigation into a young woman's murder that one of my friends has been implicated in.'

Maggie felt a twinge of guilt. It was a plausible excuse: his friendship with Bailey had been important to him.

'Let's talk about it at home,' she said.

Umpire looked sheepish.

'I've booked into a hotel.'

'Are you serious?'

'I've got a lot to get through before tomorrow.'

Maggie was determined not to show how upset she was. 'Yes, that's sensible.'

'You don't mind?'

'Why would I?' She tried to sound nonchalant, but inside she was fuming at the rejection. 'I'm going to head off now, unless you need me for anything else?'

He smiled and she hated the effect he had on her. She wasn't ready to let go of her anger.

'No, you can go. I'll call you later.'

She walked away, not answering.

Her flat occupied the top floor of a four-storey Victorian house. The flat below hers was spread over the first and ground floors, while the bottom flat was in the basement, accessed down a small set of wrought-iron stairs. Maggie didn't know the owner of the bottom flat – it was a man, living alone, that much she had worked out – so she never paid much attention when she walked up the steps to the main front door.

Today she did.

Sitting halfway down the metal steps, huddled over as though he was cold was a rangy young man. He appeared agitated and upset, was possibly even crying.

Maggie faltered.

'Are you okay?'

The young man's head snapped up and Maggie saw instantly he was actually a teenager. Then she gasped.

'Jude?'

He clambered to his feet and rushed up the steps to her, almost sending her flying in his eagerness to hug her.

'Whoa, whoa, Jude, calm down,' she laughed. She gently pushed her nephew away and held him at arm's length. In seven months he'd shot up by inches and the soft edges of his childhood were melting away to reveal a sharp, adolescent bone structure that he'd inherited from Lou. But everything else about him – his skin tone, his nose, his eyes – was Jerome's.

'Jude, what on earth are you doing here?'

His eyes filled with tears but she could see from his expression they were the product of anger, not sorrow.

'I can't stay there any more,' he said through clenched teeth. 'I want to live with you. Please don't send me back.'

73

The story came tumbling out as they sat together on the sofa, arms entwined. Maggie wanted to drink in every moment of being with her nephew because she knew, once the conversation ended, she had no choice but to call Lou and let her know Jude had run away to Mansell.

But first she listened.

'We stayed with Nana and Granddad for about a month, so we could get into a school near them. Then I think Granddad gave Mum the money so we could get our own flat. It's about a five-minute walk from theirs so at first we saw them all the time. They'd get Scotty from school and helped Mum with Mae.'

'At first?'

A shadow crossed Jude's face.

'Before Terry.'

'That's your mum's new partner?'

'Fiancé.'

Maggie couldn't hide her disappointment.

'She's marrying him? How long have they been together?'

'Three months. I hate him. He shouts at us and tells us

what to do.' Jude slammed his fist down on the sofa in frustration. 'I don't want him to be my new fucking dad.'

'Whoa, mister, I know you're upset but it's not okay to swear like that.'

Jude's eyes glistened with tears.

'Can I please come and live here? Please, Auntie Maggie.'

'You know your mum isn't going to let that happen. Whatever else she's done she loves you with all her heart. Have you told her how you feel about Terry?'

'I've tried, but you know what Mum's like when she meets a new bloke. Nothing else matters.'

Maggie understood. For years she'd watched a revolving door of men come in and out of her sister's life and saw how the first flush of passion always turned Lou into a giddy, distracted mess. When the children were younger it didn't seem to trouble them so much, plus she had been there to step in and make sure they weren't neglected. But the toll of this latest relationship was evident now on Jude's pinched, tear-streaked face.

'Has Terry ever got physical with you?' she asked.

'No, but he threatens it all the time. He raises his fist like he's going to hit us, so we'll get scared. He's even done it to Mae.'

Anger coursed through her.

'Why doesn't your mum stop him?'

'He does it when she's not there.'

'Have you told Nana and Granddad?'

'We hardly see them now. They don't like Terry either and Mum says until they're nice to him they're not welcome at ours. I want to see them but I'm worried what Mum will say. We talk on the phone, though.'

Maggie was frustrated her parents hadn't contacted her for help and she wondered if it was their pride stopping them. They'd whisked Lou down to the south coast in the hope of rebuilding their oft-fraught relationship with her but in a matter of months it had soured again.

For now, though, she needed to focus on practical matters.

'Does anyone know you've run away to Mansell? Did you leave a note?'

Jude looked puzzled. 'I haven't run away. We've been here all weekend and I didn't want to go back so I came here. Mum thinks I'm at Toby's house, saying bye.'

Maggie reeled at his comment.

'You've been here, in Mansell, this weekend?'

'Yeah, we came up to see our friends. Mum's kept us off school today so we could stay an extra day.'

Maggie didn't want Jude to see how hurt she was but failed miserably.

'Auntie Maggie, why are you getting upset?'

'I miss you guys so much and I can't believe you've been round the corner this whole time and I didn't know. Are Scotty and Mae here too?'

'Yeah, they're with Mum.'

'Is this the first time you've been back?'

Jude looked sheepish. 'No.'

Maggie thought being estranged from her family was painful enough, but this was something else, like a punch to her guts with a sledgehammer.

'Where's your mum right now?'

'Denise's.'

'What, that woman she worked with years ago? I didn't know they were friends still.'

Jude shrugged. 'That's where we've been.'

Maggie weighed up what to do. If she agreed to let Jude stay even for one night Lou would go mental. But if she rejected his request, when would she get to see him again? It could be years.

But, ultimately, she had to do what was right.

'I need to tell your mum that you're here.'

Jude was crestfallen. 'Really?'

'I'm afraid so. I know it's not the answer you want, but she's your parent and I'm not. As much as I'd love you to stay with me, I can't decide where you live.' She held out her hand. 'Give me your phone. I don't have her new number so I can't call her from mine.'

'If she comes to get me maybe you two can make things up.'

'I would like nothing more,' said Maggie, 'but it's up to your mum.'

'Did you love my dad?'

The question was so unexpected that she fumbled the phone and dropped it into her lap.

'I – well, I don't –'

'Did you or didn't you?'

She studied his face, which was so like his father's, especially his eyes. For a second she closed hers, remembering. When she opened them again she smiled.

'I loved him very much. He was my first love.' She hesitated; there was only so much detail she should burden her nephew with. 'What I did was wrong, so wrong. I should never have gone behind your mum's back like that, nor should your dad. The thing is, he loved us both. He was so excited about being a dad and starting a family with your mum. With me it was –' she let out a huge sigh, her body loosening cathartically – 'different. He wasn't a bad man. He just couldn't decide between us.'

Jude nodded but Maggie could see he was getting upset again.

'Let me ring your mum.'

Lou picked up immediately.

'Where the hell are you? I'm outside Toby's and he's saying he hasn't seen you all afternoon. The car's packed and ready to go.'

'Lou, it's Maggie.'

The silence was deafening, so Maggie spoke quickly to fill it.

'I got home from work to find Jude on my doorstep. He's here with me now.'

'Let me talk to him.'

That was it. The full sum of what her sister was prepared to say to her. Maggie handed the mobile to Jude.

From the squawking she could hear as he spoke to his mum Maggie could tell Lou was apoplectic with rage. Jude, on the other hand, said nothing, letting the tirade wash over him.

Then he put his hand over the receiver.

'She wants me to walk into the town centre so she can pick me up.'

Nearly fourteen, Jude was perfectly able to get himself to their meeting point – the walk would only take him a few minutes. But that would let Lou off the hook and, even though she might not care what she thought, Maggie felt a duty to warn her about her new fiancé.

'Tell her I'm not letting you leave. She needs to come and get you.'

Jude relayed the message and the squawking got louder. Then he passed the phone over.

'She wants to talk to you.'

Maggie's hand trembled as she held the device to her ear. Regularly in her job she came up against people who were aggressive and behaved alarmingly but none of them ever intimidated her as much as Lou did when she was angry.

Yet to her surprise, Lou didn't let rip.

'I've got to get Mae in the car, then we'll come round to get him.'

'Oh, okay. See you in a bit.'

Ten minutes later Lou, Scotty and Mae ascended the three flights to her flat. Scotty threw himself at her with the same enthusiasm Jude had but Mae, now walking confidently, hid behind her mother's legs. It killed Maggie that she didn't seem to recognize her.

'She's grown up so much in a few months,' she smiled, unable to take her eyes off the little blonde girl.

'You look tired,' said Lou.

Their eyes met and it took every ounce of Maggie's self-control not to burst into tears and beg her for forgiveness. But she'd already done that seven months ago and it didn't work then and, knowing her sister, it wouldn't now. When Lou put her mind to something she was as stubborn as a grass stain on silk.

'I'm fine. How are you?'

Jude and Scotty watched the awkward exchange with furrowed brows. It must've been as strange to them to see the sisters talk so stiltedly to one another as it was to Maggie.

'Good. We like living by the sea, don't we, Mae?'

Maggie's niece peeped out from behind Lou's legs, then shot back again.

Seaside life did seem to suit Lou. Her hair, previously in a bob and dyed bright red, was now cropped short and back to its natural blonde, and her face was softer, her skin plumped with rude health. She looked younger, fitter and markedly less weary.

'How are Mum and Dad?' asked Maggie.

'Oh, you know, the usual.'

A wry look of understanding passed between them briefly, the familiarity of which made Maggie ache with sadness.

'We have to go,' Lou said to Jude. 'It's a long drive.'

'I don't want to,' he said, exhibiting the same stubborn streak as hers.

'Me neither,' said Scotty. 'I want to live in Mansell.'

'This isn't your home any more,' said Lou.

'I'm not going back!' yelled Jude.

In the row that ensued no one noticed Mae step out from behind Lou and shuffle across to Maggie. The first she realized was when she felt a tiny hand in hers.

'Oh, hello, sweetheart,' she said, smiling down at Mae. 'Do you remember me now?' She crouched down and the little girl beamed at her.

'Aun-tay Maggie!' she giggled.

'Jude, enough, we're going,' said Lou.

Maggie decided she had to say something, even if it made Lou even angrier with her.

'Jude's worried about your fiancé. He's been threatening to hit him. Scotty and Mae too, by the sound of things.'

Lou's eyes narrowed. Maggie braced for the onslaught her interference was bound to provoke but instead her sister turned to her kids.

'Is that true?' The boys nodded. 'Why didn't you tell me?'

'Because we didn't want you to be sad again,' said Scotty in a small voice. 'You were really sad before Terry came to live with us.'

A huge pregnant pause filled the room before Lou punctured it.

'I like Terry a lot but not as much as I love you three. If that's what he's been doing, he can pack his bags and do one.'

Maggie's surprise must've shown. Lou glared at her.

'What? You don't think I'd put my kids before a bloke? Been there, done that and I'll never do it again.'

'You're a great mum,' said Maggie softly. 'No one could love them more.'

Now it was Lou's turn to be flustered. 'Um . . . thanks. Right, come on, kids.'

'Mum, can we come and see Auntie Maggie again, please?' Scotty begged.

'Aun-tay Maggie!' said Mae, clapping her hands in delight.

'Yeah, I wanna see her,' said Jude, sticking his chin out defiantly.

Maggie could tell Lou was feeling hemmed in but didn't

want to say no in front of the kids. 'Maybe next time you're up,' she fibbed.

'Actually, yeah, we could sort something,' said Lou. 'Just because you and me aren't – well, there's no reason the kids can't see you. I could drop them round.'

'Can we come and stay for a whole weekend?' asked Scott excitedly.

Maggie laughed and gave him a cuddle. 'One visit at a time, eh.' She gave her sister a searching look. 'Do you mean it?'

Lou's eyes met hers and they glistened with unshed tears. 'Yeah, I do.'

74

Tuesday

Mrs Pullman had offered to let Poppy come into school via a side entrance used exclusively by staff. Julia was concerned that skulking in would make people think they were ashamed or had something to hide, but Ewan felt it showed the school was fully supportive of their daughter – and them – and overruled her. But as they entered the playground Julia's legs threatened to give way on her and suddenly she was grateful they didn't need to hang around. The looks being thrown their way as they moved steadily towards the side entrance ranged from curiosity to outright hostility.

In her peripheral vision she spotted Siobhan standing with a group of mums that included Tess, the one who loved to gossip. She'd be having a field day with this.

Poppy suddenly stopped.

'I don't want to go inside,' she said morosely. 'Why can't I stay out here until the bell goes and our teacher comes, like I always do?'

'Mrs Pullman said it was probably best if you went straight inside today,' said Ewan. 'Come on, you don't want to be late.'

Poppy dropped her rucksack on the ground in protest.

Julia's face burned red, acutely aware of the audience they were attracting.

'Please, darling, don't be difficult,' she said in a low voice.

'I want to stay out here with my friends,' she whined.

While Julia and Ewan tried to placate and cajole Poppy, they didn't notice someone approaching them.

'Hi. It's good to see you all.'

Julia turned to face Siobhan. To her astonishment the mum stepped forward and hugged her.

'I'm sorry I was so hard on you the other day,' she said as she pulled away. 'I should've been more understanding. I can see how tough this has been on you all.'

'Thanks. It's nice to see a friendly face,' said Ewan.

Julia was grateful she hadn't told him about her confrontation with Siobhan: he wouldn't have been half as receptive to her apology had he known about it.

'Right, let's get inside,' said Ewan.

Siobhan was puzzled. 'Aren't you waiting in the line?'

'The head thinks we shouldn't.'

'That's ridiculous,' said Siobhan. 'Poppy, isn't that your friend Samira over there? Why don't you go and wait with her?'

Julia glanced warily at Ewan, who didn't seem happy at being undermined but wasn't about to cause another row.

'I guess there's no harm,' he said.

Poppy skipped off to join her friends, who greeted her as normal with giggles and smiles.

Julia didn't fully relax until the bell went and the children were indoors, but she had to admit it hadn't been half as bad as she'd feared.

Her happiness lasted until they got back to their car –

and found a sullen-faced DS Renshaw leaning against its bonnet, her arms folded. Julia's pulse spiked.

Now what?

'How did drop-off go?' the detective asked, no trace of warmth in her voice.

'Fine,' said Ewan tersely. 'Can I ask why you're here?'

'Just checking up.'

'You couldn't wait until we were home?' said Julia as a line of parents passed them on the way to their own vehicles.

'How's Poppy?'

'She'll be doing a lot better when you lot leave her alone. This is harassment. I'm calling our solicitor.' Ewan went to get his phone, then stopped. 'Hang on, you're not even working on the case any more.'

Renshaw's expression shifted, apprehension replacing the belligerence.

'When I got to the station yesterday to collect Poppy I asked for you on the front desk and they said you were on indefinite leave and off the case,' said Ewan. 'So why the hell are you here now giving us grief?'

'Poppy needs to answer for what she did,' said Renshaw falteringly. 'A violent act has been committed and needs to be investigated.'

'But not by you,' sneered Ewan.

Renshaw had no comeback for that and moved out of the way to let them get in the car. As they drove off Julia peered in the wing mirror and saw her watching them, arms still folded, face still fixed in a frown.

75

Maggie was running late. Four cars had rear-ended in the middle of a roundabout junction that even on the calmest days was a nightmare to negotiate and now the traffic was backed up in three directions. She gave it twenty minutes in the hope that the traffic would shift before calling Umpire to let him know she was stuck.

'There's no briefing until later so you're fine. We detained four of Violet Castle's clients for questioning this morning and I want statements from them first. In fact, I'd rather you went round to have a word with Benji Tyler's mum instead of coming here,' he said.

Maggie was confused. 'Yesterday you told me to keep my distance.'

'That was before she got herself plastered all over the Internet.'

Maggie's stomach plummeted to her feet. '*What?*'

'She gave the *Echo* an exclusive interview for their website that's already been picked up by the *Mail*, the *Mirror* and the BBC. Would you like to know what the headline is?'

Maggie didn't, sensing how bad it was, but Umpire enlightened her regardless.

'It's "Why won't they arrest my son's killer?" next to a fetching picture of Imogen holding up Benji's school photograph and clutching a sodden tissue. Goes right for the heart strings.'

Maggie slammed the heel of her hand against the steering wheel. Fucking Jennifer Jones. And bloody Grace, pushing her agenda.

'I'm sorry, we should've known.'

'Yes, you bloody well should.'

She knew Umpire was bollocking her as her boss, not her boyfriend, but she still found it uncomfortable. Likewise, she wanted to tell him about Jude turning up yesterday and how happy she was that Lou was going to let her see the children, but felt it inappropriate to mention when he was briefing her as SIO.

'What does she say in the interview?'

'Someone informed her that Rushbrooke was reopening today and Poppy was being allowed back, so she thinks it's disgraceful the child involved in her son's death is being given free rein by us to continue her life.'

'I can't believe the *Echo* has named Poppy,' said Maggie.

A horn tooted behind her and she inched her car forward as a small gap appeared between her bumper and the one in front.

'It hasn't, and it's been careful not to mention her gender either – it describes her as "the child" or "them". Then there's loads of guff about Imogen's grief.'

'Don't call it guff, Will – she *is* devastated.'

'I know, but I wish she'd kept it to herself.'

This was why Umpire didn't get family liaison. His focus was always more on the offender than the victim and it meant he sometimes lacked empathy when their relatives got in the way of him investigating. He would view the *Echo* report as a spanner in his works rather than a grieving mother venting in frustration.

'The Chief Constable wants an explanation as to why we didn't know.'

Maggie bit back the answer she wanted to give: that had she still been their FLO she might've got wind and put a stop to it, because she had a far better idea of what Grace was like than Carmichael did after only twenty-four hours on the job.

'I can't even think when she could've done the interview,' she mused.

'Carmichael says it must've been yesterday evening, after she'd clocked off.'

'I categorically told Imogen and her mum that we should handle the press because we didn't want it to impede the investigation.'

'Well, it's certainly done that. We're going to be under huge pressure from the media and public now to show that we're taking Benji's death seriously. We need a result, Maggie.'

'What have you decided about the second post-mortem?'

'You said yesterday that you thought Poppy was close to confessing. I want you to have another crack at her first. If we can avoid the PM, we should. I can only imagine what his mum would say to the press if we forced that on her.'

'I'll have to get Poppy from Rushbrooke if she's gone back today,' said Maggie.

Umpire paused. 'While it's tempting to think that frog-marching her out in front of her classmates might shock her into talking, I think you should speak to her parents first and get them to collect her. Their solicitor's just been on to complain about the *Echo* story and also about Renshaw harassing them and I don't want to rattle his cage again.'

Maggie's hands tightened on the steering wheel. 'Anna's been harassing them? When?'

'Outside the school just now. I don't know what the hell she was playing at. She's not answering her phone.'

'She hasn't answered any of the texts I've sent to see how she's doing either,' said Maggie, concerned.

'Keep trying. I like Anna, she's a good officer, but she's going to land herself in serious trouble if she interferes in the investigation when she's meant to be on leave. Right, you need to get round to Imogen's and do some damage limitation before she talks to anyone else. If the Chief Constable sees her popping up on the bloody news we'll be back in uniform before the lunchtime bulletin.'

76

Alan had planned to spend the morning in his basement cocoon on the pretext of catching up with paperwork, but Mrs Pullen insisted every member of staff currently on site be present for assembly. School attendance might be skeletal with the lower years elsewhere, but those remaining were required to present a united front.

This she'd announced in a hastily arranged meeting in the staffroom before the children arrived, when she'd also relayed the news that the police investigation was, for the time being, focusing away from the school and on the construction firm behind the new classrooms. Alan caught Mr Lincoln's eye and they traded grim but relieved smiles.

Alan left the meeting already thinking about the next thing on his to-do list, which was to check a faulty water fountain in the playground, and as a consequence he almost didn't notice her until they were level.

Poppy Hepworth.

He pressed his back against the wall as the class streamed past, hoping she wouldn't notice him. Why hadn't anyone warned him she'd be back at school today? Yet her appearance pulled him up short: she looked miserable, her head bent low so her hair fell over her face to partly obscure it. She wasn't walking with her friends either, but was tailing them at the back of the queue.

Alan's chest tightened. Had something happened? Their fates were intrinsically linked and if she'd had bad news, should he be braced for the same?

She was about to pass him when she suddenly looked up and her eyes locked on his. In that moment it was as though everyone and everything around them had melted away, the clamour of excited children and their clumping footsteps quieting to nothing. Alan tried to back away, but it was as though her stare was sucking him in, welding him to the secret they shared.

Then she smiled and said hello.

77

She hung back as her friends headed towards their class-room, until it was only the two of them left in the corridor.

'You'll be late for the register,' said Alan feebly.

Poppy shrugged, but didn't say anything. She hitched her rucksack from one shoulder to the other and rage burned through him. How could she stand there pretending like nothing was wrong?

'What do you want?' he snarled.

She blinked and to his surprise he saw she was close to tears. Suddenly he imagined Gayle's voice in his head, chiding him. *She's only eleven, Alan,* he heard his ex-wife say. *Remember when Lacey was that age? Full of bravado and pre-adolescent arrogance when really she was still just a scared little girl.* But he shook his head to dispel the voice. This wasn't the same: Lacey would never do what Poppy had done.

'I don't know what to do,' she said, her voice small and tight.

'How's that any concern of mine?'

'Because I know you saw what I did.'

Alan held his breath, stunned.

'Why haven't you said?' she asked.

He couldn't answer. The shock of her confessing had rendered him mute.

Poppy bit down hard on her bottom lip. He could see the skin was already scabbed and swollen as she drew fresh blood.

'Is it because you know?'

'Know what?' he croaked.

'About the bad men coming into the school at night.' Poppy looked quickly up and down the corridor to check no one was coming. 'Benji *knew*,' she whispered. 'He saw –' she choked back a sob – 'there were bad men inside the school and he saw them and he told me.'

'I don't know what you're going on about,' said Alan, his guts twisting in fear. 'You need to get to your class now, before we both end up in trouble.' He began to back away from her but she followed him.

'I didn't mean to push him,' she said, openly crying now. 'It wasn't my fault. It was because of the bad men.'

Alan put his hand out to stop her but lost his footing so he ended up slumped halfway down the wall as she loomed over him.

'Please don't tell me anything else,' he said, almost crying too now.

Poppy's eyebrows knitted and her mouth formed a perfect 'o'.

'No!' she exclaimed, her hand fluttering to her chest. 'You're one of them too. You're one of the bad men.'

Then she turned and ran for the door.

78

Imogen was unrepentant about the *Echo* piece but Maggie couldn't tell if she genuinely felt that way or if her show of defiance was down to the towering presence of Grace. She certainly had no regrets about her daughter doing it.

'She has every right to talk to the press,' she said snappily. 'If you were doing your jobs properly she wouldn't have had to.'

'The piece accuses Poppy Hepworth of being a killer when we haven't even charged her or come close to it,' Maggie admonished, while Carmichael stood beside her in a show of unity. Maggie had assured the FLO it wasn't her fault the Tylers had gone against advice by doing an interview but she felt responsible nonetheless.

'They haven't said it was her,' Grace huffed.

Maggie ignored her and directed the rest of her rebuke at Imogen.

'We know how devastated you are about Benji dying and how much you want answers, and we're all working really hard to get them for you. But you need to understand how difficult this will make things now. Anyone connected with Rushbrooke will know the child referred to in the interview is Poppy and they'll probably tell everyone they know, who will then pass it on to everyone they know, and so on, until her name is public knowledge. If she is charged with causing Benji's death, her lawyers may try to argue she won't get a fair trial because everyone will have pre-judged her.'

Imogen's eyes flickered away from Maggie's face to Carmichael's.

'Hazel?'

'I would have cautioned you against proceeding with the interview had I known,' she said solemnly.

Imogen looked mortified. 'I'm sorry—'

'Don't you dare apologize,' shrieked Grace, spittle flying from her tongue as she thrust her face into her daughter's. 'This is about getting justice for my grandson. That girl needs to pay for what she's done. We will not let that family win, not this time.'

Imogen's eyes widened and she shook her head at Grace, who caught herself and stopped. She sat down next to her daughter, breathing heavily from her outburst.

Maggie stared at them both, riveted.

'What do you mean by that?' she asked Grace.

'It doesn't matter.'

'If there is some other history between your families that might have had a bearing on what's happened we need to know about it,' said Carmichael.

'It's none of your business.'

Maggie decided the only way to get through to Grace was to be as forthright as she was.

'I would hate to have to arrest you for obstructing the course of justice,' she said, 'but I will if that's what you're doing.'

Imogen gasped. 'Mum, please tell them. I don't want you to get into trouble.'

Grace was beside herself with anger.

'I do not have to explain myself to you.'

Maggie went to speak but Carmichael put a hand on her arm to stop her.

'Grace, if this is something that might help us with our investigation, it makes no sense for you not to tell us. It goes against everything you've been saying about wanting to help us solve Benji's death,' said the FLO.

Carmichael's words were wise and delivered calmly and with kindness – the way Maggie knew she should've spoken to Grace. With a start she realized she didn't want to be a DS if it meant she lost that part of herself.

Imogen squeezed her mum's hand.

'I've told you, there's nothing for you to be embarrassed about.' She raised her eyes to meet Maggie's. 'Something else did happen involving our families. Mum wanted to tell you but I said no, because I'd already lied to you about remembering Julia.' Imogen faltered. 'I remember exactly who she is and what she accused me of doing in the past is sort of true.'

'You did bully her at school?'

'I'll admit I gave her a hard time.'

'Why lie about it?'

'I didn't want you to feel sorry for her and not feel sorry for Benji.' Imogen flared up suddenly. 'It's pathetic she's playing the victim card after all this time. All this "woe is me" when I'm the one suffering. She should grow up.'

Evidently Imogen's feelings towards her old classmate

were still as brittle as Julia's were towards her. Maggie wasn't interested in discussing that though.

'What did you mean about your family winning this time, Grace? What happened previously when you "lost"?'

Mother and daughter shared a loaded look, then Imogen took a deep breath.

'Well, it's more about Julia's mum. She was a horrible, horrible woman and she ruined our lives – mine, Mum's and Ed's.'

'How?'

Grace cleared her throat. 'She stole my husband, that's how.'

79

Alan stumbled after Poppy but his legs were weak with shock and by the time he got into the playground she'd vanished. Thinking she was hiding, he looked in the obvious places but she wasn't in any of them. She must've left the school grounds.

He held his head in despair. Benji hadn't died because he and Poppy had been mucking about on the wall – it was because of Gus and the Pavilion. And *he* had made it happen. That boy's blood was on his hands.

He pulled his phone out of his pocket and called Gus. It went straight to voicemail so he left a message.

'It's me. It's as bad as it gets. The kids *knew*.'

He didn't want to say anything more damning and hoped Gus would be able to decipher the meaning behind his message. If anyone else heard it, he'd explain it away by saying he was talking about his kids.

Hanging up, he had no idea what to do next. Telling the police what Poppy had said would mean admitting everything. He wasn't ready to do that, but it was only a matter of time before Poppy mentioned 'the bad men' to the police. Whichever way he looked at it, he was in serious shit.

He wished he could talk to Gayle about it. Before their split, before the damage had set in like dry rot, they'd talked about everything and anything. She was great at dispensing advice and always knew the right thing to say. Alan was the worrier, she the pragmatist.

God, he missed her.

Before he could talk himself out of it, he called her number. His heart skipped a beat as she picked up after only two rings.

'What do you want, Alan?'

She didn't sound angry, though, more resigned. The sound of her voice made his own stall in his throat.

'Alan?'

'I'm here,' he managed to say.

'What's going on? Aren't you at work?'

'I am.'

Shit, he wished he'd planned what he was going to say before he called. He sounded like an idiot.

'Okay, so why the call?'

He gazed across the playing field, where the charred remains of the Pavilion taunted him.

'Have you ever done something you regretted so much you'd do anything to put it right?' he asked her softly.

'*You're* asking *me* that?'

'I didn't mean about us,' he said quickly. 'This is about something else.'

'Right. Well, I guess it depended on whether it was too late to do something about it.'

'No, it can still be put right.'

'Then of course, you should do whatever needs doing.'

To his mortification he began to weep. He couldn't stop himself.

'I wish I could take back what I did to you and the kids.'

'Please don't cry,' she said, her voice softening. 'I know you're having a rough time, but things will calm down soon. Look, I have to go now, my supervisor's calling me back inside. I'm working at that cash-and-carry on the Stockdale Road. Remember it?'

'That's where we stocked up for the New Year's Eve party after Kyra was born.'

'When my mum started doing shots with your mate Clive and fell into the bath when she was meant to be going to the loo because she couldn't see straight.'

They both laughed at the memory, but Alan's insides were gripped by misery. He wanted his old life back, with Gayle and the kids, back in Newark.

'Gayle, I feel like I'm drowning.'

'You should talk to someone. The school should arrange it,' she said. 'They have a duty of care.'

'But I want to talk to you. We used to talk about everything.'

He heard the awkwardness in her voice and it hurt so much to.

'That was a long time ago, Alan. We've both moved on.'

'I haven't. I'm stuck here in this town where I don't know anyone and I'm in trouble up to my neck and I can't see a way out.'

'What do you mean, you're in trouble? What's going on, Alan? What have you done?'

'I just want it all to end.'

'What does that mean?' she asked worriedly.

The bell sounded to signal assembly.

'I've got to go,' he said. 'Tell the kids I love them and I'm sorry for hurting them.'

He hung up before she could reply. When she called back a second later, he let it ring.

80

Maggie and Carmichael took the seats Imogen offered them as Grace began to talk. Her voice was faltering at first but growing firmer as her account progressed.

'My husband, Ray, was one of those men who didn't know how attractive he was. He was a bit dim when it came to things like that. I used to say the only reason he married me was because I literally had to make him fall for me – he'd be in the Legion when I went with my dad on a Friday night but he never noticed me. So one evening when he walked past I stuck my foot out to trip him up: we got talking and that was that.'

Imogen smiled but Grace remained stony-faced.

'I never minded other women flirting with him because he never reciprocated. Most of the time Ray ran a mile. That all changed when he met Ruth Hepworth.' Grace sucked in a breath to steady herself. 'I can't remember what the occasion was – it might've been a school dance or a bingo night – but I remember how she was with him, constantly touching his arm, laughing at his jokes when they weren't even funny. As I said, normally I would laugh it off, but I knew she was trouble. I could see it in his eyes. I *knew*.'

'When did the affair begin?' asked Carmichael.

'I couldn't say for sure, but it was soon afterwards. Oh, the signs were all there: it was like he'd read some kind of manual for cheating husbands. New haircut, different after-shave, excuses about working late. He must've thought I was an idiot.'

'Me and Ed knew something was up,' said Imogen. 'It was like Dad just checked out of the family. Even when he was at home he wasn't really here, if you know what I mean.'

'It must've been a hard time for you all,' said Maggie sympathetically.

'No, it was after that things were hard,' said Grace. 'After he left.'

'They got together?' asked Maggie, the implications of what Grace was telling them racing around her mind and slotting together like a jigsaw to produce a picture she wished they'd known about sooner.

'Yes. She left her family and he left his. They rented a flat in town but it didn't last. From what I gathered, her husband gave her an ultimatum and she returned home after three months.'

From the sharp way in which Grace imparted that particular nugget of information, Maggie guessed her marriage didn't work out in the same way.

'You and your husband never reconciled,' she stated.

'Ray was heartbroken when she went back to her husband. He said she was the love of his life.' As Grace said this, her features twisted in pain. Even now, all these years later, it still hurt like hell. 'I couldn't take him back knowing that. So we divorced and eventually he married someone else. But he left me with nothing. The house was in his name and all the money coming in was his, as I didn't work. He sold up and moved away because he couldn't face bumping into Ruth and the council had to house the children and me. I was destitute. Ray never gave me a penny.'

Maggie looked at Imogen. 'Is that why you picked on Julia at school?'

Her face mottled. 'Imagine what it was like for me, knowing her mum had stolen my dad.'

'Her mum walked out on her as well,' Carmichael pointed out and Maggie flashed her a warning look. Even the smallest hint of sympathy for Julia could inflame the situation.

'Her family wasn't irrevocably broken,' said Imogen, annoyed. 'Mine was.'

'I can understand why you were upset,' said Maggie carefully. 'What I'm struggling with is why neither of you told us about this.'

'It's what I said – if you thought I'd bullied Julia, you might have been on their side and not ours,' said Imogen.

'Did Benji know about the relationship between his grandfather and Poppy's grandmother?'

'No,' said Grace sharply.

Maggie regarded Imogen for a moment, an idea percolating in her mind.

'Given how you felt about Julia and her family, why befriend Ewan?' she asked.

Imogen twisted nervously in her seat. 'I didn't know who he was at first. By the time I found out, the kids were already friends and it would've been too complicated to explain to Benji why I didn't want Poppy coming round.'

Maggie wasn't sure whether she believed her.

'Did you discuss the past with Ewan?'

Another fidget.

'No.'

Maggie took a breath, aware how incendiary her next question was.

'Imogen, have you been having an affair with Ewan Hepworth?'

Grace gasped and reeled round in her seat to confront her daughter.

'Don't you dare say yes!'

'Mum, I'm not having, nor have I had, an affair with him.' She eyeballed Maggie. 'I was tempted, though, and it would've served Julia right if I had.'

'Why?' asked Maggie.

'So she'd know what it feels like when your family goes to shit because of another woman.'

Talk about keeping your enemies close.

'What stopped you then?' Maggie wanted to know.

Imogen looked embarrassed and fiddled with the rings on her right hand.

'Ewan wasn't interested in me like that. He'd been texting me stuff that made me think something could happen between us, but when the opportunity presented itself, well – Ewan was very sweet and polite about it, but he didn't want to reciprocate.' Imogen shrugged but it was a poor attempt to appear nonchalant. The rejection had obviously stung. 'It was probably a good thing nothing happened,' she added airily. 'Benji wasn't very keen on Ewan and he would've hated it if I'd got involved with him.'

'Why didn't Benji like him?' Carmichael pressed.

'It wasn't anything he said explicitly. I could tell from how he'd behave when Ewan came round to collect Poppy.

If Ewan stayed for a drink Benji would get really huffy and moody and refuse to talk to him.' Imogen cocked her head, as though she was thinking. 'Actually, he did once say Ewan wasn't very nice to women and didn't treat them well, but that's never been my experience of him. Really Benji was jealous I was giving Ewan attention.'

'Are you sure that's all it was?' asked Maggie.

'What else would it have been? Benji was used to having me to himself and suddenly there's a man on the scene getting in the way.'

'How would you describe Poppy's relationship with her dad?'

'They're really close, although I did notice her being a bit off with him recently. That was around the time she cried off coming round for tea.'

'Why did she cancel?'

Imogen shrugged. 'I asked Benji and he said he didn't know.'

Maggie leaned back in her chair, troubled by what she was hearing. She had a niggling feeling that Imogen's association with Ewan was somehow tied to what happened on that wall between their children. Benji didn't like him and yesterday at the police station Poppy couldn't have made it clearer that she didn't want to go with her dad. What was behind—

She stopped, stunned.

The final piece of the puzzle had fallen into place.

81

The interview came up on Julia's phone as an alert. She did a double-take as she clicked through to the *Echo*'s website, not believing her eyes as the headline swam in front of them. The blood drained to her lower body and her heartbeat thumped in her ears as it accelerated with shock. How could the police let Imogen get away with it?

Her heart thudded harder at the thought of Poppy seeing the headline, let alone any of her friends and their parents. It didn't matter that her name was omitted – they'd still know which child Imogen was referring to. Julia thought it was despicable she had been allowed to put her lies across to the public in a way that made it impossible for them to defend Poppy.

She went downstairs in search of Ewan but the front room and kitchen were empty. Malcolm was still out after taking Dylan to school; he'd gone to meet an old neighbour from when he'd lived in Mansell and they weren't expecting him back until later that afternoon.

The back door in the kitchen was open and standing on the threshold she spied Ewan down the bottom of the garden. He was half shielded from the house by the kids' trampoline but she could see he was on the phone and was agitated, gesticulating into thin air as he rammed home whatever point he was trying to make.

She assumed it was a work call, although it was unusual for Ewan to be the one doing the shouting. In his self-employed world the client was always king, even if they didn't warrant it.

She backed into the kitchen. If she brought up the *Echo* interview Ewan might get even angrier and take it out on her. However upset she was about it, now wasn't the time to tell him.

Ewan stalked into the kitchen, phone clenched in his hand. White-hot anger leached from every pore.

'I'm going out.'

'Where?'

Immediately Julia wished she'd kept her mouth shut. Ewan didn't like being questioned on his movements – she'd learned that the hard way when she queried his going out three nights a week to play squash with a friend she'd never heard of, someone called Gus. Ewan hadn't taken kindly to her challenging it and had raged so loudly at her that Dylan had come into their bedroom crying for him to stop.

'Why do you do it, Julia? Do you get a kick out of winding me up?'

She shrank away from him.

'You don't have to know every fucking thing that I do.'

He grabbed his keys from the table.

'If the police call or come round, you don't tell them anything, especially if they ask where I am.'

'Why would they ask about you?' she asked, alarmed.

'For fuck's sake, Julia, will you just back off—'

'But—'

His hand was a blur as he struck her swiftly across the side of the head.

Winded from the shock and her temple throbbing in pain, Julia staggered across the kitchen to clutch the counter for support. Ewan had never hit her before and she couldn't believe he had just done so.

'I don't think you should be here right now,' she said hoarsely.

'Come on, Jules.'

He took a step towards her but she shook her head. He looked sorry for what he'd done, his face veiled with concern, but for once she wasn't falling for it.

'Please go.'

When he reached the doorway to the hall he turned back, as if he'd changed his mind. She flinched, certain he was going to hit her again.

'You're really scared of me, aren't you?' His tone was devoid of any emotion; it was like a stranger standing there in the guise of her once-loving husband. 'It's really pathetic and unbecoming, Julia.'

She gazed up at him, too frightened to speak.

'I suppose you'll tell your dad and Cath that I hit you. Well, be sure to tell them pushed me to it, because you know you did. Don't try to deny it. I wouldn't have done half the things I've done if you weren't such a crap wife. So remember that, when people try to tell you things I've done. It's all down to you.' He looked her up and down, contempt stamped all over his face. 'I could've done so much better.'

As the front door clicked shut behind him Julia slid to the floor and cried.

82

Maggie raced into the incident room and flung herself down in front of her computer, ignoring the startled looks from others. She spied Belmar across the room and hollered to him.

'I need your help. Yours too, Nath.'

Curiosity piqued, the pair of them crowded behind her as she began frantically tapping out words on her keyboard.

'What are you looking for?' asked Nathan.

'Statements from Violet Castle's mates.'

'Why?'

'I'll tell you in a minute.'

Accessing the case file on HOLMES, Maggie found the statement given by Violet's flatmate, a girl called Lila. Scrolling down, disappointment set in. The information she hoped might confirm the first part of her theory wasn't there.

'Tell us what you're looking for and we might be able to help,' said Belmar.

'I want to confirm the nickname Violet went by.'

Burton came up behind them.

'Someone wasn't listening properly in the briefing,' he

chuckled. 'Umpire said she was known as Ruby, because of her red hair.'

Maggie swivelled round in her chair to address Burton. 'As in "Ruby Tuesday"?'

His eyes widened as he caught her drift. 'You mean . . .?'

'I think so,' said Maggie, adrenaline accelerating through her veins. 'We need to talk to Lila, now.'

'I'll come with you,' said Belmar. 'You can fill me in on the way.'

'Will someone please tell me what's going on?' pleaded Nathan.

'I will in a minute,' said Burton. To Maggie he added, 'What else do you need?'

'Start cross-reffing everything. Dates, phone numbers, associates. And tell Umpire I think I know why Poppy Hepworth pushed Benji off that wall.'

83

Two things were abundantly clear to Maggie as she observed Lila Morris. The first was that someone had beaten the girl to a bloody pulp in the last week or so. The black eyes she'd been given were still swollen but yellowing, same for the bruises smattering her cheeks, temples and, most disturbingly, her chest, made visible by the clingy, low-cut top she was wearing. There were claw marks on her shoulders and down her arms, etching the handful of tattoos already marking them.

The second thing that was clear was that she wasn't going to tell them who'd inflicted the injuries no matter how hard they tried to persuade her.

'I keep telling you, I didn't know their name, it was a punter I've not been with before,' she said, swinging her bare legs onto the stained sofa and crossing them. She put a pouch of tobacco on her lap and began the process of making a roll-up.

'It's GBH,' said Maggie. 'They shouldn't be allowed to get away with it.'

'I'm not bothered so I don't know why you are. Besides,

that's not the reason you're here. It's Ruby you want to know about, not me.'

Her voice belied her tough exterior. It was soft, fragile. Young. Maggie hated to think of what had happened to Lila in her childhood that led her into prostitution even before she was out of her teens.

Home for Lila was a studio flat that was dominated by a sofa bed she and Ruby used to share. The girls had done their best to make the place homely, covering most of the grotty carpet with a brightly coloured rug and by pinning posters and sparkly scarves to the peeling wallpaper, but an underlying sense of dilapidation lingered nonetheless.

'I still can't believe she's gone,' said Lila, licking the edge of a Rizla. 'I should've noticed sooner she was missing but I thought she was in London, 'cause that's often where she took herself off to when things got a bit much.'

'In what way?' asked Belmar.

'Sometimes doing this makes you feel like you aren't human, that you're no better than the shittiest animal. You'll get a john who won't even look at you, who acts like you're disgusting or worse, and it makes you wanna die inside. I've been doing this for –' Lila paused and did a weary count on her fingers – 'eleven months but Ruby was longer than me and it was getting to her.'

Maggie pulled two printouts from her bag and laid them neatly on her lap, face down. Lila eyed them warily.

'I want to ask you about Rushbrooke,' said Maggie. 'Did you know Lila was taking clients into the school grounds?'

'No chance. An' before you ask, I ain't *never* done that. Not where kids go,' she said, her nose wrinkling in disdain. 'I've been nearby, though – sometimes when a john don't have a car we can use, I'll take them to that new estate, the one that's half built.' She caught Maggie's eye. 'Don't you look all hoity-toity at me. It's not illegal, what I do. You should know that, being the police an' all.'

'Yes, I am aware prostitution is legal,' said Maggie, 'but owning or managing a brothel and pimping out girls isn't. It's illegal if you're being procured to have sex with strangers for money. Who do you work for, Lila?'

'I shan't tell you and you can't make me. Besides, my clients call me direct so really I'm pimping myself out, aren't I?'

'Did Ruby work for the same person?'

'I told you, I won't say.'

'Are you sure Ruby never mentioned going inside the school with a client?'

'No.'

'Have you ever seen Ruby with this man?'

Maggie found the head shot she'd printed off the Internet and held it up.

Lila's features shuttered. 'No.'

She was clearly lying but, instead of pushing her, Maggie nudged her foot against Belmar's – his cue to change tack.

'Was it because of her hair she was nicknamed Ruby?' he asked.

It was a question Maggie had primed him to pose, because she already knew the answer but wanted to see how Lila would react.

'Yeah, I suppose.'

Maggie stepped in.

'Not because she was Ruby Tuesday to your Lady Jane? They're both titles of Stones' songs, right?' She pointed to the wall above Lila's head and a poster for a long-finished Rolling Stones tour featuring the band's infamous lips-and-lolling-tongue logo.

A look of fright flitted across Lila's face but she tried to brazen it out.

'Don't know what you mean.'

Maggie handed the second printout to Lila.

'Did you leave this message on Facebook under the name Lady Jane? We know it's your nickname: we're questioning some of Ruby's clients down the station at the moment and one of them has confirmed it. Apparently he's familiar with your services as well.'

Lila twitched as she thrust the piece of paper back at Maggie.

'I ain't done anything on Facebook.'

Frustrated, Maggie was about to say they could check Lila's devices but her phone rang. The caller was Umpire, so she excused herself and went into the hallway outside Lila's flat to answer. The space smelled of rotten food and damp and where there should've been carpet there were old sheets of newspaper.

'Where are you?'

'With Lila. Did Burton fill you in?'

'He did and that's why I'm ringing,' said Umpire. 'I need you and Belmar out of there now to assist with a search.'

Maggie frowned. 'Search for who?'

'Poppy Hepworth. She's missing.'

84

Alan locked up his office and went home. He didn't tell anyone he was leaving – they'd find out the reason soon enough.

He went straight upstairs and into the back bedroom, which was filled with boxes he hadn't bothered to unpack despite moving in three years ago. They were filled with his parents' books, paperwork, and the dinner set they were given for their silver anniversary. He didn't have the heart to throw the contents out but nor did he have the space downstairs to put them anywhere.

It was the same with their old tallboy chest of drawers. Unwieldy and probably riddled with woodworm, it was hardly worth him hanging on to but it was his mum's favourite piece of furniture and so for sentimental reasons he didn't want to part with it. He pulled open the top drawer and rooted around for the writing pad his mum always kept in there, and a pen.

Alan returned downstairs and sat on the sofa, resting the sheaf of paper on an old magazine. Then he began to write.

It wasn't so much a confession as a truthful account of what really happened on the wall and everything that had happened since. He left nothing out – Gus, Ruby, the Pavilion, and Poppy's confession to him that morning. Every detail filling up eight pieces of paper and by the time he'd finished his hand hurt.

Alan set his notes down next to him on the sofa and stared at them. The right thing would be to give them to the police and accept the consequences, but was he ready to do that?

Yes, he was. The time had come to put an end to the whole sorry saga. He would have a shower, smarten himself up, then hand himself in to the police.

Standing under the streaming hot water, he could feel the tension washing away. He actually felt good about the decision he'd made. Finally the boy's mother would be getting the justice she deserved.

He dried himself off in the bathroom, then fastened the damp towel around his waist to head into the bedroom, stepping over the clothes he'd discarded on the floor on his way.

The doorbell rang as he pulled on a clean T-shirt. He moved stealthily to the window to see if he could spot who was on the doorstep, but the angle of the bay meant he couldn't tell. But he heard more than one voice, so he knew it wasn't Mr Lincoln again, coming back to use his shoulder for another self-pitying cry.

It was probably house-to-house chuggers, who he hated even more than the ones who stopped him in the street. It felt intrusive, being asked to cough up on his doorstep. He pulled on a pair of jeans and headed downstairs ready to tell them to sod off, but as he yanked the front door open his heart leapt into his mouth.

'What are you lot doing here?'

'Don't sound so pleased to see us,' said Gayle, smiling.

Alan barely had time to react before Freddie launched himself forward. Stunned, Alan hugged his son back, then he reached an arm out to grab his youngest daughter, Kyra. His eldest, Lacey, hung back, trying to look as though she was unmoved by seeing him, but as tears began to steadily roll down her cheeks she stepped forward to be enveloped into the same embrace with her siblings.

'I've missed you all so much,' said Alan tearfully, raining kisses down on his children's heads. 'I can't believe you're all here.'

He looked up at Gayle, who was also in tears.

'I don't understand,' he said.

'I was worried when we spoke earlier and then when I tried calling again and you didn't answer I thought you might've –' Her voice cracked. 'I would never have forgiven myself if the kids never got to see you again. I told their schools I needed to pull them out for an emergency and we drove straight down.'

Alan was too choked to respond. His family had come for him. He couldn't believe it. As he ushered them into the house, wiping his tears with the back of his hand, he remembered the notes on the sofa.

'Go into the kitchen and I'll stick the kettle on. There's some Coke in the fridge. I wasn't expecting guests, so the house is a bit untidy. Just give me a second to clear a bit of space.'

He dashed into the lounge and snatched the sheets of paper up. If Gayle read what he'd written about the Pavilion and Gus and Benji and everything else he'd been caught up in, any hope he had of prolonging this reunion would be destroyed.

Taking a deep breath, Alan ripped the sheets into tiny pieces and tossed them in the bin.

85

Belmar floored it down Mansell's backstreets, gears grinding on the steeper inclines, while Maggie relayed the details Umpire had given her.

'Poppy was dropped off in the playground by her parents but never made it to her classroom. Her teacher remembers seeing her at the back of the line as the kids came inside but then she vanished. The school can't check CCTV to see exactly what time she went and in which direction because – get this – the caretaker's buggered off and his office is locked and the spare key can't be found.'

'Donnelly's gone as well?'

'Yep. Umpire's sent Nathan round to pick him up.'

'I can't see Poppy being with Donnelly, though.'

'I can't either. Right now I don't think she'll trust any man.'

'Not even her dad.'

'*Especially* not her dad.'

They exchanged grim glances. Thanks to Maggie slotting the last piece of the puzzle together, Ewan Hepworth was now their main suspect in the murder of Violet 'Ruby' Castle. A warrant had been issued for his arrest and Maggie and Belmar were on their way to the Hepworths' address to bring him in.

'How did you guess Ewan was one of Ruby's clients?'

'It was what Imogen said to me and Carmichael about Benji taking a dislike to Ewan because he was horrible to women. She said Ewan had turned down her advances in a nice way, so I knew it couldn't have been how he was with Imogen that made Benji wary of him – the kid must've witnessed Ewan mistreating someone else. My next guess was Julia, but then Benji had never met her as far as we know, and Ewan was a devoted dad to Poppy so it couldn't have been her either. So it must've been some other woman – and then it dawned on me Ewan was the man in the story Benji wrote. He described the man as having a round, shiny head like a skeleton's – well, Ewan's is like that because he shaves his hair down to a grade one. Then everything about Benji and Poppy being on that wall started to make sense.'

'In what way?'

'I think Benji told Poppy what he'd seen her dad getting up to and they were on that wall because he offered to show her exactly where it happened, but she refused to believe him and possibly pushed him to shut him up,' said Maggie. 'That's why she screamed the place down when we said we thought Benji had in fact witnessed Ruby's murder – Poppy thought he was making the whole thing up and there we were confirming it.'

'So she killed Benji and her dad murdered Ruby.'

'Exactly.'

'Jesus,' Belmar breathed. 'That poor kid.'

'Which one?'

They lapsed into silence for a few seconds and Maggie

384

tried to imagine how Poppy must've felt when she found out the friend she'd pushed to his death had been telling the truth all along. Benji had been trying to warn her, not upset her.

'Do you think Julia has any inkling of what her husband's done?'

'The murder, definitely not, and I don't imagine she's aware he's been sleeping with prostitutes either. Renshaw didn't know about her partner and she's a detective. I think men like Ewan probably go to great lengths to cover their tracks,' Maggie mused. 'Lila definitely recognized his picture when I showed her, though, you could tell by her reaction. Hopefully once we arrest him she'll ID him properly. Here, take a right at the next junction, it's a short cut.'

As Belmar slowed down at the traffic lights, he nervously cleared his throat.

'I know now's probably not the time, but I'm dying to tell you something and I don't know when I'll get another chance today. It's good news,' he said quickly.

'What's that?'

'Allie's pregnant.'

'Whaaat?'

Maggie screeched so loudly Belmar's foot slipped off the clutch and the car bunny-hopped forward, almost bouncing them through a red light.

'Bloody hell, Maggie! I would actually like to live long enough to be a dad if you don't mind!'

'You're having a baby!' she cried. 'Oh, mate, that's brilliant news.'

Belmar's grin stretched from ear to ear. 'We can't believe it ourselves. When the last IVF failed we didn't know if we could put ourselves through it again so we gave ourselves a break. Then one evening of cocktails later – boom!' Belmar mimed himself dropping the mic and Maggie laughed.

'When's Allie due?'

'Not for ages. She's only six weeks gone. We're not telling everyone, just immediate family and best friends.'

Maggie was flattered to be put in that category. 'You are going to be such a great dad,' she said. 'I cannot wait to see you handle a shitty nappy though.'

'Nah,' said Belmar, shaking his head. 'Compared to all the crap we deal with in this job it'll be a doddle.'

86

The chair wobbled beneath Alan's feet as he reached up into the airing cupboard.

'Careful, you could fall,' said Gayle.

She reached over and held the back of the chair with one hand, then hesitantly placed her other on Alan's calf to steady him. Her touch jolted through him like an electric shock and the chair shifted again beneath his weight before he managed to steady himself. His breathing ragged, he reached up again and pulled down a pillow from the wooden slatted shelves stacked above the immersion heater.

'There should be one each now,' he said, dropping it onto the carpet. 'Here are some pillowcases too.'

He pulled out a bundle of them and climbed down from the chair, wishing Gayle didn't have to let go of him.

'These have seen better days,' she scoffed, taking the pillowcases from him. 'Weren't these your mum's?'

Alan smiled sheepishly. 'I never got round to replacing them.'

'Oh well, they'll do for tonight.'

He hoped their visit might last longer than one night but daren't ask Gayle what her plans were for returning home.

He didn't want to rock the boat: having his family sleep under the same roof as him for one night was already beyond his expectation and he didn't want to ruin it.

'I'll change the sheets on my bed so you can have that as well. I'll kip on the sofa,' he said.

'Thanks,' said Gayle.

They were standing so close he could see tiny dark hairs feathering her top lip, the only giveaway of the brunette she used to be. She'd had brown hair when he first met her – the blonde came later, after Lacey was born.

'You've got nothing to thank me for,' he said, choked again.

'When did you become such a crybaby?' she teased, but he could see she was emotional too. He was about to reach out for her hand when Freddie's voice echoed up the stairs, asking if he could have a packet of crisps from a forgotten multipack Alan had unearthed from the back of a cupboard. With no other food in the house, he'd already decided to splash out and order a pizza delivery for tea, much to the children's delight.

'Can he have a packet, is that okay?' Alan asked Gayle nervously, not wanting to make the wrong call. 'Or will it spoil his tea?'

'Yeah, that's fine. He's got hollow legs, that one – never stops eating and never gets full up. Go on, say it's fine.'

Alan cleared his throat, then shouted down the stairs.

'Yes, that's fine, help yourself, Freddie.'

'Thanks, Daddy!'

It caught him by surprise, being called Daddy again after so long. Half smiling, half crying, he told Gayle it was the best thing he'd heard in ages.

'Good, I'm glad,' she said 'I know you've had a rough time and I'm sorry I shouted at you on the phone about that text you sent. I should've stopped to think how you must have been feeling after watching that boy die. Did you know him well, before it happened?'

'Not really. He was pretty new to the school. I think I'd only spoken to him once, and that was to tell him off.'

'What had he done?'

'I caught him in the art cupboard one break time. He should've been outside and it's out of bounds to the kids.'

'Was he nicking stuff?'

'Nah, I think he was just exploring. He hadn't been at the school long.'

Alan was suddenly assailed by sadness as he remembered how apologetic Benji had been when he'd caught him in the cupboard. He was a polite lad.

Gayle touched his arm. 'Al, what is it?'

He stared into her eyes, saw how concerned she was and before he could stop himself everything came tumbling out – what he'd seen on the wall, the Pavilion, Gus, the fire, everything. He didn't pause, not even when Gayle's face froze in horror and she shrank away from him – he had to get it all out, he needed to.

When he finally finished, Gayle slumped down on the chair and buried her face in her hands. He was desperate for her to say something but he knew he should wait and let her speak first.

Eventually she sat up, her expression set like granite.

'Here's what's going to happen next. You're going to go downstairs and tell our children that you've got to go out for a bit – tell them you're needed up at the school. Then you're going to go straight to the police and tell them everything you just told me.'

He didn't contradict her, just nodded.

'Will you still be here when I get back, though?'

'No, no, you don't get to put this on me. Because if I say we won't be, I know you won't go through with it and that's not fair, Alan.'

'I will, I promise. I *want* to tell them. I want this all to be over. Seeing you, and the kids . . . I want to put things right.'

'You doing that doesn't mean we –' she gestured at both of them – 'are okay. I need time to think. What you've done, the lies you've told . . . and you letting them use the school for, for *that* . . . It's disgusting.'

'I know, but Gus found out I had serious debts and threatened me with my job. If I got sacked from Rush-brooke I couldn't make my repayments and I wouldn't have got a decent reference to get another position. I'd have gone under and where would that have left you and the kids?'

'You could've told me. I'd have understood.'

Alan didn't believe her. 'You didn't understand last time.'

'That's because you lied to me and went behind my back and it cost us almost every penny we had. This isn't the same – this is someone in authority blackmailing you and exploiting you and putting you in a position where you couldn't say no to them. I know you're not a bad man, Alan. Stupid, definitely, but not bad.'

He managed a smile at that.

'I never did anything with the girls at the Pavilion. There's not been anyone since you. I need you to know that.'

'That's not a conversation for now. Go on, you need to go and tell the kids.'

He was halfway down the stairs when the doorbell went. Opening it to find DC Thomas, an odd feeling of calm settled over him.

'I need you to come with me, Mr Donnelly,' said the detective.

'I know. It's time I told you the truth.'

87

It took a few minutes for Julia to answer the door and when she did it was immediately obvious why.

'Who did that to you, Mrs Hepworth?' asked Belmar gently.

Julia slowly raised her hand to the side of her face, as though she was only noticing for the first time that she was in pain. Her fingertips gingerly traced the vivid red welt joining her temple to her cheekbone.

Maggie stepped forward.

'Is Ewan at home?'

Julia jolted at the mention of her husband and her hand flew to her throat, an involuntary gesture of protection.

'Is he here?' asked Belmar, when she didn't answer.

'No, he's not. I don't know where he is.'

'What about Poppy? Has she shown up here?'

'Poppy? She's at school.'

Maggie exchanged a worried glance with Belmar.

'Has no one from the school been in touch?' he asked.

Now Julia looked worried too.

'No, why? What's going on?'

'Poppy didn't go into class after you dropped her off this morning. The school doesn't know where she is.'

Julia's knees gave way and Maggie sprang forward to catch her.

'Let's get you inside.'

They helped her into the kitchen and sat her down at the table.

'I – I haven't had my phone switched on,' she said. 'It's over there charging.' She pointed to the counter next to the cooker where Maggie saw a mobile plugged into a USB socket. Going over, she could see the notification light was flashing.

'You've had missed calls from the school by the looks of it.'

Julia clasped her hands anxiously. 'Oh God, how can they not know where she is?'

'Could she be with her dad?' asked Maggie.

Julia looked stricken. 'I don't know.'

'Where is he?'

'I told you, he's not here.'

'Did he hit you, Mrs Hepworth?' asked Belmar, sitting down next to her. 'That looks nasty.'

Julia began to cry. 'It's my fault, not his. I was nagging him to tell me something and I should've stopped.'

'Don't blame yourself for his actions,' said Belmar gently.

'But I goaded him! He wouldn't have hit me otherwise. He's never done it before.'

Maggie took a breath. 'I'm sorry to have to tell you this, but we think your husband has been violent towards other women he's come into contact with. We believe him to be dangerous and it's vital we find him before he hurts anyone else. Do you have any idea where he might be?'

'Sorry, you're not making sense. What other women?'

In the phone call with Umpire before they left Lila's bedsit, Maggie had asked how much they should tell Julia about her husband. Umpire said he would leave it to her discretion, but what they must avoid at all costs was Julia tipping Ewan off. Now, watching her reaction, Maggie knew they couldn't trust Julia not to warn him. The bit she'd seized on wasn't him being violent or considered dangerous, but that there were other women involved – put a different way, possible replacements for her. Despite how appallingly he treated her, Julia would put Ewan first and always believe the best of him; it was the classic, desperate mentality of a woman indoctrinated by an emotionally abusive spouse.

'Julia, we need to find your husband,' said Maggie, shooting Belmar a look so he understood not to say anything else. 'If he was with Poppy, where would he have taken her?'

Julia wiped her tears as she tried to think. 'Maybe swimming? They like going to the Lido.'

'I don't think your husband will have taken her to do an activity.'

Julia's confusion turned to alarm. 'Wait, you said Ewan's dangerous – you think he would hurt our daughter? That's the most ridiculous thing I've ever heard.'

'Poppy didn't want to go home with him yesterday. She seemed scared.'

'Not of him. It was the situation and all those questions you were asking her. That's why she was upset . . .' She tailed off. 'Ewan said people would try to tell me things about him and that it was my fault.' She got to her feet. 'I think you need to go now. I want you to leave.'

Belmar got to his feet too. 'What about Poppy? Don't you want to help us to find your daughter?'

'Of course I do,' she said. 'But if Ewan comes back and finds you here he'll be really upset.'

Maggie could see they were getting nowhere and they couldn't afford to waste any more time. Poppy was the one person who could implicate Ewan in Ruby's death because of what Benji had told her.

They needed to find her before he did.

88

Driving back to the station, Maggie called Umpire and put him on loudspeaker so Belmar could hear too.

'Ewan's not here and Julia says she doesn't know where he is,' said Maggie. 'Any sightings of Poppy yet?'

'No, but Donnelly's been brought in and he's admitted being the last person to see her at school. They had words, then she ran off and he doesn't know where she might've gone. But that's not all – he's about to give a statement confirming he did witness her push Benji off the wall to his death.'

'What he said during his 999 call was correct then?'

'Yes.'

'So why's he been lying?' asked Belmar.

'Donnelly's been covering up for the people running the prostitution ring that Ruby was part of, and presumably Lila still is. You know the Pavilion building in Rushbrooke's grounds, the one that burned down? That was where the girls took their punters – Donnelly claims he was forced to open up the building for them to use. He thought that if we wrote Benji's death off as an accident we wouldn't find out.'

'Bloody hell,' remarked Belmar. 'I can't believe he'd let

396

prostitutes use a primary school for meeting johns. I damn well hope we're throwing the book at him.'

'He's asking for a deal. He says he'll give us the names of the people behind the racket in return for immunity. He's implied that some of Mansell's best-known public figures are involved.'

'You can't let him off the hook,' said Maggie angrily. 'What about Imogen? He should be punished for her sake, for telling lies and holding up the investigation.'

'But, Maggie, if more senior officers like ACC Bailey are involved, we need to put a stop to it and that means cutting a deal with Donnelly to get the information. For all we know some of the girls involved could've been trafficked and let's not forget one of them was murdered.'

'The thought of Donnelly walking scot-free makes me sick,' said Maggie.

'We'll still go after him for perverting the course of justice by giving a false statement about Poppy,' said Umpire. 'But, no, it's very likely he won't be implicated in the racket.'

'Does this mean we should be arresting Poppy too now?' asked Belmar.

'Yes. And before you say anything, Maggie, I know there are mitigating circumstances. But those are for a court to hear, not us.'

'I know, I just hate the thought of having to arrest her.'

'You need to find her first. Where could she have gone?'

Maggie wracked her brains but she was stumped. 'She could be anywhere in Mansell.'

'All right, let's try a different approach,' said Umpire, 'and assume she's with her dad then. Where would he take her?'

Belmar suddenly clicked his fingers.

'Hawley Ridge.'

'Oh my God,' breathed Maggie, 'that's it.'

'The viaduct?' queried Umpire. 'Why would he take her there?'

'Julia had PND that lasted for ages after Poppy was born and she was experiencing suicidal thoughts. One day she flipped and took Poppy up to Hawley Ridge with the intention of jumping. Ewan might've taken Poppy there because he'll be desperate too by now.'

'Get up there now,' said Umpire. 'I'll meet you there and I'll put a call out for backup.'

'We're on our way,' said Maggie, then she hung up. 'Put your foot down,' she said to Belmar.

He didn't need to be told twice.

89

Julia was putting her shoes on in the hallway when Malcolm let himself in. He took one look at the welt on her face and demanded an explanation.

'I caught it on a door,' she lied, knowing if she told him the truth he'd never look at Ewan in the same way again. 'Listen, Dad, I can't stop, Poppy ran out of school this morning and the police are looking for her and –' she couldn't bring herself to say they were looking for Ewan too – 'I can't get hold of Ewan to let him know. I'm heading out to see if I can find them.'

Malcolm was ashen. 'Why did she run away?'

'She probably wants to escape all the stress. I know I do.'

'Have you tried calling her?'

'I did just now but her phone is switched off.'

'I'll come with you.'

'I'd rather you stay here in case she comes home. I don't want her to find the house empty.'

Malcolm nodded solemnly, then stared at the side of her head again.

'Are you sure that was just a door?'

She stopped. 'Of course it was.'

399

He appeared unconvinced but to her relief he let it pass. 'Call me when you hear anything,' he said, hugging her. 'I will.'

She went straight round to Cath's. She wasn't expecting Poppy to be there, but Ewan must've taken their car as it wasn't parked outside the house and she needed her friend to give her a lift.

Unlike Malcolm, Cath didn't beat about the bush when she saw Julia's face.

'So Ewan's graduated from name calling to using his fists now,' she said matter-of-factly.

'It was an accident. He caught me with his hand as he was reaching to get something out of a cupboard,' said Julia unconvincingly.

'Oh, Julia, I don't know what's worse – you covering up for him or you telling yourself that he didn't mean it when he hit you.'

'It wasn't like that.'

'There's a name for what Ewan does – it's called gaslighting,' said Cath. 'It's when the dominant person in a relationship manipulates their partner into thinking everything is their fault. It's a form of abuse.'

Julia's eyes pricked with tears. 'Don't start, Cath, please. I just need to find him.'

'No, you don't, you need to find your daughter. Now, think – where could she have gone?'

'I don't know. All her friends are still at school so she can't have gone round to one of their houses—'

There was a sudden hammering on the front door. Cath opened it to find Malcolm bent double on her doorstep, hand propped against the wall to support himself.

'Are you okay, Malcolm?'

'Julia . . . needs to come . . . police,' he panted between breaths. 'I . . . ran here.'

'Julia!' Cath yelled down the hallway. She came running. 'Dad, what's going on?'

Malcolm gulped down some deep breaths. 'The police are at yours. They want you to go with them. Ewan's taken Poppy to Hawley Ridge.'

90

Hawley Ridge railway viaduct was taken out of commission in the mid-sixties and passed over to Railway Paths Ltd, who turned the old line into one of the county's most popular tourist attractions. At weekends the wide, grassy footpath where trains once passed bustled with families, dog walkers and abseilers taking in the spectacular view of the Chilterns it afforded them. Today it was empty except for three people: Ewan, Poppy – and DS Anna Renshaw.

'What the hell is she doing here?' huffed Belmar as he and Maggie reached the summit of the steps leading from the car park to the viaduct footpath. The arches were fifty metres high and it was a steep climb.

'No idea, but I don't like it,' Maggie panted back.

Ewan and Poppy were standing by the edge of the footpath and there was a sheer drop on the other side of the brick-and-flint wall they were leaning against. Ewan had his arm clamped around her shoulders and the way Poppy was leaning in to him meant her face was hidden from view. Renshaw was standing a few metres back from them, towards the middle of the footpath. She was in casual clothes – jeans, T-shirt, flip-flops – and her usually groomed hair hung limp about her face. When she saw Maggie and Belmar approaching, she held up her hand to stop them.

'Leave this to me,' she ordered.

'Anna, you need to step down. You're not meant to be here,' said Maggie firmly.

'This is *my* case,' she shot back.

'No, it isn't.'

Ewan suddenly shouted.

'All of you leave us alone!'

'Mr Hepworth, I need you to step away from the wall with Poppy,' said Maggie. 'We can sort this out.'

Renshaw clenched her fists. 'I said leave it, Maggie.' She took a step forward. 'Poppy,' she hollered to the girl, 'why did you push Benji Tyler to his death?'

'Call Umpire,' said Maggie in an undertone to Belmar. 'Find out how long he's going to be. Then stay here while I try to get Renshaw away from them.'

'How are you going to do that?'

'God knows.'

Maggie moved closer to the group.

'Anna, can I have a quick word?'

Renshaw stared resolutely ahead as if she hadn't heard her.

'I've got some intel I need to share with you about Poppy.'

That got her attention – and also Poppy's. The girl pulled away from her dad's grasp and turned towards Maggie. She looked frightened, but unscathed.

'What is it?' asked Renshaw, moving towards Maggie but keeping her gaze trained on Ewan and Poppy. The second she was within reach, Maggie grabbed her by the upper arm and yanked her towards where Belmar was waiting. Renshaw protested, but Maggie wouldn't relinquish her grip and Renshaw's flip-flops couldn't get purchase on the grass to stop her being pulled along.

'You shouldn't be here. Go home,' said Maggie as they reached Belmar.

'She can't get away with it,' said Renshaw, agitated.

'That's not your call,' said Belmar.

Renshaw looked wild-eyed as she shook her head. 'I've lost my home, my future, the love of my life. I can't have my case taken off me as well.'

'Anna, we're so sorry for what's happened, but you being here isn't helping,' said Maggie, keeping one eye on Ewan and Poppy. She could see the child was trying to wriggle out of her dad's embrace but he wasn't happy about it. In the distance was the faint sound of police sirens approaching.

'Please, Maggie, I need to do this. My job's the only thing I've got. I want to put this case to bed.'

'How did you even know they were here?' asked Belmar.

'I went to the school this morning. I wanted to talk to Poppy, to get the truth out of her. I was still parked up there when I saw her run out so I followed her. She was almost home when her dad came roaring up in his car and made her get in. Then they came up here.'

'Did she willingly get in the car with him?' asked Maggie.

'No. He had to force her.'

'Right, you can stay here with Belmar. If I see you move an inch I'll have him arrest you,' she warned. 'Do not get in the way.'

Knowing she was beaten, Renshaw nodded grudgingly

and Maggie moved slowly back across the path towards father and daughter, who were still tussling.

'You have to stay with me,' Ewan was saying. 'I'm not letting you go.'

'Please, Daddy, you're hurting me. I want to go home.'

'But that's the problem, honey, you won't be going home. The police are going to take you away because of what you did to Benji. You'll never see me, Mummy or Dylan again. That's why we must stay together now.'

'It was your fault,' wailed Poppy. 'If Benji hadn't seen you and told me, it wouldn't have happened!' She tried to pull away again and shrieked as her dad held her even tighter.

Maggie cautiously stepped forward.

'Mr Hepworth, please move away from the wall.' To her side she heard voices and from the corner of her eye saw that Umpire had arrived with backup. She held a finger up to show him she wanted them all to stay where they were. Ewan might freak out even more if they crowded him.

'I can't help if you don't listen to me,' she added.

'Help us? You want to lock us both up!' Ewan retorted.

Maggie had been trained to deal with hostile witnesses but this situation was something else. Her back and under-arms were drenched with sweat that had nothing whatsoever to do with the warm weather and she daren't move a muscle in case Ewan took it as a sign of aggression.

'I just want to talk to you,' she said.

'Please help me,' Poppy wailed. 'I want to go home.'

'I'm trying to, but I need your dad to calm down first.'

'He's not going to. He's a bad, bad man,' she sobbed. 'He did bad things with the dead woman. Benji told me.'

Maggie felt wretched for the girl. She'd killed her friend

405

not realizing he was simply trying to help her understand the kind of man her father was.

'Don't you dare call me that,' Ewan shouted at her. 'I am your father and you will respect me!'

To Maggie's horror, he swung his leg astride the wall so he was straddling it and jerked Poppy upwards so she was next to him. She cried out in pain as the jagged flint scraped her back through her thin cotton school dress.

Maggie stepped forward. Barely three metres separated her from them.

'I understand you're upset, Ewan, but this is not the answer.'

'POPPY!'

The agonizing scream splitting the still air came from Julia, who had arrived on top of the viaduct with an older woman in tow. Umpire held her back to stop her from getting any closer.

'I want my daughter,' she sobbed.

'Maggie knows what she's doing,' he reassured her.

Maggie wished she shared his belief in her. She was starting to feel out of her depth as Ewan continued to ignore her entreaties to let Poppy go and move off the wall. Then she hit on a brainwave.

'Do you remember when your mum brought you here, Poppy?'

'She was too little,' snarled her dad.

'But you remember it, don't you, Ewan? I bet you can recall like it was yesterday how scared you were seeing your wife balancing on that wall with Poppy in her arms, and how desperate you were to stop her falling to certain death.

And you did, you saved your little girl's life that day,' said Maggie. 'So why are you risking it now?'

There was a sharp intake of breath from Ewan as he struggled with the emotions Maggie's reminder had unleashed. His expression raced from anger to hurt to alarm as his mind took him back to that moment eight years ago when it was Julia standing where he now sat, threatening to kill herself and their child.

'I'm not like her,' he said through clenched teeth.

'Right now you're putting Poppy in harm's way just like she did,' said Maggie. 'But I know you don't mean to. I know you wouldn't really hurt her.'

He shook his head vehemently. 'I wouldn't, I wouldn't.'

Maggie extended her hand. 'So let me help you. Let me help you keep her safe.'

'No! You want to lock her up because she pushed the boy.'

Maggie stopped.

'How did you know she did it?'

Poppy went rigid with fear as Ewan stroked her hair.

'You told me at the school after it happened, didn't you, darling?' He looked back at Maggie. 'And she told me what Benji had said about me. I said he was lying, but she mustn't tell the truth because the police wouldn't understand and you'd take her away from us.'

'Is that why you killed Ruby, to keep her quiet as well?'

'Don't be stupid. She wanted more money than I was prepared to pay. She started yelling so I had to silence her. I won't have any woman yell at me.'

Maggie thought carefully how to respond. She daren't promise anything she couldn't deliver.

'What Poppy did to Benji – there are mitigating circumstances. Reasons, good reasons, that will be taken into account,' she said.

She could see Ewan was listening intently and it filled her with hope.

'I'll make sure everyone knows about those reasons, I swear. I'll look after her.'

She saw his arm begin to unfurl from Poppy's shoulders and, heart beating wildly, she stepped closer, stretching out both her arms, ready to grab her. But as she did, there was a shout to her left, from where the others were, and she looked round to see Renshaw bearing down on them, with Belmar in close pursuit.

'Don't you dare let her get away with it!' Renshaw screamed.

On hearing that, Julia elbowed Umpire in the stomach, forcing him to release his hold on her. Then she started running too.

'Stay back,' Maggie yelled at them. 'Don't come any closer!'

Ewan bellowed in anger and Poppy shrieked as he leaned back precariously. Maggie made a grab for the front of the girl's school dress but as she did someone crashed into her and knocked her sideways onto the grass. Winded, she tried to get up but it all happened too quickly . . . Ewan's face twisting in shock . . . a blur of red gingham . . . a hand reaching out . . . streaming blonde hair . . . a high-pitched scream . . . a thud.

Then, silence.

91

Two weeks later

Mrs Pullman sighed, then slowly folded the piece of paper up, slid it inside the envelope, and handed it back to Alan.

'I don't want to accept your resignation.'

Once again Alan marvelled at the woman's compassion. Despite everything he'd done and the terrible shame he'd helped heap on her beloved school, she didn't hate him or even blame him. He'd told her everything, as he had the police, and somehow she'd found it in her heart to understand, acknowledging that it was an impossible situation he'd been in, given the breadth of Gus's operation, the players involved and the enormous pressure he'd put Alan under. Burning down the Pavilion had proved how much he wanted to put an end to the racket and she'd even offered to act as a character witness if Alan was charged with any offences. He was really going to miss her.

'I'm afraid you're going to have to accept it. I'm leaving Mansell.'

She gazed up at him.

'But why? I understand you want a break – frankly, we all need one. But the summer holidays are coming up and that will give us all pause to regroup and get Rushbrooke back on its feet.'

'It's not about what's happened. It's my family. I'm going back to Nottinghamshire to be closer to them.'

Happiness radiated from his every pore. Straight after work he was driving up to see Gayle and the children again. He'd spent the past weekend there, visiting old haunts and establishing a couple of new ones, but this time he'd be flat hunting. He couldn't believe it when Gayle suggested he think about moving back. They could find him somewhere to rent near to her house, she'd said, adding, 'I'm not promising anything with you and me, but I don't want you not to be in the kids' lives. Whatever happens with the police investigation, we'll be there to support you.'

It was enough bait to make him say yes.

'What about your dealings with the police?' asked Mrs Pullman. 'Won't they mind you moving away?'

'I'm bailed until October pending further inquiries. I think they're more interested in Gus and the others for now.'

He hadn't told her he was going to be a witness for the prosecution in Gus's trial, whose arrest had shocked everyone. It was another reason he couldn't stay at Rushbrooke: Mrs Pullman might be magnanimous about his involvement, but he didn't imagine any parents would be once he took the stand and explained in detail exactly how Gus had schemed to defile the grounds where their precious kids were taught and how he had been involved.

'Who will I get to replace you? I've already got to find a new deputy head and several more teachers,' she said.

The innocuous way in which she stated Mr Lincoln's old

position needed to be filled made Alan suspect she didn't yet know her deputy head had been a client of Gus's enterprise. The last Alan heard, Lincoln was moving with his family to Wales.

'I know someone who can cover for me until you find a permanent replacement. He used to be the site manager at Loxley Green Primary and has just come to the end of a temporary contract to look after the grounds at Twitchmoor Manor. He's available to shadow me while I work out my notice during the holidays.'

'You have it all planned out,' said Mrs Pullman with a sigh.

'I do. I need to be closer to my kids.'

'Of course you do. And they need their father.'

Alan couldn't meet her eyes, fearing that if he did she'd see how choked he was. He didn't deserve her kindness. He'd allowed her school to be exploited and abused by the greed of others. He had let her down.

'I should get back to work now,' he said. 'I need to get the lunch tables out.'

'I shall bid you a good weekend then,' she replied, getting to her feet. 'I shan't be here this afternoon as I've decided to go to the funeral of the police officer who died on Hawley Ridge. I want to represent Rushbrooke and pay our respects. It feels like the least I can do.'

92

'I can't go in,' said Maggie tearfully. 'I can't do this.'

Umpire slipped his hand into hers. They were inside his car, in the crematorium car park. Climbing out of vehicles around them were dozens of officers from across their force, pinch-faced but purposeful as they readied themselves to say goodbye to their colleague.

Maggie still couldn't believe Renshaw was dead.

In her attempt to grab Poppy Hepworth on Hawley Ridge, Renshaw had shoulder-barged Maggie onto the grass, causing her to lose her grip on the girl. What Renshaw had failed to take into account, however, was Julia Hepworth being right behind her, gaining fast – and determined to protect her daughter. Julia had cannoned into Renshaw's back, sending her flying towards the wall, and in doing so had managed to reach out and grab Poppy's arm and yank her to safety. Maggie, dazed on the ground, saw Renshaw correct her balance, but then Ewan started to topple backwards and he'd reached out in desperation and grabbed Renshaw . . . and pulled her over the side of the viaduct with him.

Renshaw died instantly and by landing first had broken

Ewan's fall. He was now recovering in hospital with a broken pelvis and multiple leg fractures, under police guard after being charged with the murder of Violet 'Ruby' Castle.

'This will be one of the hardest things either of us will ever have to do, but we must,' said Umpire, his voice thick with emotion. 'We owe it to her family.'

The thought of Renshaw's parents prompted a fresh wave of tears. Maggie had spoken to them a couple of times on the phone since they'd learned of their daughter's death and their bewilderment at her passing was heart-wrenching. Anna had left their home in Newcastle to return to Mansell after telling them she'd been called back in to work, so to discover she was still on compassionate leave at the time of her death was baffling. Why had she gone to Hawley Ridge that day? Maggie had tried her best to explain that, however misguidedly, Renshaw had simply been trying to do her job, but they still didn't understand.

'Come on,' said Umpire. 'Let's go and wait with the others.'

Maggie kept her head down and her hand clenched in Umpire's as they walked slowly across the car park to the entrance of the crematorium, to the slip road where the hearse would draw up. There must've been at least three hundred mourners there. So many faces, many of them strangers, but plenty she did recognize: Nathan; Burton; Pearl and Omana, the CID admins; Imogen Tyler and her mother, Grace. Julia Hepworth had wanted to come but had been advised against it: emotions were too raw for it to be acceptable for her to attend. The CPS were presently decid-ing whether it was in the public interest to charge Poppy with

Benji's involuntary manslaughter but to widespread surprise his mum was petitioning against her being prosecuted. Imogen felt Poppy had already been through enough at the hands of her father.

Glancing up, Maggie saw DI Gant, the FL Coordinator, approaching. Normally reticent, he gave her a hug and when they moved apart she could see he was choked up too.

'Such a waste,' he said sadly.

She nodded, too upset to speak.

'I never told you this but I approached Anna a few years back to see if she had what it took to be a FLO. Fair play to her, she turned me down saying she wasn't nice enough to be one.'

Maggie managed a smile at that. They could never accuse Renshaw of not being honest.

'She was a great DS, though,' she replied. 'I keep thinking, if she'd been in charge still, if I hadn't been Acting DS . . .'

Gant stared at her beadily.

'Maggie, you can't blame yourself for her death.'

'But if I had handled the situation better and got Poppy away from her dad sooner –'

'Ifs and buts don't do anyone any good. I know it sounds harsh, but you need to stop with the self-recrimination and move on from this. Talking of which –' he lowered his voice – 'our conversation the other day about you joining the Met . . . well, I made some calls. There's a position going with the Homicide and Serious Crime Command, at one of their units based in north London. They're after a DC who's a fully trained and experienced FLO. I told my contact all about you and he wants you to apply.'

Despite the solemnity of the occasion, Maggie couldn't suppress the surge of excitement she felt. After everything that had happened, the prospect of leaving Mansell was suddenly an appealing one. Everywhere and everything reminded her of Renshaw and she couldn't shake the feeling that she was responsible for her death due to being in charge that day. A clean start with a new force in a new city might help exorcize some ghosts.

'Are you interested?' Gant pressed.

Maggie glanced round to see where Umpire was and saw him deep in conversation with someone. Would he be supportive of her moving to London? Deep down she knew he wouldn't stand in her way, but what would it mean for their relationship? Umpire caught her looking at him and flashed her a smile. She turned back to Gant.

'Yes, I am. But please keep it quiet. I don't want anyone else to find out. It might not come to anything,' she said.

'I'll let my contact know you're keen. Call me in the morning and I'll give you his details for applying.'

Gant clammed up as Belmar and his wife, Allie, arrived. It was the first time Maggie had seen Allie since Belmar had shared the news of her pregnancy and the sight of her prompted another stab of grief: Renshaw had spoken often about wanting to have children and now she would never have the chance.

'How are you doing?' Allie asked, after they'd hugged.

Maggie blinked back tears. 'For such a long time me and Anna couldn't stand the sight of each other, but this past year we got on well. I grew to really like her. I can't get my head round not ever seeing her again.'

'Me neither,' said Belmar. 'Wait up, she's here.'

They stood back as the hearse slowly pulled up beside them. Maggie's stomach gave a lurch. Resting against Renshaw's coffin was a garland of pink and red flowers spelling out the word 'Daughter'. She felt Umpire's hand find hers again and she clung to him as Renshaw's parents emerged from the car that had followed the hearse, their postures and expressions stiffened by grief. A young man climbed out after them and it shook Maggie to see how similar he was to Renshaw, from the winsome button nose and thick eyelashes right down to the same shade of red hair.

'I didn't know she had a brother,' Belmar whispered in her ear. 'She never talked about him.'

Nathan, who was standing with them, nodded. 'His name's Ben,' he said in an undertone, as the family walked into the crematorium. 'He's only twenty-one and still at uni. I don't think they were that close.'

Walking past, Ben caught Maggie's eye – but there was nothing friendly about the way he looked at her. Did he know she'd been in charge that day on Hawley Ridge? Or was it her guilt making her assume the worst? Either way, her instinct was to recoil from his stare.

Then a fourth person suddenly emerged from the back of the car – and to everyone's surprise it was ACC Marcus Bailey. He hurried inside to catch up with the family, head bowed to ignore the obvious stares.

'Her parents are a lot more forgiving than I would be,' remarked Nathan sourly. 'After the way he cheated on Anna I would've banned him from coming.'

'Renshaw loved him,' said Maggie, her throat tightening again. 'I think she would've wanted him here.'

The melancholic strains of classical music began to float

through the open crematorium doors and the mourners started to file inside. Their group was among the last to go in. Umpire put his arm around Maggie's shoulder and kissed her tenderly on her cheek, which was wet with tears.

'It's time to say goodbye.'

Acknowledgements

I am, as ever, indebted to the many brilliant and talented people who helped me get this book into your hands. Special thanks to my editor, Vicki Mellor, whose encouragement and tough love elevated the book to beyond even my expectations, and to everyone at Pan Macmillan for their support, in particular Natalie McCourt for erasing my mistakes and James Annal for designing another zinger of a cover. Also to Catherine Richards, for starting this one off. Thanks must also go to my agent Jane Gregory, for never doubting I could finish this one when I seriously doubted it myself, and to colleagues old and new at the agency's new home with David Higham Associates. I also owe a debt of gratitude to Julie Seddon for patiently taking me through the process of juvenile arrest and prosecution, and for helping me nail a crucial piece of plot! Any mistakes are mine alone. Likewise to Matt Johnson, for the police insight. I sincerely apologize to friends and family for having to put up with the vagueness and distractedness that descends like fog when I'm writing – please know that even though I'm lost in a world of my own I still think the world of you and your support is what keeps me going. Finally, to Sophie, for being (mostly) understanding when writing gets in the way of Lego assembling, and to Rory, for being the best sounding-board and for always telling me what I need to hear, even if I don't always like it! I love you both more than Arsenal.

Keep reading for an exclusive extract
from the thrilling new novel featuring
DC Maggie Neville, publishing in 2019

DEAD GUILTY

Ten years ago a young British woman was brutally murdered in Mallorca while holidaying with her parents and fiancé. Her killer was never caught, despite a major joint investigation between the British and Spanish police – and the fact that the girl's mother was one of the Met's highest-ranking female officers at the time.

Now, as the anniversary of Katy Pope's death approaches, the family return to the Spanish island to launch a fresh appeal for information, taking the now-skeletal team of Met officers looking into Katy's murder.

For DC Maggie Neville, recently seconded to the Met team, it's her first opportunity to work on an international investigation. But nothing is ever straight forward and when another girl goes missing in identical circumstances, Maggie and her team have to consider the possibility that Katy's killer has returned . . .

1

Philip Pope stood at the end of the bed and surveyed the chaos. A week's worth of his wife's knickers lay strewn across a mound of T-shirts that had slipped from their folds on the journey from drawer to bed, and on top of them was a flip-flop that had lost its mate. Then, jumbled alongside, he counted three dresses in prints his wife loved but were too lurid for his taste, a pair of similarly bright shorts and two pairs of sunglasses minus their cases.

Laid neatly upon his pillow was his own packing: two pairs of cream shorts, both knee-length, two pairs of light-weight stone-coloured trousers, five polo shirts for the daytime, all white, three short-sleeved shirts for evenings, striped, and enough underpants to last the trip.

Missing from both piles were his trunks and his wife's swimsuit. Patricia was insisting there should be no swimming or sunbathing; it would be improper, she argued, no matter how inviting the pool was, or how much they longed to warm themselves beneath the sun's glorious rays. They had an image to project in the coming week and 'carefree tourist' was not it. Philip gazed down at the bed and wondered how the brightly coloured dresses and shorts fitted in with her vision.

The bedroom door swung open and Patricia entered

carrying two folded beach towels. He winced as his wife threw them down on the bed with the rest of her stuff. For someone who had spent her entire professional life being orderly, and demanding the highest of standards from those she managed, she had all too willingly embraced chaos in retirement. It drove him mad.

'Why haven't you got the suitcases out of the garage yet? I asked you ages ago.'

Impatience nipped at her words, making them sound brittle and unfriendly. Philip mentally counted to ten as his counsellor had taught him, and his irritation at being nagged ebbed by the time he reached the end. It's the stress of the occasion making her like this, he told himself. Don't rise to it.

'I'll get them now,' he said. 'I was sorting my clothes out.'

Patricia eyed the neat stack on his pillow.

'Is that all you're taking?'

'What else do I need?'

'You don't want to be photographed wearing the same thing every day.'

'I don't want to be photographed at all, I told you.'

'Oh please, don't start that again,' said Patricia, sweeping across the bedroom to her glass-topped dressing table and picking through the bottles of scents and creams lining the top of it. Philip resumed his counting as she lobbed her selection onto the bed.

'You know how important it is that we make ourselves as accessible as possible to the media throughout the holiday.'

'I thought this wasn't a holiday,' said Philip. 'What was it you said? "A holiday implies relaxation and fun and time to gather one's thoughts away from the demands of daily life.

This trip will provide none of those things".' He quoted her primly, like the art curator he had once been.

She turned on him, her blue eyes flashing with anger. Forty-nine years ago those eyes had stopped Philip's seventeen-year-old self in his tracks outside a Soho coffee shop: Patricia was sitting with her friends, had looked up as he'd passed and smiled, and that was it, he was smitten. Age might've dulled their colour, but his wife's eyes could still pin him to the spot all these years later.

Their daughter's had been the exact same shade.

'You're twisting my words. I know we're not off on our jollies, but you could at least act as though what we're doing out there isn't the worst thing imaginable.'

But in his mind it was.

On the back of the bedroom door, snuggled together on the same hanger for convenience, was a knee-length black dress Patricia had purchased especially for the trip and Philip's most formal suit, dusted free of mothballs. Binding them together at the neck of the hook was a loosely knotted black tie. These clothes would go in last, carefully laid out over the shorts and the flip-flops and the bottles of sun cream Patricia had bought in bulk from Boots. They were to be worn only once – as they honoured their daughter's memory at the place where her remains were recovered.

'This week is about reminding people that Katy's killer is still at large,' said Patricia.

Philip was suddenly assailed by a memory of the four of them sitting at a table in that lovely Italian restaurant on the Pine Walk, faces tinged pink from too much sun. It was their first evening in Puerto Pollensa and Katy's fiancé Declan had treated them to champagne and they'd laughed and chatted and marvelled at the view across the bay as the sun languidly melted below the horizon and stars as ripe as diamonds filled the sky.

It had been the most idyllic holiday destination, until it wasn't.

'I – I don't think I can go,' he stuttered.

Patricia looked across at him, and for a fleeting moment he saw in her expression the sorrow she'd held at bay for the past ten years by focusing every ounce of her energy on finding whoever had murdered their daughter. The campaign had distracted her from her grief and given her purpose, but privately Philip wished she would, just occasionally, give in to tears and, in doing so, let him comfort her. Then perhaps she might do the same to him.

His wife gathered herself, pushing her desolation back down from wherever it had sprung.

'Don't be silly, it's all arranged,' she said briskly. 'We can't cancel now. What would the police think after all the fuss we've made?'

She had a point. Once they – well, Patricia – had decided to go ahead with the trip and memorial service, she'd begun pressuring the Met to send officers to join them. Katy's case was still open, under the name Operation Pivot, and Patricia had argued that a British police presence was needed on the island for the anniversary to remind everyone, particularly the Majorcan police, that the search for the murderer was still ongoing. The Met had eventually conceded – possibly, Philip suspected, to shut Patricia up and avoid any more negative press.

Indeed, Philip suspected Operation Pivot only continued *because* of Patricia and her previous standing as one of the highest-ranking female officers in the Met. She was a chief superintendent in line to be made a borough commander when Katy was murdered on their family holiday in September 2009. Returning after an extended period of compassionate leave, she found she couldn't pretend to care about solving other crimes while their daughter's death remained a mystery and had accepted early retirement.

Since then she'd devoted all her time to keeping Katy in the public conscience with endless appeals, headline-grabbing speculative claims about who might be responsible, and fierce, relentless criticism of the joint investigation by British and Majorcan police for failing to meet her exacting investigative standards.

However, in spite of her exhaustive efforts, the ranks of Operation Pivot had dwindled from the dozens of officers deployed at the start. Now the team was down to a detective chief inspector, two lower-ranking detectives and a family liaison officer, the most recent of which had been replaced a month ago because Patricia felt she was becoming over-familiar. They had yet to meet her replacement, a DC called Maggie Neville, but she was to join them on the trip.

'Have you dug your passport out?' asked Patricia, the change in subject signalling that, for her, the matter of Philip not wanting to go to Majorca was now resolved. 'Put it on the bed with mine.'

With a resigned sigh, he began rooting around his bedside table for it. The landline phone on Patricia's side began to ring and she snatched up the receiver.

'The Pope residence,' she said officiously.

Philip paid no attention to the conversation until his

wife remarked, 'This is rather out of the blue. Why now, Declan?'

'Declan Morris?' he hissed at her, seeking confirmation that it was indeed the man their daughter had once been engaged to, whom they hadn't spoken to in more than a decade. The same man who had, at one point, been the police's prime suspect.

Patricia nodded vehemently.

She listened for a few moments then replied in a faltering voice, 'Are you sure? Could it be a joke?'

Another pause.

'Fine. Yes, we shall both be here. See you shortly.'

She hung up and turned to her husband, her shock palpable.

'He's coming round now.'

'Whatever for?'

'He read about the memorial on my blog and wants to come to Majorca for it. But that's not all.' Patricia sank down on the bed, clearly too stunned to stay standing. 'He's received an anonymous email from someone saying they know why Katy was murdered – because they were the person who did it.'